KU-216-799

Can't Take My Eyes Off You

By Clare Dowling and available from Headline Review

Expecting Emily
Amazing Grace
My Fabulous Divorce
No Strings Attached
Going It Alone
Just the Three of Us
Too Close for Comfort
Would I Lie To You?
Can't Take My Eyes Off You

Can't Take My Eyes Off You

CLARE DOWLING

headline
review

Copyright © 2013 Clare Dowling

The right of Clare Dowling to be identified as the Author of
the Work has been asserted by her in accordance with the
Copyright, Designs and Patents Act 1988.

First published in 2013 by Headline Review
An imprint of HEADLINE PUBLISHING GROUP

1

Apart from any use permitted under UK copyright law, this publication may
only be reproduced, stored, or transmitted, in any form, or by any means,
with prior permission in writing of the publishers or, in the case of
reprographic production, in accordance with the terms of licences
issued by the Copyright Licensing Agency.

All characters in this publication are fictitious and any resemblance
to real persons, living or dead, is purely coincidental.

Cataloguing in Publication Data is available from the British Library

Hardback ISBN 978 0 7553 9267 4
Trade paperback ISBN 978 0 7553 9268 1

Typeset in Bembo by Palimpsest Book Production Limited,
Falkirk, Stirlingshire

Printed and bound in Great Britain by Clays Ltd, St Ives plc

Headline's policy is to use papers that are natural, renewable and recyclable
products and made from wood grown in sustainable forests. The logging and
manufacturing processes are expected to conform to the environmental
regulations of the country of origin.

HEADLINE PUBLISHING GROUP
An Hachette UK company
338 Euston Road
London NW1 3BH

www.headline.co.uk
www.hachette.co.uk

For Stewart

ACKNOWLEDGEMENTS

Huge thanks go to my editor Clare Foss for all her guidance during the writing of this book, and to all at Headline for their enthusiasm, support and talent. Thanks also to my agent, Darley Anderson, and all at the agency. And a big thank you too to Breda Purdue and the team in Hachette Ireland. Many thanks to Stewart, Seán and Ella for continuing to get excited about my books, and to our guide dog puppy Huw for making this particular writing experience a lively one.

Chapter One

I had booked the wrong ferry. Somehow I'd confused an a.m. with a p.m., and so now we would end up crossing the Irish Sea in the middle of the night.

'It could be worse,' Matthew said. 'Although don't ask me how.'

He didn't look great. His face was a pukey green, and his upper lip sported a layer of clammy sweat. I wasn't much better. Both of us badly wanted to lie down on the sofa and rock and moan, but couldn't because we had to emigrate twelve hours earlier than anticipated.

'Where's my passport?' I began to shout. 'I left it right here.'

'You're always leaving things "right here", usually on top of the cooker, and then getting very excited when they aren't still there five days later.'

I was stung at this observation, even though it was true. 'Well, if you weren't such a neat freak, and left my stuff alone instead of continually moving it somewhere else all the time . . .'

But he wasn't listening. 'Where the hell is *my* passport? Jesus. I left it right there.'

It wasn't what you'd call a great start. It didn't help that we'd begun the day hungover to hell – Jo's fault, but more about that later. Then we were faced with the dilemma of how to fit a decade's worth of clothes, shoes, CDs (Matthew's), books (mine), ornaments (unwanted presents

1

from elderly relatives), and leftover boxes of corn flakes from the flat into the modest confines of a Renault Mégane.

'Just give me five minutes,' Matthew croaked.

Both of us were a little out of practice with hangovers. We were getting very settled, Jo was always saying, as though it was the onset of some awful disease.

Matthew spent two hours packing, before standing back and scratching his head for a long time. There was still plenty of stuff by his feet. He then proceeded to take everything out of the boot, lay it all out on the driveway again, and repack the whole lot, 'only tighter this time'.

When he was finished, there was even more stuff by his feet, unpacked, and he eventually broke the news to me. 'We're going to have to leave some things behind.'

'No.'

'Clara, I know this is hard, but—'

'I can't, Matthew.'

'That horrible green lamp, at least.'

'I said NO.'

Matthew held up his hands warily. 'It was just a suggestion.'

'Sorry.' I took it down a notch. 'It's just, everything we're taking, it *means* something. We can't leave it behind.'

We'd made the inexplicable decision that we wouldn't have anything shipped over to our new house in Ireland; whatever we took with us would have to fit in the car, and everything else we would give away. It had sounded exciting and a bit mad at the time, like we were brave settlers heading for the western frontier with nothing, only the shirts on our backs. And our Gaggia coffee maker, of course, and my hair straighteners.

'Maybe we should have shipped some stuff after all,' Matthew ventured.

'No kidding.'

He looked doubtfully again at the green lamp — it was the first thing I'd bought when we'd moved into the flat three years ago; admittedly, it had looked better in the shop. I'd wanted something to mark the significance of us becoming permanent, and the lamp seemed more romantic than, say, a kitchen bin, although we really could have done with one of those.

'OK.' He sighed. 'I'll try again.'

He was great like that. He was always bringing me cups of tea in the mornings, and listening to me when I needed an almighty bitch about Brenda at work – which was about once every two days – and he never once butted in with annoying, male-type comments such as, 'Well, do you know what *I* would do?'

So he took the whole lot out of the boot for a second time, and laid it all back out on the drive. It took him hours, but he got everything into the car in the end, finding little nooks under seats, in the tyre well, anywhere at all that he could stuff a scented candle or two.

'I've made you sandwiches for the trip.' Matthew's mother, Di, came out of the flat now and pressed a large foil-wrapped package into my hands. The underside of it was warm, and it reeked of sausage and fried egg.

'Lovely,' Matthew managed. He slung an arm around her shoulders, more to support himself than anything else.

'You won't drive too fast, will you?' Di was a bit bewildered by this move to Ireland, although she was gamely playing along. We had good jobs, the two of us, a nice flat, great friends – why would we want to uproot and start all over again, in a place that wasn't Australia, or even Spain? Di loved Spain. She went to the same resort for two weeks every year with her friends Sharon and Liz. There was some insurance money coming down the line any year now and when it did, she planned to retire out there full time, and maybe even meet a fella. 'Only joking!' she always added, although nobody would have had any objection.

She would miss Matthew hugely. He was her only child. Matthew senior had died many years ago. I felt guilty, taking her son away like this. But, as Matthew said, 'We have to live our lives.'

'You take care of him now,' she said to me, her lip wobbling.

I hugged her. She was great. We would miss her too.

'I'll stick to the speed limit,' Matthew promised her. 'And we'll ring when we arrive.'

He gave one final look into the bowels of the car. 'It's going to be a squash,' he warned me.

He wasn't exaggerating. We drove across England with our noses pressed up against the windscreen, bullied forward by bulging duvets and pillows that had seen better days, and passing the hours by singing along to 'YMCA' by Village People. Matthew, who had far too much time on his hands at work, had made up a CD of travelling songs, including 'Leaving on a Jet Plane' and 'Like a Rolling Stone'.

'Isn't this fecking great!' he said.

Since our decision to relocate to Ireland, Matthew had brushed up on his Irishisms. Naturally, there was 'feck', which he used liberally and often. He was also very fond of 'bockety' – broken/useless – 'gombeen' – idiot – and 'hup-you-boy-ya', which very loosely translated into 'Go for it, mate'. Sometimes he used them all in the same sentence, even though I told him not to.

Then I had to go and spoil the fun by welling up.

'Clara? What's wrong?' He quickly switched off 'There's a Tear in My Beer' by Hank Williams (his nod to country) in case it was the culprit.

I wasn't sure myself. 'I'm just going to miss everybody, that's all.'

We'd had this conversation before. Naturally, it was going to be a wrench, leaving behind friends and colleagues and family – although I didn't actually have any family in London apart from a cousin called Fionnan, who lived in Kilburn and was a sober accountant by day and a wild cross-dresser by night. ('You won't tell them back home, will you?' he always said urgently. 'Oh, super lipstick! Can I borrow it?')

It was worse for Matthew, leaving his mother. Poor Di had lost it at the last minute and there had been tears and more tears. Fair play to her, though, she never once gave me a blameful look, although I'm sure she must have been thinking, if only he'd met a nice girl from Croydon.

'Look, we're only moving to Ireland,' Matthew said reasonably. 'It's barely a different country. We'll be flying back to visit all the time.'

'You say that now, but we probably won't. Just like everybody says they'll email us and come over to see us all the time, but they probably won't either.'

Well, people were feckers like that. I included myself. I'd sworn blind to Julia from work, who'd emigrated to New York last year, that Jo and I would fly over for a shopping trip; definitely, no question about it, looking up the flights as we speak. And had we?

Had we heck. I don't think I'd picked up the phone to her more than once.

I felt awful now. What if nobody came over to visit *us*, despite all their promises? Not even Pauline and Tim, who'd go anywhere if there was a chance of a free bed for the weekend? Maybe all of them – Jo and Jane and Mad Mags and Cool Art and horrible Brenda – would get on with their busy lives in London while we ended up in the backwater I'd been born in.

A small, post-drinking-session burp escaped me with the fright of it all.

The whole thing was hitting me only now. Since we'd made the decision, there hadn't been a whole lot of time for thought; Matthew getting the new job so quickly had brought everything forward. Instead of taking a leisurely six months or so to pack up and say our goodbyes, we'd ended up with only a matter of weeks before he had to show up in Dublin city centre, at the offices of Moore & Byrne, a huge law firm, where he would take up a position in computer support.

I never really understood what that meant. Once, he told me that it involved going around all the computers in the mornings and saying to them, 'So tell me, how are you feeling today? They still working you too hard, hmm?'

Suddenly, life became a blur of packing and writing letters to utility companies. We had to find somewhere to live in Ireland at very short notice. It was exciting and kind of glamorous, at least to us.

Mostly, it had felt right. I'd been away for ten long years. In the back of my mind, I was always going to go home.

But now that we were on the road I wasn't so sure. I was leaving absolutely everything behind.

Even more sobering: what was I walking *into*? A decade was a long time to be away. But was it long enough?

'We'll just have to make them visit,' Matthew was saying cheerily. 'The minute we move into the new house, we'll have an almighty piss-up, and invite the whole lot of them, even Mad Mags.' He thought about that. He was always a bit wary of her. 'Although she's not allowed to bring a man, OK? Make sure she knows that. We'll have rakes of floor space for all of them in a three-thousand-square-foot house.'

We loved saying that. 'When we move into our three-thousand-square-foot house,' we were always beginning sentences with. 'Shut UP about your three-thousand-square-foot house,' our friends had begun to moan. 'Certainly,' Matthew would reply. 'Did we mention our four-hundred-and-fifty-square-foot garage out the back?'

The garage was almost as big as our flat. So you could see why we were a little giddy.

We stopped for chips at a late-night chipper in Newport, 'for soakage, after that blooming Jo last night', and for the rest of the journey I was able to forget any misgivings as we belted out 'It's a Long Way to Tipperary' over and over again to his CD, even though we were actually moving to County Kildare.

We were hoarse and very tired when we arrived at Holyhead at some point past one a.m. The place was deserted, apart from a few trucks trundling into the bowels of the ferry.

'Mistake the a.m. for the p.m., then?' the sole man in the ticket booth drawled as he looked at our tickets.

Ours was the only car on the ferry deck. Well, most normal people tended to move country during the day. We looked like we were fleeing from a murder. Every other vehicle was a towering articulated truck. The Mégane looked tiny, parked beside them.

Matthew gave the car a nervous pat. 'Stay strong, baby.'

We held hands as the ferry slowly pulled away from the dock. Holyhead, and our old lives, began to recede into the distance.

'Did I remember to put the handbrake on?' Matthew wondered.

Chapter Two

It was through Jo that Matthew and I met. When I'd first arrived in London a decade ago, and taken up work at Kitchen Queens, Jo had been the one to train me in.

'So you've only worked in restaurants before?'

'Yes.' I wasn't sure if I should apologise.

'Why did you apply for a job in a private catering company?'

'I fancied a change.'

Her bright blue eyes were on my face. I felt like I was being interviewed all over again. 'The money isn't any better,' she said.

'I know.'

'In fact, it's worse. Brenda is tighter than a gnat's arse.'

According to Jo, Brenda was also moodier than a toddler with chicken pox and nastier than Joan Crawford. Brenda also made sure that people were often bitterly disappointed when we turned up to cater their party and weren't six foot one and decked out in full drag. 'Your company promised us Kitchen Queens,' one old chap said to us peevishly, clearly a queen himself.

I thought Jo was exaggerating about Brenda at first. I mean, come on. But over the course of the next ten years I came round to the view that she'd actually been playing her down.

'Have you worked in London before?' Jo enquired chirpily.

'No.' Other people from college had gone on to train under some of the big names – Ramsay was a dote underneath it all, apparently – but I'd stayed put. 'I'd a job in a restaurant in Dublin. Blinis.'

Jo blinked. 'You made blinis?'

'No. The name of the restaurant was Blinis.'

Its fame hadn't extended to London, judging by the blank look on Jo's face.

'A good job,' I clarified.

It hadn't been that good. But it had been safe and steady, like everything else in my life then; three long years had passed before itchy feet had belatedly set in.

Jo kept darting looks at me as though knowing there was something cagey about me. Was I in the witness protection programme? Or on the run from some court of law? To make matters worse, I was trapped beside her in the Kitchen Queens van, gridlocked on the M25 on our way to cater a golden wedding anniversary. Occasionally the van would get beeped at by moustachioed men who would look over to give us lewd winks.

'So!' A brief pause to unsettle me, then she was off again. 'Do you miss Ireland?'

'A bit. But I can go back at weekends.'

'You haven't yet, though.'

'Are you keeping *tabs*?'

'It's just, you've been here two months so far. No sign of that visit home yet.' She brightened. 'Are the pubs as good as they say?'

'They're OK.' I'd had vast experience of them myself, but I wouldn't give it to her.

'I've never been to Ireland. I'd love to go.' Then, as if it was the most natural thing in the world, 'Hey! You could take me over some weekend. That's if you're sure you don't have some filthy big secret to hide.'

'I do not have a filthy big secret.'

Jesus, she was relentless.

Then, a lob from left of field. 'Did you have a boyfriend over there?'

A nerve jumped under my eye. She was on it like Columbo.

'You broke up with someone, didn't you?'

'Yes, alright! I did! A man, OK? I broke up with a man, but these things happen. And in fact in turned out to be for the best, because I'm only twenty-three and the break-up seemed like a great time to finally leave home and try something new.' If not exactly in that sequence. 'Are you happy now? Is there anything else I can help you with, or can we just drive on to this bloody job?'

Jo merely shrugged in the face of my outburst. 'You should have just said.'

Well, yes. Maybe I should have. But I wasn't exactly feeling the best about myself after the whole thing, and I just wanted to leave it all behind.

'I hope you're not going to be all sensitive,' Jo announced. 'I can't work with sensitive people.'

Amazingly, we survived that day. It turned out that Jo lived near my new flat, and it wasn't long before she was round there too, mostly to give out about Brenda. 'Fucking Brenda . . . lousy menus . . . sits on her arse while we do all the work . . . rant, rant . . .'

'Oh, here,' she said one night, 'I'm fed up of giving out about Brenda. Shall we go for a drink?' She looked at me persuasively. 'I know you're just getting over a broken heart and all that, but I've got two VIP passes.' Jo's brother, Art – hereafter known as Cool Art – directed commercials or something desperately trendy like that, and was a great source of freebies.

'I don't know, Jo.' I nearly felt too guilty to go out and have a good time.

Jo, the eternal optimist, waved this away. 'Feel the fear and do it anyway. And for God's sake, change out of those awful jeans. You're in London now, girl. You have to look the part.'

I went. We had a marvellous night and didn't leave the club till four in the morning. Jo had been fantastic company until her sixth drink, after which she'd got very sleepy and snuggled up on my shoulder making mewling noises.

'There're plenty of men in London, you know,' she stated in the taxi on the way home. I was beginning to realise that she had my best interests

9

at heart, and that she was going to be a really good friend, whether I liked it or not. 'Isn't there, Nirajit? For Clara here?'

Nirajit was the taxi driver. He'd very kindly picked us up where many others had refused.

'Yes,' he agreed. I suppose anything for a quiet life. 'Many, many men. Some very attractive.'

'See?' said Jo. 'So that fellow back home. Forget all about him.'

Guiltily, I realised that I already had.

Five years passed very quickly. Or was it six? I was having such a good time I didn't bother to count. By that time I was deeply in love with London: I adored my job, apart from Brenda, who was truly awful. I was mad about my friends, my flat, the Tube (we only had buses in Ireland, and a pretend Tube called the Luas). I loved the markets and the shops and the variety of food. Dean, a friend of Cool Art's, taught me to cook amazing curries, and we ended up dating for a while. I went to exhibitions for the first time, and to musicals with Mad Mags. In London I could walk down my street in the middle of the night and not feel afraid, because now this felt like my town. After the first year had passed away from home, when I figured the dust had settled, I began to go back for sporadic weekends to Castlemoy. Later, when Dad got sick, I upped my visits to once or twice a month. I managed to get four weeks off work during his final summer, which I spent with him, and after he died later that year, there were trips home to help my mother go through his things and sort his papers out. I was always glad to see her and Róisín, and to spend some time in the town. But towards the end of these weekends, I felt an itch to get back. I'd spent twenty-three years in Castlemoy, but London was my home now.

I was pretty sure I'd be there for the rest of my life.

Then Jo said we were going to The Hawley Arms in Camden one Friday night. She'd arranged to hook up with Cool Art. That wasn't unusual.

'He has this friend I really want you to meet,' she said casually, once we were *in situ*.

Naturally, alarm bells went off.

'He's good-looking,' she insisted.

'If he's that good-looking, why aren't you going out with him yourself?'

Jo had a history of relationships with, let's say, unusual men. 'Freaks,' said Brenda, who could be very cruel. Examples would be thrice-divorced men in their fifties; local fishermen she would meet on foreign holidays and get engaged to ('That was just once,' Jo always insisted), only for the whole thing to be off a week later; a meat-delivery guy at work with seventeen tattoos and an artificial leg but also a primitive maleness that Jo found irresistible.

'He's not my type,' she told me now, with a sigh. Too normal, in other words.

I steeled myself. 'Bring him over.'

Neither of us was in a great mood. It had been a long, hard week with Brenda, who seemed to be gradually losing the run of herself. She no longer did any of the actual catering, preferring to be more involved in the social aspect of things. She'd turn up at our higher-profile events and totter about the place on outrageous heels, glass in hand, and pretend she didn't know us.

'She's delusional. She thinks she's one of the guests,' Jo kept hissing. 'Here, Brenda! The cocktail sausages are burning!' She clutched my arm. 'See? She didn't even turn round.'

There were rumours she wanted to change the name of the company from Kitchen Queens to Brenda's Fabulous Catering Company to the Stars, or something equally self-congratulatory. The day that happened, Jo insisted ominously, she'd be moving on. I had a feeling I would be, too.

That Friday night, I just wanted to have a few drinks and forget about work, not entertain some man that Jo had already passed over because he was boring as hell.

But it was best to keep on Cool Art's good side. Jo would be raging if the freebies dried up because I wouldn't have a friendly chat with his mate for five minutes.

Jo flung us together – 'Matthew, Clara – Clara, Matthew' – before disappearing off into the crowd. Rumour had it there was a one-armed ex-bank robber in the building and no doubt her lust was up.

I turned out to be right: this Matthew wasn't devastatingly good-looking, as per Jo's advertisement. At the same time he was attractive in a clean, non-fussy kind of way. For some reason I found myself thinking that he had the kind of face you would trust.

Just when I thought he might be OK, he lurched forward urgently and hissed, 'Don't look now.'

'What? Where?' I was a bit unnerved. Did he mean, don't look at *him*? Or was there some terrible sight behind me that he was trying to protect me from?

'Over your left shoulder,' he instructed in another hiss. 'It's Pete Doherty.'

It was, too. Both of us tried to be really cool about it, turning away and sipping our drinks nonchalantly, and agreeing that we 'just weren't into that kind of music' but when the door opened again ten minutes later, he leaned in urgently again.

'Kate Moss just walked in.'

She had, too. I'd never seen her in real life before. She was really beautiful.

'I thought they'd split up?'

'They have.'

'How do you know?'

'I'm an avid reader of celeb magazines,' he assured me.

'Really?'

'Ask me about anybody and I'll be able to tell you. Mick Jagger. The Beckhams.' He thought for a bit. 'No, I think that's about it.' Then, 'Ah, she smiles. I was wondering if you would.'

I blushed. 'I just wasn't much in the humour tonight for, you know . . . match-making.'

'I wasn't either,' he admitted. 'You know the way. Art says he has this really good-looking friend, and you think, well, if she's that good-looking, why isn't he going out with her himself?'

I went even redder. I was pretty sure he noticed.

'In this instance, though,' Matthew said, his eyes dancing into mine, 'I'm happy to declare that Art's loss in my gain.'

I laughed.

'You're Irish,' he stated.

'Top marks.'

'How did you end up over here?' His head dipped to one side as he watched me. 'Or is that a dirty question?'

'Not at all. It's just a bit of a long story.'

He folded his arms and settled in. 'I've got all night.'

We didn't talk about why I'd moved to London. Somehow I wound up telling him about my rotten day with Brenda, and he cheered me up by making up celebrity gossip headlines about her – 'Cruel Catering Boss Invites Us into Her Beautiful Home', and 'My Anguish at Hands of Bully Brenda', until in the end I began to wonder if he really *was* an avid reader of trashy magazines.

When Jo found us again two hours later, she had to clear her throat twice before we noticed her.

'You two seem to be enjoying yourselves,' she observed indiscreetly. 'Listen, we're going to a club. Are you coming or what?'

I looked at Matthew. He looked at me. Did we want to break off our conversation and head on with the gang to a noisy club, and shout at each other over the music, and probably end up going home our separate ways?

'Actually,' Matthew said, 'I think I'd rather stay here.'

It took me only a moment to decide. 'Me, too.'

We let Jo and Cool Art and the rest head off without us, and we moved closer as the pub grew quieter. Not that we noticed. We were too caught up in each other.

But after a while I noticed that Matthew seemed to lose interest in the conversation. He grew quiet and he stopped turning towards the door to wind me up over what new celebrity might be walking in. My heart began to sink. Just when I'd decided that he was cool and funny and nice, and really very good-looking after all.

I'd been resolutely single for a year at that point, not even a date here

13

or there. I'd got a little tired of the whole scene, having been a hectic partaker for several years up to then. Matthew was the first one I'd felt really interested in for a long time.

'Nobody new in, then?' It was a vain attempt to kick-start the conversation. I suspected in a minute he'd make his excuses and head off.

'I don't know,' he said simply. 'I'm too busy looking at you.'

The girls always made me tell this story, and they always went 'Aww,' at that bit. But I never minded, because it was how we met, and it was the best night of my life.

Chapter Three

We had decided to rent out our flat in London. Jo was going to keep an eye on it for us. It would have been easier just to sell it, of course, but there hadn't been time.

I was glad. I was very sentimental over it because I'd never owned property before; plus, of course, it was our love-shack, as we called it. The flat was also an insurance policy in case anything went wrong with our great plan. Not that it would. But you just never knew, did you?

'We can move back when we're retired and old and sick,' Matthew said happily. 'I'm sure the NHS will welcome us with open arms.'

We'd never been landlords before, either. Matthew was quite excited about it. For a few weeks before our move, he wandered around with a paintbrush touching things up and moving a few boxes of stuff into storage, figuring that we had all the time in the world.

But the weeks flew past and suddenly there we were, on what we thought was our second last night in London (we hadn't yet discovered the ferry booking mistake), frantically getting the place ready for the new tenants.

'You mean you're staying *in*?' Jo couldn't believe it. She'd arrived all glammed up, like she was off for a night on the tiles. 'When you said you were struggling with your wardrobe, I didn't think you meant *literally*.'

The tenants we'd found for the flat wanted it unfurnished. Which was grand in theory, until we realised that we had to find new homes for our much-loved, if slightly sagging, furniture. More worrying was that each time we moved a set of drawers or a locker, a patch of startlingly clean carpet jumped out at us from underneath, making the rest of the carpet look like shite.

When we moved the wardrobe, there was no carpet at all; nothing except a neat, cut-out hole revealing bare floorboards.

'Could it be mice?' Jo wondered nervously. She didn't really do animals or, indeed, nature of any kind. Once outside the city boundaries, she began to wilt and lose her colour very quickly.

'Mice tend not to gnaw in straight lines,' Matthew assured her.

But I could see that he was as stressed as I was. Who would have thought there would be so much to do at the last minute? And now there was Jo, looking to be entertained. We'd said goodbye to her the previous evening; it had been a quiet affair where we'd cooked her a special dinner and made her a present of our bookcase, which was too old and fragile to survive the journey home, and which we wouldn't entrust to anybody else.

She poked the wardrobe with her high-heeled boot. 'Just move the stupid thing back. They probably won't even notice.'

The new tenants – two rather scruffy, studenty-looking types – had been insistent that the place come unfurnished. 'We want nothing left behind at all,' they'd said several times. One of them had quite starey eyes. 'Nothing.'

Matthew hadn't been keen on the look of them. 'We'll be getting phone calls all the time about them having drug-fuelled parties. Did you see the one who was stoned out of his head? Lucky bastard.'

But the fact was that we didn't have an awful lot of choice. The flat, though lovely to our eyes, was small even by city standards, and we just weren't going to attract the holy grail of tenants – a gay, professional couple in their thirties who would keep the place pristine, and plant some coriander on the windowsill while they were at it.

We put the wardrobe back. The students might be glad of it in the end, we decided, if only as a place to store trays of Bulmers in preparation for their parties.

'You'll ring us, won't you?' Matthew reminded Jo again. 'If they put a foot wrong?'

'I'll be all over them like a rash,' Jo assured him. 'I'll quite enjoy it. Right,' she said. 'Let's go.'

Matthew and I exchanged a look; so much to do, so little time, et cetera. And now Jo wanted us to go out?

Jo clarified, 'It's just a quiet evening with the Girls.'

The Girls were me, Jo, Jane and Mad Mags (although she doesn't like being called that to her face). The venue, I learned, was Falvio's, an Italian place we knew so well by now that we'd slept with half the staff. Well, Mags had. She was fabulous, but a sexual deviant after three glasses of wine. She'd tell you herself.

Matthew had been invited to be an Honorary Girl, as in, he would be allowed to drop me and pick me up from these affairs, and sometimes we'd invite him to stay for a beer or a coffee, depending on how we felt.

He'd thought long and hard about the invitation. 'It's not a compliment, is it?' he'd said at last.

What he really wanted to know was, did he somehow come across as gay?

'It's a *fabulous* compliment. It goes to show how much the Girls like and respect you. You don't see them asking Don, do you?'

Don was Jane's husband, a tall, fussy man fond of polo necks, and who was always talking about traffic routes and the euro. Mad Mags couldn't stand him. She literally came out in a rash.

But Matthew only truly relaxed into the group when Cool Art was invited to be an Honorary Girl too. Art had recently directed several car ads and was having regular and vigorous relations with a model called Anya. No one could possibly accuse him of being gay.

'One drink,' Jo cajoled. 'Come on. It won't be a late one.'

'They might have bought us a goodbye present,' Matthew murmured to me, as a clincher.

17

We grabbed our coats. I didn't bother changing my clothes. Well, Jane always showed up in things like slacks.

Matthew gave the wardrobe a stern look. 'I'll be back.'

'SURPRISE!'

We stopped in shock at the door of Falvio's. A sea of faces grinned back at us, amid much whooping and cheering.

'Surprise!' everybody shouted again, in case we hadn't got it the first time.

My eyes skidded over the crowd. There were the Girls – Mad Mags and Jane and Cool Art and his model girlfriend, Anya – looking gorgeous as ever – waving to us. And yes, Jane's husband, Don, too, but thankfully at the back. Jo had rustled up a gang from work as well: Brenda, dressed in, oh my Christ, a pair of leather trousers, and already necking a bottle of wine. Miranda and Chloe and Sandra, waitresses from Kitchen Queens, had also shown up. Oh, and there was Di, Matthew's mother, and Sharon and Liz, in a little huddle at the end of the table, Liz already looking around to see if she could nip out for a smoke.

'Matthew!' A bit of a shout went up from his side now, led by Sebastian, who had the cubicle beside Matthew at work, and who was a decent bloke, most notable for his prolific ordering online of items that arrived at his workplace in plain brown packaging. I could see their boss, Cassandra, beside him, plus a whole gang of assorted young IT men swigging bottled beer and eyeing up Anya.

Several sets of our neighbours were also there. I spotted the two girls from the flat below ours (active sex lives, judging by the noise), and Rita and Brian from upstairs (no sex life), and there were Pauline and Tim, the freeloaders, but who were very cuddly and lovable.

There were others smiling and waving at us from the back of the crowd, but I couldn't see them properly over the bobbing heads and I was a little overwhelmed.

Jo was delighted with herself. She was grinning from ear to ear. 'Bet you wish you'd changed out of those manky jeans now.'

'Oh, Jo.' I didn't know what to say. I'd no idea she was planning this.

I knew from Matthew's face that he hadn't either. Already he was inching his way towards his IT mates, and a bottle of cold beer.

'Don't say anything,' Jo told me. 'Just do the same for me when I emigrate.'

'Where are you emigrating to?'

'Maybe Ireland. I could join you.' Suddenly, her eyes looked wet. She began to fan her face furiously. 'Fuck. I *swore* I wouldn't do this.'

'Jo.'

But she wasn't having any of it. 'No, no, don't encourage me. It's your night. We'll cry later, OK?' she promised.

The Girls took charge of me then. Mad Mags was the first on the scene, guiding me to a table in the middle, sweeping aside several assorted IT guys who had homed in on our Kitchen Queen colleagues. 'You'll have a drink,' she stated warmly. 'Logan!' She grabbed one of the waiters as he went past. 'Another bottle of red, when you have a chance.' When he was gone she explained to us, 'He's American, over here on a two-year visa to study art and politics.'

'Why don't you ask to see his teeth while you're at it?' Jane enquired. Jane was the nice one of us; decent, kind, an excellent friend, with occasional and appropriate flashes of humour. She was forever worrying that all this made her boring. Still, in any group of friends, there has to be one nice-but-boring one, Jo often consoled her.

'The night is young,' Mags assured her. 'And so am I. Relatively speaking, of course.'

She turned to me, and gave a big sigh. 'We're going to miss you, you know.'

Jane nodded earnestly. 'We've known each other, how long? Your thirtieth birthday, Mags, wasn't it?'

'Why do you always have to bring that up?' Mags exploded.

'I didn't mean—'

'Because every time you do, people start wondering how old I am now. I see them looking at my neck and things.'

Mags was very paranoid about her neck. She thought it was like the trunk of a tree: the numbers of rings you had equated to your age. 'Yes, but only if they chop your head off and have a look inside,' Jo always told her.

Mags's answer was to always wear a scarf. She was the eldest of us all by some distance; her fortieth was coming up soon and we weren't sure how she'd cope. Probably by having an almighty party that would go on for a week.

Jane hurried the conversation on. 'You must be looking forward to seeing the family again, though.'

She hadn't met my mother. None of them had. Well, Anita hadn't been in a position to fly for a number of years now, or at least not unless she purchased more than one seat. She was one of the reasons we were going home.

They knew my sister, Róisín, of course. 'Pronounced Roe-sheen,' she'd eventually explained to them, after they'd called her everything under the sun.

She'd made many a trip to London over the years, and knew the Girls well. She and Mad Mags had even snogged the same fella on one particularly wild night out, before Róisín had finally 'come clean', as our mother, Anita, called it. 'Useless!' they'd both heartily agreed afterwards.

'And your friends,' Jo chimed in, in a very cheery voice. I noticed she was laying into the white wine, which wasn't like her. Well, it was, but I knew she had to work in the morning.

'Oh, I don't really know anybody any more. Not after ten years away.'

Although there were still a few knocking around. Róisín kept me abreast of events. I knew how lucky I'd be to have her when I got back, to smooth the way.

'What about your ex?' Jane said. Then she clapped a hand over her mouth. 'I can't believe I just said that. I'm usually so sensitive.'

'Are you?' said Mags.

'It's fine,' I assured Jane.

'Is it? I'll lie awake all night now, worrying that I've put my foot in it.' She continued to writhe in mortification.

Jo waved a hand. 'Jesus, Jane. They split up ten years ago. You hardly think she's still carrying a torch, when she's got that hunk over there?'

Matthew had the IT crowd in thrall. He was making shapes with his hands. Big shapes. With panels that opened and closed.

'It looks like he's describing a wardrobe,' Mags mused.

It was a great night. By the time I'd got round to everybody, it was nearly midnight. I must have looked thirsty because they all said, 'Oh, you'll have a drink,' and another glass of wine would materialise in my hand.

Matthew briefly surfaced at one point. He called to me over the crowd, 'We should go . . . ferry . . . packing . . .' But then he was swallowed up and I didn't see him for another hour.

By then it got too *late* to go. Well, we had to see everybody out the door, didn't we? It would be rude to leave before them.

I only vaguely remembered saying goodbye to Cool Art.

'Good luck,' he said.

Jo told me afterwards that I replied, kind of belligerently, 'What's that supposed to mean? You think it's all going to go pear-shaped? I haven't done anything wrong, you know. I was only young.' Then, apparently I told Anya, the model, that she was very, very beautiful, and I was quite fawning and disgusting, Jo said.

Jane, who was driving, bore Mad Mags off, amid promises that they would visit soon (lies, probably).

Eventually the place was empty except for Jo, me, Matthew, and Logan the waiter, who had given up any notion of getting us out of the place. Matthew was badgering him about taking the wardrobe.

'We'll have it delivered to you and everything.'

'But I already have a wardrobe—'

'Just take the damn thing, man.'

Jo and I sat over pint glasses of water. Far, far too late for that, of course, but God loves a trier.

'Do you want to cry now?' I asked her.

'No.' She sighed. 'I haven't the blooming energy. But I'm a bit cheesed off at being left behind on my own.' She gave herself a little shake. 'Don't mind me. I'm just feeling lonely and friendless at the moment. And don't tell me I've still got Jane and Mad Mags. Jane is pregnant, so how much fun is *she* going to be?'

'Jane's pregnant?'

Jo's face fell. 'Sorry. I wasn't supposed to say anything. She only just found out.'

'That's OK.' But I was hurt. Could it be happening already? That I was being eased out of the group?

'She keeps coming out with insensitive remarks and forgetting all her PIN numbers.' Jo sighed. 'And Mags is great, but she likes to do her own thing at the same time.'

Mags had gazillions of friends. The Girls were just one of her many groups. She was also a member of two supper clubs, the Thames Ladies' Rowing Club, an internet swingers club, and a book club somewhere in Clapham. She wouldn't be the type who'd be pinned down too often for a trip to a cinema, for instance.

'Sorry,' said Jo. 'I know I shouldn't be bringing you down like this. I know I should be supportive and delighted for you and all that, but what the hell am I going to do without you?'

She looked so woebegone that I almost wanted to laugh. But I would probably miss her just as much; even more so, because at least she had the rest of the gang here; I had nobody, only distant memories of friends from school, and I couldn't even remember whether I'd liked them or not.

'What the hell am *I* going to do?' I wailed, and burst into tears.

'Oh, good,' said Jo, breaking down too. 'I thought we'd never start.'

At that, Logan gently hustled us out of the restaurant, still bawling our heads off.

Chapter Four

We heard Anita before we saw her. There was a puff, puff, puff on the other side of the front door, then it was flung open and there she was, in a flowery nightie so voluminous that for a minute I thought we'd strayed by accident into a field of daisies.

'Welcome home, welcome home, even though it's the crack of dawn.' She was delighted at all the excitement. She gathered us both into big hugs and planted kisses on our cheeks. 'How was the crossing? What a mix-up! Anyway, never mind, you're here now – close that door, will you, before the dogs get out.'

She had two massive, skangery-looking dogs, named Bangers and Mash, who dashed out of the kitchen with ferocious growls. They knew me well enough by now to tolerate me but, as always, they went straight for Matthew's throat, ignoring his firm but friendly, 'Hello there, boys—'

'Get down, lads,' Anita bellowed, just in time.

The dogs gave Matthew a look that said, 'Later . . .' and slunk off.

'They just have to get to know you,' Anita assured him, even though they'd known him going on five years at that point, give or take a few months. 'Is that all your things out there?'

She looked past us to the Mégane, amazed. It had survived the ferry journey, even if the poor old thing was nearly sitting on the ground from the weight of all the stuff in it.

'We're hoping it'll make it as far as the house,' I told her.

She was thrown into a flurry of activity. 'You're not going anywhere until you've had a cup of tea.' She gathered the massive nightie in around her ankles so that nobody tripped themselves up, before turning and puff-puffing her way back into the kitchen. The smell of a fry-up hit me in the face.

'Anita . . .' I began.

We'd called her Anita for as long as I could remember. She felt that 'Mum' made her sound ancient, and we were to call her by her proper name, or else, she said, she wouldn't answer. 'Touched' was how Róisín always described her. All the other kids in the town thought we were very cool and hip, though, and so we went along with it.

She flapped her hands at me. 'Giving out to me already, and she's only back in the country five minutes. Don't I get enough of that from Róisín? That girl needs to seriously lighten up. Besides,' she said, 'it's for Matthew.' She squeezed his arm, conspiratorial. 'Rashers, sausages, fried potato and that black pudding that you like.'

A blooming heart attack waiting to happen. Matthew knew what he had to do. Politely decline and walk away. No point in encouraging the madness.

'I won't take no for an answer,' Anita told him nicely.

What could he do? Except give me a sheepish look as he let himself be folded into a chair while a cup of tea was pressed into his hand. 'Um, thanks, Anita. Honestly, you shouldn't have.'

Anita was very fond of Matthew. When she phoned up for her regular Sunday night chat, she never hung up without a detailed enquiry into his wellbeing. 'Did he shake that cold yet? He sounded terrible last week. And is there any news on who's been robbing that photocopy paper in his office?'

I was raging that Matthew had told her about that – it was us, of course, but just a packet or two, mostly because it was so convenient. We'd had no idea they would start an *inquiry*.

'We think it's Sebastian,' Matthew fobbed Anita off on the phone, and defaming an innocent man in the process. He gave me an apologetic look. 'I was just trying to move the conversation on,' he hissed. 'She keeps on at me to wear vests.'

My sister, Róisín, pinned my mother's fondness for Matthew on his ability to fix things around the house. Anita's only son was our brother, Eddie, who was an actor, and so didn't really count when it came to changing light bulbs and tightening up the washer on a leaky tap. Róisín maintained that Anita had semi-adopted Matthew in a bid to get him to keep the house from falling down around her. For free.

Róisín sounded horrible and bitter, but in actual fact she was one of the nicest people you could ever meet. And she put up with Anita all year round, whereas I was only a day-tripper, home to hide the biscuit tin only for weekends here and there.

And it was true that Matthew fixed a lot of things for Anita. She'd been on her own in the house for six years now, since Dad had died (we called him Dad, not Colin). And it wasn't like she'd started with a clean slate either, with his passing. Dad's approach to DIY was a hammer and a mouthful of nails; stick enough of them in and it was job done.

The result was that Anita was left with a large, run-down house, half eaten by ivy, and held together by a few rusty nails. And Matthew was a good fixer-upper. After spending a hard week at the office browsing eBay and illegally downloading music, he was bursting with energy at the weekends, and would roam around our flat restlessly, hoping that the bedroom door had inexplicably fallen off during the night. It never had, and in the end he often put on his coat and hat and informed me, 'I'm just going to do some work in the garden.'

'We don't have a garden, Matthew.'

'I know. I just wanted to say it, OK?'

So when Anita said to him on the second weekend I brought him over, 'I wonder would you be able to go outside and chop a few logs for me?' he was nearly overcome with excitement.

He set off, axe in hand, and wearing some kind of a cap thing he'd bought in an outdoors shop in central London, and that had two tartan flaps that came down over his ears.

How we laughed at that cap. Every Christmas it was still brought up after everybody had had a few drinks. 'Here, Matthew! Do you remember that cap you brought when you first came here? With the tartan earflaps?'

'Yes, I do!' Matthew would always say gamely back. 'What an eejit I was back then!'

'He's certainly different from the other lad you used to go out with, isn't he?' Anita said to me carefully one day.

She never said his name because she knew I didn't like talking about him. 'You'd think he was Darth Vader or something, the way she goes on,' I'd heard her complain to Róisín once. But Anita was still a bit baffled about the whole thing; such a fine, tall man, always in those nice suits, and even now, years after it had ended between me and him, he still enquired after Anita's health.

Not that Matthew wasn't nice. At the same time, I could have been a solicitor's wife, instead of a something-vague-in-IT's wife.

'Thank God,' I said shortly. Anita always made me feel defensive, like the whole thing had been my fault.

'Who are we talking about?' said Matthew, walking into the kitchen.

Anita looked worried; she didn't want to frighten a second potential husband off. 'Oh, nobody. Some fellow from around here. It broke up just before she went to London.'

Now she looked at me, more worried; had she said too much?

'I know,' said Matthew. 'She told me.'

Anita was relieved. She had enough deceit going on as it was, what with the whole food thing. But I was hardly going to keep my history from Matthew. He'd told me about his ex-girlfriends too. Leggy Lisa and Busty Beatrice, as he always insisted on calling them, whilst staring wistfully into the distance until I gave him a thump.

So it was all fine.

'And he *is* much nicer,' I said, plonking a kiss on Matthew's cheek, while Anita looked on in approval.

And now we were home for good her delight was obvious. Bangers and Mash were good guard dogs, but it wasn't like having a houseful of people, the way it used to be.

Here she came now with the greasiest fry-up you ever saw. Accompanied by – oh, no – four slices of French toast.

'Will you have some?' she said to me generously.

'No, Anita. Thanks, anyway.'

Her brow creased. 'But I've done enough for two.'

Didn't she mean for eight? I looked at her hard. I was wise to her tricks. Well, Róisín was wise to them and had filled me in.

'The dogs will eat it,' I told her.

'The dogs? Give good food to the *dogs*?' She looked highly indignant. 'I certainly will not. I might just have one of those rashers myself.' She went on chattily, 'It's grilled, not fried, you know.'

'Oh, well, that's OK then,' I said sarcastically. 'Why don't you have those sausages while you're at it?'

She had the gall to tell me primly, 'Oh, no. I'm not allowed sausages.'

'You're not allowed those rashers either, Anita. Or that spoon of sugar you slipped into your mug of tea when you thought nobody was looking.'

Rumbled, her rounded chin rose up in super defensive mode. 'It's the weekend. I've been good all week. My normal breakfast is a bowl of porridge. Every single morning. With some raspberries on top,' she added modestly.

I'd heard the bowl-of-porridge-with-raspberries-on-top tale before.

'Don't listen to her.' Róisín was at the door. 'She must be eating nineteen bowls of the blooming stuff at every sitting, judging by her last doctor's visit. Eh, Anita?'

Then she caught sight of the frying pan in Anita's hand. From her horrified intake of breath, you'd think it was a semi-automatic machine gun.

Anita looked hunted. 'What are you doing here at this hour?' she bleated.

Róisín looked at me, and gave a great sigh of relief. 'Thank God you're home.'

Chapter Five

Home was Castlemoy, both a reasonable drive from the city (thirty-five minutes if you took the motorway), yet an oasis of peace and calm.

I didn't write this, by the way. It was on the official tourist information leaflet that was issued in the hope of luring tourists to the town. The town 'derived its name from the old Gaelic term *Caislean Moy*, which means the castle set on the low lands. Leprechauns optional'. Again, from the tourist information leaflet. OK, so I added the Leprechaun bit myself. And, in fairness, there *was* a bit of a castle on a hill at the top of the town, and an alleged fairy fort on Tommy Moynihan's farm two miles out, but otherwise the place was flat as a pancake.

We didn't get many tourists in Castlemoy. I couldn't remember any great influx, not even when I was a child and the Americans used to come over in their droves. Even now, when the Tourist Board was talking the country up for all it was worth, and writing pithy leaflets, we still didn't get any.

Nobody much cared. Anyway, the main street wasn't wide enough for those huge tourist coaches with their television sets and massive wing mirrors. Legend had it that one had tried to pull up once outside Dirty Harry's pub for a rest stop, but Harry had chased the visitors away before they destroyed his trade.

'They'd be demanding smoked wild salmon on brown soda bread, and we only do toasted cheese and ham sandwiches here,' he said, sweating after the close shave.

Nor was there enough to attract tourists, apart from the crumbling castle on the bit of a hill. No thatched roofs or charming stone-built rows of cottages. There were just pubs, lots of them, and Drennan's Drapers that still had yellow Perspex in the window to stop the twinsets fading in the non-existent sun.

Modernisation had come too, though. There was a twenty-four-hour Esso garage at the top of the town that could flog you anything from nappies to Rizla papers at two o'clock in the morning, depending on your preferences. There was also a well-resourced supermarket on the outskirts, a popular Chinese fast-food joint called The Big Panda, and a primary school, which was being hurriedly extended to accommodate the offspring of all the Dubliners.

In recent years Castlemoy had become a commuter town for the many disaffected Dubliners who'd been forced out of their own city by the shocking prices being demanded for three-bedroom semis in dodgy parts of town. By the time they'd finished giving out about it, they realised they had two choices: they could either emigrate to Australia or buy on purpose-built estates on the outskirts of towns like Castlemoy.

'Hmm, Tony, what do you think? Castlemoy, or sunny Sydney with its beautiful beaches, relaxed lifestyle and fantastic job opportunities?'

'God, Karen, I don't know. A thirty-five-minute commute in heavy traffic every morning – my arse, it's forty-five minutes, never mind that tourist information leaflet – or an outdoors life of surfing and barbecues, and fabulous houses with swimming pools? It's very hard, isn't it?'

You wouldn't believe how many of them had plumped for Castlemoy.

When we'd come over for weekend visits, Matthew would tell me that I wasn't being fair to the place. 'You grew up here so you're not seeing it the way outsiders do.'

'Rubbish.'

'You're always making fun of it.'

'What do you want me to say? That Flanagan's hardware shop is the ultimate in shopping experiences? That the school has produced several notable luminaries, myself included?' I had a good laugh to show him I wasn't serious.

'You were happy in that school, though, weren't you?'

'Well, yes.' I had a sudden memory of Mrs Mulligan, with her wire-rimmed glasses, giving me two of her cream crackers when I'd forgotten my lunch. And I remembered singing in the choir, fifty clear little voices soaring.

'There's nothing wrong with the place,' I conceded to Matthew. 'It's just a small town, that's all.'

I also remembered endless school holidays with flip all to do except hang around outside the sweet shop, watching tractors go by. Mostly, though, we sat on the wall outside our house, me, Róisín and Dominique Fitzgibbons, and tried to come up with a new surname for Dominique. She wanted to be a famous actress, and had the rest of the package – blond hair, upturned nose, the illusion of being French, but the *surname*. 'There's no way I'll crack Hollywood with that clanger,' she said crisply, no daw even at the age of ten. 'What do you think of Dominique Duverne?'

'Oh, shut up, would you?' Róisín and Dominique had never really got on. But in a town the size of Castlemoy, there wasn't a huge selection of potential friends to choose from, and so we were all reluctantly joined at the hip – until Dominique and Róisín's last, spectacular falling-out, that was. There was no friendship after that.

When we were a bit older, and on the rare occasions that there was some sun, we'd carefully lay ourselves out in the back garden in our bikinis, having first sprinkled lemon juice in our hair to give it natural streaks, as instructed by *Jackie* magazine, which Dominique read religiously.

'See? No difference whatsoever,' Róisín would say, examining her hair after several hours of waiting for it to turn into Farrah Fawcett's.

Dominique would languidly turn over onto her back. She was already in full puberty and I was terribly envious of her 32B chest. I could see

Róisín sneaking glances at it too. 'It doesn't work on coarse, horrible hair like yours.'

'Shut up and go home, Dominique Fitzgibbons!' Róisín would end up shouting in a temper.

But Dominique would only smile like a cat, as she looked Róisín's thin, flat body up and down, clearly finding her wanting.

'What?' poor Róisín would end up demanding. 'What are you looking at?'

'It's just that you don't look much like a girl.'

'Well, I *am* a girl.'

'You don't dress much like one either. You don't do the things girls do, like paint your nails or do your hair.'

I felt guilty. She'd just named my twin obsessions. Róisín had scant interest in either.

'So what?' Róisín said defensively. 'Just because I'm not an airhead like you.'

'I'm just saying.' And Dominique flopped back down on the towel, giving Róisín one last canny look, already able to smell out difference.

Eventually Dad would shout at us to go and put some clothes on and not be giving the postman a heart attack.

It was like we were biding our time: Dominique, to go to Hollywood, Róisín to train as a nurse (she was always bandaging me up) and me to go, well, *anywhere*.

I told Matthew all this, trying to make him laugh. Usually I could. But he was looking off into the middle distance with great gloom. 'Well, when *I* was young . . .' he began.

Oh God. Now I was in for it. His version of *Angela's Ashes*.

'. . . at school, the kids would slice the uniform off you with Stanley knives if you couldn't run fast enough,' he lectured me. 'I used to love sitting in classrooms like the ones you're complaining about now, because at least you were safe until the bell went. Once, when school was over—'

'You had to run home like a bat out of hell before you got your hair shaved into the shape of a penis in the toilets. I know, you've told me.'

31

Matthew had been brought up in a council flat on a rough estate. Apparently he'd regularly sprinted for his life from various assorted low-lifes and thugs who would try to beat him up just because he was wearing a sleeveless black T-shirt (Bon Jovi was big at the time).

'It wasn't funny,' he said mildly, as I played my imaginary violin.

'You always said it toughened you up.'

'I know, and it did. But at the same time, I wouldn't want it for my own kids.'

I thought about it. I wouldn't either.

'I'd want this,' he said.

I knew what he meant: the simplicity, the country air, the safety of small-town life. And, looking back, the boredom we'd been suffering in our teens had really only been innocence.

We were having this conversation on a walk through the town. We were home from London for the weekend for Anita's birthday. She was back at the house happily baking up a massive cake that she assured us she was 'only going to have one small slice of, because what's a birthday without a cake?'

We came to a stop outside my old school.

'Let's go in,' Matthew said.

'No.' I thought he was joking. Anyway, the school gate was locked. 'We'd be trespassing.'

'I just think you're afraid to scale the gate,' he scoffed.

That did it, of course. I could never let a challenge like that go past. I threw one leg over, then another, and then I landed into the playground that had seemed so huge when I was a child, but now was *tiny*.

'Come here. Look at this.' Matthew had jumped over the gate too, and was examining the playground wall.

He'd found my initials, scrawled by me as a nine-year-old, probably with a piece of stone. It was complete with the date, and I got a little lump in my throat at the sight.

'Bless,' Matthew said. 'Hey.' He squinted closer at the wall. 'Who's this Thomas character that you say you love? Take me to him,' he said fiercely. 'I'll knock his block off.'

On the way home, we passed by one of the commuter estates on the outskirts of the town. 'They're very tastefully built,' Matthew decided, peering in. The houses were in a crescent, two rows facing each other across a wide road. It was nice and cosy, yet you weren't on top of your neighbours. Best of all, behind the houses were mature woods, giving the place a lovely, rustic feel. 'And look, they've all got big back gardens,' Matthew detailed. 'Plenty of room for a dog, or kids, or whatever.'

A dog. *Kids?*

Both of us looked at the other, a little bug-eyed. How had that slipped out?

'So . . . what do you think?' Matthew said eventually.

'About the dog?'

'Yes. And the kids.'

I really admired him. Well, you never knew how the other person was going to react when the subject of the future was introduced, did you? You couldn't even remark on a cute baby in the park without thinking, Jesus, does he think I'm trying to entrap him? We had friends who'd dated for six or seven years, each too petrified to bring the subject up in case the other person ran for the hills.

No pussy-footing around for Matthew. He wasn't going to pretend he was too cool to talk about the whole for-keeps thing. He was a guy who knew what he wanted.

And he wanted me.

'Will we settle down then?' he said.

I felt hot and cold at the same time. This was serious. But I was ready, too. 'In Castlemoy?'

'Can you think of somewhere better?'

Chapter Six

Róisín and Anita had the usual jousting before we got down to business.

'Do you know how many calories are in a single sausage?' Róisín looked as if the thought alone scalded her. 'The salt? The *fat* content?'

'No, but I bet you can tell me.' Anita was unperturbed. 'At least I have my favourite child home now to protect me from all this abuse.'

'What she means is that you're a soft touch,' Róisín confided in me. 'Don't fall for it.'

Between the two of them, I was wondering what I'd let myself in for.

'Have you checked your blood sugar today?' Róisín was looking about in vain for the sheet Anita was supposed to record things on. 'You need to do it every day, Anita. It's not good enough to say you feel OK.'

'Don't lecture me. I get enough of that from Mooney.'

Dr Mooney was her long-suffering doctor.

'He's just trying to save your life.'

'Well, he's not doing a very good job.'

'You're still alive, aren't you?' Róisín said wearily.

'Oh,' said Anita. 'You're right. I am.' And she squealed with laughter. She had a little girl laugh, tee-hee-hee, and her eyes nearly disappeared into her cheeks.

'Sweet Jesus, do you see what I have to put up with?' Róisín said to me, smiling too. She looked me up and down admiringly. 'You look great, Clara. Doesn't she, Anita? I love those boots and your fancy jacket and . . . what's that you've done to your hair?'

I'd got it cut and coloured the previous Saturday. A final treat to myself before I left.

I waited in some trepidation as Anita and Róisín gathered round. Whenever I came home, the latest aspect of my 'London look' was always closely examined by the pair of them. You wouldn't know which way it would go.

'It's nice,' Anita declared cautiously, rifling through my hair as though checking for nits.

'Highlights, is it?' said Róisín, uncertainly.

Róisín's own hair was beautiful and glossy without any interference from hairstylists. Her look was dressed down and hip; jeans and quirky tops and Converse runners, on her days off. When she'd been younger, and doing her nursing training in Dublin, she'd gone through a rebellious period of cropped hair and military jackets and T-shirts that said things like, 'Playing for the Other Team'. 'I wonder what team she could mean?' Anita and Dad used to ponder idly over cups of tea. 'It's not like any of us is particularly sporty.' Clueless, God love them. But the T-shirts were only short-lived. When Róisín got a permanent job and moved back home to Castlemoy, the T-shirts swiftly disappeared and she retreated behind 'regular' clothes again.

I wondered if she still had the T-shirts in a drawer somewhere, biding their time until they were worn again.

'Floodlights, actually,' I said.

'*Floodlights?*' Anita and Róisín looked at each other, eyebrows jumping up. This was even dafter than the time I'd come home wearing short dungarees, the kind you used to see in photos of little boys in the 1960s.

'She got it done by a guy called Dylan,' Matthew murmured. He loved whipping them up.

'*Dylan.*' Anita was duly scornful. A very pretentious-sounding name altogether. She'd once had her hair cut up in Dublin in some trendy place, and she'd only wanted a trim and a blow-dry, like usual, but she'd been accosted by someone called Rex, who was wearing more make-up than she was, and who'd cut her hair into what could only be described as a wedge. It had taken her a full six months to grow it out.

I gave Matthew a warning look. He ignored it and silkily said, 'It cost two hundred and thirty pounds.'

'Sterling?' Anita yelped, as though there was any other kind. She did a quick conversion. 'That's nearly two hundred and eighty euro. For a *hairdo*?'

'Luckily for you, you can get it done at Cuts 'n' Curls down the town from now on,' Róisín assured me drily. 'Thirty-five euro for a cut and blow-dry.'

'Oh, yes, it's very good value,' said Anita. 'And they'll make you a cappuccino and everything, for free.'

'Great.' I was going to put a stop to this city-girl-slumming-it nonsense from the off. 'I'll make an appointment the next time I need it done. Support local business and all that.'

'And I'll be doing my level best for the pub trade,' Matthew assured Róisín stoutly.

Matthew had notions of sipping pints of plain down in Dirty Harry's with the town's elders, soaking up stories about how they used to walk to school through the fields in bare feet. Matthew would be able to chime in with his own stories about how he'd run to school through the mean streets, to avoid being mugged.

'Good for you,' Róisín said. A little doubtfully.

She didn't think Matthew would cut it here. Not that she would ever *say* it, of course, but she was always reminding us how old-fashioned and backward the place was. For some reason – maybe it was the hat with the tartan earflaps – she seemed to think Matthew's interest in Castlemoy would be limited and very possibly finite. 'It's a very pretty town,' she'd warned him before we'd moved over, 'but it's just not that sophisticated. There aren't any sushi bars or anything like that.'

'When has she ever known me to hanker after sushi bars?' Matthew had said to me, a bit bewildered.

'How's Catherine?' I asked Róisín, hastily changing the subject.

'She's OK,' said Róisín, uncertainly. They'd been going out almost a year now, but she never seemed that confident about things. 'Working too hard, of course.'

I'd only met Catherine twice. The last time Matthew and I had been home, she'd been away at a conference and the time before that, we'd met up with her in Dublin, in a very trendy coffee shop where all the staff had tattoos. Catherine worked very long hours, it seemed, doing something in marketing, and Róisín said it was easier for us to go up to Dublin than for Catherine to get into the car and make the trip down (even though it was only thirty-five minutes on the motorway). Catherine was great fun, very cheerful and energetic. She'd known absolutely everybody in the café that day, and I remembered Róisín watching her shyly, as if the sun had just come out.

'Would she not think of changing jobs?' Anita wondered cautiously. She always spoke cautiously when it came to Róisín's relationships because, she said, she always seemed to say the wrong thing. 'That way you'd get to spend a bit more time together.'

It appeared she'd put her foot in it again. 'Change *jobs*?' said Róisín, flinging her eyes around the place. 'In this recession? She's lucky to have one at all.'

It was difficult to know whether she was defensive about Catherine or just defensive in general.

'Yes, yes, of course, sorry,' Anita muttered contritely, and shut up.

Matthew pounced on the break in the conversation and interjected eagerly, 'Any word on the house?'

His question was an important one. If the house wasn't ready, then we'd be beginning our new lives under Anita's roof. Which was fine, except that she'd drive us both completely mad in five minutes. She seemed to spend a lot of time wandering round the kitchen, picking up packets of food, and squinting at the ingredients before musing aloud, 'I wonder is it OK for me to eat this?' The box would be clearly marked 'BISCUITS' or 'DOUBLE CHOCOLATE EXTRA FATTY SUGARY FUDGE CAKE', or any number of other things that poorly controlled diabetics simply could not eat, or at least not in the quantities than Anita liked. She'd never dream of picking up a lettuce or a pot of low-fat yoghurt and asking the same thing. That was probably because she never had lettuce or low-fat yoghurt in the house, but plenty of biscuits and fudge cake mix.

We were saved by Róisín jingling a set of keys provocatively and giving us a big smile. 'All yours.'

Matthew and I looked at each other, delighted; the sale must have gone through without a hitch.

Then: *oh my GOD. We've bought a house. Another one.*

'Congratulations!' Anita and Róisín sang in unison.

We hadn't meant to acquire another house. Renting would have been fine. And we already owned the flat.

'We don't want to turn into property magnates,' I told Matthew, when we'd been in the planning stages.

He laughed, but I actually meant it.

'Anyway,' I said, 'we haven't the money.'

I also meant that.

Then he announced, super casually, that he had forty thousand pounds in savings.

'Funny.'

'I have.'

'Matthew, don't be stupid.' He said nothing. '*Pounds?*' Then, '*Sterling?*'

'You're your mother's daughter, aren't you?'

Just when you thought you knew him. I could never be mysterious, like him. I'm just not secure enough, and if I had forty thousand pounds in the bank, I'd have to go bragging to everybody just so they knew how sensible and forward-thinking I was.

'Matthew. Where did you get that kind of money?' I was torn between delight and fear.

He seemed mildly bewildered himself. 'I'm not really sure.'

'You didn't . . . steal it?'

'I wish I was that exciting.' He sighed.

'How then?' We'd used some savings from a joint account to buy the flat; this new fund was a mystery.

He thought about it. 'I suppose I got it the boring way. I set up a savings account when I first started working, and some of my wages goes into it every month. And I put my bonuses in there, the performance-related ones.' He raised an eyebrow at me. 'Despite what you think, I do actually work hard every day. My bonuses have been very healthy. Mind you, I didn't think they were that healthy.' He was far too casual about the whole thing.

'*Forty thousand pounds*, Matthew.' Maybe if I said it enough times nobody would ask how much was in *my* savings account.

But it turned out that I was more budget-minded than I thought. When I counted everything up, all the bits and pieces I'd saved, I had the guts of ten thousand myself. Happy days!

'One thousand,' Matthew interjected gently. 'You have *one* thousand, Clara. Not ten.'

'Oh.'

'There's no need to be embarrassed. Luckily, you've managed to bag a rich man and I'll look after you, sweetheart.' He winked at me lewdly.

He was as good as his word. He rang up O'Mahony's estate agents in Castlemoy and discovered that one of the houses in the crescent was for sale.

'What crescent? What are you talking about?'

'That nice little estate at the top of the town. With the big gardens and the woods at the back.'

It had obviously left quite an impression on him.

I hesitated. Did I really want to live in a crescent of new houses? 'What about that idea we had of an old farmhouse that we could do up?'

'Us? Come on. Lovely idea, but we're lazy as fuck. We'd never get round to it.'

And actually, even the thought of doing up an old farmhouse imme-diately filled me with feelings of despair and exhaustion.

'OK, but that crescent is full of commuters.' I made my voice very forbidding.

'Won't we be commuters ourselves? In an oasis of peace and calm, of course.' He looked at me, his head on one side, and gave me one of his very intelligent stares, the ones I usually want to run and hide from, especially when the credit card bill comes in and it turns out that, amazingly, most of it's mine. 'What's the matter, Clara? It's like I have to persuade you every step of the way. Are you having second thoughts about moving back or something?'

How could I explain to him what was wrong, except in terms of having bad karma-ish thoughts? Matthew had no time for karma, bad or otherwise, or the feeling that someone's just walked over your grave. He called it tripe and poppycock. I loved that description. So much more polite than shite.

'Maybe I'm nervous, Matthew. We're so happy in London. We have everything we want. Maybe I'm thinking, why risk it by moving?'

Matthew put his arms around me and pulled me close. 'Because maybe it can be even better. But we won't find out if we don't take the risk.' He gave me one of his slow smiles, the kind that made me want to follow him to the ends of the earth. 'I've got a good feeling about this.'

Matthew was so much more reliable than I was. If he had a good feeling, that was enough to trump all of my bad karma.

I snuggled in close, reassured. 'Let's do it then.'

Chapter Seven

The house had a big 'Sold' sign plonked in the front garden.

I swallowed hard; there was nothing like the taking on of a second mortgage to wipe the just-happily-arrived smile off your face.

Matthew suddenly came over all serious. He had some kind of a snag list in his hand, which he'd mysteriously produced from somewhere. He immediately began strutting up and down in front of the house in a very testosteroney way, muttering things like, '. . . guttering intact . . . check . . . hydrangea in front garden . . . yes, but only a puny one . . .' followed by some feverish scribbling.

At one point he sneaked a look at Róisín. Maybe she would be impressed and see him as more than just some city boy with an inclination towards Asian food.

Róisín was paying him no attention; she was helping Anita out of her car. But Anita clearly felt patronised and tried to fend her off. There was a bit of sumo-type wrestling until they both emerged from it, with a popping sound in Anita's case, like a cork coming out of a bottle.

But it was actually Róisín, opening champagne she'd taken from the boot.

'Before you get excited, it's only sparkling wine, not proper champagne. But we have to have a toast to your new home.'

I felt guilty now. We'd tried to leave the two of them behind at Anita's.

I'd kind of hoped that Matthew would carry me over the threshold, just the two of us starting our new life together. But Anita had nothing on for the day, and when she was bored she was dangerous. Also, what with having finally managed to get us both home from London, she wasn't going to let us out of her sight. There was no room for her in the car, unless we stuffed her into the top box, so Róisín had to drive her instead.

We stood around the front garden as Róisín poured the warm wine into plastic cups.

'Am I allowed to have sparkling wine?' Anita said doubtfully. I realised this was directed at me.

'Well—' I began. Then, remembering I needed to toughen up, I said, 'No, Anita. You're not.' Her face fell pathetically. I did a U-turn. 'But as Róisín has only poured you a very, very little one, you can go ahead.'

I surreptitiously glanced at Róisín: was that acceptable?

Róisín gave a tiny indication that yes, I had done OK on my first outing. But not to give in *all* the time.

It was hard not to defer to Róisín, as she was a community care nurse and, technically, was Anita's designated nurse. When Anita annoyed her she half-heartedly threatened to hand her file over to Nurse Harriet Newman, the other community care nurse, who 'isn't half as nice and won't put up with a quarter of your nonsense'.

Róisín loved her job. She'd worked in a big hospital in Dublin for a while, but it had been too anonymous for her and she'd only really come into her own when she got back home, to people that she knew and understood, and with whom she was able to sit down and have a laugh and a chat, which was half the battle. They liked the fact that she was very calm and competent, even though she always maintained she wasn't really, it was just that they were trained that way. Even when things were going horrifically wrong, and there was blood spurting everywhere, and, worse, it was all your fault, you still had to smile serenely at the patient and say things like, 'Now, Mr Duffy, this won't hurt a bit,' even while you plunged a needle straight into his heart. (But that was only in the movies, apparently. In day-to-day nursing life you never plunged anything into anybody's heart. And if you did, they'd probably sue your arse off.)

The house was nicer than I'd remembered. I'd only seen it twice; the first time with Matthew on our walk through the town that evening, and then when we'd flown back to view it with the estate agent. The day had been dark and drizzly, and we'd been rushing to get back for our flight home, as Matthew had a meeting the following morning. The estate agent – Deirdre, I remembered now – had been very confused when we'd announced, only five minutes into her spiel, that we wanted to buy it.

'You don't have to make up your minds today,' she said suspiciously. Apparently, what with the property crash, she hadn't sold a house in months.

'I know, but we're moving in six weeks' time and we need a house.'

This wasn't adding up for her, you could see that. Plus, we had the money all lined up; no chain, and a mortgage offer in writing. It was very untoward.

'I have more houses,' she said stoutly.

'We like this one. Do you want a deposit now?'

This was the final straw for her. 'Are you not even going to haggle?'

Haggle? We were getting the house for half nothing as it was. Since the property crash, there was no longer any demand for houses on the very periphery of Dublin, when you could get one actually *in* Dublin for the price of a packet of crisps.

'Well, no.' Matthew, desperate by now, let his voice drop. 'Look, we're new to these parts. Just blow-ins.'

'Ah.' Her brow cleared. She hissed, 'I shouldn't tell you this, but if you wait a month, it'll probably have halved in price again.'

In the end Matthew practically had to strong-arm her into taking our deposit cheque; she rang us a few days later to tell us it had cleared, still sounding suspicious.

Today was bright and sunny, if cold, and the little crescent with its double row of houses looked cosy and inviting. Each house, although apparently identical to the others at first glance, was actually a little different. Ours had a big bay window to the left of the front door, and I was already planning a comfy chair there, and a desk where I would

43

do my paperwork and process all my hundreds of orders, with a lovely view across the crescent and to the trees beyond.

Róisín was delighted with our back garden. She kept standing on tiptoe to look over the wall, and saying, 'Would you look at that. It's massive.' She lived in the middle of the town, in a small terraced house with only a patio at the back, which was too small even to swing a cat in. She kept insisting that she'd tried.

Matthew was now running his hand over window-ledges, and giving the windows a sharp rap with his knuckles. Then he leaned suddenly against the outside wall, hard. Yep, definitely solid brick; we hadn't been palmed off with straw or anything like that.

'Happy it's not going to fall down around our ears?' I called to him.

'I'll be the judge of that,' he said darkly, and went off to give the door to the side passage a good seeing-to.

Anita looked around covertly at the other houses and said, 'I wonder what the neighbours are like.'

'They're probably wondering what *we're* like, quaffing sparkling wine on the front lawn in the middle of the morning, accompanied by a man who's clearly unbalanced.'

Róisín had the inside story. 'Maura Kiernan lives in number four. Do you remember her from school?' She helped me along. 'The class above you, tall, lanky, dark hair that used to be cut into a mullet?'

'Oh, yes. She was the spit of, oh, what's his name . . . '

'Keith Richards from the Rolling Stones,' Anita said triumphantly. 'Yes!'

We all tee-heed at that and then we had to sober up before someone saw us.

'Anyway,' Róisín went on low, 'she's married to Thomas Doors. A.k.a. The Knob? Sister of Patsy Doors, a.k.a. Wide Open? No? Anyway, their father had Parkinson's, God love him; he died last year. I used to visit him at home.'

Anita blessed herself. Róisín had nursed Dad too, in his final year. I used to be a bit jealous of that, even though at the same time it was relief to know that he was being looked after by family when I couldn't be there. There was little I could do from London, and nothing I could offer him in the way of my own profession, unless he suddenly developed a craving for chicken satay skewers.

'I don't know anybody else,' Róisín said, looking at the houses. 'Probably commuters.'

The house next door to Maura and The Knob's, number six, had a 'To Let' sign. The blinds were drawn and the lawn overgrown. Clearly it was vacant. Next to us, I saw a scooter strewn on the front lawn: kids there, obviously. And a Harley-Davidson motorbike outside number eleven, up the way. An overgrown kid there.

But otherwise the drives were all empty. Everybody was in Dublin, working their socks off, just like we would be soon. Or, Matthew, anyway. I had fond hopes of seeing them in the mornings, when we'd call out to each other merrily, 'Hello! Nice day! See you at Frank's barbecue Friday? We're bringing the wine!' and then we'd all leap into our cars and drive off up the motorway, happy as Larry, whoever he was.

Matthew had finally completed his snag list. 'The place is perfect,' he declared confidently. Then, and only then, did he take the key out of his pocket and open the front door. He was careful not to single any of us out for particular attention as he stood back and said, 'Ladies first.'

There was a box of teabags and a packet of Rich Tea biscuits on the kitchen floor (we had no table yet, or furniture of any kind). Matthew found a Post-it sticker attached to the teabags: 'Enjoy your new home.' 'It's from Deirdre. The estate agent.'

It was a lovely surprise. We dug the kettle out of the car, and had a cup of black tea (no milk, unfortunately) sitting on our coats by the patio window – Anita was worried she'd never be able to get up again – and watched as the early spring sun warmed our east-facing back garden.

'Isn't this lovely?' said Róisín with a contented sigh.

Then Anita gave a sharp intake of breath and clutched my arm. 'You've no telly,' she said, as though the roof had just fallen in.

'We've no couch either, Anita.'

She dismissed this as unimportant. 'You'll need a wide-screen. And a decent brand, too. Panasonic, or one of those.'

I knew I'd have to break it to her gently. 'Matthew and I, we don't really watch that much telly.'

Anita was looking at me as though I'd confessed that we enjoyed threesomes.

'You don't watch *telly*?' she repeated, just to be sure she'd heard right. Anita herself adored the telly; ever since I could remember, she'd been planted on the couch from about six o'clock in the evening onwards, and she wouldn't budge until it was bedtime, except to get numerous cups of tea and biscuits. 'A bomb wouldn't shift her,' Dad used to often declare.

'No,' I told her. It wasn't anything sanctimonious on our part. I'd love to say we spent our evenings in high-minded pursuits such as crocheting and listening to plays on Radio Four. The fact was that we did too much gallivanting, most of it ill-advised, and if I'd spent more time watching *EastEnders* and less in noodle bars in Soho then I'd probably be a lot richer and my skin would be better.

'There's a great new series after starting,' Anita told me. 'A reality show about Irish dancing – oh, what's it called, Róisín?'

Róisín's face froze in a 'not-this-fecking-yoke-again' expression. '*Dance for Your Supper*,' she said, wearily.

'That's it!' Anita squealed. 'You'll love it, Clara. The standard is quite good. And there're kids on it too. Little fellas tap-dancing away in shiny shirts, they're marvellous, aren't they, Róisín?'

'Marvellous.' Róisín fixed me with a gaze: *Yes, I'm looking at you, sis. I've done it for long enough, and now I want to go to Dublin and hang out in cool bars with my girlfriend, while you put up with Anita.*

I looked at Matthew, alarm making my slick new hairdo feel as if it were rising up in a Mohican on my head.

He leaned in reassuringly and whispered, 'No telly, honey. No little lads tap-dancing up a storm. Life will be infinitely more varied than that.'

Chapter Eight

S omething woke me in the middle of the night. I lay there in the darkness, my heart thudding, and reached for my alarm clock. Except that it wasn't there. *Nothing* was in its usual place. Where was I?

Then: this was the new house. Phew. I was on the floor, on a blow-up bed, which Róisín had lent us. Matthew was beside me, splayed on his back and snoring for Ireland. That would explain the waking-up-in-terror bit.

I gave him a vicious dig in the ribs.

'Wassup?' he mumbled, before laughing like a lunatic. The hour he'd spent manually inflating the mattress had obviously taken its toll. Then he turned over violently on the blow-up bed, almost catapulting me out onto the floor.

We settled down again and I tried to go back to sleep but my eyes kept opening with a *ping*, and darting around my new bedroom. My new home, as I kept reminding myself. I couldn't shake the feeling that I was in temporary accommodation and would be heading back to London, as usual, on Sunday night.

Eventually I got up. I'd have a little explore. Familiarise myself with my surroundings. Then I would feel more comfortable, and able to sleep.

Matthew and I had already had a good poke around, once we'd finally managed to get rid of Anita and Róisín. We'd unpacked the car and piled all the bags, boxes, duvets, CDs and the green lamp on the floor of the living room, and stood there, looking around.

'I suppose we'd better pick a bedroom,' Matthew decided.

There were three. A double at the front, a single bedroom beside it, and then another double at the back, overlooking the garden and the woods beyond.

'How about the one at the front?' I said. It would be noisier, I figured; more like the flat in London.

'Good idea. Anyway, it'll be quieter for the twins at the back.'

'Steady on. We've only just arrived. Let me settle in before I start popping them out.'

We were giddy with the excitement of moving in. There was much laughter and nonsense as we struggled upstairs with our stuff. Every five minutes one of us would say, 'I can't believe we have so much room!'

Matthew christened our big new bedroom the West Wing. The guest bedroom at the back was the East Wing. Because we had no furniture, there was a bit of an echo, which added to the allusion that we were living in a mansion. 'Honey,' Matthew said, pretending to call me from a great distance, 'I'm just going to the bathroom over in the annexe. If you want anything, just ring me, OK? I'll be back in ten minutes.'

It was getting dark by the time we finished unpacking. Everything was in neat piles on the floor, until such time as we acquired furniture to put things in. Apart from the blow-up bed in our room, there wasn't another stick.

Matthew went off up the town eventually in search of provisions, and arrived back with a takeaway from The Big Panda, and something in a bag from the off-licence.

'Proper champagne this time,' he told me.

'Matthew. We can't afford that. We've just bought a house. I have no job.'

But he shushed me. 'We're not broke yet. And it's my treat, OK?'

He poured the champagne into two mugs, and handed me one. His eyes smiled into mine. 'Welcome home.'

★

The woods behind the house, so eco and inviting during the day, were a dark solid mass at night. I'd left Matthew fogging it on the blow-up bed and wandered into the back bedroom – the East Wing – to look out. We had no blinds on any of the windows, and the only light I could see came from the few streetlights to the front, and a sliver of light on the landing in the house next door. Probably for their kids, Jennifer and Kian.

We knew their names because we'd heard them in the garden earlier.

'Ma! Jennifer just gave me the middle finger!'

'Jennifer! If I have to come out to you . . .' Ma sounded very harassed.

'It's not my fault!' Jennifer now, turning on the tears. 'He called me fat!'

'That's because you are.' Kian, gloating. Then, 'She did it again, Ma! She gave me the middle finger!'

What would Ma do now? Matthew and I stood by our open back door and waited, agog. We didn't want to seem like we were spying. But we had no radio, no television, and we'd run out of conversation about half an hour previously; Matthew said he'd rather slit his own throat than engage in any more discussion about kitchen tables and chairs and whether we should go rustic or keep it modern. We were delighted when Kian and Jennifer had stepped out of the house to provide the entertainment.

'I bet she's blonde and wears too much eyeliner,' Matthew whispered.

I could see Ma through a break in the wooden fence. She was about my age, with bobbed auburn hair and a stocky body that was clearly about five months pregnant. There was no way she was going to be able to run fast enough to catch Jennifer.

'I didn't mean it,' Jennifer was wailing.

'She did,' Matthew whispered.

'She gave me the middle finger four times in total,' said Kian, the little snitch.

'Will you just stop saying that?' Ma roared. 'Or I'll tell your da *exactly* what you've been up to.'

That shut them up. The da must be ferocious altogether.

'Bet he'll be short and dark, with a vile temper,' Matthew whispered, even though he'd got it completely wrong with Ma. 'Mark my words.'

Ma was shepherding the kids back towards the house. 'Get in there now before you disturb the new neighbours.'

Guiltily, Matthew and I both inched back into the kitchen, even though they couldn't possibly know we were there.

'The lady has ten million pairs of shoes,' said Jennifer knowledgeably. 'I saw her taking them out of the car.'

I slunk further inside, while Matthew raised his eyebrows at me in an 'out of the mouths of babes' way. I could almost hear Ma thinking, Silly cow. She'll only need a pair of runners around here.

Kian deliberated, 'The man looked kind of . . .'

I could see Matthew waiting hopefully. Cool? Successful? Intelligent?

'Green,' Jennifer chimed in.

'Yeah. Green. Like Da looks on a Sunday morning when he goes out with the lads the night before.'

Matthew slumped dejectedly. Served him right.

Jennifer and Kian would be long asleep by now. In the meagre light, I could see their toys strewn across the lawn: scooters and footballs and a pogo stick. They looked a bit abandoned and desolate.

Then I was drawn again to the woods, dark and a little creepy against the night sky. It was weird, but I felt like they were watching me back. And now the wind was rising a bit, blowing the trees back and forth. It was probably making a rustling noise, but to me it sounded like a scary movie laugh, *Mwuhh huh huh . . . MWUHH huh huh . . .*

I nearly jumped ten feet into the air when I felt hands on my shoulders.

'For feck's sake, Matthew!'

'What?' He was naked and sleepy-looking.

'You nearly gave me a bloody heart attack.'

'What are you doing, wandering round in the middle of the night?'

'Nothing. Just trying to feel more settled in. Get away from the window in case somebody sees you.'

'Who's going to see me out there?'

Blinds, I decided. We needed blinds. For every window in the house. In shocking pink. That ought to cheer the place up and give Ma something to talk about.

'Come back to bed,' said Matthew.

He shepherded me back to the West Wing. The blow-up bed heaved violently as we lowered ourselves gingerly onto it. I suspected it was over-inflated. How we'd managed to christen it so energetically earlier without it exploding was anybody's guess.

'Are you OK?' Matthew said. 'You're cold.'

'I'm fine. Just knackered after the move.' It was true. I suddenly realised how bone-tired I was.

Matthew put his arms around me to warm me. We lay on our backs looking at the ceiling.

'Do you hear that?' he whispered.

Feck. What was it now? More scary movie laughter? Mice? *Ghosts?* That's if ghosts had any interest at all in new-builds on the edges of commuter towns.

'I can't hear anything,' I bleated.

'Neither can I. No traffic, no ambulances. Just . . . peace.'

I wondered was he taking the mickey. Since when had he hankered after all this solitude? But he seemed to be in a state of some bliss as he bobbed gently up and down on the mattress.

I listened for a while too. It really was peaceful. If I closed my eyes, I could imagine that we were floating gently in the middle of the sea.

In seconds I was asleep.

Chapter Nine

I finally ran into him while I was having coffee in the hotel one morning.

'Hello, Clara.' Sophie came to serve me, as usual. She worked mornings only, as in the afternoons she had to look after her two kids, who were by different fathers, which was none of my business but she insisted on telling me anyway. Her mother, who used to mind them, couldn't do it any more as she'd decided at the age of fifty-two to go to do a diploma in music at college, which was MENTAL but she loved it, and if she didn't do it now, when would she ever?

I learned all this within the first five minutes. Sophie had needed a puff of her inhaler afterwards. She had very bad asthma, she said. 'One of these days I'm going to give up the smokes for sure.'

'Any sign of the fridge?' she enquired today.

We were good friends by now. Matthew had started work in Dublin on Monday, officially becoming a commuter, and there was only so much time I could spend in a house with only a blow-up bed for company ('Whey-hey,' Jo had said). None of our new furniture had arrived yet. I was waiting for my bespoke cooker from Cork and my massive catering fridge from Germany – long story – until I could officially start work myself.

So, to fill in the time, I painted the skirting boards, and sanded down and varnished all the floors in readiness. Only joking; I actually went for coffee every morning to the Coffee Dock, which wasn't a dock at all, just an elevated section of the hotel bar, but they did pastries and there was a great selection of locals to watch and be watched by.

'I rang. It might arrive on Monday,' I told Sophie. 'Are your croissants fresh?'

She looked affronted. 'Our croissants are always fresh.'

'Grand. I'll have one. And a skinny cappuccino with an extra shot.'

Sophie nodded in approval. She'd have been very disappointed if I'd ordered tea, like a proper Irish person. After a decade in London, I was expected to bring a dash of glamour to the hotel. This put a certain amount of pressure on me. I'd gone for a walk on Wednesday up around the falling-down castle and come in afterwards in my tracksuit, like a lot of the other patrons, and I felt that I'd somehow let Sophie down. Today, to make it up to her, I was wearing a pair of skinny jeans, wedge heel boots that came up over my knees and that had a hooker look about them, all topped off by an aviator jacket. I'd perched a pair of sunglasses atop my head even though there wasn't a whiff of the sun. Sophie had nodded in approval; she read *Style* and *Company* on her break and she knew what was what.

She wrote down my order whilst getting through the usual pleasantries. 'Nice day, isn't it?' (You had to talk about the weather, apparently. She said you'd nearly get fired if you didn't.)

'A little windy, though,' I said. The previous day I'd merely agreed, but I felt it was time to spread my wings.

'Yes, but it's not a *chilly* wind.' She put me in my place, like the professional that she was. Then she turned towards the coffee-making part of the operation and bellowed, 'CROISSANT AND SKINNY CAPPUCCINO, VALERIE. EXTRA SHOT.

I didn't know Valerie that well yet, but she seemed like a nice lady in her forties who was relentlessly bullied by the exuberant Sophie. 'Copy,' Valerie muttered.

'What?' said Sophie.

'I said COPY.'

Sophie hadn't wanted to introduce military commands, apparently. But that Valerie one was so dozy.

The hotel kept a nice selection of free newspapers for the guests, and I was delighted to find that they stocked the *Guardian*, even though it was a day out of date. I got up to fetch myself a copy as I had a great longing to know what was going on without me in London. How was Jo? (Not that I'd find out in the *Guardian*.) What was the girl like who had taken over my job? Had Mad Mags had her way with that waiter in Falvio's? I couldn't remember his name now. Damn it. I'd been gone mere days. Surely things couldn't be going fuzzy already.

But then again, maybe it was a sign that I was settling in, and not obsessing about trees and such like. Yes. I would text Matthew with news of same, even though he was getting a bit paranoid about me phoning him and texting on his first week in the new job with queries such as, 'Will I order a king-size bed or do we feel that we need something bigger? Go, baby!'

'*Clara?* Is that you?'

It was one of those moments: a voice comes from behind you, completely wrong-footing you and causing your stomach to drop.

I turned round to find myself looking into the face of my ex-boyfriend, Jason.

My first thought was, shite. Then, once I'd collected myself a little, I saw that he hadn't changed a bit. A couple of lines around his mouth, maybe, but lots of thick curly hair still, and those *eyes*. Jo had seen a photo of him once and she'd immediately squealed, 'Paul Newman!'

He wasn't really like Paul Newman, though. He didn't have the same ready smile, or a playful look in those very blue eyes. Jason had always been quite a serious person.

'Jason,' I said. I wasn't long in collecting myself. I'd known this moment would come. How could it not, with us both living in the same town? I just hadn't expected it so soon. 'Nice to see you again.'

We kind of smiled at each other. I was relieved. But then again, we were in a public place. Niceties had to be observed. Out of the corner of my eye I could see Sophie planting a warmed croissant on my table. If I wasn't back in a minute she'd probably come and hunt me down.

'It must be . . . how many years now?' he said.

'Ten. Well, almost ten.'

'Ten.' He shook his head like he couldn't believe it.

I couldn't either. In one way it seemed hard to believe I'd ever dated this man, let alone for two years. Yet everything was disconcertingly familiar: his aftershave, the little scar on his chin.

'You look well, Clara.'

The tone was neutral. It could have meant anything. I was suddenly conscious of my hooker boots and my expensive jacket. It was a far cry from the girlish clobber I used to throw on around Castlemoy ten years ago, still carrying a hint of puppy fat.

I thought I saw a hint of judgement scudding across his face: Christ, look at your woman, she's after developing notions.

But no. He was smiling again; openly, pleasantly, like we were just two acquaintances. Which of course was what we were now.

'Thanks. You, too. I like the sideburns.' I was joking. It just popped out. Maybe it was the relief.

He laughed. Not a big belly laugh or anything; it wasn't *that* funny. But a chuckle. 'And you haven't changed a bit. Still the same old Clara.' Then, as if worried that it might look like he was enjoying himself, he dug his hands into his pockets efficiently; back to business. 'I hear you've moved back.'

'That's right.' I didn't mention Matthew. I presumed he'd heard that too.

'I never left.' That was delivered sardonically.

I didn't know what to say. Anything would seem like I was passing verdict. Instead I said, 'How's the business?'

'Not too bad, given the recession. You know that Dad retired?'

Of course I did. It was one of the first things Anita had told me. I even knew he'd gone on a cruise to Mexico to celebrate.

But I feigned polite ignorance. 'Has he?'

'I've been able to make a few changes around the place.'

We exchanged a wry smile. Mr Farrell's legendary love of tradition and 'the old ways' had been a hot topic of conversation for the duration of our relationship. He wouldn't even get in new filing cabinets for fear they might make the place look 'fast'.

'I was sorry to hear about your mother.' Well, I couldn't not say it. She'd passed away a year before Dad; cancer too.

Jason had called up to the house to see Anita the week after Dad's funeral.

I'd made no such journey to his, and I felt a bit small now.

'Thanks,' he said.

Then a glance at his watch; things to see, people to do. I realised that I was going to be dismissed. He had a file in his hand, I realised only now. 'Listen, it's been nice meeting you again, Clara.'

'Oh. Um, you too.'

'Good luck with things.'

I wanted to say something like, 'No hard feelings, eh?' but it would be inappropriate, and anyway, we'd had such a civil and friendly encounter that I didn't want to spoil it by raking up a now-redundant past. It would be as crass as whipping my top up.

I have no idea where that had come from. Sometimes, under pressure, I have wildly inappropriate thoughts.

'Thanks,' I said.

And with a pleasant nod, he walked out.

Chapter Ten

'Clara?'

'Jo!' It was so lovely to hear from her.

'I'm ringing from work so I can't stay long or I'll have Brenda flogging me.'

'You're just trying to make me jealous now.' I was even nostalgic for Brenda.

'How are you getting on? Oh, and your tenants have moved in, by the way. Two guys, right? I met them and gave them the keys.' She paused. 'One of them looked really strange but the other was OK. Anyway, I left them my number and said in my big voice that I'd be round to check on them next Friday. Hey, do I get a cut for doing all this work?'

'You get a new handbag,' I promised her. 'We'll go shopping the next time I'm over.'

I said that to make us both feel a bit better. I was homesick already and I knew Jo was missing me too, but she was a chin-up kind of girl.

'Did you get the fridge?' she wanted to know immediately.

I know, the fridge again, but we loved fridges. They were our thing. People always think chefs obsess about cookers, and how many rings we can squash onto a hob, and a lot of chefs did. But as for Jo and me, fridges were our thing.

Jo was excitable on the subject. 'Size matters, yes, but so do shelves, light, storage boxes and, hello, what about an alarm that tells you if you've left the door open?'

We'd been to catering expos over the years and seen some amazing fridges on display. They were like tanks: sleek, smooth, shiny on the outside and enormous on the inside. You could fit a week's shop in the cheese drawer alone. We'd run our hands up and down the cool, stainless steel, and sometimes Jo would moan. Then we'd climb in to explore it. But the *cost* of them. Sweet Jesus. Even Brenda, the queen of splash, would recoil.

The one that was coming from Germany I'd found on the internet. A restaurateur was hanging up his spatula, and was selling his kitchen off cheap and fast. I'd never have managed the shipping cost, except a friend of his happened to be travelling to Northern Ireland with a truckload of other stuff and was willing to bring my fridge if I paid some petrol money. A courier would drive my baby on the rest of its journey home.

'It's coming on Monday.' I was a bit worried about Matthew's reaction. I wasn't sure I'd adequately described the size of it to him.

'Then you've no excuse,' she said. I could feel her wagging her finger down the line at me. Jo was following my plans very carefully. If I succeeded, then she might follow suit. But if I bombed, then she could say, 'Thank Christ I let you fail first.'

'Send me a picture,' she instructed me. 'The minute it arrives.'

'How are the Girls?' I demanded. I was desperate for news. 'Has Jane's morning sickness abated?'

'Oh, *please.*' Jo was disgusted. 'It's not just morning sickness. It's afternoon sickness, evening sickness, night sickness . . . honestly, myself and Mags feel sick just listening to her.' She cackled with laughter. 'Still,' she said belatedly, 'poor Jane. And Mags is looking into getting her eggs frozen. Her own eggs, I mean. But that's just her birthday coming up. Remember what she was like last birthday? She was going to get a tummy tuck, but that passed too.'

Casually, I said, 'I ran into Jason in the Coffee Dock yesterday.'

'You did?' This was better than the fridge. 'What happened?'

Jo knew about Jason. She'd prised it all out of me over the course of the first three months after my move to London. Resistance had been futile. Under her precision questioning, I'd revealed how our relationship had all started with a family invitation to his parents' Christmas drinks party. ('I hope it gets more interesting than this,' said Jo.) How we'd hit it off. How there had followed a two-year relationship that was great in many respects, including the sex. ('Nice!' said Jo.) Then things had got a little more serious. Well, on his part, anyway; he'd wanted to take things further. Marriage. ('Aargh!' said Jo. 'Intense, intense.') That was when I'd tried to slow things down. But when one person is trying to speed things up and the other is trying to slow them down, it's bound to end badly.

And it had.

Naturally I was a little worried that he might still be bitter and twisted about the whole thing. In fairness, I might have been, had I been the one who was dumped.

But it appeared he wasn't. So, in answer to Jo's question about what had happened, I was able to tell her with happy relief, 'Nothing.'

'Nothing? You rang me up to tell me *nothing*?'

'*You* rang *me*,' I reminded her. 'Anyway, it was grand, Jo. We chatted, and he even laughed at one point, and then we went our separate ways.'

'See? I told you.'

'I know, but I must have been worried all the same.'

'But why?' Jo could never really understand it. 'You were only twenty-three at the time. A mere child. Who knows their own mind at that age?'

And who observed proper breaking-up etiquette? I hadn't anyway, that was for sure.

'He, on the other hand,' said Jo, 'was qualified and in a practice and settled.' She said it like he was from a different time. And, in a way, he'd always seemed much older than his twenty-six years, his age when we first met. He'd even looked older; it was all those well-cut clothes, and the other trappings of manhood.

Women, of course, had found all of that very attractive. Jason was considered a ride around Castlemoy – and indeed lots of local ladies tried to. I remembered them flirting madly with him in the various pubs on a Saturday night. He even went out with one or two of them, and word filtered back of expensive dinners out, and fast drives around in his car. At one point rumours went around Castlemoy that he was dating a model from Dublin, even though nobody actually saw her.

So when he set his sights on me, innocent and chubby-cheeked and fresh out of college, I admit I was flattered. He'd seemed so sophisticated to me back then.

'Twenty-three is far too young to settle down,' Jo was saying. 'You hadn't even begun to squander your youth.'

'In fairness, I had. I'd squandered a fair bit in Dublin at catering college.'

'The thing is— Jesus,' Jo broke off suddenly. 'How much is this phone call costing Brenda? Look,' she said, clearly anxious to wrap things up, 'you're both adults now. Yes, mistakes have been made, blah, blah, but it was ten years ago. The mists of time and all that. So of *course* he was fine to you in the hotel. He'd want to be a very uptight kind of character to hold it against you now. Right?' she finished up brightly.

The only flaw in her argument was that he *was* a bit uptight, or at least he had been then. Although uptight wasn't quite the right word. Proud described him better. But that seemed to have mellowed too.

'Anyway,' Jo said on the phone. 'I'm looking up flights to Dublin. I think it's only fair to warn you.'

I was surprised at how relieved I was, having met Jason. He'd been at the back of my mind for ten years now; firmly buried, but there all the time. Occasionally, on visits home, I'd step out into Dublin Airport and I'd think, I wonder, will I run into him this weekend?

The first year or so I'd been a bit cowardly. You know, avoiding the Esso garage, that kind of thing. Skulking about the supermarket in case I bumped into him by the jam tarts. I wasn't even that keen on running into old friends much, especially his. Well, they'd probably heard, hadn't they? I kept a keen ear out for any gossip Anita might bring home from Mass. She always had something: 'Did you hear Yvonne Harris slipped a disc at Pilates last week?'

If Yvonne Harris's slipped disc could get prime airtime in Castlemoy, then my break-up with Jason must be the star attraction.

But Jason said nothing about my bad behaviour. Nobody gave me sideways looks as I walked down the street. In fact, I got a surprise when, six months down the line, and it was all receding nicely in my mind, a friend of his father's stopped me in the chemists to ask how me and Jason were managing the long-distance commute, now that I'd moved to London.

'I'm sorry?' I remember stuttering, trying to buy time.

'I suppose you've worked something out,' she said with a beam.

That's when I realised – he hadn't even told people we'd broken up.

I was stumped. So *I* began to tell people; well, someone had to. And every time I set foot outside my mother's door, I prepared myself to run into him. In a way I wanted it to happen, just to get that awkwardness over with, so we could both move on.

In ten years it had never happened.

Chapter Eleven

Matthew and I had tossed around names for weeks. I'd wondered whether I should go for something ironic, like 'Feast', but Matthew was adamant that the world had changed. There was no money any more for feasting; a decent lamb casserole maybe, and an honest lemon meringue pie, but the days of smoked Gruyère rarebit with tomato relish – cheese on toast with ketchup on the side – had gone.

'Since when did you become such a foodie?' I teased him.

'Since I've been watching Brenda disappear up her own fundament,' he said bluntly.

He didn't like Brenda any more than the rest of us. She sometimes made me cry and then he got very mad. The pretentious Gruyère rarebit was one of her inventions.

In the end, I decided to call my new catering business Food by Clara. The menu would be small and the prices reasonable.

Matthew had got one of the tekkies in his London office to build me a basic website in his spare time before we'd left, for a fee of beer and takeaway curries. Matthew had been fine-tuning it since, adding in features such as a compose-your-own-menu section, and details of where my food was sourced from, that kind of thing.

'I've even worked it so that you can put in the calorie count of each meal if you want.' He was very pleased with himself.

'We might want to think about that one,' I said.

'Come on. Loads of people are trying to watch what they eat these days. Look at your mother, for example. It'd be a help to them if they knew how many calories were in your double chocolate soufflé, for example.'

'About four hundred and fifty,' I said.

He looked shocked. 'No.'

'And that's without cream.'

He scrapped that part of the website, and a few days later showed me the finished product. There was a photo of me on the home page, smiling out. I got a bit of a shock. It was like unexpectedly catching sight of myself in a shop window. But I looked OK. Well, normal-ish anyway, and friendly, and unlikely to poison anyone.

'You like?' he said.

'I like.'

It was Jo who'd first put the idea into my head of striking out on my own. It had been a particularly grim day at work, with Brenda insisting we remake eighty mini vodka and peach jellies, because they 'weren't vodka-ey enough'.

'That's because she's a fucking lush,' Jo raged. 'You don't hear her complaining that they're not peachy enough, do you?' She slammed the jellies into the bin. 'One of these days I'm so going to break out of this kitchen and set up on my own.'

She didn't, though. And I didn't either, even though I'd chimed in, 'Yeah! Me too! Feck Brenda.'

But the idea of opening up a new business in London was daunting. Where would I get clients? If I pilfered Brenda's she'd come after me with a kitchen knife. Plus I'd have to hire premises; the flat was too small for me to cook from home. And what about transport? And insurance? And the gazillions of other, established, catering companies I'd be up against?

At the same time I knew I was a decent chef. I had loads of recipes floating around in my head that only Matthew seemed to taste. And I was tired of the big, impersonal receptions where Jo and I would word-lessly serve up platters of delicious canapés that people would grab with fat fingers, mid-conversation, and chuck down without even tasting them;

just soakage for all the free champagne. Scabby bastards, as they were technically known in the trade.

Then Matthew mooted the idea of moving to Ireland. I had to have two glasses of wine before I confided my dreams. Could I? Should I? Was I insane, to think of running a catering company out of Castlemoy?

'Of course you're insane,' Matthew comforted me. 'But do it anyway.'

'That's easy to say, but supposing nobody hires me? You'll have to support both of us.'

'So? I have a decent job. If we're careful, we could live off my wage until you conquer the dinner party circle in Dublin.'

'I might fall flat on my face.'

'You? Nah.'

From almost the moment we met, Matthew had an unshakeable belief in my abilities. I used to think he was taking the mick, the way he'd fervently praise how I made a cappuccino, for example. When I'd cooked for him on our fifth date he'd raved over my roast lamb and baked cheesecake and declared them the best he'd ever tasted.

'Are you just trying to get me into bed?' I challenged him as we did the washing-up.

'Of course I'm not.' He'd looked horrified at the notion. Then, in case he'd offended me, he hurriedly said, 'Well, obviously I'd *like* to . . . you know . . . at some appropriate stage in the distant future.' He gave me one of his worryingly direct looks. Even then, I knew I'd never be able to pull the wool over his eyes, and if I tried, then we'd be bound for a swift conclusion. 'But if you think I'm buttering you up to try to hurry along the process, then you're wrong. I just happen to think you're great.'

We slept together that very night. How could I possibly resist?

Matthew continued to be my biggest cheerleader over the years; there was nothing I wouldn't be able to do if I set my mind to it, apparently, including starting up a business in recession-stricken Ireland, with no experience, very little capital and no calorie counts on my menus.

On the Friday evening of his first full week of work at Moore & Byrne in Dublin, Matthew arrived home with a pile of flyers under his arm. 'I thought you could put them through people's letter boxes. You know, to let people know you're open for business.'

He'd clearly designed them himself – the business's logo was from the website – and he'd put my name and details on the front, and some quotes saying things like, 'Best evening I've had in ages!', and, 'Stunning food! I'd book again in a heartbeat!'

'It's OK,' he assured me. 'I made them up.'

'Thanks, Matthew.' I was touched by his efforts.

'I'm not finished yet.' He got his bag and began to extract items from a thick Moore & Byrne folder. 'Envelopes, in case you want to post some flyers. Pens. Sellotape. Markers. I tried to rob some stamps too but they keep those locked in reception, and the girls working the desk there are really uptight, and take it in turns to go out for lunch, so I couldn't break into the drawer.'

I felt weak. 'You stole all this stuff on your first week in work?'

This was far, far worse than a pack of photocopy paper. And he was only on a short-term contract too; probation, if you like, before there was any possibility of being made permanent.

'I've got some teabags and toilet rolls in my coat as well, seeing as we've just moved in and could use them. The coffee order doesn't arrive till next week, apparently. Is Nescafé OK?'

'*What?*'

He'd turned into a kleptomaniac. It must be the stress of the move. Dear God. His bag was positively bulging with contraband.

He saw my face and broke into a laugh. 'Relax. I bought them.'

'You pig.' I tried to clobber him with a stray shoe but he dodged.

'You really think I was going to clean the place out on my first week?' He winked. 'Nah. I always wait at least a month. You know, find out where the keys are, see if they've CCTV, that kind of thing.'

'Don't you dare.'

He finished putting his spoils out on the table. There was practically an office-full of stuff there, all designed to get me off to a good start. He was so sweet.

'Thank you,' I said, full of guilt that, instead of pounding the pavements to get my name out there, I'd actually spent a lot of the week in the Coffee Dock shooting the breeze with Sophie. 'I'll start properly now. I swear.'

We'd dragged the blow-up bed down to the living room and were eating dinner on it in the dark. We had all the lights off because we had no curtains yet; they were allegedly arriving on Monday, along with the fridge.

'Tell me how your first week went,' I pressed.

Matthew squinted at me in the gloom. 'It's good,' he said carefully. 'I think Eamon and I have made some progress.'

Eamon was from Kerry. Matthew was from Clapham. All week they'd been trying to understand what the other was saying.

'We've no problem with the computer stuff,' Matthew clarified. 'It's just when we try to talk about normal things, you know, like what sandwich does the other one want from the shop.'

There had been major confusion over a BLT during the week, apparently. But from all reports Eamon was sound, and had gone out of his way to introduce Matthew to Team Tech, and had taken him out for a pint to the pub *du jour* for the IT crowd. 'It was like being in hell,' Matthew had told me, full of wonderment.

Team Tech were the IT department; there were four of them in total, and they'd arrived at their nickname by putting their initials together (it had been a slow day, apparently). There was Tim, Eamon, Chris and Henry.

Then Matthew arrived.

'I think they want me to change my name,' he confided. 'I mean, they haven't said anything, but it kind of messes things up. And they really like their name. They don't bang on about it or anything, but they're up against three hundred solicitors and secretaries and law apprentices, and it makes them feel just a little bit special, you know?' He put on a movie-trailer voice. 'Problems with your hard drive? Time for Team Techhhhh!' I could tell that he already liked these guys. 'They don't want to leave me out, but at the same time it can't be, "Time for Team-Tech-plus-Matthew", can it?'

'So what are you going to change your name to?'

He grinned. 'I don't know. But probably something beginning with an S, so that we can be Team Techs. Do you think I could be a Sam?'

'Well . . .'

'Simon, then.'

'Definitely not a Simon.'

'I'll think about it over the weekend,' Matthew resolved.

I leaned over and kissed him.

'What was that for?'

'I don't know. I'm just glad things are going well for you.'

'Why wouldn't they?' Matthew never believed that anything would ever go wrong. When it did, sometimes, he always maintained that at least he hadn't wasted any time worrying about it beforehand.

He finished his Thai chicken curry. I'd had Singapore noodles and we'd shared a plate of Smokin' Bacon Sticks, all from the Chinese restaurant, The Big Panda ('We cater for all tastes!'). 'Tell me about *your* week now.'

I didn't want to bring up the fridge; I was going to use Sunday to prepare him for the new arrival. And he already knew about my walks with Anita, and my sneaky coffees in the Coffee Dock. So there was only one other bit of significant news that I hadn't told him yet.

'I met Jason during the week.'

He winced. Well, nobody liked talking about exes, unless it had all ended in sweetness and light, which, let's face it, *never* happened. 'And?'

'It was fine.' I smiled to let him know that it really was. 'I suppose I had to get it over with at some stage.'

'Is he still very good-looking?' he asked gravely.

I'd shown him a picture of Jason once. He'd pretended to shield his eyes and writhe in agony. 'Man, he's gorgeous. How can you bear the climb-down?'

'Kind of,' I told him. Well, he *was* still pretty handsome. 'Although he might have put on a few pounds.'

'Yes!' Then Matthew looked down at his own midriff. 'Mind you, I think so have I.'

Then we stopped being jokey.

'I hope it's going to be OK. You know, meeting him around town,' Matthew said.

The last thing either of us wanted to do was move home into unpleasantness. What kind of foolishness would that be? But at the same time we couldn't let it stop us, Matthew had argued. People broke up all the time and ended up seeing each other every day. Matthew's position was that I might have ended it, but *someone* had to.

I'd been vague about the break-up. Well, you're unlikely to shine a big fat torch into the murkier recesses of your life just when you've met someone new, aren't you? And Matthew was special. I didn't want him thinking, What a bitch! Imagine if she ends it with *me* like that? and so I never told him exactly how it had all come crashing to a halt. Well, it'd probably never come up again, would it? I could feel bad about it privately – and I still did, occasionally – but it was in the past.

And what was to be gained by coming clean now? Jason wasn't saying anything. Why should I? And I was a *nice* person now. Honestly.

'It's ancient history now,' I said, bringing a close to the conversation.

Chapter Twelve

Róisín and I had done up a plan. Well, it was mostly Róisín's plan; my bit was to make sure everybody stuck to it.

It went like this: every weekday morning, I would call at Anita's house at about eleven to take her for a short walk. Nothing too energetic; no off-road stuff or anything like that. Just a gentle stroll up to the falling-down castle and home again. Couldn't be easier, right?

Wrong.

'I don't know if I have a tracksuit . . . let me just check . . . No. I don't. And runners . . . now, let me just check . . . Would you believe it, no. I only have my normal shoes and they have a bit of a heel on them and I'm just not sure it's a good idea.' Much rooting around in cupboards and presses and wardrobes, and, finally, the shed out the back. At the end of it all, she'd emerge and say chirpily, 'Listen, I'm just holding you up. Go on without me and I'll be ready tomorrow.'

'What did I say? You're a soft touch,' Róisín chided me. We were in the Coffee Dock, drinking cappuccinos made by Valerie. Our brother, Eddie, had been invited along to the discussion too, but apparently rehearsals for his new play were in full swing and so we heard nothing back.

'She can smell weakness a mile off,' Róisín lectured me. 'You're going to have to wise up, because I'm warning you – she's cunning, she's manipulative, and she'll lie her head off if she thinks she can get away with it.'

'Is this Anita we're talking about?' I was a bit taken aback. Anita had never really been known as a smooth operator; the way Róisín was going on, she'd have qualified for the role of 007.

'Are you with me on this or not?'

'Yes, yes.'

Underlying all this was my guilt that I'd been slacking for ten years on the parental front and that it was now payback time. I knew I'd better pull up my socks, and fast. Anita had at least three stone to lose before, well, who knew what would happen? 'One of your legs might rot and fall off,' Róisín had told her yesterday, to try to frighten her into action, but Anita had only laughed and said, 'So? I have another one, don't I?'

'Leave it with me,' I promised Róisín fervently. 'You've done your bit. Let's just do an orderly handover.'

Róisín nodded and took a thick notebook out. It had 'Anita' written on the front, above a picture of an elephant. 'It must have been subliminal,' Róisín said apologetically, when she saw me looking. 'I didn't notice it when I was buying it.' She consulted a list she'd written in it. 'You'll have to do her shopping for her, I'm afraid. Or at least go with her. She can't be let loose in the supermarket by herself because she'll only fill her trolley with Mr Kipling. Often she eats a pack on the way round and dumps the box before the checkout. Una Mulvaney works there and she told me. I'm worried they're going to arrest her for shoplifting but then what are they going to do? Search her stomach?'

She looked at me. We couldn't help it; we dissolved into guilty laughter.

'Does she really eat Mr Kipling on the way round?' I was sure she was exaggerating, even though Anita had always loved Mr Kipling; we'd buy two boxes after Mass every Sunday to have with a cup of tea when we got home. It was tradition. Nobody thought there was any harm in it back then.

Róisín was still smiling. 'Cherry Bakewells, mostly. Well, look, she did it once. That Una Mulvaney is a desperate gossip,' she said, suddenly vicious. 'You'd get away with nothing around here if that one gets hold of it.'

Having got that off her chest, Róisín picked up the notebook again. 'I didn't think we'd have to look after Anita for blooming years yet,' she said with a sigh. 'Anyway. I've done out weekly menus here. Just as a guide for her, you know? I've tried not to be too strict because sometimes that sends her into total revolt and you couldn't blame her, really. Your main job is to try to convince her that a plain omelette and salad is delicious.'

'Thank you, Róisín.' I didn't even like plain omelette and salad. How was Anita, a stalwart of chops and gravy and mashed potato, going to cope?

Róisín gave me a wry smile. 'Welcome home.'

'Do you think she's still in denial?'

'Anita? Of course she bloody is.'

Anita didn't really believe she was diabetic. We'd realised this when we'd printed off a piece from the internet on 'Eating Well with Diabetes', after she was first diagnosed, and she'd looked at it with interest before enquiring, 'Who is it for?'

But apparently it was a very common phenomenon, so much so that doctors actually recognised it as part of the diagnostic process. Róisín said it went a bit like this:

'I'm afraid you're diabetic.'

'Oh, no, I'm not!'

'Oh, yes, you are.'

'Oh, no, I'm not. Watch out, there's a big cream puff behind you!' (Anita, bless her, adored cream puffs. Cream anything, really.)

There was diabetes in the family. Anita's brother in Canada was diabetic, diagnosed ten years previously, and our grandmother had symptoms but had never been properly diagnosed (she didn't like doctors either, apparently). Anita unfortunately was also very overweight, the result of years of a heavy diet and very little exercise.

'But I walk down to the shops every single morning,' she always maintained.

She had an explanation for everything. Her weight? She just had heavy bones; it ran in the family. The slice of almond tart? Well, the nurse had said everything in moderation, and Anita was only having one slice, even if it was a very, very big slice (the whole tart, actually. 'You tart,' Róisín had admonished her afterwards. 'Takes one to know one,' Anita had fired back. 'See? My brain is still sharp,' she'd said, and giggled). And she couldn't very well go power walking with me if she didn't have a tracksuit or even a pair of runners, now could she?

'What does Dr Mooney say?' I asked Róisín.

'Does it matter what he says? She won't listen to him anyway.'

Anita had no respect for him, mostly because he was fresh from college, and only in the job a year and therefore 'couldn't possibly know anything'. She'd only gone to him in the first place because she'd had a sore on her leg that wouldn't heal up. She'd just been looking for a bit of ointment, but he'd got her back up by asking her all kinds of personal questions about the frequency of her toilet visits, and how much she drank every day.

'I barely drink at all,' she'd told him stiffly. 'A glass of wine at the weekends sometimes, not that it's any of your business.'

'I meant water.'

Then he'd gone on about her weight. There were samples taken of this and that, and she was hauled back to the surgery again and asked *more* leading questions on her weight. Honestly, the lad was consumed with size.

'Do you not find,' she eventually said to him, very politely, 'that we're all obsessed with celebrity culture, and that if you're not a perfect size ten, then you absolutely *must* have some kind of horrible disease, because we're simply not comfortable with real women's bodies?'

She was, she said, moments away from whipping off her bra and setting fire to it there and then, which would have frightened the life out of him, and probably alerted five units of the fire brigade due to the ferocity of the blaze (she wore a 40EE), when he said, 'You have diabetes.'

72

And he'd slapped her on medication and diets and whatnot. She'd been given a pile of literature featuring smiling, thin-looking people on bikes (why?), under cheery captions like 'Live a Fabulously Fantastic Life with Diabetes!' He talked about a care plan, and made hospital appointments for her and generally treated her like she had some kind of *disease*.

'I feel absolutely fine,' Anita had insisted to me only that morning. 'There's nothing wrong with me. So I'll lose a bit of weight. Cut down on the junk. But that's it. And I don't want you going on about it all the time. That bloody Róisín is bad enough.'

Róisín closed the notebook and handed it over a tad apologetically.

'Good luck,' she said. 'You'll need it.'

'It'll be fine.' I didn't want to let her see how unconfident I was about taking charge of Anita. But at least I had some kind of a plan now. Plus, Susie Reynolds ran a class called Get Skinny or something similar in the Community Centre every Thursday. I'd seen a flyer for it in the hotel lobby. Maybe I'd sign us both up for that and Anita would drop a couple of stone.

'What'll you do, now that you'll have all this free time on your hands?' I joked.

Róisín looked a bit startled, like she hadn't thought of it. 'I don't know. I might paint the house.'

I nodded. 'And I guess you'll be free to spend a bit more time with Catherine.'

'I hope so.' She didn't look that optimistic. 'If she'd just cut down on her hours a bit.'

'So get her to take a weekend off and come down. We could go on a walk, the four of us, or out for something to eat.'

'A whole *weekend*?' Róisín looked like it would be easier to infiltrate NASA.

'Saturday, then. She can't work *all* the time.'

'Keep your voice down a bit.'

'Sorry.' I hadn't been aware that I was talking loudly. It must be Valerie's coffee; it was so strong that day that my heart was bouncing unpleasantly in my chest.

'Look, I'll ask her, OK?' Róisín promised. 'She's so busy at the moment that I'm just trying to make life easier for her.' Which seemed to include Róisín doing all the running. She was forever driving up to Dublin with an overnight bag in the boot. Catherine didn't even keep a toothbrush in Róisín's place. I knew, because I'd looked.

'Anyway, you'll see her on Saturday,' Róisín said, as she got up to go back to work.

'She's coming down?'

Róisín was throwing a dinner for Matthew and me, to welcome us home; Catherine hadn't been mentioned.

'Don't sound so surprised. She does come down sometimes.' She plastered a smile on her face as an elderly man at a nearby table waved over cheerily. 'How're you, Róisín! See you Tuesday, to have that dressing changed!'

Róisín waved back. 'Right you are, Vinny!' She hissed to me, 'You can't move in this shagging place without bumping into someone you know.'

Sophie announced, 'I saw you talking to Jason Farrell the other day.'

Róisín was right; you *couldn't* move in this shagging place.

I said nothing, anxious to get back to the plans I was drawing up for the new business. Jo had phoned me up again wanting to know whether the fridge, due later that day, had arrived, but really she just wanted to know if I'd landed a gig yet, and I had to admit that I hadn't.

'He's a solicitor, right?' Sophie carried on regardless. 'From that practice on Bridge Street?'

'Yes.'

'He's doing well. Took on another solicitor in the last year, despite the current economic climate and the dim outlook for the euro,' she said expertly (she listened to a lot of talk radio in the hotel kitchen, she said). 'Yes, very well, I'd say. The father retired, of course, a couple of years ago.'

I realised I was merely a conduit for her thoughts.

'But everybody said he was just holding him back. A nice man, but very set in his ways. Jason's attracted a lot of new business since. He was clever; he didn't concentrate on just property, like some of them. People come from all around to see him now,' Sophie said, sounding impressed.

By that time I think she'd forgotten I was even there. I just sat quietly, not drawing attention to myself, hoping she'd go away. I really wasn't interested in how successful my ex had become since I'd last seen him.

'I think he was seeing a girl from Newbridge for a while there, a physiotherapist, oh, what was her name . . . Daisy? Darina? VALERIE? Who was that woman Jason Farrell was going out with?'

Valerie jerked upright as though she'd been shot. 'That's all off,' she called timidly.

'I *know* that,' said Sophie. She threw her eyes to heaven before turning back to me. 'Anyway, it wasn't serious,' she reassured me. 'She was good-looking, but she had a bit of a cast in her eye.'

I hoped that Matthew and I never broke up; God knows how we'd be described by Sophie to the clientele of the Coffee Dock.

'Well, that's a shame,' I said, when it became obvious that a reply was required. 'I mean, that it didn't work out for him.'

There he was, still single after all these years.

And I realised that a tiny part of me wasn't all that surprised.

'Still, he won't be on his own for too long,' Sophie said. 'There's a few of them out there past thirty and with no ring on the finger yet.' She tapped her own for emphasis.

I had to laugh at her. What's more, she was probably right. I went home to wait for my fridge to arrive, feeling like there really were no clouds on the horizon now.

And, for Ireland, that was saying something.

Chapter Thirteen

My brother, Eddie, was the baby of the family. He was an actor. 'You never know, he might grow out of it,' Dad used to say hopefully, as if it was some affliction Eddie would eventually shake off, and morph into a proper man with a job and an ability to fix things around the house.

Eddie was short, dark, intense. He wore jeans that always seemed on the brink of artfully falling down, and he had a terrible job washing dishes at a restaurant called Jimmy's. Jimmy was an appalling character who flew into wild rages, and then you'd better duck. On the plus side, Jimmy had a bad memory, due to drinking so much, and so Eddie was able to disappear for three or four weeks at a time to do some fringe show with an average nightly audience of eight, and when it was over he would apply for his old job back and Jimmy wouldn't remember him. He'd growl, 'Go on then, it's only washing dishes, if you can manage that much, you poofy-looking waster.'

Eddie took this abuse in good stead; just so long as he had enough money to pay for his bedsit in a dank tenement building, on a street where small kids threw empty whiskey bottles at him as he passed. 'We'd rob ya, ya gobshite, only ya look skint.'

We'd gone to see him perform lots of times. It was mostly in new plays, in 'alternative spaces', and to be honest we usually hadn't a clue what the plot was – modern man's disintegration, or something cheery like that – but Eddie was always fantastic. And I wasn't just saying that because he was my brother. I often forgot he even *was* my brother, when he was on the stage. He would become another person entirely: powerful, scary, sexy, and when he had sung some post-apocalyptic song in a broken-down voice at the end of one of these plays, we'd all shed a tear. Even Matthew, and he never cries.

'You should do a musical,' Anita said ardently when Eddie came off the stage after that particular performance, empty-looking and exhausted. He always looked that way, like he needed a blood transfusion or something.

'A . . . *musical?*' Eddie looked at her blankly, as though she'd just suggested he go stand under a streetlight and wave a banner saying 'Hello, boys'. And there was probably more chance of him doing that.

'You have the voice for it. Oh, go on. I'd love to get dressed up and come to Dublin to hear you sing.'

Eddie had looked particularly tortured at that; Anita would more than likely bring a box of Roses as well, and the crackling of sweet papers would drown out the soliloquy.

'You're not behind on your rent, or anything?' Róisín always dealt with him briskly, but in a kindly fashion. She was forever pressing wads of tenners into his grubby hand, which he was both grateful for and annoyed about.

'I don't think she knows what else to say to me,' he often muttered.

'That's because you keep doing crap plays that we can't understand.' I smiled to show him I was joking. Kind of.

'My work is not didactic.' And he flicked back his long hair. It was in very good condition, despite his poor diet. He shot me a look. 'Besides, you're just thick.'

'Watch it.'

We were the most alike in the family. When I'd sneak upstairs to dress up in Anita's party clothes as a kid, I'd often find that Eddie had got there before me, and would be scampering around in a flowing dress and one of her chunky necklaces.

'Fuck sake,' Dad would shout in fright when he'd catch him. 'Take those off this instant before someone sees you!'

Eddie would be baffled and confused. 'But I was being a Roman emperor, trying to stop the bloodshed in the Colosseum.'

Dad would look at Anita, slack-jawed: what tripe was she letting him watch on the telly? 'Listen, son. Boys don't dress up in girls' clothing, OK? Not unless they're soft in the head, like Bender Nolan. Got it?'

(Róisín always recounted this story as proof of how ignorant and unsophisticated our background was. It was a wonder she hadn't ended up in some kind of an institution, she maintained.)

Eddie simply confined his dressing-up episodes to when Dad was at work. We'd hear him downstairs sometimes, dying dramatically on the carpet, or shouting in outrage, 'Three blind mice! See how they run!' You really felt for those mice, that was how good he was.

Eddie and I were forever disappearing off together on some adventure, leaving Róisín to do the washing-up, which used to drive her cracked. Always in cahoots, she maintained. She wasn't a bit surprised when, one after the other, we abandoned Castlemoy altogether for the brighter lights of Dublin and London, only coming back when it suited us, it seemed.

She, on the other hand, had stuck it out, building up a whole life around the place. I often wondered whether it was just duty that kept her there, or a fear of striking out and taking a chance on somewhere completely new. But then she met Catherine and that seemed to complete it for her. I honestly don't think I'd ever seen her so happy.

Eddie rolled up ten minutes late for Róisín's dinner party. He looked like he hadn't eaten in days, and he had a bottle of something cheap and nasty under his arm.

He seemed delighted to see me. He wrapped rangy, sinewy arms around me and gave me a huge hug. 'Hey, sis.'

Matthew waited stoically, knowing he would be next. Eddie had the actory thing of kissing anything that moved.

'Good to see you, man.'

'And you too, Eddie. Whoa, there!' Matthew tried to fend him off but it was no use; he was grabbed and got an affectionate and thorough pawing before managing to release himself.

'So!' Eddie said to him.

'So!' Matthew said back.

Matthew had often tried to take Eddie to the pub for pints and bloke talk – you know, football and hot girls, that kind of thing, but Eddie, Matthew maintained anyway, always looked a little affronted, like Matthew was a lightweight or something. And anyway, Eddie didn't drink, unlike other actors, who tended to be far too fond of the stuff. He said it affected his voice. He really was the genuine article. Like, it wasn't put on.

'Hi, there.'

That's when I saw her: Eddie's girlfriend. I knew of her existence but hadn't expected it to last very long. Well, girls went mad for all that sexiness and tortured artist thing, and there was always a queue of waiflike, pale-faced girls waiting for Eddie after his shows, usually wearing long dresses and Doc Martens, and they would share a pint of water with him, if they got that far, and discuss his performance in intense voices.

'I'm Eleanora.'

This one was a little different. Skinny, of course – that went without saying – and with regulation long, wafty hair, but her jeans were good and her eyes were lucid and sharp, which made a nice change.

'Lovely to meet you.' She shook hands with us all, very friendly, before turning to me. 'Eddie's told me you've decided to move home from London?'

I wondered if her name was made up. Ooh, bitchy, bitchy, and I'd only just met her.

'Yes.' I gave her a big smile to make up for my nasty thoughts. 'We're hoping for a quieter life. You know, walks in the countryside, open fires, bridge. That kind of thing.'

I could feel Matthew's eyes on me. *Bridge?*

'I hope we'll get to know each other better,' this Eleanora said efficiently. Clearly she had aspirations to the position of long-term girlfriend to Eddie. Still, you couldn't blame the girl for stating her case.

Róisín hurried in from the kitchen. Eddie, typically, had failed to warn her about Eleanora, and now she'd have to divide six portions into seven. And it looked like it was some kind of low-fat tartlet thing too, worse luck. Anita would be eating her handbag. She was already over by the peanuts, trying not to look suspicious.

'Another drink, anybody?' Róisín gave Eleanora a stiff look; you needn't think you're going to get locked on my tab, missy. 'We have wine, beer, gin and tonic—'

'Hi, everyone!' Catherine strolled in.

'At LAST,' said Róisín, who wasn't stressed by the evening at all. 'I thought you were supposed to be here on time to help me out? The shagging tartlets are lop-sided and probably burnt.' As well as about to be butchered into an extra portion. 'And, Anita, put those peanuts down.'

'Relax,' Catherine told her, oblivious to the danger such a statement might incur.

For someone who'd allegedly been working non-stop for months now, she looked remarkably fresh. She dumped an overnight bag on the ground, squeezed a rigid Róisín – she wasn't one for public displays of affection – and waved a 'hello' at Eddie and Eleanora. Then she turned to us with a big smile. 'When's the housewarming party then?'

'Whenever all the furniture arrives,' Matthew said eagerly. He'd already had two beers out of sheer nervousness at all my family being gathered in one place, and who could blame him? 'In fact, why wait? Who needs furniture anyway?'

He was being a bit giddy, but a lot of men were like that around Catherine, because she was so good-looking. She had a lot of tumbling hair and delicate features, and a killer figure, which she showed off in tight jeans and lacy tops, and honestly, their little faces when they realised that she was gay. Matthew I'd expected to be a tad more sophisticated, but as he said himself, he was only human.

'Cool,' said Catherine. I got the impression she was a bit of a party animal. We only had to give her the date and she'd be down in a flash, and to hell with work. Which, apparently, we weren't allowed to mention, in case Catherine got all stressed. 'How're you, Anita?'

She always gave Anita a bit of time whenever they met before taking any notice of her. This was because Anita tended to panic a bit and was liable to blurt out something completely inappropriate like, 'So! What do lesbians get up to in bed, then?'

It was the second thing she'd ever said to Catherine, pretty much straight after, '*Lovely* to meet you.'

I remembered the moment well. Everybody had frozen. Matthew had looked around for an escape route. Eddie, typically, had found the whole thing hilarious and had laughed his head off.

Anita said afterwards that she didn't know what had come over her. It had popped out of her mouth before she'd known what was happening. It was like the urge she had in Mass sometimes, to stand up in the middle of the homily and shout, 'Knickers!'

'Do you think I have that Tourette's syndrome thing?' she'd fretted.

'On top of type two diabetes? You'd have to be very unlucky, Anita.'

Happily, Catherine had been unfazed by it; Anita was simply curious, she maintained. And Róisín was her daughter, after all, who had only in recent years come out to the family. Why *shouldn't* she ask? In fact, Catherine found it quite refreshing; a lot of people got all tongue-tied and embarrassed, and made a point of not looking at her breasts, for some reason.

Róisín didn't share the same view.

'What do we get up to in *bed*?' she'd thundered, apoplectic. 'What would you like us to do, Anita? Hold a demonstration? Buy you a couple of educational DVDs – *Hot Lesbian Action*, maybe?'

Anita had perked up a bit at that, but there were no DVDs from Róisín, only appalled looks and mutterings about the backwardness of Castlemoy and it was a good thing that Catherine lived far, far away in Dublin.

Anyway, Róisín made it a rule that Anita was to be given a decent lead-in time at any gathering, so that she could get her thoughts in order.

'Hello, Catherine! Lovely jacket,' said Anita. It had obviously worked. The thing was, she actually got on great with Catherine, or rather she would if they were just left to it, but Róisín was forever hovering in a paranoid fashion.

81

'How's the diet going?' Catherine asked. She was a chocolate lover herself, not that you'd know it from the way she wore those jeans, and had huge sympathy for Anita's struggles.

'Great,' Anita confided.

Róisín and I shared baffled looks. If Anita thought it was going great, then clearly we were doing something wrong.

'Listen,' said Eddie apologetically, 'I don't mean to break up the party, but I've got rehearsals in the morning so we can't stay late.'

It was a hint to eat. And that boy needed to eat. I could hear his stomach rumbling from five feet away.

'What's the play?' Matthew enquired, bracing himself.

'*The Fruits of Enlightenment.* Tolstoy.'

'Very interesting, very interesting,' we all muttered, nodding furiously. Great, another bloody one we wouldn't be able to make head or tail of.

'Not a musical, then?' Anita tried.

'The thing is,' Eddie said to me in an aside, 'we won't make the last bus back up to Dublin so . . .'

I didn't hesitate. 'Of course you can stay with us.'

The beds had arrived yesterday so himself and Eleanora could christen one of them.

'You're sure it won't put you out?'

'I have to be up early myself anyway. Can't start slacking just because I'm self-employed.'

'Ah.' Eddie nodded sagely. He'd had long experience of being self-employed himself.

Eleanora waited quietly in the corner, ignored by everyone. She had enough cop-on to realise it was a family occasion and to stay out of the way. She reminded me of somebody biding their time.

'What do you do, Eleanora?'

'I'm a singer,' she said.

Of course she was. It would be too much to expect that Eddie might hook up with someone who had a job in, say, the civil service.

'She's fantastic,' Eddie said reverently.

Eleanora blushed prettily.

'What kind of singing do you do?' Matthew pitched in. Like he would have a clue. The only live singing he ever came into contact with was me, in the shower.

But Eleanora gave it a great deal of thought. 'Probably R&B. But contemporary.'

'Sometimes with a pop edge,' Eddie interjected.

'Well, maybe *sometimes*.'

Matthew looked at me, no wiser. 'And would we have heard you on the radio?'

Both Eddie and Eleanora looked at him like he'd broken wind. 'I'm a live artist. Not a recording artist,' Eleanora told him, haughtily.

In other words, the record companies had turned her down. I knew by the hungry look in her eye that she was after more.

Anita was beaming around at us all. 'You know, I can't remember the last time we've all been together like this. Two Christmases ago, at least – far too long. But now that Clara and Matthew are home for good . . .' She squeezed Matthew's arm affectionately. He'd painted her kitchen for her earlier and she'd made him a pot of tea and heavily buttered crumpets in return. 'I just wish your dad was here to see it,' she said, blinking a bit fast.

We all rallied around with cries of, 'Ah, now, stop or you'll set us all off!', and I gave her a little hug around the waist. Dad would have loved it, alright, and I was suddenly sorry I'd left it so long to come home.

'I'm sorry.' Anita smiled around at us all through her tears. 'I'm happy, that's all.'

Chapter Fourteen

Life settled into a routine surprisingly fast.

On Monday mornings, Matthew would go off on the train to start his week's work in Dublin. He and Eamon were gradually beginning to understand each other's accents, and the receptionists, he said, were getting a little friendlier. At least two of them had started to call him by his actual name, instead of just 'You there'. The defrosting had happened after he'd managed to get a keyboard working for them again by extracting a false nail from between the letters G and H. 'Oh, *Matt*hewwwww!' the other lads in Team Tech slagged him relentlessly; the receptionists never spoke to *them*.

Once he was gone for the day, I'd make myself a coffee and retreat to the little office space I'd created in the bay window. I'd installed a desk, a lamp and a chair, although Matthew maintained it was more of a recliner than a chair. But you might as well be comfortable, right?

So I'd sit down very efficiently, pick up a pen, and say, 'Okaaay! What have we on today, then?'

I was much cheerier to work for than that awful Brenda. I couldn't believe I'd put up with her snarling for so long. Seriously, she could take some lessons from me on how to treat employees. I never shouted and I was very accommodating about toilet trips and lunch breaks. I even let

84

staff invite family members into the office occasionally (my mother, for a cup of tea in the kitchen once).

Working from home was a whole new experience for me. So relaxing. After answering some emails, if there were any, I'd go back to the kitchen and wash up after breakfast. Normally, cereal-caked bowls would be waiting for me when I trudged in from work in London, but now it was all done and put away by ten o'clock. Bliss!

After another coffee, I'd head back to my lovely, comfortable chair, and make a few calls. Then the hoovering and maybe a spot of dusting; before I knew it, it would be time to go for my walk with Anita, which pretty much took me up to lunchtime.

The afternoon was more of the same: a few more emails, a few chapters of a book while I waited for my computer to back up, then I'd knock off early to have a delicious dinner ready for when Matthew walked in the door at half-past six.

I could honestly say that I *loved* working from home. It was the best decision I'd ever made.

'You should do it too, Matthew,' I told him fervently, at the end of the second week. 'To hell with being a wage slave. The quality of my life is just so much better. I even *look* healthier. See? All rested and stress-free.'

'You do, definitely.' He assessed me carefully, nodded thoughtfully, and then said, 'This working from home business. You do know you're supposed to actually *work*?'

'I *am*.' Did he have any idea of the number of emails and phone calls I made every day? Well, anyway, it wasn't so much the quantity as the quality. I'd made a fabulous contact only that morning: a butcher who was going to supply me with organic meat at a very good price. Plus, I'd persuaded the local free newspaper to run a piece on my new business. What more did he expect? I wasn't a miracle worker. 'Besides,' I said, thinking it best not to get into specifics, 'once I start getting bookings, I'll be in that kitchen all day long, cooking.'

'Ah, yes,' Matthew said. 'All those bookings.'

Naturally, I took offence. 'I'm trying my best.'

'Like the day last week I walked in to find you asleep on the blow-up bed?'

Oh! I knew he'd bring that up. Every row we would ever have, for the rest of our lives, would end with him wagging his finger and singing triumphantly, 'Blow-up bed!'

'I told you, I was just lying down to try to visualise what colour paint would be nice on the downstairs walls.' Though we'd now got proper beds upstairs, the blow-up one had remained in the living room, awaiting its return to Róisín. I'd lain down on it one afternoon for a few minutes. But the hour walk with Anita earlier must have tired me out more than I thought, because the next thing I knew, Matthew was standing over me, carrying his briefcase.

'Clara, you shouldn't be thinking about paint during your working hours. Look, I'm not trying to make you mad, although I can see I'm succeeding.' He took my hand in his and squeezed it: *I mean no harm.* 'I know you. You're a grafter. You might be happy to take it easy for a couple of months, but then you'll go mad sitting in this house all day long with nobody to talk to and nothing to do.' He looked at me. 'I'm just saying, that's all. It can be quiet around here.'

And, of course, the minute he said it, the minute I realised just how quiet it was.

No, more than quiet: silent. Still. *Deathly* still.

Twice in one day I frightened the life out of myself with my own sneezes. I heard every tiny noise like it was amplified: a dripping tap, a distant phone ringing in another house, my own breathing. This working-from-home business was definitely on the solitary side; Brenda might be the world's biggest bitch, but when she was in the building, at least you knew it. Plus your hands wouldn't be shaking uncontrollably from too many coffee breaks to combat the monotony, because Brenda didn't believe in such things.

I noticed that I was spending a worrying amount of time watching my neighbours. I wasn't particularly proud of that. But there I was, planted in the front bay window. What was I to do? *Not* look?

Anyway, you'd want to have the concentration powers of a Tibetan monk not to notice the screaming red faux satin dressing gown of Ma, who never seemed to have time to get fully dressed, God love her. She'd bundle the kids into the car at two minutes to nine, and drive them to school, still in her dressing gown, her bump protruding incongruously under the shiny material. Matthew had gone out to help her bring in her bins last week in case she strained anything, but she'd just said stiffly, 'Thanks, but my hubby will be home at any moment.'

He'd been confused. 'Why, did she think I was trying to hit on her or something?'

True to her word, the husband roared up in a filthy-looking old banger shortly afterwards. Matthew was right: he *was* dark and bad-tempered looking. He spent a lot of time shouting at Jennifer and Kian to keep the noise down, at any rate. He and Ma were most unfriendly; if you even said 'hello' to them you would get only the gruffest of responses, and usually a door closed in your face.

I was growing fond of Jennifer and Kian, though, who now waved to me every morning on their way out to school as I sat in the bay window. Kian had cheeky freckles, and Jennifer was the most demure-looking child, and it was hard to believe that she was so fond of sticking up the middle finger.

The Harley-Davidson's owner, I observed, turned out to be Burt Reynolds. Not the real Burt Reynolds, of course, but a very good imitation. He had a massive 'tache clinging to his upper lip and a big, cheesy grin (he smiled at his motorbike every morning, and gave it a suggestive squeeze about the saddle region). One morning he stepped out in a check shirt with tufty dark hair bursting out the top, and Matthew murmured, 'The resemblance is uncanny.'

Anyway, Burt seemed to have some kind of regular job because he left the estate at ten past eight every morning and arrived home at six fourteen most evenings. From my casual observations, anyway.

Maura Kiernan – from my old school, whom Róisín had pointed out that first day on the lawn – and her husband, Thomas 'The Knob' Doors, called over soon after we moved in with an apple pie for us. One side of it had caved in.

'I'm not a very good cook,' Maura said, unnecessarily. Then something struck her and she blanched. 'Oh my God. And you're a *chef*. I should have thrown it in the bin.'

'I'm sure it'll taste great,' I consoled her.

'I wouldn't be too sure at all,' she warned.

I only remembered her vaguely. Her mullet had been her most defining feature but she'd grown that out now, into a glossy bob, and until she'd said her name, I didn't have a clue who she was.

Her husband, Thomas, had indeed the unfortunate look of a knob about him – he had a big head and shoulders, and a barrel chest that tapered abruptly to a girlishly small waist and skinny little legs.

He was a very nice man, though. Decent through and through. 'Will you come for a pint up the town some night?' he asked Matthew shyly. 'A few of us meet for darts on a Thursday night in Dirty Harry's.'

'Yeah? Thanks. That'd be great.' For all his talk, Matthew hadn't summoned the nerve yet to walk into one of the 'men's pubs' on his own in case they all made fun of his foreignness.

Maura and The Knob wouldn't come in – 'no, no, you've enough to be doing without us in on top of you' – but we all promised we'd have some kind of a get-together soon.

'Maybe when our new neighbour settles in,' Maura said.

I looked across the road to the property adjoining theirs. The 'To Let' sign had gone, and the lawn had been freshly mowed. A pink Mini sat in the driveway. Clearly, it was woman.

'We haven't met her yet,' The Knob said. He grimaced. 'But she's got wooden floorboards and she's fond of high heels.'

Maura and The Knob promised to keep an eye on the place if we were away any weekend, and with more smiles and waves they went back to their own house across the road.

'See? I told you we'd like it here.' Matthew was effusive in his praise of them. 'They're great! And did you hear the way he invited me out?'

'Relax. It's not topless darts or anything.'

'Remember in the flat it was three weeks before we met any of the neighbours? As in, we didn't even run into them on the stairs? And it

88

was another six months after that before we got to know anybody's name, and that was only because the fire alarm went off in the middle of the night? Here, we've got a ready-made community. People who bake apple pies and call round to say hello. Imagine – our kids will go to school with Maura and The Knob's!'

'Calm down, Matthew.'

But he was adamant. 'Moving here was the best decision we ever made.'

Even though I kept a close eye out over the following days, I never saw the new occupant of number six. Her pink car was nearly always in the driveway, so I knew she was home. A couple of times during the night, when I got up for the bathroom, I saw a light burning brightly in a downstairs room, so she was a bit of a night bird, but didn't venture out much during the day.

'Or maybe she's got one of those phobias,' I wondered to Matthew idly. 'You know, about people, or open spaces or something.'

'Agoraphobia,' Matthew said. 'Or anthropophobia, if it's fear of people, or social occasions.'

'How do you know that?'

'I don't know. I must have just picked it up along the way.' He looked at me. Androphobia,' he blurted without warning. 'Fear of men.' He looked troubled. 'What is *wrong* with me? And why do they all begin with an A?'

Then he gave himself a bit of a shake and said happily, 'But isn't it great, to be talking about the neighbours behind their backs like this? I've never really done it before. Life on a suburban estate rocks.'

Chapter Fifteen

Matthew turned out to be right. The day finally came to pass when I sat down in the bay window, having done the hoovering, the washing-up, put on a whites wash, watched Ma drag in the weekly shop from the boot of her car (dressed this time) and drunk three cups of industrial-strength coffee. Then I realised: I was bored out of my tree.

'Anita,' I said, ringing her up. 'Get your runners on. The honeymoon is over.'

I turned up at her door ten minutes later, full of energy, and with a big bundle of the flyers Matthew had printed for me under my arm.

'You're early,' Anita said pointedly. I knew I'd interrupted her routine, which at that time normally involved a nice sit-down with a gossipy magazine and a cup of milky coffee. She'd been doing it for years, and was naturally narky at being disturbed.

'I know, but we're working today.'

'Working?' Another filthy look. I was guessing that she'd lined up a couple of chocolate biscuits for her coffee, too.

'Handing out flyers for my new business. It'll be fun.'

'Pull the other one.'

'alright, so it won't be any fun, but at least with luck I get to drum up some orders for my struggling new business, and you get to put a smile on Dr Mooney's face, with all the walking.'

I shouldn't have mentioned his name. Her eyebrows snapped even closer together. 'He thinks it's all my fault, you know.'

'Don't be daft.'

'You're not the one sitting there, looking at him. Knowing he's thinking, that fat cow, if she'd taken a bit more care of herself she wouldn't be in this boat.'

'And if someone walks in with cancer, does he think that's their fault too? Or arthritis, or heart problems? Did you tell him it was in the family?' I knew I was pandering to her a bit, but honestly, the *mood*.

'Of course I did. But he told me lifestyle is a big part of it too.' Another sigh, as though he was the biggest buffoon she'd ever come across in her life. 'He all but told me yesterday that I'd eaten myself into the way I am. Can you believe it?'

'How would you like me to answer that?'

There was no denying that Anita had always loved food. When we were children, she was forever in the kitchen baking old-fashioned things like apple strudel and delicious rolls of spotted dick (practically banned now, of course). She adored her chips and her pies and pretty much everything else you could think of. Except vegetables, if they were green. Or orange (she hated carrots). She wasn't too fond of cauliflower either, as it gave her wind. But she'd always been a great woman for the fruit. Anything at all that could be baked, stewed, sieved, steamed or pressed lovingly into a pie was good in her book.

It was just such a blasted shame it all had to catch up on her now.

'Right,' Anita grumbled. 'Let's get this bloody walk over with and then maybe I'll be left in peace.' She sighed and mumbled as she bent over to haul on her newly bought runners. 'Bangers! Mash! Come on. The bitch is here.'

'I heard that.'

'You're not as bad as your sister yet. I'll give you that. But you're getting there.'

We set off up towards the town at a brisk pace, set by Anita. We always started out like that, with her swinging her arms energetically and throwing her bottom from side to side, like she saw experienced athletes doing on the telly.

'Anita, should we not pace ourselves—'

'Can't talk. I'm doing my breathing.'

That involved lots of impressive sucking in and blowing out of air. Beside us, Bangers and Mash trotted along, unworried. They knew it would last only about ten minutes.

Actually, only nine minutes that day. Anita slowly ground to a halt. 'I just need to catch my breath,' she said. 'Go on without me. I'll catch you up.'

Bangers and Mash gave me a look: *and if you believe that one . . .*

I wasn't going to let her get away with it. 'You're never going to get fit if you keep giving up. Come on. Just a bit further.'

'But the further we go, the further we'll have to come back. If I knew the car was parked in the town . . .'

I sometimes did that, as an incentive.

'No car today,' I said firmly. 'Anyway, it's in the garage, getting a new number plate. I lost it somehow.' Matthew had been amused, especially as I had no recollection of reversing into anything, or hearing a clatter as it hit the road behind me. 'Let's go, Anita.' I took her arm and coaxed her along. 'Look, we're nearly in the town.'

She rallied reluctantly. When we reached the outskirts of Castlemoy, I began to put a flyer through the letter box of every house and shop that we passed. Anita waited on the road with the dogs, passing commentary in between gasping for breath.

'There, try that one. That's the Nesbitts, they might hire you, they're fond of their food.' Talk about the pot calling the kettle and all that. 'Don't bother with the Dillons. They only eat Spam, no class at all.'

On we went again. I worked my way up Main Street, every shop and business getting a flyer, and we zigzagged down all the side roads too – O'Malley Place, Carragh Street and The Cottages. I'd nearly forgotten about poor Anita, who was dragging along behind me in her stiff new runners, and trying to stop Bangers and Mash from savaging innocent passers-by.

'Anita, are you OK?' Now that I stopped to look at her, I got a bit of a fright. She was looking grey around the mouth.

'Fine.' It came out as a rasp. 'I'm not as fit as I hoped. Or, rather, I'm more unfit than I thought.' She tried a little laugh but erupted instead into a terrible coughing fit, so much so that Bangers and Mash began to look hopeful; there was nothing like a fresh corpse.

'Stop talking,' I begged her. I felt awful. Imagine if she had a heart attack? And I'd be useless, not like Róisín, who would know how to unloosen clothing and perform CPR. The only thing I might possibly do to bring her round would be to produce the packet of Rolos I had in my coat pocket. 'I'm ringing Róisín. I'll tell her to come and get us.' Whatever patient she was with, they'd just have to medicate themselves.

'No. Don't. I'm better now.' She didn't look better. The thing was, we hadn't walked that far. It was worrying that she couldn't even manage that. She looked worried herself. 'You finish those flyers, I'll wait here.'

'I'm not leaving you here in this state.'

'The hotel, then. I think I need to sit down.'

'Right. Lean on my arm. Let's go.'

I left her in the Coffee Dock, drinking a glass of water. Her usual bluster gone, she insisted that I finish the flyers and come back for her in ten minutes, despite my protests. 'Now everybody's looking at us, just *go.*'

She did look a little better, so I set off. There wasn't much left to do, just Hickey's Chemist on the Main Street, which smelled the same as when I'd been a child, and then the auctioneers. I pushed open the door and a little bell pinged, announcing my arrival.

'Oh, hello.' I was delighted to see Deirdre, who'd sold us our house, sitting at a desk.

'We can't take it back,' she said immediately. 'You've signed a contract.'

'I know. And we want to keep it.'

Seeing as I came in peace, her shoulders went down a few inches. 'To be honest, we didn't think you'd stick it a week.'

I became aware of other people now, peeping out from behind desks; there she was, your woman from London, and the boyfriend who, rumour had it, threw up the minute he set foot in Ireland.

'We love it here.' I said it loud enough for all the peepers to hear.

'It's not the worst spot in the world,' Deirdre agreed.

'Listen, Deirdre, would you mind if I left a few flyers here?'

Deirdre waved me to a vacant spot on a ledge inside the door. 'Come here,' she said, 'did you get the teabags?'

For a minute I was thrown.

'And the biscuits?'

Then I remembered. 'We did! Thank you.'

'We're just trying it out. A "Welcome Pack" if you like. Some of the others – ' she jerked a head violently towards the desk behind her – 'wanted to put in a tea-towel and toilet rolls and everything, but we have to stick to a budget.'

'Well, it was a lovely touch,' I assured her.

'So I hope you'll come back to us if ever you're considering selling at some point in the future,' she said.

We were only in the place in a few weeks. But I said, 'Certainly,' and the door pinged shut behind me as I stepped back out on the street.

I looked around me. I was in what was known as the professional end of the town, without any butchers or pubs to lower the tone.

And around the corner from the auctioneers was Bridge Street; down there it was even more professional. The insurance broker had an office on Bridge Street, and the dentist, and there was an architect's practice.

Jason's office was also on Bridge Street.

I set off with my flyers. I hadn't been down the street in years. Farrell & Reddy, Solicitors, was in a nice old building with a new shop front, I saw, and a rather snazzy nameplate by the door – very minimalist, no horrible loopy handwriting like solicitors were usually guilty of. Everything was glass and chrome, and I could see that the receptionist had been updated too; Mrs Phelan used to man the place ten years ago, in sensible skirts and Margaret Thatcher-type blouses with big floppy bows. Now there was a blonde on the front desk, early twenties, glam. She was tapping carefully on a keyboard; with those nails, it probably took her half a day to produce one letter.

I found my eyes drawn to the windows above.

Jason's office had always been at the back of the building. But now that his father had retired, he must have moved into pole position: the big office at the front, looking down over the whole street.

'Can I help you?' The blonde was suddenly in front of me. She had her coat on and her purse in her hand. Out to get something low-fat, judging by her itsy-bitsy skirt (come back, Mrs Phelan!).

She looked pointedly at my runners, then the flyers in my hand. I clearly looked like some kind of undesirable.

'No. Not today, thanks,' I told her nicely, before turning and walking away fast.

'It's good that you and Jason are talking again, anyway,' Anita opined in the Coffee Dock. There are ways of doing things, her pursed lips said. She'd raised me to be a nice girl, not some scut who rode rough-shod over the town's menfolk. For months afterwards, she'd been mortified every time she'd run into his parents, she said; she'd had to leg it out of the supermarket one morning to avoid them. 'I suppose you'll have to learn to get on, now that you're living in the same town.'

'We *are* getting on. Didn't I just tell you that I ran into his receptionist?' I wish I hadn't now. I thought she'd have a laugh over how the position had been upgraded. 'Anyway, look, are you feeling better?'

'I'm grand, back to myself.'

And it appeared that she was indeed, because she'd summoned Sophie to the table with a menu for her perusal.

Sophie took me aside and whispered, 'I didn't know what to do. I mean, with the alcoholics, we just say, "Now go home to your wife, Ned, you know you're not getting any drink here." But with *diabetics*? I can hardly refuse her a scone, can I?'

'It's fine. I'll handle this,' I assured her. I decided to take advantage of her feelings of guilt. 'Oh, and can I leave some flyers here? For my new business?'

But Sophie's guilt was short-lived. 'I'll have to inspect one first,' she said officiously. 'To make sure it conforms to our standards and guidelines.'

You'd think it was a branch of the Four Seasons, but anyhow, I handed over one.

After scrutinising it closely and turning it over several times in case there was a sneaky advertisement for lap dancing on the back, Sophie declared it suitable.

'You can put them on that table over there. VALERIE. Can you clear those cups off that table, please, for Clara's flyers?' Then she took out her order book and waited for the fallout from Anita's perusal of their selection of cakes, scones and other delicacies. I saw her checking that she had a second pencil, in case the order was a particularly long one.

'Anita,' I began. How to do it? I was tired of nagging her; I don't know who was more demoralised by it, me or her.

But Anita put down the menu and said, 'Tea.'

'Tea?' Sophie and I looked at each other, waiting for the 'and'. But there was no 'and'.

'Just tea. Thank you.'

When Sophie was gone, Anita sat there in silence for a moment. I sensed a change in the air, somehow. And it was to do with how that short walk had nearly killed her, not that she'd admit it in a million years.

'I'm going to have to do it, aren't I? What that doctor says. And the nurse in the hospital.' She flexed her feet in the new runners. After three weeks, they were blindingly white and unscuffed. They could have been put back in the box and returned to the shop, no problem.

'I suppose you do, if you want to feel better.'

It was like our roles had been reversed. Whereas she had once coaxed me to have a tiny spoon of delicious rice pudding, I was now coaxing her to stay off the stuff.

She sighed. 'Right, then. I guess I'd better make SOME effort.'

It didn't exactly inspire enthusiasm.

Matthew and I were, as Americans so artfully put it, making out on the couch when there was a rumble somewhere beneath us.

'Sorry,' Matthew said, mortified.

'No, I think it was my phone.'

96

'Who's texting you at this hour of the night?'

A quick glance at the clock said 10.45 p.m. Probably Jo; she was a great one for the late-night texts. After a glass of wine or two, she'd start to miss me, and she'd text things like, 'ET phone home!' and, 'Baby, I Need Your Lovin' (but not in a pervy way).'

'This isn't over, young lady,' Matthew warned me, rolling away as I found the phone.

It wasn't Jo. I shot up on the couch and clamped a hand on Matthew's leg.

'I just got a job!'

The text wanted to know if I was free to cater a drinks party for fifty people the following Saturday night.

'Are you heck!' Matthew was more excited than I was. 'Tell them you'll do it standing on your head! Well, if they want, that is.'

I couldn't believe it. My very first gig. The flyers had worked.

'Who's it for?' Matthew was peering over my shoulder at the phone.

I didn't recognise the number. Well, why would I? Since moving back, I'd only acquired a handful of them.

I scrolled down to the end of the message – it was a long one – to see if there was a name. But it was simply signed 'J'.

Chapter Sixteen

We used to always sign texts or notes with 'J' or 'C'. 'Running late, client not here yet, J.' Or, 'No milk, gone to shop (might get a sneaky Kit Kat too), C.' We were allowed to say it out loud too, but only in an American accent (don't ask me why, I haven't a clue). It would go like this:

'Hey, J. Whaddya say we go out to eat tonight?'

'Gee, C. Now you've put it up to me. But I guess I could put away a cheese burger and fries.'

I was surprised at how silly Jason could be sometimes. He'd always seemed so mature when I first began dating him. A little strait-laced, even. So it was a bit disconcerting at first when he would break into a perfect Mid-Western twang. He always looked surprised himself. 'Look what you're doing to me,' he would marvel.

'Yeah,' I'd say back. 'You'd be a hoot if you'd just let yourself go.'

But I suppose that's the way you are when you first fall in love; you get goofy and giggly, and everything about the other person seems completely fascinating, right down to the tips of their toes.

I made Jason smile and be silly. In turn, I was impressed by the whole alpha male thing that he had going on. It's funny how the things that first bring you together are the ones that end up irritating you the most.

In the early days, he'd roar up outside the house at the weekends in his low-slung legal-eagle-type car. Nobody that presentable had ever pitched up to take any of us out before. Eddie's girlfriends always looked like they had some kind of an eating disorder, and Róisín, well, the few men that she'd tried out in her early days had looked as bewildered and mismatched as she did.

But *Jason*: a big catch in a small town. Even without the lure of the job, he was a ride; an ex-schools rugby player, with an impressive jaw-line, even if his clothes sense was slightly on the conservative side. I figured it was because he had no sisters to give him fashion advice, but then again, I was a penniless student and hardly in a position to wish that his waistbands were just an inch or two lower.

On our dates, we'd never slum it locally; he always drove me to Dublin, to nice restaurants or hotel bars, where I'd sit up on a high stool, feeling flattered that I'd been singled out. He could have had anybody in the town, and he wanted me.

It was heady stuff. We'd spend the night sipping something expensive and staring into each other's eyes before going back to his place – he *owned* his own house, swoon – and keeping each other up all night.

Then, during the week, I'd get the train to Dublin, swapping my high heels for jeans and comfy boots. There, I'd burn things in the college kitchens, and get scuttered with my mates in the smelly pub around the corner. When the weekend would come round, I'd hastily shave my legs and slap on the fake tan again.

I hadn't realised how far apart my two worlds were until I invited Jason to my graduation do. I have a crystal-clear memory of him sitting there in a well-cut suit with a stiff smile on, while my classmates knocked back vodkas and Red Bull and took silly photos of each other.

He never said a word against them. But gradually, after college, I lost touch with my college friends. In the first year or two I still went up to Dublin to meet them – on my own, as it was clear Jason wasn't enthu-siastic. But eventually the nights out died away as I became more involved with home. Jason always had plans to do things; weekends away, just the two of us, or he'd spoil me with dinners in and clever movies that he'd rent. Often we'd stay in his house the whole weekend, all loved up, not seeing another soul. It was all wonderful and intense and special. And in comparison with all that, my college friends seemed a bit young or something.

Which, of course, I was too, underneath it all. It was just that somehow it had got a little lost along the way.

Now, ten years on, Jason wanted me to cater a party in his house. It was for his father's seventieth, his text had said, only it was a surprise, so not to say anything. The menu was up to me, except that two people were coeliacs and so could I keep some things gluten-free?

'You can, can't you?' Matthew ventured.

He was being very sensible about the whole thing. There was no head throwing and outbursts of, 'That fucker! I knew he'd be sniffing round the minute we came back!'

Rather, he seemed cautiously pleased that I had finally landed my first gig.

'This is how you get started. Impress those people and they'll tell more people, and so on and so on.'

'Yes, but he's my ex.'

'That chocolate cake that you do with ground almonds, that's gluten-free, isn't it?'

'I'll say it again. He's my *ex*. Come on, Matthew, is it not just a little bit weird?'

'Well, you could look at it that way,' he admitted. 'But you could also say that he's just trying to give you a leg up, Clara. He's being nice.'

'Yes, but why?' The text seemed to be burning a hole in my phone. I hadn't even replied to it yet, a whole day on. Some businesswoman I was turning out to be.

'I don't know. He's a nice guy?'

'Nobody's that nice. I didn't even put a flyer in his office.'

'You've papered the entire town with them. He couldn't miss them.'

That much was true.

'Plus, you know his father,' Matthew went on. 'Maybe he was thinking it would be nice, rather than getting some stranger.'

'His father probably can't stand me.'

'Why?'

'Maybe because I finished with his son? Why do you think?'

'Ten years ago, Clara. Look, we might never know Jason's motives. But if you really don't want to do it . . .'

Of course I didn't want to do it. Walk around his house, where I'd once used to stroll, buck naked? Be introduced to all his dinner guests as his ex? 'She dumped me. Pretty badly, actually. She's not half as nice as she looks, you know.' I'd be *mortified*.

Naturally, I showed Matthew none of this weakness. He might be suspicious as to the depths of my guilt. Instead, I spluttered, 'What, turn down my very first gig? Ha!'

'Well, if you're sure.'

'Couldn't be surer.' But I didn't get out my phone to text back a confirmation. I'd leave things to settle for an hour or two, and then I could start mumbling, 'You know something? I think it might be a little uncomfortable after all.'

'Anyway,' I said, 'are you not jealous?'

'Do you want me to be?' Honestly. He was so reasonable sometimes.

'Well, you either are or you aren't. You know, hunky ex, steamy kitchen, late night drinks after all the other guests have gone . . . ?'

'*Will* you stay for a drink with him afterwards?' Matthew looked a bit pained, and I immediately felt bad for trying to wind him up.

'No. Of course not. In fact,' I admitted, all pride gone now, 'I don't want to do it at all.'

'I understand,' Matthew murmured, and began to massage my feet. He always did that when I was very stressed. Jo could never believe it. 'He massages *those feet*? Girl, you've got a keeper there.'

'But if I *don't*, it'll look like I've something to be guilty about.' Which of course I did, but I'd been young, blah blah.

Then: maybe this was his way of making me pay. You know, if I cooked for him like some slave in the horribly embarrassing confines of his kitchen, then he might, just *might*, think about forgiving me for skipping out on him without even an it-was-good-while-it-lasted shag.

Suddenly, I decided. 'You know, I should do it.'

Matthew looked surprised. 'Really? Because you don't owe him anything.'

'I know, but it might actually break the ice.'

Things had been cordial enough in the hotel but I'd still sensed a certain aloofness. My Insane Chocolate Cake might be just the thing to break down those final barriers – and at a whopping five hundred calories a slice, it would want to be good for something.

Chapter Seventeen

'There's something familiar about her.'

'What, exactly?'

'I can't put my finger on it. I just think I know her from somewhere.'

Róisín was over. After many delays and false starts, the curtains had finally arrived that morning and none of them fitted and, in a blind panic (no pun intended) I'd phoned her up to come and have a look at them. 'They don't fit,' she'd said, helpfully.

By now we'd abandoned the curtains and were having a good look out at the neighbours. Róisín said her own neighbours weren't really worth spying on – they were mostly elderly and routine-bound – and so she was making full use of her time in my house. She'd already passed comment on Ma's red dressing gown and Burt Reynolds' chest hair, and now we'd just caught a glimpse of the new neighbour across the way. We could see her quite clearly standing by her front window. She had a load of blond, puffy hair, and she was chatting animatedly on the telephone.

'Oh, well. Never mind.' Róisín's interest in my neighbours and my curtains waned abruptly, and she began to pack up to leave disarmingly fast. 'I'd better go. I have to drive to Dublin. I'm meeting Catherine in The Front Lounge.'

'Again?' I said.

'Do you have a better suggestion? There just aren't that many gay bars in Dublin, Clara.'

'I mean you traipsing up to her. She hasn't been down to you since that dinner party you threw.'

I really liked Catherine, but I was also beginning to suspect she was as lazy as sin.

'I didn't realise you were keeping tabs.'

'I just hope she's giving you petrol money, that's all.'

'Maybe I like getting away from Castlemoy for the night, have you thought of that? Do you know what it's like being a nurse around here? To have people sidling up to me, asking me what they should put on their sore toe, or are there any home remedies for a dose of the clap? Cut it off, I told one eejit last week, just because I was so fed up of being hit on for free advice every time I walked out my front door.'

I'd been going to ask her about a patch of dry skin on my arm, but quickly knocked that one on the head.

'Or else they're asking me when I'm going to get married. You should hear them, Clara. "Any sign of a man at all there, Róisín? No chance of you getting hitched any time soon, har, har?" Imagine if I said to them, "Are you getting the ride at all these days, Mr Power, or has your dodgy prostate put paid to that?"'

She was hamming it up, and I laughed.

'Do they really have no idea?' I asked.

'What, that I'm a raving lezzer?'

I looked at her jeans and almost old-fashioned top. She looked like she was off to Mass. 'I wouldn't exactly say raving.'

'You know what I mean. Do you want me to give them heart attacks?' She checked her watch. '*Now* look at the time. I'm late.' She grabbed her bag, all in a fluster now.

'Go on, give Catherine a ring,' I coaxed. 'Tell her to hop on a train down, and you'll pick her up.'

'And do what, exactly? Partake of the local thriving gay scene?'

The nearest thing to a gay bar was Disco Night in Murphy's Lounge, which was held once a month, and where they hung up a glittery ball and occasionally played songs by Kylie Minogue (request only). It would be difficult to walk in there and hope to run into like-minded members of the local lesbian community.

Róisín was following my thoughts. 'Yes,' she drawled. 'Harder than you might think. It's fine for me, I'm used to it, but Catherine would be bored out of her tree.'

Catherine was beginning to sound like a right pain in the arse, but I suspected I'd only drive Róisín further into her arms if I gave out any more. Why couldn't Róisín have found someone decent, who'd treat her well, instead of a party animal who wouldn't set foot outside the city boundaries?

Róisín was hurrying out the door. 'Here, will you take Anita for her walk?' she asked, like Anita was a dog.

'I always take Anita for her walk.'

Just as we opened the front door, the door of number six across the road opened at the same time.

She of the puffy hair was still on the phone. 'Don't be naughty,' we could hear her saying saucily, as she pulled the front door closed behind her. 'Anyway, I'll see you soon.'

She was making for her car, all dolled up. As she got into the car, we saw her full face for the first time.

Beside me, Róisín gave a sharp intake of breath. 'I don't believe it!' she hissed. Off she marched across the road.

I set off after her, memories stirring . . . long summer days . . . bikinis on lawns . . .

Róisín rapped sharply on the car window of my new neighbour. 'Open up, Dominique Fitzgibbons! I know it's you!'

Dominique Fitzgibbons? The last I'd heard of her, she'd been on the bus out of here, her dreams in her suitcase, ready to take the world by the scruff of the neck. I'd kept wondering would I see her on the telly in a commercial, or starring in some drama series, but I never did, and after I went to London I forgot all about her.

The car door opened, and a tanned, shapely leg ending in a red high-heeled shoe stepped out. The tan was a bit streaky in places, and the skirt, when it emerged, too short, but you wouldn't notice that, because the next thing that hit me were the boobs, and then the upturned nose, and finally I was looking into Dominique's amused blue eyes.

'Well, well,' she said, the words dripping off her red lips. 'If it isn't the Maguire sisters.'

She made it sound like we were some kind of comedy double act. But even when we were kids, she always seemed to find us amusing in some way, like we were country hicks in comparison with her sophistication.

But that would have been forgivable. What she had done to Róisín had crossed a line.

Beside me, I could feel Róisín bubbling and simmering, that crossed line clearly fresh in her mind. 'What are you doing back in Castlemoy?' she demanded.

If Dominique was taken aback at this show of hostility, she didn't let on. 'I could ask the same of you. Oh, wait, I forgot. You never left.' She turned her attention to me now. 'You're looking well, Clara. Lost all that puppy fat, then?'

Witch. 'I see you've put a bit on.'

Dominique just planted a tanned hand – also a little patchy – on her rounded hip and said, 'More of me to love.'

And she gave a big laugh. You had to hand it to her. Still full of herself after all these years.

Róisín, understandably, wasn't quite as appreciative of Dominique's reappearance in Castlemoy. The last words she'd spoken to her had been, 'I'll put you in hospital, you bitch,' or something along those lines. In comparison, she was being incredibly restrained today. 'I thought you were going to take the universe by storm? Or did someone get there before you?'

I must admit, I was just as surprised to find Dominique back. If anybody was going to make it in this world, it was going to be her. Róisín and I had once had a sneaky read of her diary, and it had said things like, 'I probably won't ever get married because I don't really have any interest in children, only in myself, and anyway, I'll most likely be too busy making movies and being very famos [sic].'

I was quite impressed. The only stuff I ever wrote in my diary was things like, 'The boys in school asked me the colour of my knickers today.' I'd never have had the wit to map out my whole life.

'Relax, would you?' Dominique told Róisín. 'Yes, I'm back. But that doesn't give you the right to come knocking on my car window like that.' One eyebrow jumped up suggestively. 'Unless, of course, you were dying to see me again?'

Róisín's face exploded into colour. 'You bitch,' she said.

Somewhat contritely, Dominique said, 'Come on, that was a joke. Look, I can't believe we're still going to fall out over that stuff. What are we talking here, nearly twenty years ago? Please. Let's just shake on it and forget about the past, eh?'

But Róisín ignored Dominique's outstretched hand. 'I have forgotten about it,' she ground out coldly.

Dominique sighed, and said crisply, 'If you must know, I came back to work.' She gave Róisín a look. 'Thankfully, it's only temporary. Now, much and all as I'd like to hang around catching up with you girls all day, I'm actually late. I'm meeting an old friend.' She got back into the car, streaky legs and all. 'Maybe we can meet up for a coffee sometime, Clara, and catch up. Your sister clearly doesn't want to.' And she closed the car door in our faces.

We had to step back hurriedly as she reversed loudly in the pink Mini, then set off out of the estate with a merry screech of the tyres.

'You're not going to go for coffee with her, are you?' Róisín looked scandalised.

'Of course not.' My friendship with Dominique hadn't been so strong that I was dying to get it back. And certainly not at the expense of good relations with my sister. 'But, you know, Róisín, maybe she's got a point. The past is the past.'

'We are not going to be friends again,' Róisín ground out. 'Got it?'

'OK, OK. Look, just go, would you? You'll be really late for Catherine.'

I wanted Róisín to have a good night now, and not dwell on Dominique

Fitzgibbons and that night at the school disco in the local hall all those years ago.

But Róisín hesitated. 'Come here. I hear you're cooking dinner for your ex.'

I hadn't said anything. Why would I?

'He's booked me to cater a party he's throwing. You make it sound like I'm going on a date with him.' I tried a laugh, just to show how professional I was being about the whole thing. 'He's just giving me my first break, that's all.'

'Don't be stupid, Clara. Why would he do that?'

'Because . . .' What, we were friends? 'What other reason would he have?' I said instead.

Róisín had never been that keen on him. 'Ancient', she'd branded him, pretty much from the moment I'd announced we were seeing each other. Mind you, he wasn't that keen on her either, puzzled by her refusal to exercise the usual feminine charms. He just couldn't work her out at all; worse, he didn't bother trying very hard, just brushed her off as Clara's weird sister. Relations had soured completely when he'd made some colourless remark about 'lezzers'.

'I'm sorry, Róisín,' I said at the time. 'He obviously doesn't know you're one.'

'He's probably heard the rumours.'

Róisín was convinced that the whole town had heard about the disco. I tried to reason with her that it had all blown over in a matter of days. But from then on, Róisín had remained convinced that she was always the number one topic of conversation in the town.

'Look, I'll educate him,' I promised her. 'He won't do it again.'

But Róisín just kept shaking her head incredulously. 'There was a time when you'd have run a mile from someone like him.'

'What's that supposed to mean?' I was still madly in love at that point; all I could see were the similarities between me and him, and not the gaping differences.

Róisín, being wise, knew there was little point in reason; that I would find out eventually for myself through bitter experience, as indeed I did.

She gave the same sigh now. 'I suppose you'll have to do it, now that you've said yes. Just keep it professional.'

'Of course I'm going to keep it professional.' What did she think I was going to do? Start rehashing the finer points of our relationships in his kitchen?

'Well, then. You don't have anything to worry about, do you?'

Chapter Eighteen

Eddie was going to be my waiter on the night of Jason's party. When I'd texted Jason to ask whether he would like to book servers on the night, he'd texted back crisply, 'Yes, please.'

Róisín had me spooked. I looked at the text this way and that. Could he have meant something else? Was there some hidden agenda between the lines? Did he think there was something else on offer apart from canapés?

But in the end I decided that he just wanted servers.

This coincided with Eddie getting fired by Jimmy. Jimmy had apparently gone on the dry. When Eddie had shown up to apply for his dishwashing job back following a two-week sojourn in a play set in someone's actual bedroom, Jimmy had said in a rare moment of lucidity, 'You used to wash dishes here before, you little fucker. Are you trying to make a fool out of Jimmy Maloney?'

'Certainly not,' Eddie said humbly, and apparently took his belongings, wrapped in a spotted handkerchief, and set off on his lonely way.

So my offer to pay Eddie to work for the night came at a particularly good time for him.

'It's just a couple of hours' work,' I told him apologetically. 'But there might be other parties, if it takes off.'

'Hey,' he said. 'Don't you start feeling sorry for me too. Anita already tried to send me a cooked chicken in the post. I think it got intercepted in Head Office and was detonated by bomb disposal.'

He'd phoned back, a few minutes later, sounding a little embarrassed. 'This gig on Saturday. I don't suppose you need a second server, do you? It's just that Eleanora wanted me to ask. No pressure or anything.'

As it happened, I did need a second server. Trust Eleanora to realise that. She was no daw.

On the other hand, she was my brother's girlfriend. She'd moved in with him to his grotty, flea-ridden bedsit two weeks ago, so it must be serious. By helping her, I was helping him, I reluctantly concluded. What did it matter if I always got the impression that she had her eye on the main chance?

'Tell her to tie up all that hair,' I warned him.

Miniature lamb koftas . . . crab cakes served warm with tartar sauce . . . sesame chicken sticks . . . stuffed mushrooms . . . spring rolls with plum sauce . . . chunky chips with garlic dip . . . sausages from Brennan's butchers with honey glaze . . .

'Just one,' said Matthew, drooling over my shoulder. He loved sausages. Brennan's in the town did lovely fat juicy ones.

'Get the feck away.' I slapped his hand.

'Hey.' He looked surprised. 'That hurt.'

'Sorry-sorry-sorry.' I felt bad. Apparently I'd rolled over in bed last night and had walloped him in the face, and hadn't even apologised, just went on snoring fitfully. 'I'm just running behind.' The miniature pies had gone the tiniest bit too brown on me because I'd taken my eye off them for a second, and I'd had to rustle up a batch of sesame chicken sticks instead, which had set me back an hour.

'Let me help,' he said.

He'd been offering to help all day. He'd hung about in the corner of the kitchen, as it would be dangerous to stray into the middle, what with all the skewers and spatulas flying around at speed. At the slightest command, I knew he would be only too willing to jump in.

The problem was, unless he could stuff a mushroom – at least, to my exacting standard – there wasn't much he could do, except make me cups

111

of tea and massage my shoulders. Which he'd tried, about mid-afternoon, and I'd nearly hit the roof. 'Are you trying to have sex with me?' I'd apparently shrieked (it had all been a blur at that point). 'I'm in the middle of trying to cater my first official party!'

It was nerve-racking. And no Jo there in the kitchen to share the stress or jolly me along. I was on my own with this one. Tonight was my big test as a chef, and an entrepreneur, and I was bricking it.

Of course, it didn't help that it was my ex's party. But I didn't dwell on that. I was fully focused on the job at hand. I needed it to go well, for myself as much as anybody else.

'Everything looks great,' Matthew tried to convince me.

'Do you think? I reckon I've probably done too much.'

I'd spent a fortune on fresh ingredients, and had offered an extensive menu. If I was going to launch Food by Clara, then I would do it with a bang.

And who knew, maybe I might get some bookings out of tonight.

'Do you want me to go with you?' Matthew said eagerly. 'You know, if you think it would help.'

'And do what?'

His brow furrowed. 'I could be a bartender or something. Ask attractive women if they'd like it shaken, not stirred.'

I laughed. 'I'm not paying you to flirt with the guests.'

'Or just even some moral support? For free? I promise I won't lurk in the kitchen like some kind of deranged boyfriend fending off your ex.'

He knew I was a little nervous about the whole Jason thing. But I reckoned I'd be too busy, as would Jason, to be mixing much. It would be fine.

'I think you should go to the pub like you keep threatening to, and make some new friends,' I told him. That morning Matthew had spoken to Burt Reynolds for the first time – just a 'Hey!' from him, but Burt had nodded back, very friendly, Matthew said, before steadying his motorbike and firmly straddling it.

'This place is feeling like home,' Matthew had declared.

Eddie and Eleanora arrived on the bus from Dublin. Eddie's cheekbones were even more razor-like than usual, which I put down to the loss of his dishwashing job and the accompanying staff meals. Eleanora had washed her masses of hair and, contrary to instructions, it hung around her shoulders in seductive coils. She was turned out in a see-through dress and high heels that looked a size too small, not that you'd know it from the determined smile on her face.

'Thanks very much for giving me the gig,' she told me effusively. 'Wow! Look at all that food! Eddie was right. You're WAY talented.'

I wanted to like her. I almost did. Then she said, 'Tonight. Is it minimum wage or more?'

She had every right to ask. Eddie hadn't. It wouldn't occur to him. Money? Pah! It was probably left to Eleanora to make sure they didn't get thrown out for non-payment of rent.

'Minimum wage,' I clarified crisply. 'Plus, sometimes people tip.'

Her eyes brightened. They dulled again quickly when I made her change into plain black trousers, black apron and a pair of my pumps (also a size too small). The long hair I whipped into a severe-looking knot on the top of her head.

'Health and safety,' I told her.

Eddie, with his great love of dressing up, had a joyous rifle through Matthew's wardrobe in search of black trousers that would fit. Matthew was very unhappy about this and stood protectively by as Eddie pulled out various garments for inspection, marvelling.

'Man, you've got some weird shit.' He'd found a cricket jumper.

'Yes, thank you, I'll take that.' Matthew leaped forward to rescue it.

'Rocking!' Eddie, fascinated, held up a pair of Lycra cycling shorts that had been purchased during Matthew's brief I'm-going-to-cycle-to-work-every-day phase in London. 'We're doing a day of improvisation next month. Centred round a guy who goes crazy in a fast-food joint as a protest against the rot of consumerism?' Eddie's eyes began to take on an otherworldly glow. Eleanora, who had somehow found her way upstairs, looked a little tight around the mouth. You could hardly blame her. If only once in a while he did a cheery, well-paid farce or something. 'We've been looking for the perfect costume,' Eddie informed us avidly. 'And I think this just might be—'

'Just take the black trousers and get the hell out of my room,' Matthew said evenly.

Eddie, always in tune with the zeitgeist, correctly determined that he had crossed a line. It wasn't always easy to recognise it with Matthew, because he was generally so balanced and non-hysterical and happy.

'If you say so.'

'I do.' Matthew clutched the Lycra shorts to his chest. You could insult him all you liked, but not his sportswear.

Eddie looked fabulous in his black gear, with his long hair slicked back. He'd found a crisp white cloth from somewhere and draped it over his arm, and wore an expression of brooding subservience. If Al Pacino had been a waiter, he'd have looked like Eddie.

'Is he playing a part?' Matthew whispered to me. 'Because he's scarily good.'

Eleanora looked good too, even though she kept trying to pull down little bits of hair to look less frumpy. 'I'll get no tips, looking like this,' I heard her fretting to Eddie. 'You'd better be nice to the women, to make up for it.'

'I'm not a gigolo.' Eddie was affronted.

'Nobody said you were.' Eleanora sounded irritable. 'But we need to pay the shagging rent, and your starring role as a nutter in Lycra shorts isn't going to do that, is it?'

It was difficult to argue with that. And Eddie hated confrontation – all that wasted energy that could be used creatively instead – so he ended up muttering, 'Sorry. You're right.'

Eleanora immediately backed down. She wound thin, pale arms around his neck. 'You'll get your break. We just have to wait. Now, let's go serve your sister's canapés for minimum bloody wage.'

Chapter Nineteen

It was strange being back in Jason's house. The minute I'd stepped through the door, the smell of the place had nearly knocked me over. Nothing *rotting*, or anything like that. Furniture polish, mostly – Pledge, I think, although I'm far from an expert in these things. In that regard, Jason wasn't your typical man, whose idea of cleanliness was firing his underpants in the vague direction of the laundry bin. Jason had always cleaned, hoovered, kept things nice.

'An OCD head!' Jo had declared, when I'd told her about his penchant for hoovering. 'You lucky bitch. I went out with one of those once, but all he ever did was open doors with a handkerchief over his hand. Nutter.'

When I told her about having landed my first catering gig, she'd immediately booked a post-mortem on the phone. 'Ring me when you get home from it, no matter how late it gets,' I'd been sternly instructed. Things with Brenda were getting desperate, apparently, and Jo needed any small diversion at all to keep from flinging herself off a window-ledge. 'You might give me some hope, or inspiration, or *something*.' According to Jo, Brenda had disappeared on a three-day bender with some lecherous client, and had left Jo and the new girl without even a key to the building. Any day now, Jo was going to jack it in and follow in my footsteps, so she was very anxious that I wow them tonight.

I wished she was there with me now. But I was on my own in Jason's kitchen. I remembered the big kitchen table, the black and white tiled floor. The cooker, the microwave, the presses by the door – none of it had changed. And the huge old-fashioned porcelain sink, of course, where once we'd re-enacted that water-sprayed sex scene from *Fatal Attraction*. Mortifying, of course, but you know the way it is when you're young. Anyway, never mind, it would do very nicely to wash up the pots and pans when I was finished.

'They're getting rowdy out there.' Eddie arrived into the kitchen with an empty platter. He was working so hard that his cheeks were ruddy. I suspected he was using the whole exercise as research; at some point in the future Eddie the Waiter would appear on a stage near you. 'Someone pinched my bottom,' he said indignantly.

I peered past to the living room. The place was jammed; lots of shiny, red faces and guffawy bursts of laughter. This lot had looked sedate enough coming in, but give them a glass or two of Prosecco . . .

'That's Ian Shanahan,' I said. The arse pincher. Long retired now, he used to own a grocery shop in the town.

'No!' said Eddie. 'Is it? I thought he was dead.'

From the way he was knocking back the drink out there, being pickled was probably what kept him going.

'Do you remember he used to call to our house at Christmas time with a box of Quality Street to thank us for our trade?'

Eddie laughed. 'God, yes. We used to fight over the purple ones.' He looked back out to the living room. 'It's a bit of an older crowd, isn't it?'

Well, it *was* a birthday party for a seventy-year-old. There was Mr and Mrs Hartigan, propping each other up, Mrs Hartigan asking her husband every two minutes, '*What* did he say?' And I could see some clients of the practice, old cronies of Jason's father, knocking back the sherry. One of them had cornered Eleanora and her platter of stuffed mushrooms. You could see she was bitterly disappointed by the calibre of the clientele; not a dashing country squire in sight.

There were hardly any younger people except for the blonde receptionist I'd seen at the office the previous week, and a few dutiful daughters here and there. I didn't see any of Jason's friends whom I would once have known, which was a bit of a relief. Now there would be no need for explanations, or embarrassing conversations like, 'Clara! YEARS since I've seen you! God, you look GREAT.' Awkward pause. Much shuffling of shoes. Then a quick scuttle off to the drinks table, muttering under their breath, 'Gone a bit brassy-looking, isn't she?'

Now I was worried that maybe I *did* look a bit brassy. I'd lashed on the make-up back at home, and had a stylish black dress on under my apron. I probably should have stayed more low-key. I was the caterer, after all, not a guest. Cripes, maybe Brenda had rubbed off on me after all.

Here came the birthday boy into the kitchen now – Jason's father, Paul, all dickied up in a suit and tie.

'Hello, Paul!' I said heartily. 'Happy birthday!' I hope to Christ he wasn't thinking, the nerve of you, woman, back in my son's kitchen after all this time.

But he just gave me a proud smile and said to Eddie, 'Any chance of another Scotch?'

Eddie immediately snapped into waiter mode. 'Certainly, sir!' he said, even though I'd explained there was no need for all that sir and madam stuff. He then clicked his heels together sharply at the back, like he was in a military movie (ah! It wasn't a waiter he was being at all, but a man in uniform) and swept out of the kitchen, leaving Mr Farrell looking rather taken aback.

'Your brother, right?' he checked cautiously, not wanting to assume it was some loon who'd strayed in the back door.

'Eddie. Yes.'

'I remember him when he was a young lad around the town. He was always wearing your mother's scarves and carrying sticks like they were spears.'

'That would have been Eddie, alright.'

There was a little silence. Mr Farrell – I'd never got used to calling him Paul – was clearly wondering what to say to me next. Nothing new there. He and Rose, Jason's mother, would always be watching television whenever

117

Jason would bring me by on a rare visit, but the minute we'd walk in, they'd feel obliged to turn the television off and we'd all sit there like lemons trying to make conversation. 'So! What have you two been up to, then?' Mr Farrell would say in an attempt at gaiety. 'Fornicating on the back seat of your son's car,' wasn't the appropriate response, so I'd mumble something about the cinema or a fictitious walk around the castle. 'Lovely,' Mrs Farrell would say valiantly, secretly dying to catch the end of *Coronation Street*. 'We often take a walk up there ourselves, don't we, Paul?' Much mutual nodding and declarations of 'yes', before it all petered out again.

Jason never seemed bothered by these silences. He would quite happily sit there, stretching his feet out towards the fire as though he were sixty himself. But eventually, I would feel a pressure begin to build inside me, and no matter how many sad things I thought of – funerals, world hunger, my credit card bill – I knew that it was only a matter of time before I burst out laughing uncontrollably. Usually I managed to escape to the loo before that happened, and once I'd got it out of my system, I could return to the stuffy living room again.

I wasn't quick enough one evening, though, and in the middle of Mrs Farrell telling us about her sister's awful holiday in Turkey – too many Turks, apparently – a massive snigger escaped me. I can still remember them all looking at me in astonishment, as I rocked on the couch in mirth, tears rolling down my face.

'Sorry. It was the Turk thing that set me off,' I apologised to Jason as we got into the car afterwards, me still mopping my eyes.

He'd looked at me, coldly cross. 'That was really rude, Clara.'

He'd been slagging them himself earlier.

'I know, I'm sorry—'

'Grow up, for God's sake. When you do that, you make me look bad too.'

And he hadn't spoken to me for two days.

I wondered if Mr Farrell remembered that night too, when Jason's inappropriate girlfriend in the torn jeans had cracked up on his couch.

'I hope you're enjoying your party,' I said gamely.

'Well, it was certainly a surprise,' he said. 'Jason's never done anything like this before. I don't know what's got into him.'

'I suppose he just wanted to mark the occasion.' Party animal that he was. Not.

'To be honest, I'd have preferred a round of golf at the club and a few drinks afterwards. For him to go to all this trouble . . .' He glanced round at all the food, troubled. Maybe he thought he'd be expected to eat it himself. 'Anyway, I was glad to hear you were back,' he said. 'And setting up your own business too. Very brave, especially in this economy.'

He was warming up now. He'd always loved talking about the economy. I could see no trace of resentment towards me at all. And to think that we had almost been related.

'Listen, I'm sorry about Mrs Farrell,' I said impulsively. It was better late than never. And he must miss her tonight, what with the celebrations and everything. They'd been decent people, and never anything but polite to me.

'Thank you, Clara.'

We could see that Eddie had procured a bottle of Scotch and was brandishing a large glass.

'I'd better go,' Mr Farrell said hurriedly. Eddie's measures were on the large side, I'd noticed. No wonder half the guests were off their heads.

He stopped by the door and looked back at me. 'I never blamed you, you know,' he said unexpectedly. 'For the way things ended. Jason's a good lad but he's not so good at reading the signals.'

There was no time to digest it, because suddenly Eleanora was back with two empty platters, and I barely saw Mr Farrell again for the rest of the evening.

Despite my worries, the time flew. Eddie and Eleanora were in and out, I was reheating and plating up and throwing away scraps. Of which there were very few, I was delighted to note. They'd scoffed the lot. Someone had even sent Eddie back in to see if there were any more lamb koftas.

Towards the end of the evening, my phone beeped with an incoming text.

'Are you surviving? Do you need me to swing by on my white steed and help out with the washing-up? I come cheap.'

Matthew. The dote.

'No steed required,' I texted back. 'The food's going down really well. Phew!'

'Everything OK?'

It was Jason this time, standing in the doorway. I put my phone down guiltily. Then I was annoyed with myself. I was thirty-three years old. Why was I behaving like a naughty schoolgirl again?

'Fine,' I told him confidently. 'No problems at all.'

I could see him looking at the sink. Was it because of the pile of washing-up I was just about to start? Or was he thinking of Glenn Close? Mortification.

'Your father seems to be enjoying himself,' I said. Mr Farrell had put away several more of Eddie's large Scotches, and was singing 'The Fields of Athenry' with some cronies in the corner.

Jason followed my gaze and smiled too. 'I might have to get you to whip up a fry to sober everybody up.'

'I don't do fry-ups. I've gone up in the world.'

It was a joke. Come on. But Jason gave me a bit of a look. Oh, feck him. I was tired and hot and I wanted to go home. I'd earned my money, and I didn't feel any obligation to stay here and make small talk with him.

He obviously took the hint, because he got a cheque book out of a drawer and referred to the invoice I'd placed on the table rather blatantly. I was able to get a good look at him, unobserved. He hadn't really aged at all in ten years; even though he was approaching middle age, there were no grey hairs or paunch. But the waistband of his trousers was still just that inch or two too high. I nearly smiled, but caught myself just in time.

Then he was tearing off the cheque with a flourish – he'd always liked to do that, like he was an oil tycoon or something, instead of a midlands solicitor – and handed it over to me.

'Thank you.' I crisply took it. 'The leftovers are in the fridge. They'll be OK to eat tomorrow, if you can face them. Although maybe not the salmon. If you got sick my reputation would be shot to hell.'

At last he smiled. Honestly, you would think it killed him. Still taking himself too seriously, after all these years.

'So!' I said. 'Nice doing business with you. And thanks again for giving me the booking.'

I wasn't too crawly. He'd got a very good deal. Fearful of overcharging him, I had probably ended up under-charging him.

I looked around for Eddie and Eleanora to help with the final bits of washing-up. Eleanora seemed to be working the room for tips. In ten minutes we'd be on our way, out by the back door, nice and discreet.

But Jason planted himself in front of me and said, 'I hope it hasn't been weird. You know, being back in the house like this.'

I was thrown. I hadn't been expecting this at all. I was here to cook. That was all.

'Jason . . .'

'You were going to move in, remember?'

Yes, I had been going to move in. A long, long, LONG time ago. Had he had too much wine?

'I suppose that's all in the past now.' My tone said: This Conversation is Wildly Inappropriate. I gave the washing-up a pointed look.

He immediately retreated. 'Sure. Sorry. I just thought I'd say something rather than ignore it, that's all.'

'Ignore what? We broke up. I hardly think we need to go over the finer points after all this time, do we?' But I made my voice friendly. Maybe he'd been trying to smooth things over but had just got it plain wrong. That would be typical of him, too, along with not reading signals. (Example: when your girlfriend says she wants to cool things off, instead of backing away in concern, you tell her, 'I know! Let's get married!')

'Thanks again for hiring me.' I'd better give a little something back. 'It was decent of you.'

He shrugged, cool and detached again. 'Why not? I needed a caterer, and you needed the business. You can hand out some business cards to people, if you want.'

'Really?' That would be great. I desperately needed to spread the word, and people had clearly enjoyed my food.

'In fact, give me a bunch and I'll do it.'

I handed him some. He took them, and with a curt nod – mortified by his faux pas, no doubt – off he went.

I was upstairs in the spare bedroom, rooting around for my coat in the pile on the bed, when a woman came in behind me.

It was Dominique.

We looked at each other for a moment, before she tossed a fluffy pink coat onto the bed with no great enthusiasm.

'Bloody hell,' she said. She nodded towards the stairs. 'It's like a geriatric ward down there. I'd sneak back out only Jason's already spotted me.'

Dominique had always been late for everything. Maybe because she took so long getting ready. Tonight she was wearing a cream dress so tight that it stuck like cling film to her generous backside. Her lips were dripping with gloss and the hair was a mad, popcorn puff. She looked a bit like a cartoon.

'What are you doing here, Dominique?' She was hardly an old friend of Mr Farrell, and she didn't look anything like the other business clients in the room downstairs.

'I was invited. You hardly think I'm here to work the room?'

I eyed the dress. One could be forgiven.

'Mind you, if I'd known it was going to be this lively . . .' She threw another doubtful look towards the stairs. 'Still, it's all good research for my book.' She enjoyed the look on my face. 'I'm a writer now, did you not know?'

I made no effort to hide my disbelief. Dominique had displayed little interest in literature at school. She'd spent most of the time in English class trying to put curls in her hair with a pencil, or else practising her name over and over again, with loops and kisses and hearts.

'I'm on my eighth novel at the moment. All of them bestsellers.'

OK, now I was a little bit impressed.

'Anyway, my publisher in New York and my agent in LA' – heavy emphasis on the LA bit – 'suggested I set it in small-town Ireland, for a change. Americans love that sort of stuff. So I sublet my apartment and flew back to write it here. There was a short-term let on the house, I took it, and now I just need to rack up the word count. I've got a deadline looming.'

That would explain her being house-bound. She was writing. And long into every night too, judging by the lights burning late in her house. Tonight, though, she was clearly letting her hair down.

'I'm glad you've done well, Dom.' Oops. I'd slipped into old nicknames. Róisín would kill me.

'So, what's your story?' she asked. 'From what I hear, you actually returned *willingly*?'

'We've decided to settle down here.'

'But there's nothing to do.' She looked baffled. 'No decent shops, no proper restaurants. It's just like when we were kids.'

Clearly her family felt the same; Róisín told me that Dominique's parents had gone back to Scotland, where her father was from.

'You should try the Coffee Dock.' Sophie would eat her for breakfast. 'It's newish.'

'Yeah? Thanks.' She looked me up and down, taking in my apron. 'So you're a cook now?'

'A chef. I own my own catering business.'

'So Jason tells me.' His name fell familiarly from her lips. Her head dipped to one side. 'You two used to go out, right? I think you started dating just before I left. He was mad about you, right from the start. Personally, I didn't know what you were doing with an old fogey like him.' And she gave a little laugh. 'Mind you, he's improved with age. Or maybe we've both got a little older too, eh?'

'It was a long time ago, Dominique.' I was tired and wanted to go home. I hadn't a whole heap of interest in this conversation. Matthew would be waiting up for me and we'd unwind with a nice glass of wine.

But Dominique was in no hurry to get down to the elderly guests. 'Jason's been helping me with my research,' she confided. 'One of the main characters in the new book works in the field of law, and when I phoned him up, he said he'd be glad to give me a few hours of his time, just for background stuff.'

123

The idea of Jason, in his sober suits, being background researched by an over-scented Dominique conjured up all kinds of scenarios, and I wanted to laugh.

'Anyway, he invited me along tonight.' She leaned in and said confidentially, 'I think it's a date.'

'Good for you,' I said confidentially back. 'I'm afraid all the food's gone, and most of the drink. Half the guests are asleep. But I'm sure you'll have a great time.'

Dominique threw back her head and laughed. If she hadn't made such an eejit out of Róisín I'd nearly have liked her again. Growing up, she'd always had the upper hand by virtue of being two years older than me. Now we were adults, equal, and I suspect we'd have got on very well in other circumstances.

She watched as I found my coat and put it on. 'I have to hand it to you,' she said cheerily. '*I* never manage to stay friends with guys who dump me. I usually end up cutting up all their clothes or pushing their car off a cliff.'

I smiled too, a little uneasily. She was talking generally, right? Because Jason hadn't dumped me. It had been the other way round.

But Dominique was looking at me very sympathetically. 'It must have been really rough for you, him breaking off your engagement like that. So for you to come and cater his party like this without poisoning him . . .' And she gave another snort of laughter. 'Fair play to you. I mean it.'

Chapter Twenty

'Are your croissants fresh?'

It had become a bit of a running joke between me and Sophie. I asked every morning whether the croissants were fresh. It was the only lightness she permitted during the transaction.

'As a daisy,' she said. 'Coffee?'

'Please.'

'VALERIE. The usual.'

She tore off my docket and plonked it down on the table. She went straight off to get my croissant, not stopping for her usual chat. Maybe she was busy.

When she arrived back, I said, 'Has anybody picked up one of my flyers from the table, did you notice?'

My first catering gig had yet to be followed by a second. Patience, Matthew said. He was talking me up for all he was worth at work. He'd nearly got me a booking to cater one of the receptionists' twenty-first birthday party – she'd looked at the website and everything, and had been very impressed – but then it turned out that she had a budget of about five euro.

'I have no idea,' said Sophie, clipped.

Something had clearly got her goat this morning. I was beginning to suspect it was me. From the way she was fingering her notebook with her sharp, French-tipped nails, I was getting the impression she wanted to get away from me, fast. Plus, she hadn't passed any comment at all on my wet-look raincoat, which I hadn't worn up to now but which was pretty kinky and deserved at least a passing mention.

'Sophie, I'm getting the impression that I've upset you in some way.'

She drew herself up to her full height of five foot three and managed to look more offended. 'I don't bring my grievances into work.'

'No, no, I wasn't suggesting that for a second—'

'But now that you've asked, I'm a bit surprised you didn't ask me to work for you on Saturday night at Jason's party. I *am* a professional waitress, you know. Unlike some.'

It hit me then. She'd obviously heard about Eddie and Eleanora doing the honours at Jason's party. Mere amateurs.

It had never occurred to me to ask Sophie. Or maybe it had, but subconsciously I'd worried that she would turn towards the kitchen mid-party and bellow, 'MORE SAUSAGE ROLLS. NOW.'

'Sorry, Sophie.' I felt terrible. Would it make her feel better if I ordered a second croissant? Left a ginormous tip?

'My mother would mind the kids, you know. I *am* available,' she bit out. 'And I thought we were friends.'

'We are . . . Look, maybe next time, how about that?' I heard myself saying.

Her smile was like the sun coming out. 'Great!' she said. 'I'm looking forward to it already.'

Ma emerged from her house as I was getting out of my car. She cast a suspicious look over at me, no doubt thinking that I was some feckless layabout who did nothing except sit at home all day long watching the neighbours out my window, interspersed with the odd bout of shopping.

And actually, I'd made a quick trip into Veronica's Boutique up the town. Well, Jo was coming over the following week and I didn't want her thinking that we Irish didn't know how to rock it, did I? So I'd bought this pair of fabulous wedge sandals in white and orange stripes that would, I hoped, give her serious shoe envy.

Ma was standing by her car, waiting for the kids. 'Jennifer! Kian!' she bawled towards the house.

I tried to get the shopping bag out of the passenger seat without her spotting it.

Kian and Jennifer emerged now. Kian waved, and Jennifer gave me the middle finger, but in a friendly way.

Ma was really staring at me now. Honestly. What did she think I was going to do? Poison them, or something? Instil a love of shopping into Jennifer?

'Can I help you?' I eventually asked, in an unfriendly voice. Well, if she could dish it out, she could take it too.

Ma looked like she wasn't going to bother answering me at all. But then she just shrugged and said, 'Your licence plate is missing again, that's all.'

Chapter Twenty-one

Anita gave me a bit of a fright.

It came at the end of a long week, most of which I'd spent cooking. Not for a string of glittering catering gigs, sadly; I still hadn't done anything since the night in Jason's except a children's birthday party.

'It's for twenty six-year-olds,' the harassed mother had told me over the phone. A pause. 'Boys.'

'How much trouble can they be?' Matthew reasoned. But he'd been a nice boy at six. He would never have been curious as to how many toasted marshmallows you could fit into another six-year-old's mouth without them choking. (Fourteen. They all came back up.) He would have appreciated my handmade sausage rolls, instead of placing them carefully into catapults and launching them at passing cars. And he would never, ever have called to me, 'Hey, you, the cook.' In fairness to me, they had only been alerting me to the fact that someone had used the birthday candles on the beautiful chocolate cake to start a small fire in the garden.

'They're an awful bunch of little shits, I'm terribly sorry.' The mother was killed apologising to me. As compensation, she'd popped my business card into all the party bags with the kids going home, along with the fake blood and the whoopie cushions, but I still didn't get a single call.

To take my mind off it, I'd spent the week cooking for Anita. A quick stock-take of her freezer had revealed all sorts of horrors – pork pies and pizzas and a frozen pavlova that she'd clearly tried to conceal beneath lots of innocent-looking bags of frozen fruit.

'Where did they come from?' Anita exclaimed, her hand leaping to her throat like all this bad junk food had picked the lock during the night while she was sleep and evilly taken up residence in her freezer.

'Anita, your nose is growing.'

'They must be in there ages,' she insisted.

'I thought you'd never seen them before?'

I was getting more like Róisín. Give her hell. All this lying was doing nobody any favours.

'I don't remember them,' she said, very convincingly. 'Obviously, I must have bought them. But it was months ago. I've hardly touched them.'

I rolled my eyes. It turned out to be the wrong thing to do.

'You don't believe me?' Anita looked very cross. But she always was when she was caught. 'Look, then. Go on. Open the box and have a look.'

'Oh, stop it, Anita.' I'd find only a few forgotten crumbs, which she'd probably be back later on to hoover up.

But she brushed me aside to whip out the box of pavlova from the freezer and unearth the sickly confectionery. 'One small slice – see? I haven't touched it since.'

She'd probably got interrupted mid-binge by the postman.

'And the pork pie. Unopened.' She held the box up, giving the flaps a good shake to demonstrate that it was, indeed, fully intact. 'And the pizzas. Past their sell-by date. Look! Look!' She was getting very excited now as more boxes of junk food made an appearance from the freezer. Bangers and Mash, sensing a blood bath, began to circle us and make lip-smacking noises. 'I've actually been really good lately. Not that you or Róisín have noticed. So busy dragging me out on walks and cooking me fecking fat-free cottage pies.' She looked a bit upset as she poked at the offerings I'd brought over. 'It wouldn't occur to you for a second that I might be capable of looking after myself.'

'In fairness, Anita, you haven't been.'

'Well, OK. Fifteen–love to you.' (She'd been watching the tennis on the telly when I'd arrived.) 'But I've changed in the last few weeks. Have you not noticed?'

'Well . . .' Frankly, no. But now that I really thought about it, since she'd turned down the chance of a buttered scone in the Coffee Dock, I hadn't seen her eating anything she shouldn't have. No sneaky biscuits in my house when she'd been over for a visit, or 'just a little taste' of whatever I might have cooling in the kitchen.

'I've lost seven pounds, I'll have you know,' Anita announced.

I was shocked. I really was. Seven pounds. That was amazing.

'Yes,' she reiterated smugly, at my face. 'I admit I was a little slow off the mark with this whole diabetes thing, but I've come to terms with it now.'

'Seven *pounds*, Anita!'

'Don't labour it, I have a good bit to go yet,' she said modestly. 'Here, lads.'

She began to empty out the junk food onto the ground for the dogs. I thought she might crack at that point, and get emotional at the waste of it all, but no. She looked calm and serene as frozen pepperoni pizza and garlic bread disappeared down the two boyos' throats at the speed of light.

'But they're frozen, Anita.'

'So? That doesn't bother these two. They ate a concrete block once, didn't you?' She held out slices of frozen apple tart for them now. 'And at least they might leave Matthew alone when he comes over later.' Friday nights had become a regular for him at hers. He pretended to be the man around the house, and she made him his tea, and occasionally bought him warm socks and things. 'You'll think we're having an affair!' she said to me once, laughing at the good of it and not noticing the expression of fear on Matthew's face.

But back to the seven pounds. This change in attitude was most disconcerting. Where had Anita gone, to be replaced by this slightly ethereal, mature woman?

'Look,' she said, seeing my surprise, 'I'm a grown woman. I'm fully cognisant of the fact that I have a life-long, chronic disease that needs careful monitoring and diligence, and which nobody is responsible for but myself.' It was like she'd swallowed a few bits off the internet, commas and all.

But I was very glad to hear it. I'd begun to get a bit worried about her constant denial. It had just been a phase, that was all, like Róisín said.

'Do you want me to take all the stuff I've cooked for you home, then?' I asked cautiously.

'No, no, I'll keep it,' she said graciously. 'Seeing as you've gone to so much trouble, and it's low carb and all that. And if you're doing nothing during the week, you might like to join me at Susie Reynolds' classes in the Community Centre. I was going to sign up for Burn That Butt –' Susie was young and direct – 'but I think I might go for Fight That Flab instead. It's more nonspecific.'

And she gave me a look as if to suggest that I could do with shaving a few pounds off myself.

But I didn't want to put her off. This new-found determination should be encouraged for all it was worth. 'I'll be there,' I promised her.

Matthew's mother rang when we were in the supermarket. I could hear her high voice clearly on Matthew's phone.

'Are you settling in OK? With the new job and the house and everything? How's the weather? Has it improved at all?' It was the fourth or fifth time she'd rung and it was always like she was expecting some terrible tale of doom. I knew she was just a little anxious; Matthew was her baby, after all, and he'd moved to a different country. But it'd be nice if every question wasn't so leading.

Matthew winked at me. 'The weather's fantastic. Twenty-four degrees today.'

'Twenty-four!' Her voice grew faint. 'Sharon! Liz! It's twenty-four degrees in Ireland!'

They must be over for coffee. They had a kind of rotation thing going on between them. I could hear them in the background: 'Ohhh!' and, 'Lucky beggar!'

I raised my eyebrows at Matthew; the supermarket roof was nearly coming down with the rain. Twenty-four degrees, my eye.

'Everything's fine, Mum,' he was saying. 'The job's good. And Clara's got her business off the ground; she'll be run off her feet in no time.'

I looked at him gratefully; my biggest cheerleader, even if the phone wasn't exactly hopping.

'Now that we're settled, you should come over for a visit,' he said.

'I suppose I could.' She sounded like the idea had never occurred to her before.

'Great. Maybe some weekend next month?'

'Oh, I can't do next month. Well, Sharon's daughter is getting married that first weekend, remember I was telling you? And then we've got our big bingo night the following Saturday night. And then Pauline is gone on *her* holidays and I'll have to cover for her at work . . .'

Already she was in a bit of a heap at the thought of it.

'Never mind,' Matthew said. He was good at managing her. 'Maybe the month after, there's no pressure.'

'OK.' She sounded relieved. 'Listen, I have to go, Liz's son is here to pick her up. Give my love to Clara, won't you?'

'Thanks,' I said to him, after he had hung up.

'For what?'

'For being so positive about everything.'

He waved this away. 'I'm only telling it like it is. I'd love her to come over and see the place. It's great.'

Not once since we'd arrived in Castlemoy for good had he really complained about anything, not even Burt's motorbike, which managed to wake us up at least once a week with its nocturnal comings and goings. He loved his job. He loved our house, especially the back garden, where he'd started to plant all kinds of strange, sad-looking plants that he was sure would 'perk up' once we got a bit of sun. He had endless time for my family: my prickly sister and my headstrong mother, and my actor brother, who came on the bus from Dublin at least twice a week to be fed and sometimes to put a coloureds wash through our machine.

The only thing he had a problem with was that someone seemed to like stealing our car number plate. We were worried that maybe it was being used in a robbery or something. We'd even watched *Crimewatch* one night, worried that it might flash up on the screen, attached to a stolen car.

'We should have reported it,' we fretted, innocent to this sort of thing. 'They might think it's us going around robbing all those post offices.'

But when we'd mentioned it to The Knob, he just nodded sagely and said, 'Kids.'

Apparently there were a few bad families – commuters, of course, from Dublin, where else? – who'd moved into one of the estates on the other side of the town. They were being blamed, probably rightly, for all kind of things, from stolen licence plates to graffiti on Father O'Reilly's gate to the odd car-jacking when the mood took them.

Matthew had instructed me to park under streetlights, if possible, and that we'd report the next incident to the Guards.

That morning, we'd had yet another brand-new licence plate fitted. This time, there was damage to the bumper too, and the whole exercise proved so expensive that we couldn't afford to go out that night, and instead would have to eat at home.

'I'll cook,' Matthew had declared, enthusiastic.

In fairness, he didn't often get a go in the kitchen. It was difficult, when you were in a relationship with a professional. He said he experienced acute feelings of paranoia and judgement when I was standing there, allegedly breathing down his neck. So the compromise was that, every so often, I would retire to the living room with a glass of white wine and he would be allowed to put on one of his terrible CDs and really go for it. He was quite a good cook, too, even if he had – whisper it – a slight tendency to over-salt things.

'I heard that thought,' Matthew said. 'Luckily for you, I'm not offended. Now, how about a nice bottle of wine to keep us going for the evening?'

He gave my bum a little squeeze. I knew what he meant. Our new bed had been *in situ* for some time now, but so far we'd only slept in it. There had been nothing doing since our last outing on the blow-up bed, when Matthew had severely bruised his shoulder after being violently catapulted off it during a quick position change.

'Maybe we should just have an early night,' I suggested doubtfully.

I didn't want him going into Team Tech banjaxed again. They would be thinking he got a tremendous amount of action.

He flexed his shoulder carefully. 'I think I'm good to go.' He looked at me sternly. 'You might have to be gentle with me, though. No rough stuff.'

That was how we were discovered by Jason; laughing at our own corniness and having a bit of a grope by the Chardonnay.

'Clara?' That voice again, behind me. 'I thought it was you.'

Jason had a habit of sneaking up on me, I was beginning to notice.

'Jason.' I swung around to face him, realising that my hand was on the backside of Matthew's jeans. My other hand was wrapped around a bottle of wine. Classy.

I looked him in the eye and announced, 'Matthew, this is Jason.' No further explanation was needed.

Matthew was the first to stick out his hand. 'How's it going?'

While the men pumped hands vigorously, probably trying to see which of them had the most upper body strength, I could see Jason flick a look into our basket. I wish I hadn't popped in those Creme Eggs, or that bumper pack of tampons.

'So!' Jason said in a boomy kind of voice. 'Are you settling in OK?'

'Pretty good, thanks.' Matthew didn't boom back. I was proud of him. 'It's a nice town. Clara's been busy showing me around.'

'Oh, yeah?' Jason was trying to play it cool, but I could see some little muscle doing a dance routine in his cheek.

'And thanks for giving her business a start,' Matthew said. He only said it out of politeness. Nothing had come out of it in terms of more work. Plus, I realised afterwards that Jason had used up all the business cards I'd brought with me. At least, they were gone from the kitchen when I went back. They'd cost money, too.

Jason brushed this off, as if he were some kind of philanthropist. 'It was the least I could do.'

Another lengthy silence. I waited for him to go away. We clearly had nothing left to say to each other. But he bullishly stood there, as if trying to make us uncomfortable.

Well, to hell with that, I decided. Suddenly I didn't give a damn about Jason. So what if we ran into him in the supermarket? It probably wouldn't be the last time. We might run into him tomorrow at the flipping Esso up the town. I was back now, for good, and there was no way I was going to worry about walking around my own town.

So I handed the bottle of wine to Matthew to put in the basket, and turned to Jason. 'You know something?' I said pleasantly. 'We've got to go now. But nice meeting you.'

Jason looked a bit taken aback at this dismissal. Well, he'd usually been the one who'd called the shots. 'Right. Sure. Nice to meet you too.'

Not.

But there was more nodding and fake smiles, and we were just about to turn away when Jason said to Matthew suddenly, 'I wouldn't go for that.'

For a minute I thought he was referring to me: steer clear, mate, she'll only dump you, and horribly, like she did me. It would be just like Jason to bring up our engagement. He had a disturbing lack of boundaries, as he'd shown in his own house the night I'd been there. And Matthew wouldn't know what he was talking about.

But it was the wine in Matthew's hand that Jason was referring to.

'It's sharp on the palate, I had a bottle last month and it really wasn't very nice.'

He officiously reached past a very surprised Matthew to pluck a different bottle off the shelf. 'This is better. More much subtle. Give it a try.'

'Er, thanks.' Matthew flashed me an amused look as Jason thrust the bottle into his hand.

Jason saw him. Colour stained his cheeks. 'Goodbye now,' he said abruptly, and disappeared around the end of the aisle.

'What the hell was that all about?' Matthew looked at me, torn between amusement and bafflement.

I reached out for another bottle of wine and put it in the basket. We might need it. 'Let's go home.'

Chapter Twenty-two

'I haven't been entirely straight with you,' I said to Matthew when we got home.

He was fiddling about with a curry; adding little bits of things and fishing others out. He sniffed at it, then took a spoon and tasted the sauce, rolling it around his tongue like it was a suspect bottle of red.

Normally at this point I would retire into the living room with a glass of wine before a row broke out.

But not tonight. Tonight I needed to 'face the past', as they say on the afternoon shows that were on in the background whilst I worked from home (I still really, really liked working from home). I was just hoping at the end of it I'd still have a boyfriend.

After some more persecution of the poor blameless curry, Matthew lifted his eyes from the pot. 'I know,' he said.

I got such a fright that I said, 'You haven't a clue what I'm even talking about!'

'Well, I'm presuming it's Jason.'

I was wrong-footed, and annoyed too; was I really that transparent? I thought I'd been better than that.

Then, I realised. 'Jo told you, didn't she? Of course she did!' I began to get excited. Jo could never keep her trap shut about anything, especially after a few scoops. 'She had a skinful and she blabbed it all out.'

I would kill her. Honestly. And I was always so loyal to *her*. I'd never, ever told anybody about the time we'd had to walk home from a club late one night, not a taxi in sight, and she'd ended up climbing into someone's back garden because she was caught short, only for us to realise that the property belonged to a keen astronomer who saw rather more than he'd bargained for at the end of his high-powered telescope.

'Jo never said a word about him,' Matthew said. 'And I think this is called time-wasting.' He looked at me mildly. 'It's clear you two have some history. In his mind, anyway. Fucker nearly broke my fingers.' He flexed them delicately. 'As well as nearly deafening me.'

The look on his face was so funny that I couldn't help laughing out loud, even though this was serious.

'And as for his advice on the wine . . ."It's a little sharp on the palate".' He mimicked Jason unmercifully. '"I know, because I'm a solicitor and you're just a lowly IT boy."'

I convulsed again. He had Jason's dry, superior voice down to a T.

'I thought he was going to break his neck looking into our basket. I should have thrown in a bumper pack of condoms. Mint flavoured.'

'He wasn't as bad as that.' I was defending myself more than Jason; I wasn't so stupid that I'd spent two years with a complete plonker. I did have *some* taste. 'I think he was just feeling a little defensive today.'

'No kidding. Paranoid, even.'

'Yes, well,' I said, all laughter gone now. 'It's never easy, is it? Meeting the new boyfriend.'

Matthew's eyebrows jumped up. 'Even after all this time? And it's not like he doesn't have a string of gorgeous girlfriends himself, by the sounds of it. Even if they have casts in their eyes.' He could be vicious when he wanted to be. 'I wouldn't think he had all that much to be defensive about, that's all.'

'He's just that kind of character.'

'Maybe. And I guess he was the one who was dumped. That always stings.' He shot me a look. 'Even if he says it was the other way around.' I wished I hadn't told him about that now. 'Why would he come out with something like that, Clara?'

He let that hang in the air for a minute.

'Because our break-up was a little messier that I've led you to believe,' I admitted.

'I think I've gathered that much. So what happened?' He looked sympathetic. 'It can't have been that bad.'

'It was. I didn't behave very well. He didn't either, but that's not any excuse.'

Suddenly I was a bit worried. What had I started here? What stupid notion had overtaken me to 'come clean'? The supermarket run-in must have softened my head. Just because Jason had made a bit of an eejit of himself in front of Matthew wasn't going to make me look any better, I realised.

I felt a bit queasy now. I should have kept my mouth shut. Or else I should have told him all this before we moved back, which would have been the sensible – and brave – thing to do.

'Just tell me,' Matthew invited. 'You can't not, now.'

He was right. We were hardly going to carry on with our curry, were we? Which he peered in at now, and gave a desultory stir to, but I knew his attention was wholly focused on me.

I sighed. 'You'd better sit down.'

'Jesus, is it *that* bad?'

'No. But I'm not proud of myself either.'

'I'm often not proud of myself,' Matthew said loyally.

'You're just trying to make me feel better now. The thing is, I was a coward, Matthew. I should have ended things properly, to his face, like decent people do, but I ran off like a thief in the night.'

That was Jo's expression. I hadn't actually left during the night at all – it was a half-past five flight in the afternoon, if I remember correctly – but Jo was fond of a bit of drama and it was she who coined the phrase. My behaviour towards Jason was always referred to as 'thief-in-the-night' stuff.

The sentiment was correct, though, which was why I said it now.

'Things hadn't been going well for a while,' I admitted. 'Maybe I was getting a little bored of doing the same things. Film on a Friday night, eat out in Dublin on a Saturday night. Stay in mine on a Tuesday night, his on a Thursday night.'

'You were that organised?' Matthew sounded impressed.

'Well, it was Jason mostly. He liked to know what was what. He wasn't fond of spontaneity, or anything that was out of his control. But it was only ever the two of us doing stuff. We never met anybody else. Or, if we did, they were his friends, and they always seemed so much older than me, stuffy, you know?' But I stopped myself there. I realised I didn't really care enough to go over it all again; it was just my own role in the break-up that I needed to get off my chest. 'So I tried to break it off. I knew it wasn't working, not for me, anyway. I invited him round one evening and said that I didn't think we were really suited. Not because of our ages, just because we were two completely different people. But he didn't really listen. Well, he seemed to at the time, but he just went and bought tickets to the theatre, took me for a weekend away, like that was supposed to make me happy.'

'I suppose you can't blame the guy.' For a minute I thought he was defending Jason. 'I'd probably try to hang on to you too.'

'Yes, but not like that. By wearing me down.'

'No. Definitely not.'

'I should have been stronger, told him clearly it was over, but he was trying so hard . . . And we were such a couple about town. I know that sounds stupid, but everybody knew us, Matthew. My parents knew his, our friends all socialised together . . . It'd have been easier to break up in a city because nobody would have given a damn. And he was always so aware of his position. The town solicitor. Nobody would ever dare jilt him.'

'Hmm. I bet.' The corner of Matthew's mouth rose up. 'But you did.'

'Yes.' A bit brutally, as it turned out. 'He asked me to marry him. Even after everything I'd said. Got the ring and everything, just to put that bit of extra pressure on. I didn't say yes.'

Matthew's face was grim. 'I'm not surprised.'

'But I didn't say no either, Matthew. And Jason's the type who, if you don't tell him no, as in N-O, he kind of assumes that everything's OK.'

I looked at a spot on the floor for the next bit. 'He went ahead and organised a night out. Dinner. He invited his parents, and mine, and I realised he was up to something, because I knew the chef there, from college. He let slip something about a special dessert to be delivered to our table, with the engagement ring in it. Jason was going to propose to me again, in front of everybody, including his sick mother – she'd just got her cancer diagnosis – and how could I say no? And then I'd be stuck. So I ran.'

The curry let out a hiss. It was probably burning. But neither of us gave a damn.

'Good for you,' Matthew said bluntly.

'You haven't heard the rest.'

'I've heard enough.'

'But I didn't say goodbye.'

'So what?'

'I didn't even say I wouldn't make the dinner. I packed a bag and got on a plane to London and I didn't come back.'

I still remembered the airport: the glare of the lights, the people, the noise. I stood there with my suitcase, blinking like a newborn, and wondering whether I should just turn round and go back home. Face the music. Then somebody bumped into me from behind, propelled me forward, and I just kept on walking.

The texts had begun a few minutes later. 'At the restaurant. See you in a bit.' I was on a train when the second one came. 'Everybody here. You delayed?' Then his number, flashing up on my screen in an incoming call. At that point I turned off my phone altogether, and when I arrived at my cousin Fionnan's flat in Kilburn, I was a guilt-ridden, hysterical mess.

'Clara!' Luckily, he was in his regular, accountant's clothes. It would have been too much had I caught him in something from Vera Wang. 'What the hell are you doing here?'

That's when it hit me. I'd stood up an entire party of people, including my elderly parents, at my own engagement party.

'Heavy,' Fionnan had breathed.

The way he looked at me made me feel even more scared. And when I turned on my phone again, there were numerous texts and phone calls from Jason, each sounding colder and angrier as the night had gone on.

'I'd better ring, let him know what's happened,' I began babbling.

But Fionnan took the phone firmly from my hands. 'I imagine he's guessed by now. Leave it for tonight. I'll ring your parents, let them know you're safe.' He gave me a look. 'Everybody else can cool their jets.'

Fionnan insisted I take his bed – his room stank to high heaven of lavender – and I lay in the dark dreading Jason's bewilderment and anger.

But mostly I felt relieved, lying there on the scented sheets. It was like a very heavy weight had been lifted from my chest and I could breathe again.

'I never heard from him again,' I finished up the sorry tale to Matthew. 'No text messages, no phone calls, nothing. Anita told me he'd met her on the street a couple of days later, and he never even asked where I was.' The spot on the floor was growing blurred, I was staring at it so hard. 'And I never got in touch with him again either.'

It wasn't behaviour you'd be proud of. Matthew must surely be wondering if I'd dump him the same way some day. No, 'Cheerio! Nice knowing you!' Just off on the next plane out.

He was looking at me with great sympathy, but something else too. A hint of amusement? 'And you've been worrying over this for ten years?'

'Well, no,' I admitted. 'To be honest, I forgot all about him. It was only when we decided to come back here that I started to think about it again.'

'Your thief-in-the-night behaviour,' Matthew clarified.

I suspected he was making fun of me.

'Well, he was a creep in the night, which was much worse,' Matthew declared. 'Imagine buying an engagement ring when he'd been told to bog off. What kind of person does that?'

'Well, I did think it was a bit odd at the time.'

'Christ, the guy just wasn't taking no for an answer, was he? Oh, Clara,' he said. 'You should have told me this years ago.'

I was feeling better and better. The way Matthew put it was so

142

reasonable. And right. Jason was the type of person that you didn't end things amicably with. Maybe if I'd been older, I'd have been able to say no. But I was young, and a little bit immature, but it was done and dusted now.

It really was time to move on. And now that I'd told Matthew, I need have no fear of him running into Jason any time or any place. He could say what he liked about me and it would only make himself look bad.

'Now,' said Matthew, 'let's eat our curry. I think we've wasted enough of our evening on your ex-boyfriend, don't you?'

And he planted a kiss on me to shut me up.

Chapter Twenty-three

'I've got bad news,' Eddie announced.

He was sitting at the kitchen table, hoofing back the contents of my fridge. I wasn't sure when he'd last eaten, but his face was starting to look shadowy and Christlike. 'These are lovely, by the way,' he said fervently, reaching for another miniature fish cake that I was trialling for a drinks party booking at the weekend.

'You didn't get the part?' said Anita, disappointed. She was sipping plain tea, and didn't throw so much as a glance at the loaf of banana bread that I put on the table for Eddie. I was proud of her.

'The part . . . ?' said Eddie. Well, there were always auditions.

'That Russian thing.' Anita looked at me: *help!* Eddie was always doing plays whose titles she couldn't remember by playwrights whose names she wasn't able to pronounce. Never *Grease* or *Grumpy Old Men*.

'Oh, the Chekhov thing.' Eddie looked glum. 'Actually,' he said, 'I did.'

'Great,' said Anita, valiantly. Another trek to bloody Dublin, and having to sit through a load of foreign stuff, when she could be cosy in front of her telly, soaking up reality Irish dancing shows, and having sneaky six-packs of crisps.

Although, in fairness to her, she was sticking to her diet this time. Rigidly. Nobody was sure what had come over her, but something had;

our nagging had become redundant as she took charge of her own healthy eating plan and, so far, had lost over a stone.

We wondered had she got a fright. Was it that walk that day in the town, and the realisation of how unfit she was? Or did she stumble across something that had put the wind up her? Last month there had been a diabetic on the radio talking from hospital after they'd had to amputate his toe. 'I didn't realise,' he kept saying, sounding shaken. We'd been standing in the kitchen at the time, myself and Anita.

Anyway, whatever it was, it was working.

At the top of the table, Eleanora emerged from behind her wall of hair. 'He's had to turn it down, though.' She wore a look of suppressed excitement. 'Because he got something much better instead.'

We turned to Eddie; things must be looking up.

'Is it a musical?' Anita ventured hopefully. Now *that* she'd stir out for.

But Eddie was scowling at Eleanora. 'I haven't turned it down yet; why do you keep saying that?'

'Yes, but you're going to.'

'Nothing's decided yet.'

'It's not like you exactly have a choice,' Eleanora insisted. 'The Chekhov's a profit-share.' Which meant that box-office takings were shared equally between cast and crew (usually a hundred-odd quid divided into twenty-two. Minus expenses).

She turned to us. 'Eddie's been offered a TV voiceover ad. It's just a couple of days' work, but the money's good, and the exposure would be fantastic for his career. Still,' she said, looking hurt, 'what do *I* know.'

Anita was thrown into a flurry of excitement. Wait till the girls at Burn That Butt heard about this (the Fight That Flab class had been full). Much better than that bloody Chekhov. 'Is it true? You're going to be on *TV*?'

Eddie was shredding a fish cake in an anguished kind of way. Clearly he wasn't sharing in the excitement.

'So what's the ad for then, Eddie?' I asked, hoping to keep it neutral.

Moody eyes jumped up to mine. 'Fried chicken.'

Anita and I looked at each other. This was certainly a new departure. 'I have to say in a fake American accent that this chicken is finger–lickin' good.' He shot a blameful look at Eleanora, who was intently examining the table.

'At least it rhymes,' Anita said at last. 'And I suppose if it's just your voice, nobody's going to know it's you.'

'*I'll* know.'

Anita ploughed on, 'And you'll be putting on an accent.'

'Oh, well, that's alright, then.'

Eleanora couldn't stay quiet any longer. 'Oh, for God's sake, it's just a bit of fun. You don't have to take everything so seriously, Eddie. At the end of the day *somebody* has to advertise chicken, and if it means you get money to live on for a while, then what's the harm?' She was clearly exasperated, and I have to say, it was hard not to see her point. 'Anybody would think you were being asked to do bloody porn.'

'I'd rather do porn than a fried fucking chicken ad,' Eddie declared.

'Would you?' Anita looked worried. Was there any danger Eddie might appear on the top shelf of the local video shop?

'At least porn has *some* integrity.'

'Integrity!' Eleanora scoffed. 'How, exactly?'

I hastily intervened before we had a full–blown domestic on our hands. 'This bad news then, Eddie . . . ?'

'Oh. Right.' His face settled into fresh folds of anxiety. 'It's about Catherine.'

'Is she back?' Anita enquired.

Catherine was on the road working again, Róisín had told us. She hadn't seen her in over a week. Phone coverage must be scant on Catherine's travels too, because there hadn't been any calls or texts either, not that we'd heard of, anyway. Anita and I had both commented on Róisín's shocking mood.

'Oh, she's back alright,' Eddie growled.

'It's very sad,' Eleanora murmured.

'Why? What's after happening? Tell us,' Anita demanded. She didn't do stress very well at the best of times, and now she couldn't even take comfort in a nice cup of milky coffee and a biscuit. She had a little frown line between her eyes now, which I hadn't noticed before. But maybe that was because of losing all that weight.

'We went to a bar after the show finished the other night,' Eddie began reluctantly. He was in some experimental show that was running for five nights; apparently everybody took their clothes off at some point, but not in an ooh-er-Matron kind of way. 'Some friends were in the audience.'

'Of five,' Eleanora interjected. 'What?' she said, off Eddie's look. 'I'm just remarking that it was a small audience.' She turned to me and Anita. 'It's such a shame. Eddie is *amazing* in it, I honestly think it's his best performance yet.' She reached out and brushed a now-bashful Eddie with her fingers. 'No, don't protest. I just wish you were reaching a wider audience, that's all.'

A TV audience, by any chance? But Eleanora looked away demurely.

'So we were in this bar,' Eddie began again. 'And Catherine was there.' He looked miserable. 'With another woman.'

Oh, no. My heart sank.

'With?' Anita might think she was all hip and in the know, but still she needed clarification. 'As in . . . ?'

'All over her like a cheap suit,' Eleanora said succinctly. She had the good sense to leave it at that.

Nobody said anything for a moment. I could see by the faces around me that nobody was really that surprised. Disappointed, yes, and annoyed, and sad for Róisín, but not surprised. Even though they'd been seeing each other for a year, there had always been something transitory about Catherine. She was forever running after some kind of excitement, it seemed, be it the highs of hard work, or the bar-hopping in Dublin. Certainly, she'd wasted little enough time down in Castlemoy with Róisín.

Surely Róisín must know by now that she had done all of the chasing. But, of course, maybe that was part of the excitement for her.

'Who's going to tell her?' Anita said at last.

Chapter Twenty-four

'We're all terribly sorry, Róisín.' A wretched pause. 'It couldn't have happened to a nicer person.' The pause turned doubtful; that didn't sound right. 'What I mean is, you're such a nice person that, frankly, Catherine doesn't deserve you.' That was better. 'And I know this sounds corny, but there *is* someone better out there for you. Someone who can make you happy. You need a bit of time to get over this,' Matthew finished up with genuine warmth and sincerity.

Which was why we'd chosen him for the job. He shot me a look – *thanks a fucking bunch* – which I returned with a hugely grateful smile. I'd inflate the blow-up bed at the weekend as payback. It wasn't that the new bed wasn't good – we'd had great nights' sleep since it had arrived – but somehow the sex didn't have the same edge. Maybe it was because there was no element of danger, not like on the blow-up bed.

'I know.' Róisín was fragile but dry-eyed. I would put money on it that she wasn't all that surprised either.

But that didn't mean she wasn't heartbroken. I could see it in the way her thin shoulders were stiff and hunched, and she looked like she couldn't get warm.

I wanted to give her a hug, but that wasn't Róisín's style and so I said instead, 'Let me drive you home.'

'No, I'm fine.'

'You're not fine, you've just had awful news. We'll open a bottle of wine. Talk.'

Matthew nodded approvingly. 'Stay over if you want,' he said to me. Get hammered, in other words. Call Catherine a cheating bitch and then order a filthy great pepperoni pizza at one in the morning. Therapy the proper way. 'I'll drive over and collect you in the morning,' he assured me.

The car was parked right outside Dirty Harry's door, under a streetlamp and within view of Hickey's Chemist's CCTV system. If any of those little scuts from the bad end of town decided to have another go at our licence plate, we'd get them this time.

I gave him a grateful smile. 'Thanks.'

He really was the best. Since I'd told him about Jason, we'd become even closer. I couldn't believe he'd been so accepting of my youthful follies. Sharing shame was fantastic, and I'd recommend it to anybody.

Now that it was behind me, my conscience was in terrific shape, not a blot on it. Jason was firmly repositioned in my head as the more culpable one in our break-up, and Matthew and I had honestly never been better. He'd even offered to break the wretched news to my poor sister. Well, in tandem with me. But once he got going, it seemed rude of me to interrupt.

'I suppose you thought I was over-reaching anyway,' Róisín said with a heavy sigh.

I looked at her. 'Of course we didn't.'

'Oh, please. Catherine's stunning. She could have anybody she wants.'

'And did, by the looks of it,' Matthew murmured.

I flicked him a look. Not helpful. 'Her looks have nothing to do with this. The fact is that she was a cow and she let you down.'

It was as close as I'd come to declaring open season on Catherine. It would do Róisín good. We could kick off with something harmless like her tendency to bite her nails, before getting down to the real, character-destroying stuff.

But Róisín just sat there looking really, really sad. 'You know what the worst thing is? I'll never find anybody else.'

'Come on. Everybody says that when they break up with someone.'

'Not everybody is a lesbian in a small town, Clara.'

'Well, true, but—'

'Look around you. We're sitting in a bar called Dirty Harry's, the only two females in the entire place, unless you count Dirty Harry's wife, Hilda.'

Several men of indeterminate age were folded over pints of Guinness at the bar, sighing deeply at intervals. Dirty Harry and Hilda morosely dried glasses on rags, and tended to toasted cheese sandwiches. Various groupings of middle-aged men were dotted round the lounge area, sipping pints and having riveting conversations: '. . . a new ride-on lawnmower . . . substituted off for the second half . . . anybody for a packet of bacon fries?'

Róisín had a point.

'Maybe there are women in the toilets,' Matthew said valiantly. Well, in his experience, that's where females tended to spend a lot of their evenings out.

But Róisín was taking no prisoners tonight. 'You think there are a crowd of lesbians in there?' She jerked a thumb towards the ancient, peeling plastic sign that said 'Ladies'. Except that the S had fallen off, so it was 'Ladie'.

'I—'

'Sitting around forlornly waiting to be ridden?'

'I didn't say lesbians. I said women,' Matthew desperately tried to clarify. He was in over his head and knew it. 'And I'm sure they would appreciate a little conversation before being ridden—'

But his voice had risen slightly and Róisín went mental. 'For fuck's sake, keep it down! I could have patients in here, you know!'

Judging by the age and condition of most of the clientele, if they weren't already patients of hers, they soon would be.

'Sorry,' Matthew whispered. He ventured, 'But I suppose you won't know who's out there until you actually stick your head above the parapet—'

'Don't!' Róisín held up a hand to stop him. 'For the love of God, do *not* give me the big fat speech about coming out to my local community. I've already told Clara – this isn't London, OK?' Róisín rolled the word around on her tongue sarcastically, like it was some out-of-this-world metropolis. 'There aren't any gay women here in Castlemoy, apart from me, I'd put money on it. So even if I *was* to come out, what's the point? It's not like they're going to be queuing up.'

At the bar, a toasted cheese sandwich popped up. Dirty Harry went to take it out, while Hilda lined up to put another in. It was the only queue in sight.

'Anyhow,' Róisín finished up dully, 'my heart has just been broken. If it's OK with everybody, I might just take five minutes for myself before I go on the pull again.'

Matthew looked at me. *More drinks?*

I looked back. *Yes. Better make them doubles. Oh, and a packet of bacon fries.*

Róisín and I sat in silence for a moment after he'd gone.

'Did you not see it coming at all, Róisín?'

Róisín just shrugged. 'I don't blame her, you know.'

'What?'

'I mean, it's not really her fault.'

OK, no way was I going with the self-flagellation bit. 'Why isn't it? I would say it's *entirely* her fault. No, just listen. Did she ever really try to make this relationship work? Did she ever turn up on your doorstep some night uninvited, just because she was desperate to see you? The number of times I watched you slog to Dublin, Róisín, making all the effort, while she sat there and let you.'

Róisín looked at her hands, silent.

'Maybe she doesn't even have time for a proper relationship. Look how busy she is with her job. There might not be room for anything except a quick fling with someone she picks up in a pub. But isn't it better to know that now, after one year in, instead of after five? Look, we've all been there, and it sucks. But when you love someone you don't treat them like that.'

Róisín started to cry.

'Oh, Róisín.' I hadn't meant to upset her. Still, maybe it was good for her to let it out.

Matthew arrived back with the drinks in time to see me dispensing tissues. He wore his 'I'm a Man Get Me Out of Here' expression.

Then, like a call from the wild, there was a fluttering over in the far corner of the pub near the Gents. 'Matthew! It's your turn, bud!'

Matthew – a.k.a. 'bud' – jerked up like he'd been shot. There was a primitive gleam in his eye; the lads awaited. 'I have to go,' he said tersely, and he grabbed a set of darts – not belonging to Dirty Harry's, but his own set, bought in a specialist shop in Dublin during his lunch break, you never saw anything like the excitement – and then he nearly upended the table in his haste to join the pack.

'I hope you feel better soon,' he said to Róisín, belatedly remembering his manners. To me, he merely threw a distracted, 'Ring me in the morning,' and then he was gone.

A group of about four men had commandeered the darts board. It was difficult to tell them apart; they all wore polo shirts, and had the beginnings of bellies, which they ruthlessly held in. Hair differed in shade, but to a man was thinning, and cut very short to hide said fact. One of them had taken the plunge and had shaved it off, to try to remain cool and young. But nothing could hide the fact that they were all 'of a certain age'.

'How's it going, lads?' Matthew joined them, beaming, his spanking new darts held out like crayons on the first day of school.

I was a bit embarrassed for him. The lads weren't used to this level of enthusiasm. You could see them looking at each other. It was just a game of darts; who the hell had invited Mr-London-Trendy-Arse to join the gang, anyway? Plus, he was a good bit younger than some of them, and with a full head of hair. Worst of all, he had not one but TWO birds over at that table there, even if one of them was bawling her head off.

'Matthew,' said The Knob, calmly. Thank God! I loved The Knob. When he'd promised to take Matthew out for darts he'd actually meant it. I was so grateful for this hand of friendship that I'd insisted that Matthew buy the drinks, despite The Knob's protestations that 'it was too much, like' and 'it was only an aul' game of darts'. But Matthew refused to let The Knob put his hand in his pocket on darts nights.

The downside was that Matthew was too polite to buy The Knob a pint without offering to buy everybody else pints too, and while the lads remained deeply suspicious of Matthew, they were quite happy to drink his beer.

'Darts night is costing me a fortune,' he revealed to me.

But it was worth it, just to see his face: the excitement, the longing. It wasn't just the darts; it was being part of the gang again. And I hadn't realised until tonight, seeing him cravenly hanging about on the fringes of the group, just how much he missed his old life. Or, rather, he hadn't let me see. Up to now he'd professed himself DELIGHTED with Castlemoy. Best place on earth, and all of that. Never a word about how he'd lost his entire network of friends. How he had nobody to go out with for pints on a Saturday night.

Oh, sure, there was Team Tech, but work tended to follow them to the pub. It wasn't the same as having your local, where you could pop in for a pint and see a dozen familiar faces.

But this was a new dawn. 'I think I'm making friends with them,' he'd revealed to me earlier. 'Them' was Macker, O'Brien, JP and, of course, The Knob. They were all pretty good at darts, having played once a week in Dirty Harry's since they were fifteen, which was the earliest that Harry would accept forged ID.

'Go on, then.' Macker, O'Brien and JP all planted meaty elbows on the bar, and took up position to have a good laugh at Matthew. Fucking amateur, with his poncy darts. *Yellow*. Hee hee.

'Right,' said Matthew, swallowing hard.

After his poor showing in the first few sessions, he'd been practising in secret in our back garden. A cheap darts board had been erected on the shed door, which was horribly pockmarked from early misses. Every night after dinner he'd go out for an hour. I'd know when he was finished, because the birds would stop circling the woods in alarmed flocks, and descend cautiously to roost again.

'Take your time,' The Knob murmured. Only for him, Matthew would have been torn apart by the pack weeks ago.

My heart was in my mouth as Matthew threw the first dart. Oooh. I didn't know much about darts, but I knew from the faces on the lads that it wasn't good.

'Never mind,' said The Knob loyally. 'You're definitely getting better.'

Much amusement from O'Brien and JP and the other one.

Matthew's second throw was indeed better. At least the lads stopped smirking.

He raised his hand for the third and final throw.

O'Brien and JP and the other one held their breaths.

Go on, go on Matthew.

Even Róisín stopped crying in order to have a look.

Matthew steadied himself, took aim . . .

The door to Dirty Harry's swung open, letting in an icy wind that blew the beer mat clean off our table and onto the floor.

Jason walked in, with Dominique on his arm.

Róisín clamped a hand on me. 'Look!' she spluttered, as though I'd somehow missed it. 'That bitch! With Jason Farrell!'

'Yes,' I agreed.

'What the hell is he doing with her? What's *she* doing with *him*?'

I looked over again. Dominique was laughing garrulously at something Jason said. I'd never remembered him being such a wit. But maybe I just hadn't got his jokes.

'They're on a date, I'd imagine.' They must have hit it off at the party, then.

Róisín blinked. 'They're *involved*?'

'I know. You wouldn't immediately put them together. But each to their own and all that.'

I was a bit annoyed at them having come into 'our' pub, though. We'd been there three Thursdays on the trot now and there had been no sign of them. I would have thought some bar in Dublin would have been more their scene.

I gave a friendly nod and wave over in their general direction. Jason didn't reciprocate. Then I saw he was holding something. I couldn't immediately see what it was. He held it up and turned around the pub, a look of concern on his face.

'Does this number plate belong to anyone?'

Chapter Twenty-five

Jo arrived from London, red-cheeked and fresh-faced, with her hair in a bouncy new bob and her neat figure tucked into a pair of white jeans.

'I look great, don't I?' she said, seeing me looking.

I laughed. 'Yes.'

She looked me up and down in turn. 'You look . . . countrified.' To Jo, anywhere beyond Fulham was the wilderness. On the drive home from the airport she'd kept screeching, 'Oh my God, is that a *cow*?'

'We think so,' Matthew had said gravely. 'And see that round, fluffy thing in that field over there? We're not a hundred per cent certain, but we suspect it's a sheep.'

Undaunted, Jo oohed and aahed over everything. The scenery was FABULOUS, the town was GORGEOUS, and the motorway was . . . well, just like the M25 back home.

'I'm so jealous,' she kept saying, which was really sweet of her, because she wouldn't move over here in a fit. 'Wow. Is this your *house*?'

Before anything else, of course, I had to take her into the kitchen and show her the fridge.

I heard her sharp intake of breath. 'Nice,' she said.

'Everything else is fabulous and wonderful but my fridge is just nice?'

She raised a hand slowly to her chest, as if trying to contain strong

156

emotion. 'Do you mind . . . could I possibly spend a moment alone with it?'

And we broke up laughing. It was like we'd seen each other only yesterday.

We gave her the grand tour of the house, all three thousand square feet of it, finishing up in the freshly decorated guest room at the back.

'There are extra towels in the chest of drawers if you need them.'

'But no getting fake tan on them, alright?' Matthew warned. Jo was a demon for the fake tan. 'They're new. Everything's new.'

But Jo was looking out the window, transfixed. 'There aren't any wolves out there, are there?'

She was looking out at the woods. They were dense with spring growth, and were much thicker and darker than when we'd first moved over.

'It's just a few trees, Jo.'

I was used to them by now. I even took a walk in them from time to time, with Matthew. They weren't that deep at all. Apart from a dense patch in the middle, you came out the other side surprisingly quickly, and it seemed silly to have been so scared of them in the beginning.

'Well, I think they're very romantic,' Jo declared. 'It's like living in the middle of a fairy tale!'

No sooner had we got back downstairs, and made a cup of tea, than Jo said, 'So!' Where are we going tonight?'

Matthew looked at me: Jesus, three days of this to go.

'You've only just arrived,' I pointed out. But we probably should have been tipped off by the enormous suitcase she'd brought, enough for a fortnight away, and the way she kept chortling, 'I'm on my holidays!'

'I don't mind staying local,' she said, generously. 'Hey. Are there any good pubs?'

Dirty Harry's sprang immediately to mind. You never knew who we might run into . . .

'I really want to try out Guinness. For ten years now I've wondered what it's like, and I'm not going home without having a pint of it.'

'Tomorrow night,' I promised her. 'But right now I just want to catch up. I thought Matthew would go for a takeaway while we open a bottle of wine.'

'Lovely,' said Jo, sinking gratefully onto the sofa. 'To be honest,' she confided, 'I'm exhausted from having to be so enthusiastic about everything.'

'You don't have to be,' I told her, surprised.

'Yeah, but you wouldn't have liked it if I'd said the place was a shithole either, would you? Now,' she said, rubbing her hands together, 'let's hit the wine.'

Once we were on our own, we curled up on the couch for a proper catch-up.

'Tell us, how's Brenda?'

'Oh, a total bitch, as usual. On the sauce big time. She threw a wooden spoon at me the other day and then she started crying and begging me not to sue, that she was going to clean up her act.' Jo didn't seem too put out by it. 'The new girl – Miranda – is finding it hard going, I think. She's OK. But I wouldn't go drinking with her or anything,' she said loyally.

'Thanks, Jo.'

'And the girls all say hello, by the way. Jane's preggers, of course, and honest to God, you would think nobody in the world had ever had a baby before.' She derisively knocked back a mouthful of wine. 'I *hate* meeting her now because all she can talk about is her darkening nipples and how the baby is the size of a grapefruit. Or maybe it was a melon, oh, some fruit anyway. *Head* wrecking. And she's going round in these hickey maternity dungarees, like something out of the 1970s.' A burst of laughter. 'Mad Mags is riding a nurse, a male nurse, that is; they do a lot of role play, she says. She gets him to put on his uniform, anyway, which mustn't seem so much role play to him as a busman's holiday, but guess what? He actually diagnosed her with a cyst last week, so wasn't that great? She always lands on her feet, that Mags. Oh, and brace yourself. Pauline and Tim were wondering if you had the spare room done up yet. Hint, hint. So you can expect the pair of them to start booking flights any day, and they won't even bring a bottle of wine with them . . .' She trailed off abruptly. 'Clara, are you *crying*?'

'Don't be stupid.' I fanned my face furiously.

'You are.' Jo was horrified. 'Pauline and Tim probably won't even come. They often say these things but never go through with them.'

'It's not Pauline and Tim.' I was embarrassed, turning on the tears like that. It must be the wine or something. 'It's just, hearing you talk about everybody. I miss them, that's all.'

'Well, of course you do!' Jo said. 'And we miss you. Ah, Jesus, you're starting me off now.' Now she was fanning her face and blinking her eyes rapidly. 'How are we going to get through the weekend if we're bawling already?'

Now she was laughing, and so was I, and we took a gulp of our wine and settled back down.

'It's such a big change, coming back here,' I told her. 'It's funny to believe I was running around London a few months ago.'

'But it's good, though, isn't it?' she probed.

'It's great. I mean, obviously, I wish the business was taking off a bit better.'

'I suppose it was a bad time to open a business.'

'*Now* you tell me.'

She rallied. 'But you just wait. Some day all those kids you've fed at birthday parties will grow up. They'll book you for sure.'

'Thanks, Jo. How reassuring.'

We laughed and she refilled our glasses with very generous measures. 'And you and Matthew?'

'What about us?'

'Is the dream working out? You know the way sometimes people up and move to a new place to start again and it doesn't end up how it's supposed to.'

'Are you sounding hopeful?'

'No!' She was mortified. 'But I'm keeping your seat warm in Falvio's.' She laughed to show me she wasn't serious.

I considered it. 'If anything, I think Matthew loves the place more than I do.'

'I'm glad you finally filled him in about Jason.'

'Me too. I don't know why I didn't before.'

'See? I told you you were being a ninny.' She was triumphant. 'Come here, is he really going out with Dominique now?'

Jo had already caught of glimpse of her out my front window. She'd marvelled at the hair, the clothes, the pink Mini; it took a lot of confidence to pull that lot off. I'd assured her that Dominique had plenty of that.

'I guess so. At least, I've seen him over at hers once or twice.'

We hadn't spoken since he'd found my number plate. It had been lying on the road outside, apparently. Those little toerags from the top of the town really seemed to have it in for us. I don't know what Matthew was more annoyed about: the hassle of getting it replaced yet again, or the fact that we'd all been so distracted by the number plate that we'd missed his bull's-eye.

'Nobody saw it! Not even the lads. Everyone was wondering who owned the licence plate!'

Out the window I could see him arriving back from the Chinese. He'd jogged, as he liked the evening air, and I knew from the bulging takeaway bag they'd given him free prawn crackers, now that they were getting to know us. He waved over at Burt Reynolds, who was putting his bins out, and he and Ma exchanged a friendly scowl. After we'd finished eating, we would sit out in our back garden and listen to the wind in the trees, and Kian and Jennifer squabbling, and some day I knew it would be our own two kids, and suddenly I didn't miss London one little bit.

Chapter Twenty-six

Matthew had been bursting to ask a question all evening. He bided his time until the washing-up was done and then he pounced.

'How's the flat?'

'Still there,' Jo reassured him.

'Yes, but are there any problems? You know, late payment of rent, cigarette burns on the carpet, that kind of thing?' he probed painfully.

'You want the truth?' said Jo.

Matthew was immediately alarmed. 'Is it bad?'

'There have been . . . complaints.'

Matthew shot me an I-knew-this-would-happen look. 'What kind of complaints? Partying, I bet. Music till four in the morning,' he said bitterly. 'I bet they're having a great old time in our property.'

'No.'

'What, then? Not putting their rubbish out, is it? Leaving it festering in the hallway? I knew by the look of them, didn't I, Clara? We should never have taken them on.'

'I mean *they're* the ones complaining.'

That set us back a bit.

'About what?'

'Look, I didn't want to go bothering you, what with you trying to settle in here and everything.' Jo looked apologetic. 'But you didn't leave any instructions about the immersion.'

Matthew looked at me. 'We did. We left them on the counter, alongside the alarm codes.'

A vague memory stirred in me.

'They said there weren't any.'

'They didn't look properly then, did they?' Matthew was getting testy.

'Their electricity bill was massive, they said, because it wasn't clear how to set the timer, and they ended up leaving it on all day for a whole month.'

'That's hardly my fault, is it? I definitely left instructions. They must be blind.'

'Actually, Matthew?' I'd just found them, tucked into a pile of travel documentation we'd stashed in a drawer. 'We were in a rush, we must have picked them up by mistake.' I took them out from where I'd semi-hidden them.

'You don't say.' He handed them over to Jo, gruff. 'Maybe you'd, um, pass on our apologies.'

'Sure.' But she wasn't finished yet. 'And the dishwasher isn't working properly.'

'*What?*'

Even I was surprised at that. Granted, the dishwasher was getting on a bit now, but had been in good working order when we'd left. The two lads looked like they subsisted on beans on toast; I doubted they needed to use it that much anyway.

'They want a new dishwasher, then?' Matthew looked like he was developing a hernia. So this landlord lark wasn't just about watching all that lovely lolly go into your bank account every month.

'Or you could just get the old one fixed.'

'It costs a fortune to get these repair guys out. It's not worth it. We're better off getting a new one.' His eyes watered at the cost. 'Thanks for letting us know, Jo.'

'No problem.'

'And, you know, I can deal with them if it's too much hassle.'

But Jo waved this away. 'I'm only up the road. And you've enough to be getting on with here.'

He thanked her profusely for her trouble, and a few minutes later retired to bed with a stack of kitchen catalogues we had left over from furnishing the house in Ireland, and we heard the door close.

'No sex tonight then,' Jo cackled.

Chapter Twenty-seven

It was two days before I realised that there was something different about Jo: she had the look of a woman in love.

'Me? You must be joking. I most certainly am not.'

'Jo, you can't fool me.'

'Rubbish.'

'So you're not seeing anybody at all?'

'No.'

'Liar.'

'I might have a casual thing going on,' she admitted reluctantly.

Her defensiveness was understandable. She had such poor taste in men that each new acquisition was usually met with a despairing chorus of, 'Oh, *Jo.*'

'What's wrong with him?' It was out before I could help myself.

Much eye flinging. 'Nothing. He's perfectly normal.'

'No offence, but you've never gone out with a normal man in your life.'

'Well, this time I have.'

'Who is it then?'

'You wouldn't know him. Look, we've only just met.'

She was being too cagey, and my heart sank. It was bound to end badly, like all the others. And I so wanted somebody nice for Jo. Even more so now, seeing as I wasn't around for her in the same way any more, and I'd feel so much better if she was, well, settled. I caught myself on – was I sounding like her mother?

Sophie pitched up, carrying a tray. 'One tall soy milk latte with an extra shot, no sugar, extra hot and with low-cal sweetener on the side?'

'Thank you, thank you,' said Jo airily, reaching out to accept the abomination.

Jo's pernicketiness when it came to ordering coffee was legendary, but Sophie had got terribly excited by the sophisticated order, and had jotted it all down importantly. Poor Val had nearly had a hernia trying to make the damn thing, and at one point I'd seen one of the barmen legging it out the door, returning a few minutes later with a carton of what was allegedly soy milk, but judging by the smell coming from the latte right now, could well be baby formula.

'And a tea,' Sophie said to me, rather witheringly. How boring.

I'd clearly been knocked off my perch by glamorous Jo, who was swinging her foot back and forth nonchalantly.

'GREAT shoes,' said Sophie.

'Thank you!'

Jo angled her foot, the better to show off the heel, and the two of them began murmuring, 'lovely' and 'surprisingly comfortable' and 'the shops are shite around here', giving me a chance to look out the window to the street beyond.

There she was: Anita, in her new runners, bombing past on the other side of the street. She wore a bright pink velour tracksuit, and her arms were pumping ferociously. A pace-counter was clamped to one wrist. I could see people clock her approach and step swiftly out of the way, gathering small children and buggies into themselves protectively.

Sophie and Jo turned to look too.

'Still going,' said Sophie, in great admiration. Well, who would have thought? Nobody had seen Anita actually walking up the Main Street in recent years; normally she just reversed up to the Spar, and piled the boot high.

As Anita passed outside, Jo leaned forward to rap sharply on the window. 'Good work!' she shouted.

Anita looked up wildly, startled. Her face was puce and her hair stringy with sweat.

'Jesus,' said Jo, recoiling. 'Is she alright?'

Well, who really knew? Her transformation was as unexpected as it was complete. You would never equate this get-fit freak with the unhealthy, morbidly obese, stubborn woman from a month ago. But it was nearly like she'd gone too far; from being delighted that she'd lost seven pounds, now she was raging if she didn't drop more than three pounds a week. Every morsel was weighed and thoroughly assessed for the twin evils of sugar or fat before she'd allow it past her lips.

Sophie put it into words for all of us. 'It's like she's turned into the poster girl for diabetes.'

Anita disappeared around a corner, throwing up a cloud of dust behind herself.

The strange thing was, I think I worried about her more now than I did before.

Róisín called over just as we were getting ready to go out for the night. Róisín knew Jo from her trips to London over the years to see me. She was very comfortable around Jo because Jo was a Londoner who had many gay friends, and didn't swallow nervously every time Róisín looked in her direction, like Róisín fancied her or something.

'I'm going to move to London,' Róisín had often declared, when she would be over visiting Matthew and me. 'I really feel I can be myself over here, you know?'

'I totally agree,' I always said heartily. 'So come on, pack a bag, you can sleep on the couch until you get your own place.' I meant it, too.

But she never did, of course. Within two days of returning home, she'd be back in the thick of it at work, and putting on her 'straight face', and making secret forays to Dublin, where nobody knew her. She'd be perfectly happy with this state of affairs until the next time she came over. Jo would take her out to some fabulous gay club, courtesy of free tickets from Cool Art, and where Róisín could just be herself, no pretending, and she'd be plunged into self-crisis all over again. 'I'm *definitely* moving this time.'

After the split with Catherine, I was sure it would be on her mind again tonight. But there was no talk of London. She walked in, her face peculiar, and announced, 'I have two words to say to you.'

Matthew, thinking this was aimed at him, immediately blurted, 'I didn't want the breakfast roll, your mother insisted on making it for me after I painted the garage for her, but I swear, not a morsel passed her lips. I ate the whole lot.'

Róisín wasn't looking at him, though.

'"Nice shoes?"' Jo tried next, raising one ankle delicately to show off a fabulous Louboutin. My new wedges looked like wellies in comparison.

But Róisín's two words were for me. 'Erotic fiction,' she enunciated slowly.

I immediately jumped guiltily. But I'd have felt just as guilty if she'd said, 'Pink dildo!' or 'Nippleless bra', even though I didn't possess either of those things.

'Two words for you. "Buy online",' I told her back.

'I'm talking about Dominique Fitzgibbons.'

We all had a little look towards the window. 'What about her?'

Róisín had the pent-up excitement of a child about to tell at school. 'Sit down. This is good.' She made us all wait until she had our full attention, and Jo was forced to lower her Clinique Eye Defining Liquid Liner mid-application. 'She calls herself a bestselling writer, but the reason none of us has seen her on the New York bestsellers list is because she writes . . .' pause for imaginary drum roll '. . . erotic fiction!'

I looked at Róisín suspiciously. 'Where did you find this out?' There was no need to ask why. Dominique's reappearance in Castlemoy had clearly brought back unpleasant memories for Róisín.

'I went on the internet, of course.' Róisín was unabashed.

'This erotic fiction. What are we talking about – dirty books?' Matthew breathed. God love him, he was very innocent in that regard. Even with access to computers all day long, he never really strayed beyond eBay.

'Filthy,' Róisín confirmed. 'Nudity, sex scenes, illicit couplings, people riding each other every time you turn a page.' She realised we were staring at her. 'Or so I believe.'

'Wow,' said Jo, suitably impressed. 'You've interesting neighbours,' she complimented me.

'Interesting?' Róisín spluttered. 'I'd call her something else.' She looked at me, excited by her discovery. 'I knew when she spun you that tale about being a writer that there was something funny going on. So I did a little research. And there's no bestselling writer called Dominique Fitzgibbons.' She eyed me, nearly bursting now. 'But there is a Dominique . . . Duverne!'

I laughed. Good old Dominique.

'It's not funny,' Róisín insisted.

'Oh, come on. It is, a little bit.'

'What? What?' Matthew and Jo wanted to know.

'When we were kids, Dominique was going to change her name to something more Hollywood. She picked Duverne. She thought it had a dash of glamour. We helped her come up with it, Róisín, so I guess we have to take some responsibility too. Hey, maybe we're due royalties.'

But Róisín refused to crack a smile. 'She has her own website and everything, with this author shot where she's holding a pen and looking into the middle distance like she's some genius at work. She prides herself on her "research" apparently – the mind boggles – and there's a list of all her dirty books, called things like *Joy Ride*, and *I've Got Your Number.*'

The titles invited infantile sniggering. Jo and I duly obliged.

Matthew cleared his throat officiously. 'And would you happen to have a copy of any of these publications?' he asked Róisín. 'Because I may have to peruse them and possibly submit them to the censor.'

More laughter from Jo and me.

Róisín seemed annoyed that I was enjoying the news so much. 'I just thought you'd be interested, that's all,' she huffed, and turned to leave.

I caught her up at the door. 'Look, Róisín, I know it's difficult having Dominique back.'

'No, it's not,' said Róisín, even though she'd obviously spent hours researching her online, trying to find something to use against her.

'What happened between you two was a long time ago,' I tried to reason. 'And I get the feeling she'd like to make the peace. Why don't you meet her halfway?'

Róisín flashed me a haughty look. 'You don't think I still remember that stupid night?'

Who was she trying to kid? I remembered it clearly myself: the vivid image of Dominique and my sister locked in a massive snog in the dingy girls' toilets at the Junior Disco on a chilly night in November. I'd no idea they were in there; I'd just followed a few other people out of the main hall. Word had discreetly spread that there was something going down in the toilets. I'd genuinely expected that someone had procured a forbidden bottle of vodka, or that a pack of Benson & Hedges was doing the rounds. I arrived just in time to see Róisín's thin, straight body pressed up against Dominique's curvier one, mouths seeking hungrily, arms on each other's waists.

For a moment, I struggled to comprehend: what did Róisín think she was doing? Why on earth was she kissing a *girl*? Then, almost as quickly, everything about my sister made sense, and I felt a bit stupid for not having realised before.

They didn't see us for a moment. We stood in the doorway, a clump of kids, wide-eyed and frozen, the silence broken only by the wet sound of their kissing.

Then: 'Go on, ya lezzer!'

The boys in front of me erupted in catcalls, jeers, whistles.

I saw Róisín rear away from Dominique, white-faced with shock. Eyes skittering about, terrified, wondering what was going on.

Dominique wasn't so shocked. In fact, I saw that she wasn't surprised at all. The looks that flew between her and the jeering boys suggested some kind of conspiracy. The kiss had been a set-up, with Róisín the one to take the fall.

It had 'just been a bit of a laugh' Dominique tried to explain afterwards. But we knew what was going on: Róisín had become the subject of mounting speculation about her sexuality, mostly due to her stoic refusal to get off with any of the boys. They figured they'd 'out' her, with Dominique – who would get off with anybody, at any time, it seemed – as the bait.

We couldn't understand how Dominique, our friend, could have gone along with it. Apparently no great planning had gone into it; it was a spur-of-the-moment dare at the disco. Everybody had had an illegal bottle or two of beer, and Róisín had somehow let her defences and good judgement slip.

'She said she fancied me,' Róisín cried in my arms that night in our bedroom. 'But all she wanted to do was make a fool of me. How could I have been so stupid? She's not even my type. All I could think of was, there's somebody else in this town like me.'

My heart broke for her. And I gave her what, looking back now, was probably a terrible piece of advice. 'Deny it. Say it never happened.'

'But everyone will know.'

'Who cares? Nobody's going to believe Dominique. She'd get up on herself,' I scoffed. 'And as for those airhead boys . . . just say it's a stupid story, and it'll all die down.'

So she did, and I was right: three days later everybody was talking about the flood in Hickey's Chemist. But I often wondered whether we'd painted Róisín into a corner that she would find it hard to get out of. She was still trying.

Anyway, the upshot of the whole thing was that, unsurprisingly, Dominique and Róisín's friendship hit a brick wall.

'Come out with us tonight,' I urged her at the door. 'It'll take your mind off things.' I didn't want her to go home and brood. She was very raw yet over Catherine. And now Dominique was stirring up bad memories.

But Róisín just pulled a face when I told her the club we were going to.

'Too many straight people?' I'd asked.

'Too many fecking eejits.' She smiled wanly. 'See you tomorrow.'

Chapter Twenty-eight

'Do you want another drink?'

'What?'

'I said, DO YOU WANT ANOTHER DRINK?'

'Oh. NO, THANKS.'

The noise in the club was deafening. But we couldn't say anything because Jo would immediately start calling us old farts, like she used to in London.

Matthew, fair play to him, jerked a thumb in the direction of the sweating, gyrating mass of bodies. 'Will we hit the dance floor?'

He took my hand, and we struck out in its general direction, but were immediately thrown back by the wall of people, and landed where we'd started.

Matthew leaned in very close, and said into my ear, 'Can we go home?'

He seemed a bit bewildered. What was worse, I was too.

'This wouldn't bother us in London. In fact, we'd love it,' I told him.

'You're right. We would. We were out every weekend over there.'

'During the week too,' I reminded him. 'Sometimes two nights in a row.'

'Really? Were we?' He blinked like it was a distant memory. 'Wow. I'm impressed by us.' He looked at me. 'So what's happened? Do you think she's right?' He looked in the direction of Jo, who was wiggling her backside energetically on the dance floor. 'Have we really turned into old farts since moving here?'

'It's entirely possible.'

We sat stiffly at the bar – we'd bagged seats, another damning indication of advancing middle age – and tried to tap our feet in time to the music, which wasn't really music at all, we'd agreed only a moment ago, not in the traditional sense anyway; it was more *noise* than anything.

'I think those youths over there are laughing at us again,' Matthew said, stopping his foot-tapping abruptly.

Jo, meanwhile, was shimmying like she was in Ibiza, while a plethora of admiring men watched from a careful distance. 'I'm going out with someone,' she'd barked at one of them earlier. 'Look, but don't touch.'

'I don't care, though,' Matthew said suddenly.

'About what?'

'I don't want my old life back. I'm exactly where I want to be in my life. Right here, with you.' He took my hands in his. 'I love you.'

'It's OK,' I teased him. 'You've pulled.'

'Will you marry me?'

I was so surprised that I just gawked at him.

'I said, WILL YOU—'

'I know, I know, I heard you the first time.'

It had always been part of the plan: the marriage and kids bit. But we'd been so busy with the first part of the plan – the move to Ireland – that I honestly hadn't given it any more thought. I presumed Matthew hadn't either.

I prepared to indulge him; we were in a club, we'd had a few drinks, I'd slag him about it in the morning.

'I've never been more sober in my life,' Matthew told me quietly, having followed my gaze to his drink. 'And I'm sorry for blurting it out like that, it probably isn't the time or the place. You'd probably have preferred somewhere a little more romantic.' He looked anxious now. 'Damn, I've messed it up, haven't I? But seeing as we were talking about having become very settled and ancient, I thought we might as well go the whole hog and tie the knot.'

'Yes, please,' I said.

Now he was the one to go very still. '. . . Yes?'

'Yes, I would love to marry you. Nothing would make me happier.' And I leaned in and gave him a big, passionate, heart-felt kiss.

I could see the nearby youths nudging each other again, and having a bit of a laugh at us. 'Go get a room!'

I didn't give a shite about them. I was going to get married. *Married*.

Jo found us holding hands, and grinning insanely at each other. She had to tap us on the shoulders before we took any notice of her.

'WE'RE ENGAGED,' Matthew shouted at her.

'I'm not deaf,' she said crossly. Then, 'Oh my *God*! Amazing! What the hell took you so long?'

And she burst into tears and hugged me, and then Matthew, and then the two of us together.

'Can I be your bridesmaid?' she sobbed, hunting for a tissue.

'Great!' said Matthew. 'One job filled. I just need to find a best man now and we can get hitched tomorrow.'

'But I'm going home tomorrow,' Jo wailed. Typical. She would miss all the fun.

'He's only joking. Knowing us, we won't get around to it for ages,' I assured her. 'Years and years.'

'One year, maybe. But not years and years,' Matthew said firmly.

I dropped Jo off at the airport the following evening.

'You can't take the smile off your face, can you?' she said indulgently.

'Nope.'

'I always knew you two were made for each other. Imagine, if I hadn't introduced you that night, you might never have met. So really, you can thank me for the whole thing.' Jo loved a happy ending.

'Thanks, Jo,' I said drily.

'Although I suppose you won't come back now, will you?' She wrinkled her nose. 'If you're getting married. You'll stay here now, and have tonnes of kids, and put down roots and all that.' She managed a smile. 'That's proper grown-up, isn't it?'

'I suppose.' There was no point in pretending otherwise. 'But now that you've made your first visit, the next one will be easier.'

'Yeah,' she said, cheering up. 'And you'd better come back to London, too. It can't be one-sided.'

'Absolutely. That's if you'll have time to see me. What with this new man.'

'Oh,' said Jo, offhand, but I could tell she was excited. It had been a long time since there had been anybody.

'At least tell me his name.

'No.'

'You would if he was normal.'

'He *is* normal. How many times do I have to tell you?' she said, clutching the pile of dishwasher catalogues that Matthew had pressed upon her before we'd left. 'They've only got a choice between the cheapest two,' he'd told her grimly in a lengthy list of instructions. 'And tell them I'm getting in contact with their college if they leave so much as a scratch on it when they leave – that should put the frighteners on them.' He'd even got poor Jo to promise to call over that very evening to the flat to 'sort this entire thing out' and to 'take no messing from that pair of penniless wasters'.

I knew from the look on her face that she had better things to be doing with her time. But she'd assured him that she'd try to call over after work during the week. The handbag we owed her was getting more and more expensive.

'Don't forget. I'm your chief bridesmaid.' She winked at me by the security gates. 'I promise I'll try not to upstage you.'

She planted a big mwah! mwah! on each of my cheeks, then, with a wave, she was gone.

I stayed smiling all the way home – fifty-two minutes on the motorway, by my count. Getting married was great crack, especially the beginning lovey-dovey bit, where you got to celebrate with lots of champagne and make emotional phone calls to relatives.

'Married!' Matthew's mother had said in a quivery voice.

'Yes. So you'll have to come over now,' Matthew had told her.

'Of course I will, of *course*. We'll *all* come over. Put me on to Clara.'

I took the phone a little worriedly. English mammies could be as fearsome as Irish mammies. Would I be warned to have a good hot meal on the table for him every evening of our married lives, for instance?

But Di wanted to know what we'd like as an engagement present. 'Matthew says I'm not to go to the expense, but I'm going to get you something anyway, so you might as well just tell me what you want.'

I could hear her anxiety. There was no point in telling her, 'Just surprise us,' because she'd spend a week trying to come up with ideas, which she'd then have to run past Sharon and Liz, and *they* would get in a heap about it, and so I said, 'Placemats. We've no placemats for the new dining table.'

She was delighted. 'Great. I'll get some for you. A nice design, nothing too fussy. And, Clara? I'm really delighted about the engagement. He couldn't have met a nicer girl.'

I knew that, on some level, she must be thinking the same as Jo; that there was no chance at all of us moving back to London now. But she was too kind to ever say it.

'Thank you, Di. I hope I can make him happy.'

I resolved there and then that we would make frequent visits back, for Di's sake, and for Matthew's. In fact, I'd look into flights straight away.

I was so wrapped up in my plans that I had a little start when I got out of my car and turned to find myself looking into Jason's face.

For a minute I was confused. What was he doing outside my house in the dark? And why was he carrying flowers and a bottle of wine?

'Hello, Clara.'

I could tell he was enjoying my confusion, just a little bit.

Then Dominique's door opened opposite, spilling light across the road. Of course: he was here to see her. She waved out at him. Soft music came from the doorway behind her.

'I hope your licence plate hasn't gone missing again?' Jason enquired softly.

I stared at him, my mouth suddenly dry. 'No.'

'Glad to hear it.' He turned, a big smile suddenly on his face for Dominique, and he crossed the road to her.

Chapter Twenty-nine

We threw a small party to celebrate our engagement.

'You *have* to have a party,' Róisín had said, scandalised when it seemed that we were going to let the happy occasion pass without getting stociously drunk and having someone get sick into the hydrangeas outside.

Now that she and Catherine were no longer together, Róisín declared herself stoically determined to 'enjoy life as a rural-based lesbian who is reconciled to remaining single for ever'.

'Talk about setting the bar high,' Matthew murmured. 'But still, she's right. We should celebrate. 'We can't let our new neighbour put us off.'

Jason visited Dominique's house a lot now. When I opened the bedroom curtains in the morning, his car was the first thing I saw. You couldn't help but notice.

'Don't tell me he's there again?' Matthew would enquire.

'Yes.'

'How many nights is that this week?'

'I don't know. Maybe five?'

'*Five?*'

I didn't know how Dominique was going to hit her deadline, what with the ferocious amount of dating she was doing. Róisín had ordered one of her books for the laugh – *I've Got Your Number* – and it was . . .

interesting. There was no plot to speak of; everybody just went at it the whole time, and page after page was filled with boobs and willies, which they were always thrusting in each other's faces, and other places too, and saying things like, 'Each stroke drove me nearer and nearer to the point of ecstasy.' I couldn't imagine Dominique tossing a few pages of her latest work to Jason, with the words, 'Here, have a look over that for any typos, would you?'

Matthew had read *I've Got Your Number* too. 'That description on page eighty-four of the heroine pleasuring herself in the shower was a shocking waste of water. Gallons and gallons of the stuff, down the drain, just like that,' he said, very concerned. A pause. 'I might have to read it again just to see exactly how much.'

I've Got Your Number had done the rounds of the whole family by now. Everybody had their favourite scene. Anita's was the one where one couple smeared each other in Nutella and licked it all off. She was quite annoyed when the man 'peaked' rather too soon into it, 'before hardly any of the Nutella was licked off. I'd have finished the job first.'

'At least we know what happens in the next one,' I said to Matthew wryly. 'A solicitor is going to ride rings round himself in some Irish country town.'

We decided to have the engagement party on Saturday night at home, with just family. I cooked up a storm in the kitchen, and Matthew put up a load of balloons. It would be a lovely end to a great week. After a spate of children's birthday parties – and it was great to get the work, I wasn't knocking it – Food by Clara had received its first corporate booking, for a luncheon event for approximately one hundred people in two weeks' time.

'Woo hoo.' Matthew had done a little dance around the kitchen.

I was desperately excited, but nervous too. 'I need to get this right, Matthew. Can you imagine the contacts I could make out of this?'

'I know. And you'll do it.'

I *had* to do it. It was close to make-or-break time for the business. The bit of money I'd invested in it was running low. Matthew insisted that his job was more than enough to support us both. Plus, we were getting married now – I could legally fleece him for all he was worth, he told me lovingly. I was grateful and all that – but it didn't diminish my determination to make Food by Clara work. Imagine Jo's face if it flopped.

The first to arrive were Eddie and Eleanora.

'Congratulations! *Look* at you two. Soon to be mister and missus!' Eleanora was suitably effervescent. Unusually, they'd come down on the train. Normally they took the bus as it was cheaper. Eleanora handed me a pretty vase as an engagement gift. Eddie immediately took Matthew into the study 'for a chat'.

'Sorry about this. But seeing as Dad's not around any more, I'd better do the duty instead. It's just to go over your prospects, stocks and shares, that kind of thing. And I'll have to warn you to treat her right, or I'll knock your block off, is that OK?'

'Fire ahead, fire ahead,' said Matthew.

Róisín took the opportunity to engage Eleanora in rather leading conversation. 'Been to any bars recently?', that kind of thing, and, 'Bumped into anyone we might know?'

'Do you mean Catherine?' Eleanora was always good for a clanger.

I watched Róisín's cheeks bloom. 'No. *As if.* Absolutely not!'

She was still in love. That was plain to see. I wanted to kill Catherine all over again for treating her so badly.

'So!' said Eleanora to me. 'Can we see the ring?'

Her eyes were already busily hunting out my ring finger.

'I haven't got it yet. Matthew didn't want to pick one on his own, so we'll go together next week.'

Matthew had joked that it would take him a few days to tot up the coins in the jam jar he kept on the windowsill for change.

'Good idea. You don't want to get landed with something awful. Besides, if you're with him, you can be sure he won't skimp!' Eleanora said, displaying once again that there were no flies on her. And, indeed, she and Eddie both looked remarkably fly- and flea-free. Her hair had received some kind of a cut – there was still loads of it, but the ends had been feathered and some highlights were scattered artistically round the crown. She didn't get those out of a home dye kit.

There was something different about Eddie too, but nobody could put their finger on it for ages. Then Róisín hissed, 'You can't see the crack of his arse. Look, it's gone, tucked away under those jeans.'

She was right. The jeans were sober and more structured than he normally favoured. His broody stare was still intact, though, thank God. In fact, he was a bit more simmering than usual today. Maybe he was trying to get into character for some new play.

I was taking the food out of the oven when Anita arrived. 'Nothing for me, nothing for me,' she announced, as she swept in wearing – Jesus, Mary and Joseph – a pair of fitted white trousers and some high heels. 'Look,' she insisted, doing a twirl.

Róisín and I exchanged wary glances.

'Very nice, Anita,' Róisín said, inspecting the trousers. 'Where did you get them, Marks & Spencer?'

'Not the trousers. My *bottom*.' And she pointed in case we were blind as well as stupid.

We all looked at her bottom. Eddie only managed a quick glance before he had to turn away. Eleanora had started to smirk but one look from me killed that one dead.

'Lovely,' Matthew eventually said loyally. He truly was the son she never had. 'Isn't it?' he challenged us.

'Yes, indeed, it's a fine, *fine* bottom,' we murmured amongst ourselves energetically.

'It's *smaller*.' Anita was very exasperated now. 'I did it! I burned it!'

It was Róisín who finally twigged. 'Burn That Butt!'

'Yes.' Anita was delighted. 'There're six inches gone from that rump. Susie measured it last night.' And she gave her bum a good slap. I half expected her to whinny and gallop off at any moment. 'I won the Burner of the Month award,' she said, a little shyly. 'I'm so hot, I'm practically sizzling!' she quipped unexpectedly, before bursting into her tee-hee laugh.

We all laughed too. You had to hand it to Anita. It must be tough keeping a sense of humour in the face of all that exercise and denial but she had done it.

'I just need to keep it up now,' she resolved, sobering. 'So don't anybody offer me anything bad. Not even a glass of wine,' she chided Matthew, who hadn't been offering anyway. 'I'm going to show that bloody Dr Mooney that he won't need to hack my leg off any time soon.'

'He was never going to hack your leg off, Anita,' Róisín interceded. 'What you had was the beginnings of an ulcer—'

'I know exactly what I had. So you needn't lecture me, thank you very much.'

'Makes a blinking change,' Róisín muttered. She might be determined to enjoy herself as a single-not-by-choice rural-based lesbian, but right now she didn't look like she was making much of a fist of it.

Anita duly eschewed all the food I'd made, which was nearly all healthy and suitable for diabetics. Instead she kept reaching into her handbag for handfuls of nuts and seeds, which she chewed on, her cheeks working furiously, like a squirrel's. 'The sunflower seeds are a right bugger,' I heard her confide to Eleanora.

Pop. Matthew had the champagne open and was handing out glasses.

'Speech, speech . . .' Eddie began to chant.

'Oh, yes, go on, Matthew,' Anita encouraged, already tearing up. Not only was she delighted that I was marrying a wonderful man, but she now had DIY on tap for the rest of her life.

Matthew looked under pressure. He wasn't a great one for the flowery stuff. Eventually he lifted his glass, turned to me, and simply said, 'To my lovely fiancée.' Then, as if there were only the two of us in the room: 'You've made me the proudest man in Ireland.'

That had Anita blubbing – 'I'm fine, I'm fine, ah, go on then, just a half glass' – and Eleanora linked her arm possessively with Eddie's, no doubt hoping the day would come for her, too. Róisín smiled and clapped valiantly, giving no indication at all that her own heart was in smithereens.

Just then a pair of headlights shone into the living room as a car drove up. The headlights turned into the drive opposite.

'They're back,' Anita said unnecessarily.

'Stop looking,' Róisín warned her.

But everybody did now, of course. There was much flattening back against walls and everybody trying to see past other people's heads. Jason stepped out of the driver's side of the car. Dominique alighted from the other side.

'Better go and check if our licence plate is still intact,' Matthew murmured.

Anita rolled her eyes. 'As if Jason is going around stealing licence plates!'

'Well, *someone* is,' Matthew commented mildly. 'And Jason seems to be the lucky man who finds them.'

'He's stealing your licence plate?' Eddie enquired.

Anita rubbished this. 'He's a solicitor. You think he's crawling about on his hands and knees vandalising cars?'

'Stranger things have happened,' Róisín piped up darkly. 'He's clearly not thinking straight if he's seeing Dominique.'

She couldn't let any chance to denigrate Dominique pass.

Matthew went over and pulled the curtains across firmly. 'I'd like to remind you all that this is our engagement party. So let's leave the neighbours out of it, will we? Even the strange ones.'

I wished I'd said nothing now about my encounter with Jason that night. I'd just thought his comment odd. But no doubt I'd been reading too much into it. At any rate, the licence plate hadn't gone missing since, so that was that.

'Does anybody want to hear Eddie's chicken ad?' Eleanora chirped.

There was nothing like a good laugh at somebody else's expense to kick a party off. We all loudly signalled our enthusiasm.

'Because I have a recording right here.' She held up a music gadget and wriggled it tantalisingly.

'Don't,' said Eddie in a strangled voice.

'Oh, stop it.' She indulgently squeezed his arm. 'It's wonderful.'

'It is not, give it to me . . . Eleanora, for fuck's sake . . .'

She held it out of his reach.

'Go on, put it on,' Anita begged. 'I just bet you're brilliant.'

Róisín was smiling too, for the first time all evening. 'I hope they paid you well,' she ribbed Eddie.

He just looked stonily back.

Belatedly I realised that Eddie must have turned down the theatre job in order to do the ad. And it wasn't sitting well; a bit like the new jeans, really. It had paid for Eleanora's new hairdo, and the train tickets down.

It was dirty money. It was *chicken* money.

'If you put that on, I'm out of here,' he warned Eleanora.

By now the rest of them were clamouring to hear it. Matthew had his computer out, and was setting up some speakers.

'Did you do it in an American accent?' Anita asked. 'Because nobody will know it's you, you know. You can be anonymous,' she said reassuringly.

'He's marvellous in it.' Eleanora was fervent. 'The producer definitely wants to work with him again.'

Eddie gave her a look and walked out.

'Anyway,' said Anita, valiantly. 'Happy engagement!'

Chapter Thirty

There was a ring on the doorbell early one morning and I opened it to find Jason standing there.

'Clara,' he said easily. 'I was hoping you'd be in.'

I didn't say anything for a minute. I felt a bit ambushed or something. He was in a suit and tie, and I guessed he was on his way out to work. Matthew had already left.

'I was actually just leaving,' I found myself saying, thanking God that at least I was dressed. Often at this time I'd still be pottering about in my pyjamas. But the big lunch booking was coming up in three days' time and I was going to collect all the cheeses and charcuterie for it today, just to have it ready.

'I won't keep you, so. Oh, and my father was saying just the other day again how much he enjoyed the food you did for his party.'

There was no mention of my licence plate this time. His entire demeanour was friendly, cheerful, almost overly so. It was disconcerting.

Across the way Dominique emerged from the side passage, in some frilly horror of a dressing gown, pushing a green bin for collection. She waved across. Jason waved back, and before I knew what I was doing, I was waving too, like this was OK, and not a little bit odd.

But maybe that was just from my perspective. 'Good,' I told him.

'Anyway, I won't keep you,' he said. 'It's just, Dominique and I were thinking of throwing a little party at the end of the week.' Then, 'You know Dominique, don't you?'

I looked at him. He knew I did. We'd been in school together for years. 'Of course I do.'

His brow bunched together, as though a thought had just occurred to him. 'I hope it's OK? Me and her dating? I mean, I wouldn't want you to feel uncomfortable or anything.'

I mightn't be too keen on bumping into him all the time, but apart from that it was nothing to do with me. It was almost like he wanted me to be uncomfortable.

'Fire away,' I assured him pleasantly.

'Great! So, listen, how are you fixed for Friday night? To cater a little something for us?' He smiled at me.

I saw immediately what he had done. How could I say no, now that I'd assured him that I had no problem with him dating Dominique?

'I'm afraid I can't,' I told him pleasantly. 'You see, I'm doing a big lunch on Friday at noon, so I wouldn't have time to prepare for yours if it was to be that evening.'

'That's a shame. It was probably a bit extravagant of us anyway. I'm sure we can knock up a few bowls of crisps ourselves!'

He was so jovial that I wondered whether I'd misread him. Maybe he genuinely didn't see how cack-handed he was being. And even if he didn't – because he wasn't the most empathetic soul in the world – would he not think that Dominique mightn't be too gone on the idea of me in her kitchen?

Jason was looking around the estate now, like he had all the time in the world. 'It's nice around here, isn't it? With the trees out the back, and it's pretty quiet too. Well, apart from that bloody motorbike. Who is that guy, anyway?'

'Burt Reynolds,' I said faintly.

Motorbikes had always annoyed Jason. 'Look at the speed of that guy!' he was forever complaining. 'What's he trying to do, get himself killed? Fool.'

'As for your woman.' He jerked a thumb towards Ma's house and lowered his voice as though we were co-conspirators. 'A bit of rough, eh? Wouldn't like to run into her up a dark alley. And those kids. Tomorrow's delinquents, mark my words.'

My face grew colder. I mightn't be that keen on Ma myself, but I'd got very fond Kian and Jennifer, and I wasn't going to listen to Jason putting them down. They were my neighbours, not his, and I felt he had no right to comment on them like that.

'Sorry,' I said to him shortly, 'but I have to go.'

'Sure. Me too. I'm hammered at work lately,' he confided. 'Still, can't complain. Not in this recession!'

I was beginning to wonder now whether he was on some kind of medication. He was carrying on like he was high, or something.

Just as he turned to go, he looked past me, into the hallway and up the stairs. 'Matthew not about?'

Something about his tone – suddenly soft, invasive – made every instinct go into overdrive. I moved my body so that his view into the house – my house – was blocked. 'Did you want him for something?'

He gave me a look that I couldn't describe. It was like that night I'd met him outside the house; he'd rattled me and was enjoying it.

He watched me closely. Then shrugged. 'Just making conversation.'

The words were out before I thought about them. 'We got engaged the other weekend, did you hear?'

I watched with satisfaction as something flared at the back of his eyes.

'I didn't. But congratulations.'

'Thank you. We had a bit of a party ourselves here, to celebrate, I hope we didn't keep you awake.'

OK, so that was twisting the knife a bit, I admit. But if anybody was playing games it was him, coming over to ask me to cater his bloody party, which I was pretty sure he'd fabricated. I had no idea what he was up to, but I wanted him to know that he'd better leave me out of it.

'Not at all,' he said, in a voice that I remembered, the one he used when things weren't going his way.

'Cheerio now.' And I closed the door on his unsmiling face.

★

185

'What did you go telling him for?' Matthew wanted to know.

'Why shouldn't I? We *are* engaged, or at least we were the last time I looked.'

'You were baiting him.'

'I was not.'

'Christ, Clara.'

'What do you think he was doing, coming to my door and asking me to cater his and his girlfriend's party?' I said hotly. I felt ashamed now in the face of Matthew's disapproval, like I'd let myself down.

'I don't *know* what he was doing,' Matthew retorted. 'I don't know if he's doing anything at all.'

It was like Jason had snuck into our lives unawares. One day we were happily settling ourselves into our new existence in Castlemoy, and the next, my ex had insinuated himself into our estate, and our conversations, without us knowing how.

Matthew took a breath. I could see that he was determined not to make a big deal out of things. 'I think the best thing we can do is ignore him.'

'Until he pinches our number plate again?'

'We have no idea if that was him. Your mother's right. Why on earth would he do something so childish?'

'You didn't see the look on his face when he asked me about it that night.' I refused to have my instincts written off too easily.

But Matthew wasn't writing them off. In a way, that was worse. 'Look, maybe the guy is a bit immature. Maybe he's still a bit sore over the way you gave him the boot.' He shrugged. 'We've all known people like that. So he's decided to rattle your cage a bit; once he sees that you don't rise to it, he'll just stop.'

I took a breath. I felt better. 'You're right.' For all his apparent sophistication, Jason *had* sometimes struck me as immature.

'Mind you, it'd be a bit easier to ignore him if he wasn't going past our house several times a week to visit his girlfriend,' Matthew grumbled.

'Well, yes. But I suppose we can't dictate his romantic choices.'

Presuming they weren't on purpose too, just to niggle me. But that would be really crazy.

When I looked at Matthew, though, I wondered if the same thought had just crossed his mind.

'Look,' I said, feeling that I had somehow ruined the evening, 'I'm sorry I said anything to him, OK? But he just annoyed me. I mean, what kind of person shows up on someone's doorstep at ten past eight in the morning? He could have come at any time, but he didn't. He wanted to catch me off guard.'

'I suppose he was on his way to work.'

He had a point.

'So you think maybe we're being a bit paranoid?'

'I don't know.' Matthew chewed his lip. 'I just don't trust the guy, that's all. He doesn't seem to read the normal signals.'

We tried to concentrate on our takeaway menus from the Chinese. I don't know why we even bothered with the menu any more, seeing as we both knew it off by heart. Our number was saved in the restaurant's phone by now. 'Ah! Miss Clara!' they always said when I rang up. Then, if more than forty-eight hours had passed since my last order, 'Long time no see!' Fat bitch, I was sure they were adding in their heads; you'd never think she was a bloody chef, with the amount of our (tasty) Chinese/Indian/Thai/North American food she puts away. But they would never say such things because they were very nice people, and their King Prawn Omelette (from their 'European' section) had been surprisingly good last week, both Matthew and I had agreed.

But neither of us seemed to have any appetite tonight. Eventually, Matthew put his menu down and said to me, 'Don't go mental when I ask you this.'

'What?

'About your break-up with Jason.'

I knew what he was going to ask straight away. 'What, you think there was more to it than I told you?'

'Don't get defensive.'

'How the fuck do you expect me to be?'

'I need to ask, Clara. Did anything else happen between you?'

I was really cross now. 'You think a broken engagement wasn't enough? You want something more salacious? That I slept with his best friend or something? Or that maybe I jilted him at the altar but watered it down for you?'

I knew I was being a little unfair. Maybe he had a right to doubt me, given that I had taken years to come clean about it in the first place.

But Matthew didn't bring that up. Instead he backtracked immediately. 'I'm sorry. Jesus. I don't even know why I asked you. I suppose I was just trying to figure out why this guy suddenly seems to be around all the time. Please, don't be mad at me.' Then, as a peace offering, 'Would you like to split some barbecued ribs?'

I loved barbecued ribs. 'I suppose I could eat one or two,' I said. Might as well meet him half-way.

'And I thought we might try the Special Soup?'

'What's in the Special Soup?'

He consulted the menu. 'Pork, chicken, sweetcorn, minced beef, shredded duck, vegetables . . . pretty much the whole restaurant.'

'Go on, then. And some chips.'

They did great chips. Frozen, of course, but 'very high quality frozen', as we had been told a number of times.

Peace restored, Matthew rang in the order – 'Yes, us again' – and we settled down to watch some TV. We hadn't wanted a television at all, but Anita had insisted on giving us her old one, and Matthew had wired it up one night. And now we were completely addicted. We *loved* the diddly-eye reality shows, and the news, and the American murder series. 'Hurry up, it's starting!' was the constant cry in our house. There was an indentation in the new couch from where our bottoms sat, night after night, often with a takeaway in our laps.

'Will this be what married life will be like?' Matthew asked, after the food had been delivered and paid for, and we'd installed ourselves in front of the box.

'Yes. Although we might get some TV trays, for the food.'

'Good,' said Matthew in satisfaction.

We watched some dire cop show, so bad it was brilliant, and we nibbled our ribs and waded through the soup. Then we opened a bottle of wine, and held hands on the couch and everything was fine again.

'We can't let him get to us,' Matthew said suddenly.

I looked at him.

'If, you know, that's what he's trying to do.'

Chapter Thirty-one

I was gutted. There was no other word for it.

'It's the recession,' Sophie consoled me. 'There's a lot of instability out there in the markets, and consumer confidence is suffering, especially for high-end products and services like the one you're offering,' she said expertly.

The radio must be set to the news station in the hotel kitchens again. A few weeks back it had been stuck on Classic FM and Sophie had gone around humming the *1812 Overture* under her breath.

'I know,' I said, 'but to pull out with less than twenty-four hours to go?'

The next time I should charge a booking deposit; at least it would cover all the cheese and salami I was now stuck with in my fridge.

And all they'd sent me was a lousy email saying the circumstances were beyond their control. I'd emailed them back, saying I wanted a cancellation fee to cover my costs. I'd got no reply. I emailed again. And again. I never heard from them again, and the phone number they'd given me didn't connect.

'They could have gone bust.' Sophie was sanguine. 'It's happening all the time. Everything's great until they call a staff meeting at five o'clock and tell everybody not to turn up in the morning.'

That would make sense; the whole operation closed down overnight, phones and everything. On the bright side, I'd learned a lot from all the planning that had gone into it, so it wasn't completely wasted. It was just a shame that I was sitting in the Coffee Dock right now instead of networking at my first business booking.

'I could help you,' Sophie announced.

'With what?'

'The business. Handing out flyers and stuff.'

Alarm bells immediately went off.

'I could start one end of the town, and you at the other and we could meet in the middle. It wouldn't take us more than an hour or two.'

'Thanks anyway, Sophie, but I've already done that, with Anita.'

She sensed my reticence. 'What, were you not happy with me the other day?'

'No, no, you were great.'

Sophie had waitressed for me at a First Communion party I'd catered for the previous weekend. She'd been ultra professional, turning up early, in a starched uniform, and with her hair in a pristine bun. Her professionalism had extended to correcting people on which cutlery they should be using, and insisting that the Communion children get OFF the trampoline so that she could write down their lunch orders. Luckily, the child's mother – who was also paying my bill – had been too harassed to notice, and the father too locked, and so I'd got away with Sophie's tendencies that time.

'It's just that Eddie and Eleanora will probably want to do it next time,' I said, diplomatic.

I'd offered the Communion gig to them, but Eddie was rehearsing, apparently. Some new show. So he was going to be busy for the next while.

'Where?'

'What?'

'Where is it going to be put on? The play.'

'Oh, the usual,' he said vaguely. Some warehouse on a dark street, in other words, where you'd be lucky not to be stabbed on your way home.

'Let us know the dates and we'll come up and see it,' I told him.

'You don't have to come to *every* one.'

'I know, but we like to.'

'You don't.'

'Well, no, but we'll come anyway. Anita could do with a night out. She hasn't dropped any more weight since she won her award, and the distraction would be good for her.'

'She's probably just plateauing. She should stay in Castlemoy and concentrate on it,' was Eddie's advice, like he was some kind of weight-loss expert. And, thinking about it, he probably was.

'Oh, listen, maybe Eleanora's free? To do some waitressing?' I figured they could probably do with the money, especially if Eddie was back doing serious theatre again.

But Eddie went all vague on me again. These blooming method actors. 'I'll ask her, but I think she's busy too.'

He never got back to me. So Sophie had landed the Communion waitressing job instead. I wasn't sure which was more stressful – Eleanora tottering around with her falling-down hair and harassing guests for tips, or Sophie, ordering people about and whipping glasses off them before they'd finished.

'Sure,' Sophie said now, clearly disappointed. 'I understand.' She looked around, before leaning in suddenly. 'Between you and me, I'm looking round for something else. I don't want to be stuck serving tea and coffee all my life. I have kids, you know. I want to set them a good example. I want them to see that their mum is more than just a waitress in some crummy hotel.'

'Well, if I hear of anything . . .' I said to her.

'I meant if you were looking for a business partner, I'd be interested.'

To be honest, the words struck fear into my heart. Me and Sophie? Working in a kitchen together all day long? Suddenly I felt a deep and heartfelt sympathy for Valerie, even though you had to admire Sophie's ambition.

'I know what you think of me,' Sophie said unexpectedly. 'But I have savings. I'm not looking for a free ride or anything. I'll pay my way.'

God knows what would have happened next – I'd probably have ended up selling her a half-stake in the business – had we not been joined by Róisín, from work. She had a jacket on over her nurse's uniform, but I could see that the front of it was spattered with red, like she'd walked off the set of a Freddy Krueger movie.

'A bleeder,' she explained unnecessarily. 'A lot of them are on blood thinners after operations. I nearly had to sit on the poor man to make it stop.' She turned to Sophie. 'I'll have a cup of your best coffee, please, Sophie.'

'What, you think we have two tins of it, shite coffee and good coffee?' Sophie barked. '*All* our coffee is good.'

And she stomped off.

'Jesus Christ,' Róisín exploded. 'That one would give you a pain in your face with all her airs and graces.'

'What's wrong, Róisín?'

'Me? Nothing.'

'Come on. You're in an even worse mood than usual.'

She gave a furtive look round, like she was about to enter a sex shop, before leaning forward and speaking in a very, very low voice. 'Catherine phoned . . . would I meet her . . . try again . . . don't know what to do . . .'

'For God's sake, Róisín. Nobody's minding us. Would you stop getting your knickers in a twist and speak up?'

Róisín gave me a look. 'Anyway, I don't even know why I'm telling you, because I've made up my mind.'

'And?'

'I've decided that I'm not going to meet her.'

I was getting some mixed signals. Her lips were saying no, but the hope on her face was stark. There was nothing she wanted more than to leap into her car and zoom up to Dublin.

'Well, I think you're doing the right thing,' I said.

'I know.'

'Once the trust is broken it's very difficult to win it back.'

'I know.'

'She can't just snap her fingers and expect you to come running to Dublin like everything's OK.'

'I get the picture. Jesus, Clara, sometimes you think you know everything.'

She often tried this one on me; that I knew nothing about 'the scene', that I was just some heterosexual hick – although not as bad as Anita, obviously – who didn't have a clue how things actually worked. But Róisín wasn't all that experienced in the scene herself, and had never shown any interest in it, which was probably why Catherine had had the freedom to flirt all over Dublin without Róisín finding out.

'No,' I said, 'but you have to admit that I know most things.'

Another look. Then she cracked a small smile.

'Look, I just don't want you to get hurt again.' It was the nearest I could come to actually declaring Catherine a cad. I really liked Catherine; I just felt strongly that being promiscuous was the same thing no matter what scene you were in.

'And you think I do?'

I knew that look on her face. That wavering look. 'Róisín Maguire. Don't you dare weaken.'

'I'm not.' She looked bleak. 'I can't.'

We met Dominique in the supermarket where, it seemed, all portentous meetings seemed destined to take place. We'd gone there to stock up on Pringles Sour Cream & Onion and Double Decker bars, both clinically proven to cheer people up who'd lost catering gigs and hot girls.

Anita would have been appalled. Or, rather, the new Anita. The old Anita would have clapped her hands and said, 'Girls, girls! You forgot the two litres of Coke!'

But we hadn't.

'Full fat or diet?' Róisín mused.

'Do you even need to *ask*?'

Full fat, then. Anita (the old one) would have been proud.

Then all the sugar-fuelled happiness drained from Róisín's face as she looked to her left. 'For feck's sake,' she said crossly. 'Just as I was starting to enjoy myself. Now I have to look at *her*.'

Dominique was in the Personal Hygiene section, languidly filling her basket.

'I wonder how did she get into those jeans?' Róisín jeered. 'I'd say the zipper must have been made in an iron foundry, to hold that lot in.'

'Now, stop it, Róisín.'

'What are you defending her for?'

'I'm not.' I was just getting a little tired of Róisín's continuing hostility.

'Could have fooled me. Besides, she's brought that ex of yours back into your life.'

'Well, yes, but she didn't do it on purpose.'

We'd become very good at ignoring Jason, actually, just like we'd said we would. Sure, there was the occasional glimpse of his car coming or going from Dominique's house, and we'd crossed each other on foot at the entrance of the estate, but we didn't let it bother us. And he hadn't come near us either.

'OK,' I said, 'are we done here?' I wasn't about to entertain Dominique either.

'I'm not going to run out of the place just because she's here,' Róisín said defiantly.

It was too late, anyway. Dominique must have sensed some bad vibes coming her way because her heavily made-up eyes swivelled round, narrowed, and honed in on us. A flick of the fake, candy-floss hair, and here she came, wriggling along in those jeans.

'I still ask myself: how could I have snogged her?' Róisín moaned in anguish.

'You must have fancied her at the time.'

'I did not! I was young and confused! Stop talking about it before she hears us,' she begged.

'You're the one who brought it up, not me.'

Róisín clamped a hand on my arm to shut me up as Dominique arrived, basket swinging. 'Girls,' she said in greeting.

I had a sneaky look into her basket. Well, it would be impossible not to. It was full of razors, shampoo and other scented assortments.

She, in turn, gave our full-fat Coke and junk food a good going-over.

'Comfort eating, girls?'

'I'm surprised you're not at home writing,' Róisín retaliated. 'Dominique *Duverne.*'

If we'd expected Dominique to hang her head in shame and confess to being the Queen of Smut, we'd have been disappointed. Instead she threw back her head and laughed. 'I thought you might be tickled by it, alright. Do you remember all those hours we spent trying to come up with a new name?' At least I got to use it in the end.'

I almost found myself smiling back. It was nice to think back to our younger selves — at least, before the falling-out. But I could see that Róisín wouldn't be budged.

'Have you read any of my books?' Dominique enquired.

'Yes,' I said.

'No,' Róisín said, at the same time.

Clearly, one of us was telling porkies. Róisín blushed wildly, giving herself away.

Dominique, amused, let her get away with it.

'*I've Got Your Number,*' I said.

'What did you think?' she asked me.

'That I'm not as sexually sophisticated as you.'

That drew a wry smile. 'And what about you, Róisín?' Dominique looked at her, jokey. 'Did you like the girl-on-girl scene in chapter nineteen? I put a lot of work into that.'

Róisín went into a sort of spasm, the way she always did when anything vaguely lesbian was mentioned in public. She cast a look over her shoulder before she could stop herself.

Dominique, of course, saw. She looked alarmed. 'Ah, Jesus. Don't tell me you're still not out?'

Róisín looked at her, malevolent. 'My personal life has nothing to do with you any more. Do you understand me?'

Dominique suddenly dropped her haughty mask. 'Listen, that night at the disco. I'm sorry. I just thought it'd be a bit of fun.' She shrugged. 'And I wanted to know what it would be like to kiss a girl.'

'Stop speaking to me.' Róisín's voice was forbidding.

Dominique gave her a wicked smile. 'And you know something? It was really, really nice. You're a good kisser, Róisín Maguire.'

I thought Róisín's knees were going to give way and she was going to end up ón the floor, writhing in mortification.

'So do yourself a favour and stop hiding yourself away.' Then Dominique was turning to me, her face suddenly cold. 'Congratulations on your engagement.'

'Er, thanks.' I had no idea what I'd done to her.

'You have your man, and I have my mine, so let's just keep out of each other's way, OK?'

Now I was really puzzled. 'We are.'

'That includes summoning Jason over for cosy early morning chats on your doorstep.'

I was so surprised I said nothing for a minute. Which probably made me look guilty as hell. 'Hang on here,' I spluttered. 'I didn't "summon" him. *He* called over to *me*.'

She gave me a sharp look. 'I'm surprised at you, playing games. You were never like that. Don't start now.'

Chapter Thirty-two

Matthew finally took me to buy an engagement ring.
'I suppose we'd better,' he said, 'or else people will think we're just making it up.'

'Are you going to spend the full three months' salary on it?' I teased.

'Let's just say that I've emptied every jam jar in the house,' he assured me.

That must surely mean a trip to some swanky place in Dublin, where normally they try to discourage people like us from going in. I put on my new linen dress in anticipation, but there was no sign of the car being started up, and then Matthew declared we were going to 'shop local'.

'You mean O'Toole's on Main Street?' They had displays of Swatch watches in the window, and millions of carriage clocks, and ornamental cats. I felt my heart sink, but didn't want to spoil the moment by whinging.

'They keep their best stuff inside,' Matthew assured me. 'Besides, I think it's important to start building a relationship with them, seeing as I'll be buying your eternity ring there in a couple of years, once the kids start coming along.'

'Oh, really?' I tried to keep it light even as the horror deepened. Two awful rings, that I'd have to wear for the rest of my life. I'd probably be buried in them too, because the family would be too fearful that I'd pass them on in my will, and *they'd* be forced to wear them.

Then Matthew said, 'Joking! We're going to a swanky place in Dublin. And in that nice dress of yours, they're bound to let us in.'

Off we set, as happy as Larry (I'd made no mention of my encounter with Dominique, and Róisín, upon my instruction, hadn't either). We took only one small detour, to a massive, industrial-looking building that turned out to be an electrical suppliers, where we wandered amongst the blindingly white fridge-freezers, washing machines and dishwashers.

'I just need to check some prices.' Matthew feverishly scribbled on a scrap of paper. 'Those wasters are trying to take me for a ride.'

The tenants had bought the dishwasher themselves at what Matthew maintained was an extortionate price. Naturally, they wanted to be reimbursed.

There was another problem too, they said. Apparently there was no car parking. Well, there was some, but it was always taken, allegedly, and they had nowhere to park their cars. This was via Jo.

'And how is that our problem?' Matthew had said, baffled. Then, 'They have *cars*?'

'Apparently you told them when they viewed the flat that there was parking, but there isn't any,' Jo relayed on the phone.

'There *is*. There's an underground car park. It's not designated, but it's there, they just have to get in early. And there's parking on the street.'

'I know, but that's not the same, though, is it? As saying, "yes, there is parking"?'

'I suppose not.' Beads of sweat had broken out on his upper lip. Another landlord cock-up. 'What could we do to make it up to them?'

'They suggested a small reduction in rent.'

'*What?*'

'Sorry about this.' Jo sounded mortified.

'No, *we're* sorry, putting you through all this. Here, they're not being cheeky to you or anything, are they? Because if they are . . .' Nobody knew what Matthew would do, but we all assumed it would be something terrible.

'No, no.'

'Well, if it gets too much, just say, and we'll get a letting agency to deal with them.'

'I'll stick it out for the moment. Let me know what you decide about the rent reduction and I'll pass it on.'

'Isn't she just *great?*' we said, when she'd hung up. 'Dealing with those brats for us. I think we owe her shoes as well as a handbag at this stage.'

In the electrical appliance place, Matthew seemed to be reluctantly conceding that dishwashers cost more than he'd realised. He put his scrap of paper away at any rate.

'These damn tenants, and their fecking rights,' I said, to cheer him up.

'Exactly. Shouldn't be allowed.' It seemed to have done the trick. 'Now, let's go get that ring.'

We had a lovely time on the motorway to Dublin. We spent the whole journey planning the wedding.

'We'll have the ceremony in Castlemoy, I suppose,' said Matthew.

'Yes, in that church at the top of the town that neither of us ever sets foot in.'

'Well, yes . . .'

'Officiated over by the priest whose name we don't know.'

We exchanged a look. 'It's OK,' he said. 'It's what everybody does. I'll find out his name on Wednesday night at darts.'

Reassured, I reached over and squeezed his leg. 'What about the reception?'

'Would we have it in the hotel?' Matthew ventured.

'The hotel? You mean, the *hotel* hotel?'

'I know what you're thinking—'

'With Sophie pissing the guests off and Valerie poisoning everybody with her awful coffee? And all our London guests – Mad Mags and Cool Art and Jo and *everybody* – wandering around trying to find the spa and wondering why their rooms don't have forty-two-inch plasma TVs?'

I didn't want to be a snob. But it would be *carnage*.

'Just listen,' said Matthew. 'I know I was joking earlier about getting the ring in O'Toole's, but if we're going to live in Castlemoy, then I think we should celebrate our wedding there. It mightn't be the swankiest place in the world but I'd rather have it in the local hotel than some flash but soulless castle.'

'We can't afford a flash but soulless castle.'

'I know, honey, but that's not the point. Castlemoy is your home town, Clara. And it's going to be mine now, too.'

Well, how could you argue with that? His intentions, as always, were clear and honourable. And, thinking about it, it was the right thing to do. Why *wouldn't* we get married amongst family and friends, close to home? We'd be able to say to our kids as we drove past, 'Look! That's where Mummy and Daddy got married, in that church there – we'll go in some day, I promise – and there's the hotel where we had our reception. Well, it used to be a hotel, now it's a multistorey business hub run by a lady called Sophie.'

'You always make me look like such a lightweight, next to you,' I grumbled to Matthew.

'I know,' he soothed. 'Look, it won't be so bad. We'll tell all the guests that the hotel is deliberately retro. They'll love it.'

'I suppose.'

'But if you really want the castle . . .'

'Haven't we got one at the top of the town?'

His face lit up. 'We'll have the wedding photos taken there. It's going to be perfect.'

The ring was stunning. The sales assistant – who wasn't at all snobby and let us in no bother – was murmuring away to Matthew about carats and clarity and six-prong settings but all I could see was this solitaire on my finger, and it was GORGEOUS.

'Clara, would you like to try on a different one?' Matthew was clearly fired up by the sales assistant and determined to test-run everything in the shop.

'No. I'd like this one.'

'Are you sure? Because there are other ones here, beautiful ones. We have all day.'

'Please,' I begged him, 'can we just get this?'

He knew when my mind was made up. He looked at me for a minute, his eyes smiling into mine. 'Of course we can.'

I lowered my voice to a hiss. 'That's if it doesn't cost too much.'

It wasn't the kind of jewellers that had price tags attached by little pieces of string, like O'Toole's, so that you nearly had to dislocate your neck trying to see how much the Swatch watches were. Instead Matthew was led away, given a stiff brandy and half a Valium (or so he said) and the damage was revealed to him gently, and in stages.

Eventually he rejoined me, a little pale, but otherwise OK. 'It's all sorted,' he said. He turned to the sales assistant. 'May I?'

'Of course, of course.'

Before I knew what was happening, the ring was handed to Matthew, and a stray chair was whisked away. So was the sales assistant, by some other, higher up assistant, until the shop was empty except for Matthew and me, and presumably a hundred CCTV units.

Matthew dropped to one knee in front of me, the ring in his hand. 'Matthew . . .'

'It's OK,' he said, 'I have the receipt, it's a hundred per cent yours.'

He took my hand and looked up at me. The joking fell away and he became very serious. 'I don't think I asked properly the first time. Clara, will you marry me?'

His eyes looked a bit shiny. And I realised that my own were wet too, even though this was just a formality.

'Definitely,' I said, and we had a lovely, romantic kiss that was probably being watched in the staff room on the CCTV.

★

Matthew put on 'Should I Stay or Should I Go' in the car on the way home. 'Just to keep things fresh,' he told me. 'Marriage isn't all a bed of roses, you know. We'll have to work at it. Starting with that blow-up bed.'

I was glad he'd brought that up. 'I agree, let's get rid of it.' It had been fun for a while, but we should embrace the marital bed from now on, like proper grown-ups.

'I meant we should repair that puncture in it.' He put on a fresh CD: Queen, and 'I Want to Break Free'.

I gave him a dig. 'You could be free sooner than you think.'

We sang loudly along to Matthew's hit list until we pulled off the motorway into a McDonald's. While Matthew was inside getting us a quick burger, I admired my ring again. It was just so . . . sparkly. I'm pretty sure there was a far more elegant and sophisticated way to describe it, but that's what struck me the most. Like a child, I turned it this way and that, making the light bounce off it. Then I held it out to the side mirror, just to see how it might look to other people. Well, to Jo, who would probably be the most critical.

In the side mirror I saw Jason's car.

Was it? No, probably just one like it. I was getting paranoid. It was parked near the drive-thru area. The windows were slightly tinted, making it difficult to see in . . . but then I recognised the licence plate.

I felt my nerves jangle. What was Jason doing here?

Reason kicked in again almost immediately: he might simply be hungry. Or he could have stopped by for a coffee. Why not? He might have pulled in to take a phone call, or to use the bathroom. There could be any number of perfectly valid reasons why he was in this restaurant car park, on this afternoon, in his car, just like us. There was absolutely no reason to get into a tizzy.

And so I deliberately turned my eyes away from the side mirror and stuck another CD on. I was glad of the noise, but it meant I didn't hear footsteps approach the car and when the driver's door flew open, and something landed in my lap, I nearly passed out with fright. 'Jesus Christ Almighty!'

It was Matthew. He looked taken aback. 'I got you a Big Mac, is that OK?'

'Yes. Lovely.' My heart felt like it was going to burst out of my chest. I scrabbled to rescue the warm takeaway bag that was sliding off my knees.

'Everything OK?'

'Yes, yes, fine.' I made my voice nice and normal. 'Will we go?'

Normally we'd have eaten our burgers in the car but I just wanted to get away.

'Sure. I can eat on the run.' With another quizzical look, he started the car.

Jason's car started up behind us.

'Clara, I can't see with your head.' Matthew indicated apologetically for me to sit back; that he couldn't see into the side mirror as he manoeuvred his way out into the traffic.

'Sorry.' I flattened myself back against the seat. I tried to listen to the song as we set off for home again.

'You're very quiet.' Matthew looked over at me.

'I'm eating.' Actually, I'd hardly touched my burger.

'Don't tell me you're having second thoughts already?' he teased.

Jason's car was behind us. Not directly behind, but two cars behind, like you see in cop shows on the telly. Or maybe I was just going mad.

'Clara,' Matthew prompted me.

Should I say something? But it would just sound hysterical: 'Don't look now, but my ex is on our tail!' Matthew might slow down and try to confront him. We could have an awful accident. And when the ambulance people came to cut us out, I would look like an awful eejit when Jason explained to them, traumatised, 'I just stopped in for coffee on my way home from a meeting with a client. I didn't even see them until they tried to ram me.'

I took a calming breath. This thing was big only if I let it be. We'd just come from buying my engagement ring; my fiancé had gone down on one knee, just like in all the best fairy tales – was I going to let Jason find his way into our perfect day and spoil it?

'I was just trying to think up some stunning riposte,' I said to Matthew, spirited. 'But I can't. I still want to marry you.'

Matthew gave a sigh. 'I was afraid you'd say that.'

And I laughed. I didn't look in the mirror the rest of the way home.

Chapter Thirty-three

'What are we going to do about Róisín?' Anita wondered. 'Why, is she worse?'

'Well, she's not any better, is she? Not that she'd talk to you or anything. That one's so paranoid that she wouldn't give you the time of day in case it got out and her reputation was ruined.' Anita sniffed at Róisín's crookedness. 'But a mother knows when her lesbian daughter is pining over the woman who shafted her for another, probably more fun, lesbian.' She sighed. 'Oh, I wish she'd had an easier life. Sometimes I lie awake at night, and think, if only we lived in Tokyo.'

I looked at her. '*Tokyo?*' I don't think I'd ever heard her mention Tokyo before. Ever.

'Well, it'd be so much easier for Róisín in a big city, wouldn't it? Like New York, or LA, better still. Nearly everybody in LA is gay,' she announced.

'Are you sure about that?'

'Long Beach is. I've been on the internet. Same-sex couples are very accepted there. There are robust LGBT communities all over the place.'

'Do you even know what LGBT stands for?'

'I certainly do. It's Lesbian, Gay, Bisexual and . . . oh feck.' The T was stumping her. 'Trying-It-Out?'

'That's three words. And no. It's for Transgender.'

Anita couldn't help herself; she burst into a volley of laughter, and it was great to hear, as she'd been a bit short on laughter recently. 'I was close enough,' she said, wiping tears from her eyes. 'God, isn't the world a great place nowadays, when you think about it. All these things you can be. When I was growing up, you either married whatever man asked you, or else you stayed home to look after your ailing mother.'

'You can stop giving me that hopeful look, Anita. I'm not calling off my engagement to look after you.'

'Who asked you to? Haven't I turned over a whole new leaf all by myself? I'm practically a new woman.' The words were feisty, but I thought her tone lacked a certain oomph. Still, she might well be tired. Six miles of power walking would knock the stuffing out of anybody. 'And why do you keep looking in the rear-view mirror?' she asked.

'Because I'm driving. It's what you're supposed to do.'

We drove on. The silence stretched. Now there was no denying Anita's little sighs.

'Anita,' I said, 'is everything OK?'

'Great, great.'

It was clear it was not. I wondered if she missed Dad. More than usual, that was. His anniversary was coming up and, even though it had been seven years now, she could get a bit in on herself. It was only normal.

And it wasn't like her life had changed in any dramatic way since he'd gone. Some people who'd been widowed discovered a passion for chess, or they joined set-dancing, or they might even have met someone new.

Anita had just kept going on like before, except that she didn't get out as much − Dad had liked picking mushrooms in the woods, and would often drag her along, or else the two of them would take a trip up to Dublin. But since he'd died it was the telly and a trip to Mass on a Sunday.

'It's just that you seem a bit down.'

'You'll only think it's stupid.'

'I won't.'

'I haven't lost any weight in two weeks.'

'Is that all?'

'See? I knew you'd only laugh.'

'I'm not laughing, Anita.' But I was a little surprised she was taking it so badly. 'Anyway, aren't you doing great? You've already lost loads of weight. Plus there's all the exercise you've been getting. Isn't Dr Mooney delighted with you?'

'He just tells me to keep up the good work.'

'Well, isn't that great?'

'Great?' Mam burst out unexpectedly. 'Eating rabbit food, day in, day out? Not able to cook anything I like? Walking for miles and miles, drinking litres of water, even though I hate the bloody stuff. Oh, it's great fun, alright. What else would I want to be doing, except torturing myself day in, day out, my whole life changed overnight? I used to enjoy myself, you know. Now it's just misery.'

She sounded completely fed up, in stark contrast to her gung-ho attitude of the last few weeks. Surely it couldn't have worn off already.

'I know it's tough, but do you think maybe you'll get used to it?'

Anita shot me a look. 'That's the thing. I keep thinking, it's only for another few weeks, like those diets I used to go on, but it's not, is it? It's for the rest of my life. I'll never be able to sit down with a steak and chips again, or make one of my luxury Christmas cakes, or at least not for me to eat. Oh, why did I do this to myself?'

My heart went out to her. It must be how a lot of people ended up: in some consultant's room wishing they'd taken more care of themselves years ago. You just never think it's going to catch up on you.

'Come on, Anita. You're just having a bad day.'

Róisín had said this could happen with people in Anita's position; they'd begin to take it all very seriously, and embark upon a strict diet and exercise plan, and generally get very zealous about the whole thing. Then they came a cropper when the weight stopped coming off, no matter what they did to try to shift it. It wouldn't be their fault at all; it was the disease, and the way the body dealt with sugar.

It looked like Anita had hit the roadblock. And sorry and all as I felt for her, I knew that I couldn't let her waver; it would be disastrous if she fell off the wagon.

'A session with Susie will get us focused again.' We were on our way to Burn That Butt in the Community Centre.

'Oh God!' Anita howled.

I didn't really blame her. It was a wet, miserable night, and Anita could have been at home watching the regional finals of *Dance for Your Supper*. The little lad in the waistcoat was tipped to go through.

'I know it's hard. But there're two of us in it. It'll be a bit of fun,' I cajoled her along. 'Afterwards, we'll stop off for a Diet Coke at the hotel on the way home, how about that?'

Anita crossed her arms. 'I think I preferred Róisín.'

I indicated and pulled into the Community Centre.

Behind me Jason's car slowed briefly, then drove on.

Chapter Thirty-four

Hey Hon!
I'm afraid to ring in case Matthew picks up, so I thought I'd break the news to you in an email instead.

The tenants have a situation with the bathroom. Well, it's mostly one of them. Apparently there's mould growing on the shower tiles. Now, if you want to know the truth, I had a look and there *is*. The tenants took a photo of it, which I'm attaching, and you'll see what I'm talking about. But, in my inexpert opinion, it's only a small bit and you shouldn't have to retile the whole thing. They want it fixed because one of them – the pain in the arse one – has asthma, and mould can exacerbate it, apparently. Oh, and tell Matthew not to shoot the messenger!!!

So tell us – are you demented with wedding plans? The girls are desperate to know all the details – we went to Falvio's last night, it was a 2.00 a.m. job, I had to have a snooze this morning in Brenda's office chair (I *did* tell you she's in rehab, didn't I?). The girls are *very* enthusiastic about attending a 'traditional Irish wedding'. And don't worry about the hotel. Mad Mags said that if she goes on one more luxury spa weekend, she'll puke, and that she'll actually quite enjoy a narrow single bed with nylon sheets, and with no TV (joke! joke!). Oh, and she wants to know if the invitation is a Plus One. 'Mags,' we said, roaring with laughter, 'don't be daft, won't you be picking up someone at the wedding?' And she gave us this filthy look and announced, 'Philip will be coming with me.'

For a minute we thought she meant *Prince* Philip, because you know that biography she was reading of the Royal Family the time you left? Well, she's still reading it. But it turns out that Philip is her boyfriend!! I still can't get my head round it. Jane nearly went into early labour with the surprise of it all. 'But, Mags,' we said, wondering if early dementia had set in, 'you never stick a man for more than three dates.' At that point she got very stroppy and produced this photograph of some man that actually *did* look a bit like Prince Philip; distinguished, regal bearing, etc., totally unlike Mags's usual rides. But we're not allowed to meet him, apparently, in case we contaminate him. At the moment they're getting to know each other over expensive dinners out and visits to museums. Usually Mags just takes them straight to bed to get to know them, but apparently this one is 'different' (I know! Hilarious!). I wanted to know if she was having some kind of mid-life crisis, seeing as her fortieth is coming up – we're not allowed to mention it, by the way, it's a banned topic – but then didn't Don start ringing up Jane to ask her how were her varicose veins/swollen ankles/heartburn? The guy is so over-protective. By the end of it, we all had heartburn and couldn't face dessert. Mags and me have both agreed that we're never, ever getting pregnant. Or not by Don, anyway. Mags says that baby will come out wearing a polo neck.

Then we had two more glasses of wine each (Jane had mineral water) and then I got randy and so I hopped in a taxi to F.'s place (that's all I'm telling you) and jumped on him. And promise you won't throw this back in my face in the event of it all going horribly wrong, but I think I might be in love.

Eek! Can't believe I said that.

PLEASE reply, or else I'm going to start thinking you've gone into hiding.

Jo ☺ x

PS: How's the romance going across the way? If I were you, I'd buy a big thick set of net curtains and put them up. Seriously, though, you haven't mentioned your ex, even though I've asked you several times. So I'm presuming that everything has settled down nicely.

I was trying not to notice, but Jason's car seemed to follow me a lot. I would glance in my rear-view mirror and suddenly it would be there, or maybe a car or two back, but visible all the same.

Mostly, it was on short journeys; up to the takeaway to pick up our barbecued ribs and chips, or the Esso to get milk for the morning. He never stopped or anything, just drove on past whenever I would pull in, as though he was going about his business. Once, when I'd turned into my drive, he'd been right behind me. He'd turned into Dominique's, opposite, and had got out and gone into hers, without so much as a glance in my direction, like he hadn't even noticed me.

It had to be a coincidence, right? He couldn't possibly be going out of his way to follow me; and even if he *was*, why? It didn't make sense.

Plus, this was a small town. You ran into the same people over and over again. For example: one day I'd ended up driving behind Anita in her car, all the way up the town and out to the big supermarket on the Old Dublin Road.

'Are you monitoring me?' she'd said, defensive, when I ended up bumping into her in the frozen food section.

'No, Anita. I just happen to be doing my shopping at the same time as you.'

'See?' She waved a hand at her trolley. 'Nothing but frozen peas.'

And a packet of biscuits, I saw.

'You needn't give me that look. I'm allowed a small treat every now and then. They told me that. I'm not going to eat the whole pack. And, for your information, I feel perfectly fine.'

I let it pass. She seemed in good form. I didn't want to ruin that by going on about the biscuits; and it *was* only one pack, and they were plain ones.

Then, after I'd loaded up my car and set off for home, I saw that Anita was now following *me* back into town. Oblivious, she drove behind me all the way down Main Street, before peeling off to head out to her own house.

There weren't many places you could go in a town the size of Castlemoy. People made the same journeys every day from the chemist to the super-market and to the twenty-four-hour Esso station. If you were to get excited every time you felt someone was following you, you'd end up in the loony bin.

On some days, though, it was easier just to stay at home.

Chapter Thirty-five

'Where have you been hiding away?' Róisín wanted to know. We were having a coffee in the hotel as part of her rehabilitation as a single, rural-based lesbian.

'Nowhere.'

'I haven't seen you up the town in ages. And Sophie says you haven't been in for a coffee in two weeks.'

I looked over at Sophie. She probably kept a log on every customer: date, time, type of coffee ordered and with/without stale croissant. She'd greeted me like a long-lost friend when I'd walked in.

'I've been working.'

'Bookings are up, then?'

'Well, no,' I admitted. 'I've had a lot of enquiries, though.'

Unfortunately, not all of them turned into bookings. I was currently in protracted email contact with a woman called Anne Marie who was planning a garden party. A lovely, lovely woman, no doubt, but Jesus, she'd wreck your head. She asked a million questions, each requiring a separate email response: did I do hot and cold food? Could I provide a children's menu? Was my produce organic? How long were the lamb koftas? (Matthew's eyebrows had jumped up at that.)

And now that I'd answered all of her queries, every single blasted one, she'd suddenly gone quiet on me. I'd sent her a reminder email only that morning but I knew deep down that I'd never hear from her again. It was just like what had happened with a guy called Ian Fleming who'd strung me along for weeks about some corporate do, and just when we'd got everything tied down and it was time for him to pay his deposit, he disappeared off the face of the earth.

'Didn't Ian Fleming write the James Bond books?' Matthew had said suddenly.

'Well, yes. Why?'

'I'm just saying.'

Róisín was watching me keenly. 'And the wedding? How are the preparations coming along?'

'Fine. Any more questions or is the interrogation complete?'

'I'm not interrogating you. Well, alright, I am. Anita rang me up and said you haven't been over to go out on walks, and to take her to Burn That Butt. Mind you, she didn't sound too upset about that. Anyway, I've been sent to "suss you out".'

'She's too much time on her hands.'

'Tell me about it.'

'No, Róisín. She really does have too much time on her hands. We need to do something about it.'

'Well, if you'd stick to the plan of taking her for walks . . .'

Guilt-ridden, I said, 'She's been a bit down. I think it'd be easier for her if she wasn't sitting around the house all day long, with nothing to think about apart from food. I'm worried she'll slip back into her old ways.'

But Róisín was a healthcare professional – I could never say this to her face – and possibly a little hardened to people being down. She dealt with a lot of misery in her day-to-day career, at least to hear her go on. So our mother being down didn't exactly have her running for the door with a nice big bottle of pills in her hand.

'She's going through an adjustment process,' she assured me. 'It's normal to have some ups and downs. I'll call around later and check on her, OK? Anyway, just so I can tick this off my list, you really are grand? The countryside isn't doing your head in? You and Matthew

215

aren't having big bust-ups on a weekly basis, only you're too embar-rassed to tell me?'

It was on the tip of my tongue to tell her about Jason following me around in his car. But I didn't want to create a drama where none prob-ably existed. So I said, 'Like I said. I've just been keeping my head low, working.'

Róisín waved a hand, 'Great, great,' and finished up her coffee. Today they were so weak that we were really only drinking warm milk with a load of drinking chocolate sprinkled on top. Then she gave a sigh and said, 'I'd better go home and plough through this lot.'

She had a pile of flyers in her hand, picked up from the coffee table designated for such things. It was an eclectic selection: Cheese-making. Ukulele for Beginners. Mountaineering for Fun and Fitness.

'I'm surprised you didn't pick up the one for Lion Taming or Knit Your Own House.'

'Laugh all you want. But I'm going to need something to fill my evenings now that I'm single again.'

'Or – and this is really wild – you could chuck all those flyers in the bin, get yourself a push-up bra and go on the pull. I'd even go with you.'

'Believe it or not, a push-up bra is not the solution to all my problems.'

'Nor is sitting at home with a ukulele.'

'I hear it makes a very nice sound.'

Sophie gave us a strange look as she passed us by. 'Valerie,' I heard her say, 'what are you putting in that coffee?'

'Very fecking little,' Róisín complained.

'Listen, I know you're still sore over Catherine. But is this really the solution?'

'As opposed to what? And please don't mention push-up bras again. You clearly know nothing about me if you think I'd ever be caught dead in one of those.'

'Look, I've been thinking about what Dominique said in the supermarket.'

'Not Dominique again,' Róisín exploded. Quietly, that was; there were people around, after all.

'She has a point. All these years later and you still haven't come out. Not properly, anyway. Not in your normal, everyday life.'

Róisín gathered up her flyers fast. 'I don't know what gives you the right to keep commenting on my personal life. You all do it, like it's some kind of sport. I don't comment on yours, do I? I don't wonder how often you and Matthew have sex, or whether Mam is missing it in her life now that Dad is gone, or whether Eddie and Eleanora regularly swing from the chandeliers.'

'This isn't about sex, Róisín. It's about you being happy.'

'You get on with your life and I'll get on with mine, OK?'

I bumped into Jason on the steps of the hotel.

'Hi,' I said, and made to go on by.

But somehow he angled himself so that I was hemmed in by the wall. To the casual observer, it looked like we were in intimate conversation.

'Clara,' he said. 'I haven't seen you in ages.'

'I've been busy. Actually, I've got an appointment now, so . . .'

He didn't move. 'I hope you haven't been avoiding me?'

I saw the amusement in his face. The guy was getting off on this.

I deliberately kept my voice bland. 'Why would I do that?'

'Well, as I keep telling Dominique, it can't be easy for you. Watching me and her together. And right across the road from you, too.'

He'd tried this one on me before – the fake jealousy angle – and so I was ready for it. 'You're mistaken.'

'I think it's only fair to warn you. Things are going very, very well for us. So I guess I'll be around a lot more,' he said sympathetically.

I looked him straight in the eye. 'If you really want to know, I think it's very, very sad that you're behaving like this, Jason.'

This was probably breaking our ignore-him rule, but he needed to know that his behaviour was pathetic.

But he just smiled, like we were merely jousting or something. He was enjoying himself. Anything further I might say would only add to it.

'Goodbye,' I said, and I pushed past him and onto the street.

'Oh, and, Clara?'

I turned before I could help myself.

'Nice pyjamas you were wearing this morning.' He winked at me. 'You should keep your curtains closed upstairs. Anybody can see in.'

Chapter Thirty-six

The doorbell rang. My first instinct was not to answer it.

It was hard to believe that only a few short months ago, I'd have been delighted at the distraction. The doorbell, the telephone, the postman – I welcomed them all. Any excuse to abandon my computer and have a fifteen-minute chat.

But now I had an unpleasant feeling in the pit of my stomach. I looked out the bay window; Jason's car wasn't there.

The relief lasted only a second before I felt worse; I was in my own house. What was wrong with me? Since when did I need someone's permission before I could answer my front door?

It turned out to be Maura, The Knob's wife.

'Hi,' she said. She looked at me, uncertain. 'Is this a bad time?'

'No, no. Not at all.' I gave her a big smile to show her just what a good time it was.

'I only wanted to know if you were going to cheer the lads on?'

'I might, for the laugh.'

'That's the problem,' she sighed. 'I'm afraid I actually *might* start laughing.'

The darts lads had only gone and entered a competition. Their first ever. It was at the Spring Lodge Hotel and Country Club, about twenty-five miles away, and there was much feverish discussion about who would drive, and furtive trying on of polo shirts in their bedrooms at night.

'I blame Matthew,' Maura said. 'They were perfectly content to fling a few darts around in the pub until he came along, and motivated them.'

It was Matthew's continued improvement that had got the lads' backs up. Well, they couldn't let themselves be outdone by some fella who'd only been in the country a wet weekend, with a fancy darts set he'd bought in Dublin. So they started to practise at home too, furtively, and the standard improved beyond all recognition. So much so that one night, The Knob had joked, 'Jesus, lads, we could nearly enter a competition.'

But when Maura told me the competition was taking place on Saturday night, and not on Sunday, as I had thought, I realised that I couldn't go. I had a booking, for once.

'That's a shame,' Maura said. 'I'd have liked to have caught up. Raked over the past.' And she gave me a sudden smile of friendship. 'Bad mullets and other atrocities.'

'It wasn't exactly a mullet . . .'

'You don't have to be kind. Still, everybody had them. It could have been worse.' And she looked over her shoulder at Dominique's house. '*She* hasn't changed a bit.'

'Yes, well.' I hadn't spoken to Dominique since she'd 'warned me off' in the supermarket. Jason, it seemed, was fond of telling her lies about me, and I had no interest in finding out what else he might have said to her about me.

'She told me she's a writer now.' Maura smiled. 'She gave me one of her books. *Touched*. To be honest, you'd want to be touched to make it past page three. I've had to put it away on top of the wardrobe in case it falls into the wrong hands.' She gave me a look. I could just imagine The Knob stumbling across it, and the ensuing trauma.

'When you're finished, we'll swap,' I joked. 'We have *I've Got Your Number*.'

'God only knows what the new one will be called. *Barely Legal*, maybe, given the solicitor connection,' Maura quipped.

It felt good to be laughing about Jason. It made me feel less like pulling down my blinds and hiding behind them all day.

Maybe Maura had sensed some disharmony on the estate because she said unexpectedly, 'They're not getting on great, you know. Her and him. We hear them in the back garden sometimes. Rowing, and stuff. I'd be surprised if it lasted a whole lot longer.'

She said nothing more, but it was enough. So Jason's goading that he and Dominique were practically about to tie the knot had just been to rattle me, as I'd suspected.

'Thanks, Maura.'

We both looked to my left, as the front door of the house beside mine flew open. Ma appeared, clutching a load of empty shopping bags to her vast middle, and clearly not pleased to see us.

'Hello,' we called.

She gave us a look. 'Hello,' she said at last, like it killed her.

'When are you due?' said Maura enthusiastically. Like The Knob, Maura was one of life's good people. You simply could not dislike her.

Ma was going to give it a good go, though. 'What?' she barked.

'The baby.' Maura, smiling, indicated Ma's belly. 'Not long now, I'd say!'

I wanted to tell her to stop. Ma's face grew blacker and blacker.

But Maura kept bubbling enthusiastically. 'Jennifer and Kian will be delighted to have a new brother or sister to play with.'

Ma responded with a deafening silence. Even Maura knew now that something was wrong.

'You're not pregnant, are you?' she eventually said.

'No,' Ma ground out. 'I'm not.'

Maura flashed me a look. *Oh Christ.* I felt for her. But there wasn't a person on this planet who hadn't mistaken rotundity for pregnancy at least once.

'Terribly sorry . . .' Maura began, but Ma just got into her car and slammed the door in our faces. The car exhaust backfired rudely in our direction for good measure.

'I never thought I'd say it, but fecking Dubliners,' Maura said suddenly and viciously.

I was laughing and turning to go back in when she said, 'Listen, I hope you don't mind if I mention something.'

'Fire away.'

Her face was twisted into apology. 'It's your bins. I was just wondering if you wouldn't mind storing them at the back of the house. It must be dogs or something, but yesterday one of them was overturned and all the papers blew across the road into our place.' She was in agony now. 'I picked it up and put all the rubbish back, but just for the next time . . . Jesus, I hope you're not thinking, That one's an awful moany neighbour.'

'Not at all. I'm glad you told me.' I didn't like the thought of my neighbours seeing the contents of our bins.

'I'd better go get the dinner on. All this darts practice is hard work. Thomas will be starving.'

Thomas? Oh, yes. The Knob. I forgot for a minute that he had a real name, and that his wife would probably use it. It would be impossible to, for instance, have intimate marital relations with a person you called The Knob.

I called after her as she went back across the road. 'Maura? About the bins. Has it been more than once?'

She looked embarrassed again. 'A couple of times. You were never here. But it's OK, I picked everything up, you won't get fined!'

'Watch this,' said Matthew.

We were in the back garden, drinking bottles of beer, and he was strutting his stuff. He made sure he had my full attention before lifting the dart with cool ease. He eyed the dartboard for about ten minutes, then, with a mildly alarming lurch forward, he sent the dart arching through the air.

Bingo. It was a good one.

I immediately leaped up, grabbed the two mop heads I was using as pompoms and did my cheerleader's routine (I'd been accused of not being supportive enough). 'More, MORE! C'mon, push up that SCORE.'

Matthew did a pretend flick-back of his hair and checked the dartboard.

'Ladies and gentlemen, it's another EIGHTY POINTS.'

I pretended to swoon and fan myself.

'They're not going to know what's hit them at the Spring Lodge Hotel and Country Club,' he said with grim satisfaction. 'It'll be carnage.'

'I bet I could do better,' said Kian, unimpressed. He'd pulled the slide right up to the fence on his side of it, and was standing on top of it, looking over into our garden.

'Bet you couldn't. I've put in hours of practice every night this week while you were asleep.'

'I was not,' said Kian, outraged at the idea. 'I don't go to sleep until midnight.'

'He's lying,' said Jennifer. She'd climbed up beside him. 'And he snores.'

'Shut up! I don't snore!'

'Alright, kids,' I said, calming the situation with a handful of crisps from the bowl Matthew and I were snacking out of.

'We go to bed at eight,' Jennifer informed us crisply. 'Sometimes you sit out here kissing. We watch you.'

'Yeah,' said Kian, looking disgusted.

'We kiss because we're getting married,' I told them.

'Our ma and da aren't married,' Kian announced. Then, in another random thought, 'We're from Dublin.'

'I work in Dublin,' Matthew began eagerly, but neither of them displayed any interest.

'Ma says we don't belong down here, that the place is full of culchies, but we couldn't buy a house in Dublin because they cost too much,' Jennifer said. 'And now we can't sell, because Da says nobody wants to live in the arse end of nowhere, so we're stuck.' She didn't look too put out.

The back door opened. A man's voice cut through the air. 'Kian! Jennifer! What did I tell you about looking into people's gardens?'

'Why can't we?' Kian complained. 'Everybody does it.'

'Do I have to go out there to you?' the man threatened, but in a voice that said he was already settled on the sofa for the evening with a beer and couldn't be bothered.

It worked anyhow. They scrambled down so fast that we heard the slide topple over and hit the ground. Little feet ran across the lawn and a moment later the back door slammed closed.

Matthew and I smiled at each other. If we were lucky enough to have kids, I think we'd both have wanted them to be like Kian and Jennifer, except maybe without the rude hand gestures.

When I looked at Matthew a moment later, he was still watching me. I knew that look, and I tensed.

'Are you going to ask me if I'm fine?'

'No. Why?'

'Because everybody else seems to be asking me.' I knew I sounded tetchy.

'Is there some reason why you *wouldn't* be fine?'

'No.'

He shrugged. 'So what's the problem?'

The conversation was annoying me. I just wasn't in the mood for anything else today. 'The *problem* is that everybody seems to think that just because I stop pissing away my mornings having coffee in the Coffee Dock, and actually doing some work for a change, that there must be something wrong with me. That I must be down or depressed, or having big arguments with you. Well, I'm not, OK?'

'I think I'd know if you were having big arguments with me.' His tone was mild but his eyes were wary.

I needed to take it down a notch. It was just that I felt a bit claustrophobic tonight. And my arm hurt. I'd dragged all the bins into the side passage and I think I strained a muscle or something. Then I'd tried to screw a lock onto the wooden door, but I couldn't, and then I gave up and hid the lock in a kitchen drawer because how would I explain it when Matthew came home from work? I would look like a crazy person if I was to start going on about needing to keep packs of roving wild dogs out.

'The business isn't doing so well,' I said, because I had to offer *something*.

Besides, it was perfectly true.

'It's the middle of a recession, Clara. I know you'd like things to be better but I think you're just going to have to be patient.'

I dutifully nodded as he murmured soothing things to me about growth and word-of-mouth and competitiveness.

Then he said, 'Is there anything else? You know, bothering you?'

We both knew what he meant. I hadn't told him about my meeting Jason at the hotel. I didn't know why. Maybe because I felt soiled by Jason's comment about seeing me in my pyjamas. If I told Matthew he might feel the same. He also might go mental and do something stupid and I just didn't want to be responsible for that.

Ignore, ignore. Wasn't that what we'd agreed? For now, anyway.

'No,' I said. 'Except that my beer has run out.'

He was still watching me. He knew me too well. 'You've a lot going on, Clara. What with the business, and stuff. Maybe we should put back the wedding for a bit until things settle down?'

He was so good to me. Not prying, just trying to make things better.

'Are you kidding me? Absolutely not. No way.' This time, my smile was real.

'Are you sure?'

'Positive.'

The blind going down on the bedroom next door drew my eye upwards; Kian and Jennifer going to bed. A second later, the blind went back up a few inches, and Jennifer gave us a cheeky wave.

Matthew put his arms round me. 'Come on. Let's rally. They'll be expecting us to kiss.'

'Oh, will they?'

'They're only kids. Let's not disappoint them.'

Chapter Thirty-seven

The evening of the darts tournament had finally arrived. The lads were all to meet in Dirty Harry's for a final practice session and go on from there. The excitement was immense.

'I thought you had to be a beer-swilling fat bloke to play darts?' said Eddie.

Matthew fixed him with a look. 'If you ever get a part as a darts player, then I hope you do more research than that.' He was taking the whole thing very seriously. I watched as he packed bottles of mineral water, and some energy bars, like an élite athlete.

'Chance would be a fine thing,' Eddie muttered.

'Well, I hope you have a great match,' said Eleanora swiftly.

She wasn't looking as put-together tonight as she normally did, I noted. Her hair was ever so slightly greasy, and her eyes looked tired. I hoped the pair of them hadn't been out drinking water until all hours the previous evening, seeing as they were serving at my gig tonight. Neither of them had shown much enthusiasm at the chance to make some money, but Sophie's kids had the measles and I'd pulled in a favour. They'd driven – *driven* – down in a second-hand car they'd just bought. The way things were going, they'd be arriving by private helicopter next. And I'd bet that Chekhov wouldn't be paying for it, either.

'Oh,' said Matthew to Eddie, his face lighting up, 'we heard you on that new radio ad during the week.'

Eddie's own face turned to stone, but Matthew was so busy packing some plasters in case one of the team developed life-threatening chafing from the darts that he didn't notice, and went on happily, 'It's great, especially the bit where you break into *yodel-ay-ee-oo*—'

'I know.' Eddie cut him off, clearly scarred by the experience. Eleanora looked at her shoes, her face tight.

Matthew glanced at me: *oops*.

'It doesn't matter,' said Eddie at last, 'because I'm not doing any more of them.'

Eleanora made a strangled sound somewhere in the back of her throat.

'Why not?' I asked. Eddie had been doing very well at them. OK, so he clearly wasn't mad keen, but his voice sounded great and the money was good.

'Jimmy gave me my job back. He's hit the beer again and didn't recognise me. So now I'll be available for rehearsals, and won't have to turn down any more theatre parts.'

'And we'd better cross our fingers that we win the bloody lotto, because the pay Jimmy gives you doesn't go far, does it?' Eleanora threw back.

'I think you'd better jolly your staff into better moods before you unleash them upon your guests later on,' Matthew murmured to me.

There was the sound of a car horn outside; The Knob was doing the driving, poor Maura sitting in the back.

I waved as Matthew joined them, with much bravado-filled greetings of, 'Trying to scare the competition with that shirt?' and the like. Maura threw her eyes to heaven as they drove off.

And it was time for us to go, too.

I didn't look over at Dominique's house as I loaded the food for the party into my car. We must have made three trips, Eddie, Eleanora and myself, and not once did I look across the road. I had no idea if they were in, or out, or dancing naked on their front lawn (although that might have been harder to miss). I kept my eyes firmly in front of me, blocking everything else out.

'All set?' Eddie asked, as we were ready to go. He was going to take his car, and I would take mine.

'All set.'

For the first time in a couple of weeks, I felt in control.

The party went very well. Several of the guests came into the kitchen afterwards to ask for my card, and one of them made a firm booking. The host was delighted and had already promised to have me back.

Coming home, I was so high on the success of the night that I had no idea how long Jason's car was behind me before I noticed.

I was just coming back into the town when I looked in my rear-view mirror and saw it, clearly visible under the streetlights.

My stomach jolted unpleasantly. But it could just be another of those odd, small-town coincidences, right? No sense in jumping to all kinds of conclusions. Plus, he hadn't followed me *to* the party – I'd certainly have noticed that – so how could he have known I was on my way back?

I wished to God I wasn't on my own. But I'd stayed behind to talk to the hosts and had given Eddie the house keys and sent him on with Eleanora. They were staying with Matthew and me tonight. And my mobile phone was in my handbag, in the boot of the car, I just realised.

I pulled up at the first set of traffic lights on Main Street. So did he. I stared hard into the rear-view mirror, but could see nothing in the darkness. It didn't matter, though; I could feel his gaze on the back of my neck, as if he was touching me.

The lights went green.

Without thinking about it, I suddenly swung left. No indicator, nothing. He'd have expected me to go straight on, for home.

When I dared look in my mirror, he was gone. I relaxed. I felt like a bit of a drama queen now; yes, his behaviour had crossed the line several times, but that didn't mean he was up to some kind of intimidation campaign—

He was back. When I glanced in my side mirror, there was his car again, following a careful thirty yards behind. His lights were on full, not dimmed, blinding me.

I felt a slow burn inside. Fuck this. *Fuck* this.

I slowed down and watched in the mirror as he got closer. Twenty yards, then fifteen. When he was ten yards behind me, so close that I could almost read his tax disc, I slammed my foot on the brakes as hard as I could.

There was a loud squeal of tyres as he nearly crashed into the back of me.

I was out of my car in a flash, and marching to the driver's window before he'd even got his seatbelt off.

'Get out.' I rapped sharply on the window. 'Get the fuck out of your car.'

'Jesus Christ.' Jason was climbing out now, looking a bit shaken. And no wonder. Caught red-handed crawling round in his car after his ex-girlfriend. Bet he wouldn't like his clients getting wind of *that*.

'Just what the hell do you think you're playing at?' I demanded.

I was vaguely aware that two pedestrians, unsteadily making their way home from some late-night drinking session, had stopped at the commotion. I didn't care. Let them look. The more people who saw, the better.

'You could have got us killed,' Jason said coldly. He was over his fright and managing to look convincingly outraged.

'At twenty kilometres an hour? I don't think so.'

'What did you stop like that for?'

'To see your face when I finally tell you that I'm on to you.'

'*On* to me?' He looked highly exasperated now. A car behind us hooted and was then forced to pull out and pass us in the street. Jason waved to them apologetically – like this whole thing was my fault. Silly woman driver.

'As if you don't know what I'm talking about,' I threw at him.

'I haven't a clue, if you must know.'

'Let me spell it out for you, so. You've been following me. Don't even try to deny it. Every time I go out in my car you're there.'

He said nothing for a minute. Then, '*Following* you?', like it was the most baffling thing he'd ever heard; so baffling that it was almost amusing.

'Yes, Jason! In and out of my estate! To the chipper and back. You even followed me to the Esso garage one night.'

'And why exactly would I do that?' he asked slowly.

The calmer and more logical he was, the more furious I got. Somehow I knew it was a mistake to lose my cool but I couldn't help it. 'Well, I don't know, do I? Maybe you enjoy it!'

'Following you to the Esso station?' he stated in amazement, making it sound the most ridiculous, illogical thing ever.

And it *did* sound illogical.

'Look,' he said, kind now, which was worse. 'If you think I was behind you once or twice' – I SO was not, his face said – 'then I'm sorry, but I have no memory of it.'

I wasn't going to let him turn this on me. No way. 'Well, your memory is clearly failing you. But you must be able to remember five minutes ago? When I turned left at the lights, and you suddenly did too?'

Let him explain *that*.

'We turned left because that's where I live,' he said patiently.

I realised that his house was indeed in that direction. I'd just assumed he was going straight to my estate, to Dominique's. God knows he spent enough time there.

Then: he'd said 'we'.

Just as I realised that, the passenger door opened. Dominique climbed out. She shoved a load of puffy blond hair back from her face and glared at me. 'I nearly got whiplash because of you. You'll be lucky if I don't sue your ass, as we say in the US of A.'

Oh Christ. Dominique had been there the whole time. Listening to our conversation through the open driver's door; every word, clear as a bell.

'He's been following me,' I told her hotly. 'And probably stealing my licence plates too. Every time we're alone he makes some kind of off comment.' Why the hell should I protect him? 'The last time, he insinuated he'd been spying on me in my bedroom.'

230

There. It was all out.

But Jason just gave me a pitying look, and murmured to Dominique, 'What did I tell you? Deluded.'

'I am not deluded.' I appealed to Dominique this time. She would believe me, right?

But her eyes just narrowed further. 'I thought I told you to stay away? Spying on you. Would you give me a break?' Dominique snapped. She said to Jason, 'I told her to stay away.'

Now Jason was fussing over Dominique, ignoring me as though I were an irritating distraction. 'Are you sure you're OK?' His voice was warm with concern for her. 'Maybe we should get you checked out.'

'I told you, I'm fine. Let's just go before the whole night is ruined.' She looked back at me, with pity. 'Clara,' she said, 'speaking as an old friend . . .'

I wanted to vomit.

'. . . don't do this to yourself. It's just sad, OK?'

Then, with another swipe at her hair – the sudden stop had clearly unbalanced it – she got back into the car and shut the door.

I was left looking at Jason.

And his expression was different now. Unmasked. I was beginning to realise that he had two faces: a public one, and a private one just for me.

'Have a nice evening,' he said silkily.

When they pulled out, their car made a wide circle around me, like I was poison.

Matthew wasn't home yet when I got in. Just Eddie and Eleanora, fighting in the sitting room. As I slipped past to the kitchen I could hear them: '. . . such a jerk . . .', '. . . nothing wrong with washing dishes . . .', '. . . except for the crappy money . . .' '. . . oh, here we go! . . . money again . . . all you ever talk about . . .'

I got a beer from the fridge. I needed it. I looked at my hands. They were shaking.

'. . . maybe you'd be better off finding someone with a proper job . . .'

'. . . we're nearly thirty, sick of living like students . . .'

I desperately wanted to ring Matthew; even just to hear his voice. But what if he was in the car going home right now, squashed in with all the lads, and he put me on speakerphone, like he sometimes did without realising it, and everybody witnessed my shame? Because that's how I felt right now. Weird, and scared, and inexplicably ashamed, like the whole thing was my fault. Logically I knew it wasn't, but that wasn't washing right now.

Things were really kicking off in the sitting room.

'. . . why is it always my fault? . . . why don't YOU . . . ?'

'. . . don't shout at me . . .'

'. . . no, had enough of this . . .'

'. . . oh, cop on . . .'

I slipped out into the back garden and sat down on the grass, hugging my knees to my chin. It was the place where I was beginning to spend the most time. It was secluded and quiet out there, with the woods to look at, and not Dominique's house.

And nobody could see me out there. Well, except Kian and Jennifer, and I didn't mind them. They must be gone away for the weekend, though, maybe back to Dublin to visit, because their house was quiet and locked up, and I wished they were home.

Tonight I felt afraid, vulnerable. And shocked that somebody I knew was making me feel that way.

The back door opened and I nearly jumped out of my skin.

'Oh. Hi. Sorry, I didn't know you were out here.' It was Eleanora, shoulders hunched.

'It's OK. Do you want a beer?' I was even anxious for Eleanora's company; that's how bad things were.

'No, thanks.' She sounded a bit hoarse. When she lifted her face I saw that she'd been crying.

I heard the front door slam. Eddie, probably gone for a walk to cool down. Honestly, I'd had about as much drama as I could handle tonight.

'Look, Eleanora,' I said, sharper than I intended, 'you're not going to change him, OK? You can try, but he doesn't want to be a voiceover artist, or a TV presenter or whatever it is you're trying to push him into. He wants to do serious acting. There mightn't be any money in it, but it's his life, and he's managed so far.'

'Yeah, but only because he's been mollycoddled by you lot.' There were no chirpy smiles now; only a bitter look. 'Sending him cooked chickens and giving him money and coming up to Dublin to tell him how FANTASTIC he is.'

She was upset, I reminded myself. She was just letting off a bit of steam. 'There's nothing wrong with supporting him.'

'Yeah? I'd call it facilitating his immaturity and making him think he doesn't have to live in the real world.'

Whoa. That got my back up. 'You've only been going out with him a short while,' I reminded her. She knew nothing about our family, in other words, or about Eddie.

'And in that time he's never really bothered with your mother, for instance, even though she's not well. He always ducks out of anything resembling responsibility. Because everybody just thinks, Oh, isn't he so great to do his dishwashing job! So noble, so proud!' She skewered me with a look. 'Do you know what he spent his last pay cheque on? Costumes for an abstract production of *King Lear* that nobody came to see.' She wrinkled her nose. 'It looked kind of stupid, to be honest,' she said. 'The king in a boiler suit.'

The boiler suit would be Eddie, alright. But, irresponsible? No. And as for us mollycoddling him, well, that was ridiculous. It was just that he was the youngest, that was all. So we cut him some slack, big deal. The way Eleanora was going on, you'd think we'd ruined him.

Defensive, I said, 'Your money worries are your own business, Eleanora. It's nothing to do with me.'

'He thinks we can go on like this for ever. Him acting, me singing in shitty pubs for twenty euro a time. And I haven't even done one of those gigs in a month.'

All this whinging was beginning to grate on my nerves.

'How come the whole thing is Eddie's fault? If you're so desperate for the good life, then why don't *you* get a job?'

233

'The good life?' she said, a funny look on her face. 'Is that what you think I'm after?'

'Yes,' I said frankly. Anybody could see she had ambitions for herself. Let her get off her pert behind and do something about them then.

She said nothing for ages, then raised red-rimmed eyes to mine. 'I haven't told him yet. But I'm pregnant.'

Chapter Thirty-eight

'We're going to keep a log,' said Matthew grimly. I'd told him everything. I knew what it was like, keeping things from him, and I didn't want to do it again.

'Everything that happens, no matter how small, we're going to write it down, OK? I'll steal a new pen from work just for the job.'

It was an attempt to lighten the atmosphere but his little joke fell flat on its face.

'Hey.' He took my hand. 'Come on. OK, so this isn't pleasant, but there's no point in getting upset about it. We're on to him now. He's not going to get away with this.'

Matthew was so reassuring, so calm, that I was already feeling better. He took my hands now, and rubbed them.

'I'm sorry,' I said.

Matthew was amazed. 'Why are you sorry? You haven't done anything.'

'You know what I mean. It's spoiling everything.'

And Matthew had been on such a high, too. The darts team had won the cup, actually *won it*. It had been an iconic sporting moment, apparently; after a gruelling evening where six teams of portly men had slugged it out, dart for dart, The Knob had stepped up to the board and clinched it with a final, perfect bull's-eye.

Maura had cried. The Knob had cried. The lads had cried. It had all been very, very emotional and they'd had to have about seven pints each to dampen things down enough so that Maura, the only sober one, could drive them all home.

The cup – a magnificent eight-inch-high vessel of tarnished hue – had come with them. There had been much tooting of the horn as they'd arrived in Castlemoy in the small hours, and pulled up outside Dirty Harry's. Harry was woken up and let them in by the back door. Hilda had fired up the sandwich maker and they'd had a feed of toasted cheese and tomato sandwiches, washed down with a bottle of fine Scotch that Harry had reverently taken from the top shelf of the pub and dusted off.

Then The Knob had looked at them all very seriously and said, 'There's a team tournament on in Naas in a month's time. It's serious stuff, lads. Will we go for it?'

The roars of 'yes' had woken the cattle in the fields, by all accounts.

But the dream ended abruptly for Matthew when he'd arrived home to tales of creepy ex-boyfriends and a distraught fiancée.

'He *was* following me, Matthew,' I reiterated now.

'I know.'

'And all those other times too. It wasn't just accidental, like he was trying to make out.'

Well, if Dominique could swallow Jason's version of events so easily, maybe Matthew was wondering about this whole thing too. Jason hadn't followed him, after all, or indeed done a single thing to him. Was Matthew sitting there now, nodding and smiling at me, but really doing a furtive assessment of my mental health? 'She was fine until she started working from home,' he might be telling our friends gravely.

'Clara,' he said. 'I believe you. OK?'

'Really?'

'One hundred per cent.'

I sagged with relief. But only momentarily, because then Matthew got up, saying, 'Stay here. I'll be back in a few minutes.'

'Where are you going?'

'To ring the police.'

'What? No.'

But he stood his ground, calm and determined. 'Just to ask their advice. They might go and have a word with him if we wanted, let him know that this kind of thing is unacceptable and that they'll be keeping an eye on him from now on.'

'You can't.' I was filled with sudden panic. Matthew was losing the run of himself. 'And, anyway, there aren't any police in Ireland. We call them Guards here, the station is at the top of the town. People go in mostly to get their passport photos signed, and to complain about noise from their neighbours. Nobody goes in to say they're being stalked.'

I had a horrible vision of myself standing there, and them looking at me, baffled: 'Jason Farrell was driving around the town *in his car*, you say?' Was this a wind-up? 'So he hasn't actually murdered anyone?'

Jason probably met the Guards all the time, what with representing local petty thieves and acting in land disputes. He also knew the law like the back of his hand; nothing he'd done so far would be in any way easy to pin on him.

But Matthew seemed to think we were back in London, and that Operation Stalker would go into full swing, with fifty men on the case. 'It doesn't matter,' he insisted. 'What he's doing is wrong, and the police – Guards – will know that. Once we make a complaint, that should stop him.'

'No.'

'Clara, I realise it might be a little embarrassing, as it's a small town.'

A little? But he didn't seem to recognise his naïvety.

'We can't let this pass. We need to sort it out now.'

What did he think was going to happen? That the Guards would march into Jason's office – on my say so – and Jason would hold up his hands: 'Got me! Look, sorry, Sarge, I won't do it again.'

'I said no.'

Matthew looked at me. 'What's wrong?'

'We don't even have any proof, for starters! So he's followed me a few times. You want the whole town talking about it? I'm only back from

London, I don't want to start some massive fuss. Not when we don't even have anything to complain about.'

'We do. He's following you.'

'A couple of times, Matthew.' I was now desperately trying to downplay it. I honestly couldn't bear it if our whole move to Ireland was blighted by gossip and conjecture. Things like this just didn't happen in Castlemoy and there was no way I was going to be the focus of some awful drama.

'There's the stolen licence plate,' Matthew kept arguing. 'And the way he keeps intimidating you verbally, talking about pyjamas, for Christ's sake. What kind of a sicko is he?'

When he'd heard that, he'd pulled our bedroom blinds down permanently. Jason wouldn't be able to see in any more. But nor could we see out, and our nice, bright room was now gloomy and dim.

'Please,' I begged. 'Let's just keep our log. We can think about the Guards down the line. If it gets worse.'

Matthew wasn't happy. 'What harm will it do to mention it to them?'

'Look, none of this happened until I taunted him about the engagement.'

'Oh, so what, all of this is your fault?' Now he was exasperated. 'That's just daft.'

Well, yes. But it was difficult to believe that I wasn't in some way to blame. And now I was going to further damage things by bringing in the local Guards?

'Look,' I said. 'I've already confronted him, OK?'

'Which I don't want you doing again.'

'So I should have just driven on like some kind of victim?'

'You should never get involved with these people.' He was adamant. 'That much I *do* know.'

It was a little late to worry about getting involved with Jason.

'Listen to me,' I pleaded. 'We're just going to let things die down a bit, OK? We're not going to rush in there, making things worse.'

At last I seemed to be getting through to him.

'I suppose there's that risk,' he conceded reluctantly.

'Exactly.' I knew Jason in a way that Matthew didn't. He was like a chess player; watching and waiting and planning his next move. Calling in the Guards might just be the catalyst.

'But if he puts a foot wrong again, I don't care what you say – we're contacting the Guards.'

'Absolutely.' My panicky feeling subsided somewhat. If we could just keep this thing contained, low-key, then maybe Jason would get bored and back off. That was all I wanted right now. The thought of it escalating was just too much.

Matthew put his arms around me and hugged me close. 'I'm sorry you have to go through this.'

'It's not your fault.'

'And it's not yours either.'

We sat in silence for a minute. We were in the kitchen, with the door closed. There was no possibility of accidentally catching a glimpse of Dominique's house, or seeing a pair of headlights swing into her drive.

Matthew was the one to ask the question. 'Why do you think he's doing it?'

We looked at each other; it was a mystery. He had his own practice, car, house, and a curvy girlfriend who wrote erotic fiction. It didn't get much jammier than that. Why the hell would he be bothered needling me?

'Do you think he's making you pay? You know, for breaking off the engagement?'

'We weren't engaged in the first place—'

'I know, I know, I'm just telling it from his perspective, OK? Trying to get inside his head.'

Who knew what was going on inside Jason's head? Ten years was a long time to hold a grudge. But maybe he didn't even know he *had* a grudge until I decided to move back to Castlemoy, and stirred up memories after all this time.

'I don't know.'

Matthew galvanised. 'Enough about Jason. We've a plan now, so let's just put him and his stupid antics to the backs of our minds.'

'Alright.'

And we got out our wedding folder – brochures and sample menus and invitations, and we had a spirited discussion over whether more people preferred lamb over beef, and for a little while Matthew made everything OK again.

Chapter Thirty-nine

'I can't believe I'm going to be a grandmother,' Anita kept saying. Well, she'd practically given up hope, seeing as I was such a slow starter, and Róisín was unlikely to produce much in that department, at least given that she had split with Catherine and taken up with a ukulele instead.

Who'd have thought it would be Eddie, the actor, the one officially for the birds, who'd seek to carry on the family line?

And if only it was that simple.

'You're not,' Eddie told her shortly. 'Well, technically you are, but Eleanora says that we'll get access over her dead body.'

Eleanora could certainly be on the bossy side which, we all agreed, he needed. But for her to act so decisively, so fearlessly, well, we were all a bit blind-sided. Eddie's reaction to the pregnancy – something along the lines of 'oh shit' – had prompted her to pack a bag for him and throw him out.

He still looked like he wasn't sure what had hit him.

'Don't talk like that,' said Anita, highly distressed by Eleanora's threat. This was coming on top of Dr Mooney telling her that her blood sugar levels were still not under control, despite all her sterling efforts; despite not having eaten anything but salad for a whole shagging week previously. If she didn't lamp the poor man there and then, she said, she never would.

But a *grandchild*. The pitter-patter of tiny feet in her big old house again . . . I could see that she was clinging onto this, as though a baby was what her life had been missing all along.

'Never heard of condoms?' Róisín asked Eddie baldly. 'Or did you use them all up in one of your plays, to tie the scenery together?'

Róisín, being broken-hearted and depressed, wasn't a bit surprised at the way it had all turned out. 'I knew it,' she kept saying morosely, even though she couldn't possibly have. 'There's no such thing as lasting love or commitment in this world. People might have great *intentions*, but if you look at the break-up rate of relationships and the number of divorces . . .' Usually at that point we all zoned out.

'There's no point in talking about condoms now that the horse has bolted,' Anita chastised Róisín.

Róisín backed down. 'Look,' she said to Eddie, 'why don't you go and talk to her? Be more positive about the whole thing.'

'I can't pretend to be delighted, Róisín. Neither of us wants a kid, so what's the point in fooling ourselves?'

'Róisín's right,' Anita implored him. 'I'll drive you to the train station now; you could be up by lunchtime.'

Eddie was living back home, ensconced in his old room upstairs. He had nice clean sheets and hot water that came freely from the taps without you having to stick a euro coin into a meter out in the hall first. Anita was cooking him mountains of lovely food and driving him to the train station and back so that he could attend rehearsals for some new play.

'And how is Eleanora?' I enquired. Presumably alone and pregnant in the manky bedsit.

Sensing blame, Eddie said defensively, 'Well enough to be drawing up a plan.'

We all looked at each other.

'What sort of a plan?'

'A financial plan. Obviously, we're going to need, you know, something to live on.'

'You mean money?' I prompted.

'Yes. Money. Babies are expensive.' You would think he was talking about running a car. But sure, he hadn't a clue. None of us had any contact with babies. I didn't think Eddie had ever held one, even though he'd once played a baby in some comedy during the Dublin Theatre Festival. He probably didn't know anybody who had a baby. All his friends were actors in their twenties for whom parenthood was a long, long way off. Unless your contraception malfunctioned, that was. Then you were in the shit.

'She's given me a list of costs for food, clothes, childcare, that kind of thing.' He dug in his pocket and extracted it. From the way his eyes watered, I was guessing the figures were frightening and bewildering.

'Nothing but the best for our Eleanora,' Róisín murmured, looking over his shoulder.

'Don't worry,' said Anita, anxious to square things. 'We'll work something out.'

'We'll all pitch in,' Róisín assured him.

'Or else,' I said, 'Eddie could get a job. A proper job, I mean.'

Eddie looked at me. 'I don't know why you're being like this.'

'Like what?'

'Anita and Róisín are being very supportive, but all I've got so far from you is negativity.'

'Don't mind that, she's the same with everybody these days,' Anita interjected. 'Taking the heads off us all.'

'I'm just trying to be realistic here. She's pregnant, you need money and right now only one of you can work.'

'So you mean putting on a shirt and tie and pushing papers around a desk all day long?'

'If that's what it takes.'

'The voiceover work . . .' Anita began. She didn't look well tonight. The stress really was getting to her.

Eddie looked embarrassed. 'I think I might have burned my boats there. I turned down some jobs, and I'm not sure I'm that popular with certain directors any more.'

Great. So he'd blacklisted himself from some lucrative work by mouthing off. Typical Eddie.

'Then it looks like you don't have any choice,' I told him.

'You were a bit hard on him back there,' Róisín said on the way home.

'Why? For pointing out that somebody's going to have to pay for his failure to cover up his pecker, and that someone is him?'

Róisín sighed. 'I just feel so bad for him. He's barely able to look after himself, never mind a girlfriend and child.'

'I suppose he's going to have to learn, and fast.'

I looked in the rear-view mirror. All clear. Only a tractor behind us, and the farmer driving it looked genuine, not Jason in disguise.

'Will we go visit Jo in London?' I said impulsively. I felt a strong urge to go myself. To get away from Castlemoy for a while. 'She might take us to some clubs.'

Actually, I wasn't at all sure that Jo would have time for us. She seemed to be heavily involved with her new boyfriend, so much so that it was difficult to get her to respond even to a text message these days.

And I could have done with talking to her. But it was true; when you moved away from a place, you drifted apart from your friends a little bit. Life went on.

I realised that, beside me, Róisín was crying.

'Róisín?'

'Oh, fuck it, sorry.' She was scrabbling about for a tissue, mortified.

'What's wrong?'

'Nothing.'

'Clearly *something* is. So come on. Spit it out.'

'It's stupid.'

'Not if you're crying about it.'

'I just feel so alone.' She dabbed at her eyes, refusing to look at me. 'I know things are a mess for Eddie. The guy couldn't find his way out of a paper bag. But he's going to have a baby, Clara, whether he likes it or not. A family of his own. And you have Matthew, you're getting married, you'll have babies too, your whole life ahead of you, full of people you love.' Her chin sank lower. 'Me? I'll just turn up at all the births and the weddings and the christenings, poor old Auntie Róisín, be nice to her now because that racy lady broke her heart years ago and there are no other lesbians once you get past the outer reaches of Dublin.'

I didn't know what to say. I felt desperately sorry that she was feeling like that. She was always so strong, so full of it, that you forgot that underneath it all she was as vulnerable as anybody else. All I could do was reach across and squeeze her hand.

'And there's Anita, going on about me moving to Tokyo.' She sniffed. 'What the hell is that all about?'

'She thinks Tokyo is coming down with lesbians.'

'Is it?'

'Jesus, I don't know, Róisín. Maybe you should go and see.'

'Maybe I will.' She was cheering up now. 'Take my magnifying glass and look under every stone.'

'And don't forget Dad's old duck caller too. Give a few blasts of it in downtown Tokyo and see if they come running.'

'You never know, I might arrive back to Castlemoy with an Asian babe and set up home. That would really set tongues wagging.'

We were laughing now – only because the idea was so preposterous. The idea of Róisín setting up home in Castlemoy with *any* babe was preposterous.

'I suppose it's nice that I'm going to be an auntie, anyway,' Róisín said, with a little sigh.

'I'll be an auntie too.'

'Yes, but I'll be the favourite auntie,' Róisín said smugly. A pause. 'Clara, you *do* know that Mace is illegal in Ireland, don't you?'

'What are you talking about?'

'It's just that there's a can of it rolling around my feet.'

I looked down in horror. I thought I'd put it securely under the passenger seat – more accessible than the glove compartment, I figured – but I clearly hadn't secured it enough because it was, indeed, bouncing merrily around Róisín's shoes.

'I can explain.'

'I'm listening.' I could see she was taking a very dim view of it. As a nurse she saw first-hand what an encounter with these things could do.

'Look, I bought it off some dodgy site on the internet, OK? It's just to make myself feel better, I swear. I mean, I don't intend to actually *use* it.'

'So what the hell did you get it for, so? My God, Clara, if you're found with this you're in very serious trouble, do you realise that?'

She wasn't going to be easy to buy off, I could see that. 'I got it because my licence plate keeps getting stolen, Róisín. And someone's following me around, OK? Matthew doesn't know I have it, and he'd only worry more if he did know, so will you just say nothing?'

'Clara . . .' She was shocked. Incredulous. Worried. And full of questions.

'Please. I can't say anything more. So don't ask.'

'Don't *ask*? My God, what on earth is going on?'

I wished I'd said nothing now, but I was spared any further interrogation because as I swung into Róisín's road, we almost collided with another car – being driven rather fast – which pulled in outside Róisín's house and came to a stop.

A woman jumped out. it was Catherine.

For a second Róisín's face melted; then it was back on with the outrage, full blast. 'What the hell is she doing here?'

I saw her do a quick look round at the neighbouring houses; was anybody home?

'Obviously she's not keen on taking no for an answer,' I offered.

'Well, she'll just have to. She has no right to come here unannounced. No right at all.'

But Catherine didn't look like she was going anywhere. When we stopped the car, in front of hers, she marched over to the passenger side and looked in at Róisín.

'Are you going to get out?' Catherine called, 'or will I just shout from here?'

Róisín nearly jumped a foot into the air. 'I have nothing to say to you, so you might as well go home!'

'At least get out and talk to her, Róisín,' I urged.

'No. Look, just drive on, would you?'

'What? Drive on where? You *live* here.'

'Please,' she begged. 'Just get me out of here before she makes a scene.'

Catherine stepped back from the car. For a moment I thought she'd given up and was leaving. So did Róisín, because she relaxed a bit. Instead Catherine cupped her hands to her mouth and shouted at the top of her voice for the world to hear, 'I love you, Róisín Maguire!'

I never saw Róisín move so fast. She'd scrambled out of her seatbelt and was on the pavement before you could say 'paranoia'. I got out after her.

'Shut the fuck up.' She was really angry. 'This isn't funny, Catherine.'

Catherine seemed to be nearly as angry. 'You're right. It isn't. We were good together.'

Róisín cast a look up and down the street. If people weren't already looking, they would be now. 'You threw it away.'

'No, you *drove* me away, with your refusal to acknowledge us properly. Was it worth it, Róisín? Being respectable? Has it made you happier, pretending to be someone you're not?'

Róisín's face was a dull red now. 'Stop talking like you're in a cheap movie,' she hissed. 'You haven't a clue. This is Castlemoy, not Tokyo.'

Catherine blinked a bit at that. 'I'm starting to think you're using the Castlemoy thing as an excuse.'

'Don't be stupid.'

Catherine swung towards me now. 'I was never allowed down here, did you know that? It was one of her rules. Our dates were strictly in Dublin.'

I hadn't felt I had any place in this conversation up to now, but I couldn't let that pass. 'Oh, come on, Catherine. You were always working. You can hardly complain about not having any dates in Castlemoy when you were forever making Róisín drive up and down that motorway just to get five minutes with you.'

'What job? I lost my job a year ago, just before I met Róisín.' She swung around to Róisín accusingly. 'Have you been using my so-called job as yet another excuse?'

I looked at Róisín; her eyes slid away from mine in mortification. It was all the answer I needed.

'It doesn't surprise me. She was so petrified that people were going to find out.' Catherine nailed Róisín with a look. 'You know, because you're such dinosaurs down here. Actually, you're insulting all your friends and neighbours as well with your behaviour, you do realise that, don't you?' she said to Róisín.

'Just go,' Róisín said dully.

'I'll go when I'm good and finished. So I was hidden away in Dublin,' she told me, 'only let down here for the odd day trip when it was completely unavoidable. And one night, I thought, Fuck this. There I was, sitting in Dublin on my own, because my girlfriend was too ashamed to be seen with me. So I went out and got off with someone else.' Another look, flung at Róisín. 'And I'm sorry about that, but what the hell else did you expect to happen when you refused to give us a chance?'

'Why aren't you with her then?' Róisín threw back. 'Go on, go back to her if she's such a ride.'

'I don't want her,' Catherine said. She grew quiet now. 'I want you.'

Róisín blushed and squirmed and looked over her shoulder right and left.

'Yes, well . . .' she began to splutter and huff.

'And you want me too.'

Róisín nearly died. Jesus Christ. In the middle of the *street*. If somebody walked by now it'd be all over town, about the lezzer love-fest outside that nurse's house, best thing since Jerry Cronin was caught *in flagrante* with a brand-new piece of farm machinery.

But Róisín didn't deny that she wanted Catherine too. She looked at her like she wanted to run into her arms.

She wouldn't let herself, though. She stood there like her feet were set in concrete, no matter what her heart wanted to do. 'I've been burned before.' She looked at Catherine, appealing to her to understand.

'Yes, we all know about that stupid disco. If you ask me, that girl did you a favour. She did half the work for you, all you had to do was brazen it out. But you didn't.'

I felt I had some responsibility to take there. 'She was only a kid.'

Catherine addressed Róisín. 'You're not a kid any more. You're a thirty-something woman, Róisín. It's way past time you decided what you want to be in life.' She turned back to her car. 'Ring me if you want. I won't come after you again.'

Chapter Forty

Jason hadn't followed me since the night I'd confronted him. We'd been all ready for it; Matthew had even come in the car with me several times, scrunched down in the passenger seat, our video camera in his hand. It would have been funny in other circumstances. But there was no sign of Jason's car. I'd even taken to driving up the town for things I didn't need; inviting him to follow me. Goading him. Because a few more incidents of that and I'd have grounds for a complaint against him, right?

But he'd changed tack. Wrong-footed us again with new stuff, petty stuff. If indeed it was him at all.

For instance: the dogs had got at our bins again when we'd both been out, even though they were now stored in the side passage. Our rubbish had been strewn all over the estate for everybody to see. Burt Reynolds had complained. Matthew, tight-faced, had cleaned the mess up, dragged the bins back into the side passage and rooted out the lock I'd bought. He screwed it on tight to the side door.

'That ought to sort that out,' he said, looking across the road to Dominique's house.

Then our car got keyed while we were in Dirty Harry's one night for darts. We didn't see it till the next morning – a long, angry scratch all along the side of Matthew's beloved Renault Mégane.

'Could it have been an accident?'

'I suppose. Maybe.' But I heard him whispering to the car, 'It's OK, baby. I know a man with a spray gun.' He looked at me. 'Write it down.'

'You think it was . . . ?'

'I don't know.' Of course he did. We both did. 'Let's write it down anyway.'

He got the notebook out of the drawer and we both sat down at the table, as we always did when we added to the 'list' of things that seemed to happen to me.

It was getting longer, I saw; things I would never have put down as anything other than bad luck were now listed.

'You wrote down about our post?' It had been stuffed through our letter box one morning sodden and muddy, as though the postman had dropped it into a puddle by accident. Just the post addressed to me. Not Matthew's.

'Well, it wasn't raining that day, was it?' Matthew said.

Listed also were the two terrible reviews someone had posted about my company on a consumer website. I'd got one star out of a possible five, with the reviewer, who described themselves as guests at a function I'd catered, saying that my food was 'appalling' and 'not fit for pigs'.

It had never entered my head that they'd been anything other than genuine. Clearly Matthew had different ideas.

He'd written down two separate incidents of our house alarm going off when we weren't there, an incidence of my supermarket clubcard being cancelled. Which was hardly life-shattering, as often I didn't remember to use the blasted thing, but apparently it had been cancelled by someone, at some point.

'Please don't put that down, it's embarrassing.'

'Why? It happened. It's down.' And he slapped the notebook shut. 'We could go to the Guards with all this.'

'All what? Accusations of him interfering with my shopping experience? Come on, Matthew. Besides, we can't prove a damn thing.'

'We don't have to.'

'I'm not sure they can swoop in and arrest him on the basis of, "well,

251

it might have been him, but on the other hand it might have been some dogs, or a ham-fisted postman, we're not really sure".'

'Well, not if you put it like that.'

It was the first time I'd seen his mask of positivity slip. I couldn't really blame him. There were so many niggling things to deal with recently. And I couldn't help feeling responsible for the little furrow that had appeared in his brow lately, or the way he seemed to be permanently on guard. When we relaxed in the evenings in front of the television now, I noticed that he never fully managed it.

Matthew put the notebook back in the drawer. Then he went out to practise his darts.

The tenants in our flat sent us written notification of their dissatisfaction that we hadn't fixed the mould problem in the bathroom. The 'substandard living conditions' were causing continued health problems for one of the tenants. The letter, they warned, was the first step in their taking things further. They declined to go into the specifics, but reading between the lines we envisaged tussles with tenancy associations, solicitors and possible public tarrings and featherings.

'These guys are unreal. I swear to God.' Matthew was furious.

Jo offered to talk to them on our behalf. Smooth things over. But Matthew wouldn't hear of it. Jo had done far too much as it was. She would get a handbag, as promised – she wasn't to go too mad, no Stella McCartney or anything like that – and we would send in workmen to get the whole bathroom replastered and retiled for that pair of moaning, snivelling pains-in-the-arse.

'And then we'll take our own photographs of it and send them a copy,' Matthew decided, his mouth tight.

'We were just unlucky,' I said. There seemed to be nothing but problems these days. 'The next tenants will be better.'

'Do you think?'

After months of auditions, preliminary rounds, regional finals, and a spin-off series, *Dance for Your Supper* had reached the dizzying semi-final stage.

The little fella in the shiny waistcoat was tipped to tap-dance his way into the final and I'd made an extra big bowl of popcorn in readiness when the phone rang.

I looked at it suspiciously, as always, before answering. 'Hello?'

'Clara? It's Di.'

I was surprised. Normally Matthew's mother rang on Sunday morning. It was only Thursday. 'He's not here,' I told her. 'My mother developed a leak and he's gone to fix it. Her water tank, I mean.'

I'd stayed at home, in case. In case of what, neither of us said. But it felt better to have a presence in the house and so there I was, in the front room.

'It's just about the wedding,' Di began. Rather delicately, I thought.

Dominique's front door opened across the way. I'd forgotten to pull the blinds across before I sat down to watch the telly. I couldn't do it now; they would see me.

'I really don't mean to stick my oar in,' Di was saying, 'and I'm sure you've enough to be getting on with, what with all the arrangements . . . It's just that you haven't sent out any invitations yet.'

There they were: Dominique and Jason, coming out of her house. Dominique was all dressed up. They may well have been heading out to dinner.

She turned to lock the door, her mouth fixed in a sulky pout. She didn't look like a woman in love. She looked like one spoiling for a fight.

Jason didn't look much happier. I recognised that tight-lipped, impatient look. It used to be directed at me a lot of the time, when I'd be late, or not dressed up enough, or too dressed up, or any number of infractions that used to piss him off. When he turned to speak to her, he barely met her eyes. She spoke back, sharp, her hand on her hip, and his face grew darker.

I found myself rooting for her. She certainly wasn't going to let herself be cowed by his disapproval.

I wondered if Maura was right. Was the gloss wearing off on that particular relationship?

Dominique looked over at our house suddenly, even though I knew she couldn't possibly see me, sitting there on the couch. Her expression was strange, or curious, or something. I turned away as I saw them get into the car. Great. They were going out. I could relax for the evening.

'It's just that you need to give people notice,' Di was saying on the phone. 'If they're travelling. Lord knows, it's criminal the way they put up the price of flights the later you book, but if people knew the date for certain, they could get in early.'

'Yes, of course.' I was contrite. 'You're right.'

'I don't mean to interfere . . .'

'You're not. Honestly.' Di didn't have money to throw away, nor did her friends Liz and Sharon, or anybody else who would have to pay through the nose to come over to watch us get married. I was embarrassed. It was just that we'd got a little distracted from our wedding preparation, what with having to rescue bins and keep lengthening logs. Naturally, I wasn't going to say any of this to Di. 'We just didn't think of it.'

'That's what I thought.' Di sounded pleased for having stepped in and rescued the whole thing. 'So I just thought I'd remind you.'

'Invitations?' Matthew looked more stressed after he finally got home. Anita's leak had been a bad one and it was late.

'She was just reminding us.'

'Fine. Let's do the invitations then.'

'Not now, it's late.'

'Well, when else? I've been at your mother's all evening, so unless we get up extra early or something . . .'

'I'm sorry,' I said.

He looked at me. 'No, *I'm* sorry.' He rubbed his face. 'I'm just tired and I couldn't fix the leak properly. Don't mind me.'

We had a big hug. He smelled of sweat and oil. And sausages. Oh, Anita. And I just bet that she'd kept one or two over for herself to have later on. Anita, when stressed, had always turned to food. She was allegedly sticking to her diet but her trousers were growing suspiciously tight.

'Do you know what I was thinking about on the drive back?' he said into my hair. 'Your ex. I was wondering whether I would bump into him.

I was thinking, has he done something else, only we just don't know about it yet?' He said it to me like he was ashamed. Like it was somehow his fault.

'They've gone out. I saw them.'

It was small comfort, but we both held on to it.

'I just wish we could do something. Instead of sitting here, like rabbits in headlights, writing it down in a notebook.'

I was shocked to see how frustrated he looked. All the exuberance and optimism of the big move had gone.

'He can't keep it up. He'll get tired eventually.' I was desperate to convince us both.

'And what if he doesn't? What if it gets worse?'

'Then I suppose we'll have to do something.'

The little fella won the semi-finals of *Dance for Your Supper*, like everybody thought he would. We were just watching him accept the standing ovation of the studio audience, after which there was a much-anticipated interview with his demon of a mother (well, she had to be, if he was to make any money out of his autobiography, *My Dancing Hell*, later down the line), when the doorbell rang.

We opened it to find a pizza delivery guy there, holding out a large pizza. 'Number sixteen? There you go.'

We explained that there must be some kind of mistake. 'We didn't order that.'

'Eighteen euro twenty,' said the delivery guy, not giving a damn who'd ordered it. 'The address was given as number sixteen.'

Matthew and I looked at each other. In the end Matthew handed over the money, because we couldn't think what else to do.

The pizza was ham and pineapple. Matthew hated pineapple. He was probably allergic to it because it always made him sneeze.

He clapped a hand to his forehead. 'Jesus, don't tell me he's got into my medical records too!'

For a minute I thought he was serious. Then we cracked up laughing. It was a great release, and we laughed and laughed until my sides hurt.

'Fuck him,' Matthew said, suddenly cheerful again. 'Sad loser.'

And we threw the pizza in the bin.

Chapter Forty-one

The blonde receptionist ran a finger down her screen doubtfully. 'And you don't have an appointment?'

'No. But if you could just tell him I'm here, I'm sure he can spare five minutes.' My voice said, Look, love, this isn't Fort Knox.

It did the trick. She flicked another look at me – I was in heels, and an edgy little suit I'd bought on sale in a boutique once, and that screamed confidence, even if I felt like a bowl of porridge inside. 'Take a seat.'

Jason made me wait ten minutes. Then I heard him running lightly down the stairs, a look of fixed surprise on his face. 'Clara.'

He held out his hand. I ignored it.

'Could we talk somewhere in private?'

'I'm actually busy,' he said, enjoying turning me down.

'So am I,' I said loudly. 'My car is parked outside and I can't leave it for long in case someone nicks my number plate.'

The receptionist's head snapped up. It would be all round the office in five minutes if I kicked up a stink.

'Let's go up to my office,' Jason agreed quickly.

Upstairs had been refurbished over the years too; it was expensive, bare, no imagination whatsoever in the slatted blinds and the seaside prints mounted on the wall.

Jason closed the door behind him. I immediately felt claustrophobic, hot. I could smell him from here – aftershave, fresh sweat, a faint trace of Dominique's perfume – and it made me want to gag.

I moved as close to the open window as I could, and I faced him and said, 'I want you to stop.'

'Stop?'

'Yes. You know exactly what I mean. I'm very sorry if I hurt you in the past, but harassing me and my fiancé isn't going to solve anything. All it's going to do is make everybody miserable and make you look like a fool.'

I'd spent a lot of time of planning what I was going to say. I needed to be clear. I needed him to realise how destructive it was to him, as well as us.

Most of all, I needed to look him in the face and tell him to leave me alone.

He said nothing for a long time. He walked around to the other side of the desk and sat down. He indicated the seat opposite for me and I sat too.

I searched his face for some understanding. Some break-through.

'You'd want to be very careful about throwing around accusations, Clara. Whatever they might be.' His eyes were like two stones.

'You're harassing me.'

His face didn't change. 'Oh? I think you'll find that's your opinion only.'

OK. On to Plan B. I'd hoped I wouldn't need it; that a direct appeal might somehow cause the scales to fall from his eyes, and he would realise what he'd been doing was just plain wrong.

But I might have known that wouldn't happen. It had been naïve of me. He was never going to meet me half-way.

I took a breath. Made my eyes as hard as his. Harder. 'If you keep this up, I'm going to start telling people. My mother and my sister and all the neighbours. Your receptionist downstairs. I'm going to ask them to watch out for you, to be alert. That you're bothering me.'

I waited.

What piece of solicitor-speak would he throw back at me next? Would he be angered by my threats? Would he be, for a split second, worried?

257

Instead he threw his head back and laughed at the good of it.

It was horrible. He found it amusing; me, my fears, what he was doing to me. 'Ah, Clara,' he said. 'I'll say one thing for you. You always had a sense of humour.'

He laughed again. I looked at his open, gaping mouth and I felt fury like never before.

'You're disgusting, do you know that? You're a vile, cowardly, stupid man. In fact, you're not a man. No proper man would behave like you're doing.' This wasn't part of the script, but I couldn't stop myself. The words just kept coming and I spat them out like weapons. 'To think that you get a kick out of overturning people's bins. Does it make you feel good, does it? Is it the highlight of your day? My God. You're pathetic.'

He was still smiling, trying to look like he didn't give a damn, but he wasn't pulling it off.

'You should know all about pathetic behaviour,' he said back pleasantly.

I knew it would come up, sooner or later. His justification to himself.

'Like I said. I'm sorry if I hurt you.'

The smile disappeared. 'And that's it? That's your apology?' He looked at me incredulously. 'To be honest, I'd have expected a bit more.'

'A bit more than what? We broke up. Deal with it.'

But his face was really coming alive now. It was full of bitterness and old anger. He'd been waiting for this moment, I saw. 'Two years we'd been going out. Two years. And you didn't even send me a lousy postcard from London. But you think I can be palmed off now with a quick sorry?'

I began to wonder about the wisdom of coming here like this. I'd thought that maybe it would be cathartic; put the past to rest and all that. But one look at Jason's face told me it wasn't in the past for him at all.

'What's the point in going over all this?'

'Oh, that would suit you just fine, wouldn't it, Clara? Never mention it. Just move back here, into my hometown with your boyfriend, like everything's OK.'

'I didn't say that.'

'You didn't warn me you were coming. No courtesy telephone call. Nothing. I just hear from the dogs on the street that my fiancée had moved back here permanently. But, then again, you never had any manners, did you? All your new fancy clothes and your shiny hairdo can't hide that.'

I felt my cheeks burn, even though it was just a cheap jibe on his part. Put-downs had been his way of keeping me from leaving him much sooner. If you have low self-esteem, it's much easier to stay where you are, even if you're miserable.

'I was not your fiancée. You just assumed I was. I never wanted to marry you but I was too afraid to say no.'

There. It was out. I was telling myself as much as him. The fault was on his side, for making me feel like that.

'So you leave me sitting in a restaurant with my parents and yours, making me look like a fucking fool?' This was said calmly, every syllable enunciated perfectly.

It was more frightening because of that. I'd have felt better had he had a right go at me, screamed and roared. But it was the *control*.

And I wondered now which he'd been more upset about: me, leaving, or being made to look stupid in the restaurant that night.

'And now you're paying me back, is that it? Ten years on? By conducting some kind of campaign against me?' I filled my voice with scorn, even though I felt like running out of the place. And maybe that was the wisest thing to do; I clearly wasn't getting anywhere. But I wouldn't give it to him.

'I have no idea what you mean,' he said blandly.

'Oh, come on. It's just us here.' I gestured around at the office. 'You can admit it. Or are you afraid?'

But he wasn't going to rise to it. 'If you feel you've got a complaint against me, Clara, then I would strongly advise you to take it to the Guards. They'd take immediate action, I'm sure.' He left a little pause. 'That's if you've got some kind of proof.'

In other words, he knew exactly what he was doing. They wouldn't be able to touch him; he was a solicitor and he knew the law; how far he could go and what he could do without getting nailed, or making it very difficult for them, anyway.

'Or maybe that boyfriend of yours could sort it out. What's his name again?'

I didn't answer.

'Matthew. That's it, isn't it?' He smiled at me. 'Frankly, I'm surprised he sent you in here today. If it was my fiancée who was having a problem, I wouldn't hide behind her. I'd sort it out myself.'

There was no reasoning with him, I knew that, and anything I said now was only making matters worse, but I couldn't let him malign Matthew like that behind his back.

'He doesn't know I'm here, OK?'

'Ah.' He made a steeple out of his fingers and looked at me. His eyes twinkled. 'Was that wise? I hope he doesn't find out and jump to the wrong conclusions!'

Jesus. *Jesus*. Was this guy for real?

'Relax, Clara. I have no interest in getting back with you.' His eyes flickered dismissively over me. 'Even if you've scrubbed up a bit from the old days.'

I decided to have one last attempt. I swallowed hard, knowing every word would stick in my craw. 'Alright, if it's an apology you're looking for, you've got one. Unreservedly. I was in the wrong ten years ago. I shouldn't have embarrassed you like that.' He seemed to be listening intently so I made my voice as conciliatory as possible. 'Please. Can we just leave all this behind us and move on? That way nobody needs to know about it.'

For a moment I thought it had worked.

'One more time,' he said, 'with feeling.'

I stood up fast. I should never have come here. All I'd done was feed some sick desire of his to make me crawl. I had an overwhelming urge to get into a hot shower and scrub myself raw.

'I wonder how Dominique would feel about all of this?' I flung, trying to reclaim some of my dignity.

260

He shrugged, seemingly not too bothered. 'Who knows?' he said. 'She spends all day writing that stuff.' And he gave a bit of a shudder of distaste. 'I don't know how she does it, to be honest. It's a bit sick.'

He was talking to me like we were having a normal conversation. As if there was nothing wrong.

'Goodbye, Jason.'

I walked out on him.

Chapter Forty-two

'I can't believe you went round there without telling me.'

'Because I knew you'd try to stop me.'

'Damn right I would. What if something had happened?' Matthew was looking at me like I'd lost my mind. 'Jesus, Clara, you can't mess with these people. He could be dangerous, have you thought of that?'

'Which was why I went to his office in the day time, when there were plenty of people around. I'm not stupid, you know. I knew what I was doing.' I was annoyed at his response. Did he think I'd be content to sit around like some victim and not do anything about it?

Also, I was still a little shaken by the whole thing, and now here was Matthew, getting at me too.

'You had no idea how he was going to react,' he said.

'No, but it worked, didn't it?'

Since I'd gone to his office, Jason seemed to have backed off completely. No more pizza deliveries, no mean stuff happening to our car. In fact, he'd disappeared so much that we'd started to get spooked by his absence.

'You think?' This was delivered flatly. 'He's probably just regrouping, like before.'

I didn't want to think about that. 'Jesus, Matthew, can you not back me up here, just a little bit? Unless you think I should just lie down and take whatever crap he's prepared to dish out?'

I admit it: I was a little bit proud of myself. I'd taken matters into my own hands for once.

Except that Matthew didn't seem to agree. 'We had a plan. We agreed we weren't going to approach him. But you decided to hell with that, and you go provoking him?'

'I wasn't provoking him. Just because your way didn't work.'

His face went funny. 'You think this is some kind of competition?'

'Don't be stupid. But it was better than sitting here writing things down.'

I didn't mean for it to come out like that; that his methods were piddling and ineffectual. But his face grew blacker.

'Oh, really. Maybe you think I should have gone round there too, is that it? Pulled the jealous boyfriend act? Leave my girlfriend alone or I'll knock your block off type of thing?'

'Stop it, Matthew.' We never rowed like this, it was awful.

'That might make us both feel better for five minutes, but we'd just be playing into that bastard's hands. Which you've already done, if you don't mind me saying so, by going round there. It's probably exactly what he wanted.'

I was afraid now. Matthew was right about so many things; what if he was right about that too? 'He can't stand the sight of me,' I argued, more to myself than anybody else. 'The last thing he wants is me turning up at his place of work, and risking people finding out what he's been doing. I know what he's like, remember? Mr Respectable. Always careful about what people might think of him. I've given him a warning shot.'

But Matthew took no comfort from that. He sighed. 'Oh, Clara. I just bet he's sitting at home going over and over the whole thing in his head, like the sick weirdo he is.'

'Can you please stop that?'

'Calling him a weirdo? I'm sorry, but that's what he is.'

'I honestly think he'll back off now.'

'Maybe he will. Who knows? But we'll still be talking about him, won't we? Or trying not to look over our shoulders, or out the windows, or checking our number plate to see if it's still there. The guy has already won.'

The prospect was frightening. 'Well, let's forget about him then. Let's not mention him again tonight.' I grabbed a pile of papers. 'Come on. Let's go through some wedding stuff.' I knew I was trying too hard. I could hear it in my voice.

Matthew looked at the papers, and looked away again. 'I think we should go back to London.'

The air in the room went dead.

'Matthew,' I said. 'That's not funny.'

'As if I'd joke about a thing like that.'

'But . . . what are you talking about? This is our home now. We live here.'

'And I'd like to continue living here but I don't know if we can, Clara.'

He was being completely serious. I couldn't believe it.

'So we're going to let him drive us out, is that it? Let him win?'

'It's not like that.'

'Yes, it is!' I looked at him. 'You want us to pack our bags, to give up this lovely house, to leave my family, because Jason is sending us unwanted pizzas?'

'Let's not water this thing down. It's a lot more than that and you know it.'

'Yes, but none of it's enough to make me want to leave.'

'It's enough to make *me* want to leave.' He took a breath. 'And it's nothing to do with being a coward, Clara.'

'I didn't say that.'

'You meant it, though.' His face was almost hard. He had changed too, through this. 'I don't want to live my life looking out from behind my net curtains, simply to prove a point. I have nobody to prove a point to. And certainly not him.' His lip curled in contempt. 'But what I do want is a normal, happy existence with my fiancée, just like I used to have in London.'

I had a sudden vision of it too; life had seemed so busy and crowded in London. It was partly why we had moved here. Now, it seemed the essence of simplicity.

'There would be no shame in it, Clara. It would be the best decision.'

All this was going too fast for me. I couldn't get my head around it. We had to give up our dreams, our new lives, just like that?

Matthew was so pragmatic: if something didn't work, then change it. But it was different for him. He didn't have the same emotional attachment. He had no family here. And he wasn't the one being driven out. In a way, he was just collateral damage.

'I think he's going to stop,' I reiterated, determined to believe it myself. 'At least let's wait and see.'

Matthew gave me a long look and quietly left the room.

Chapter Forty-three

'You look awful,' Sophie said.

'Cheers.'

Undaunted by my sarcasm, she bristled with motherly concern. 'And you haven't ordered a croissant in days. Are you off your food?'

'I'm on a diet,' I lied.

'I hear your brother got a girl pregnant.'

As always, I struggled to keep up with Sophie's unpredictable train of thought. 'He's going to be a father, yes. He's very happy about it. Can I have a coffee, please, Sophie?'

Her head snapped back defensively. She knew when she was being dismissed. 'Fine.'

God knows what kind of brew Valerie would be instructed to make me.

The truth was, Eddie was giving me the cold shoulder since I'd advised him to get a proper job. But I heard plenty about it from Anita, who seemed to have ended up as some kind of reluctant go-between.

'Oh, it's awful,' she'd said on the phone to me earlier. 'Eleanora's parents are in on the act now, did you know that? I had her mother on the phone to me last night, giving out yards. You'd think I had gone up to Dublin and impregnated her myself. The mother said I was just as bad, harbouring Eddie, while her daughter was stuck in that bedsit.'

'Tell her to mind her own business.'

'How can I do that?' Anita wailed. 'And there's Eddie, stubborn as ever, saying that he won't bow down to an ultimatum. I think Eleanora's given him another one. That she's going to move abroad and raise the baby in a kibbutz or something like that.'

'Mam,' I said, just to try to get through to her, 'I think you should mind your own business too. They're adults. They're going to have to sort this one out themselves.'

Anita was on a roll, though. 'And then Róisín said something about your having lethal weapons in your car? This was after Mrs Finn told me at Mass that there was a commotion around Róisín's house, some woman shouting about Róisín and making a holy show of her. I don't know,' she said, 'I just don't know.'

There was a crackling noise on the other end of the phone.

'Anita? Are you eating something?'

'Oh, so now I can't *eat*?' And she hung up smartly on me.

I should have gone over; a short visit at least, just to check that she wasn't overdosing on Mr Kipling. But I was just so tired these days. When the alarm went off in the mornings all I wanted to do was burrow back under the covers and sleep; anything to avoid having to lift those blinds and look out onto another day.

It was the watching, the waiting. That was the exhausting part; the wondering what Jason would do next, or if he would do anything at all. I felt like I was in a holding pattern, wondering whether it was really over or whether it would all start again.

I knew Matthew felt the same. We were OK in the house. It was our territory, and as long as we kept the blinds at half-mast, blocking out the view, we could carry on pretty much as normal. Well, as normal as you could be when you lived more or less in your kitchen.

But any little noise, any sound at all, and we were both on super alert – eyes wide open, necks swivelling around to see what, who, where.

'The postman,' one of us would eventually deduce.

And we would relax, only for it to start all over again when Burt Reynolds revved up his motorbike, nearly giving us heart attacks, or when

Kian and Jennifer would burst out of their back door and into the garden. 'Ma! Ma! She pushed me!'

We still managed all the normal things, though: work, and the Saturday trip to the supermarket, darts and (occasionally) Susie's Burn That Butt. Matthew still talked energetically about Team Tech and occasionally went out with them. Once or twice he had come home very drunk.

But the good had gone out of things, somehow. We no longer drew up plans for the back garden, and what great things we would do with it when we finally had time. The wedding plans had been more or less put on ice. We were in the grip of inertia, waiting for the unknown.

We were careful with each other, too. Cautious of feelings and insecurities. There were no impromptu darts sessions out the back any more, even though we stuck together like glue. But since our row things felt tense between us. Oh, we were pretending for all we were worth, but Jason had managed to drive a little wedge between us, of hurt and stress and unspoken accusations.

London hadn't been spoken about again. Not yet, anyway.

Róisín caught up with me in Dirty Harry's on darts night.

'Not avoiding me, by any chance?' She plonked herself down at the Wives & Girlfriends table. Tonight there was only me; Maura had gone to her mother-in-law's, and the rest usually didn't show up. 'You haven't been answering my calls. And when I called to the house last week, you didn't answer the door. I know you were home, I could see you sitting in the kitchen.'

'I'm sorry, I've just been really busy. How are you? Did you do anything about Catherine?'

'Don't try to deflect.' Her face was creased in worry. 'I'm worried about you, Clara.'

I was sorry I'd told her that day. It just seemed to complicate things even more; to take things further out of my control. 'Look, you were right about the Mace,' I said, low. 'It was stupid. I've thrown it out and it's over, OK?'

Over at the darts board, a small cheer went up. Matthew had scored well, it seemed; The Knob was giving him an enthusiastic high-five. Thank God for darts night, the only thing keeping us sane right now.

Róisín wasn't going to be budged. 'If you don't tell me what's going on, I'll ask Matthew. Because I know something is.'

I opened my mouth but closed it again. I was afraid that once I started to speak I wouldn't be able to stop.

'It's him, isn't it?' she said. 'Jason. What's he been doing, Clara? Has he been following you around?'

She got her answer when the door to Dirty Harry's opened and in walked Dominique and Jason.

My knee bounced up so hard that it jolted the table. Róisín rescued our drinks just in time.

Jason stood for a moment, like he was on a stage, then he nodded pleasantly to me as he walked past to the bar. 'Evening, Clara.'

I hadn't seen him since the day in his office. It was as though it had never happened.

Dominique trailed behind. She wasn't her usually polished self. Her face was cold, angry, as she looked at me wordlessly. She was in a right vicious mood and I had a sinking feeling that it was to do with me.

'Bloody hell,' Róisín whispered beside me. 'What have you done to her?'

Who knew? Jason had probably told her that I'd come to his office and tried to ravish him behind her back.

I was shaking inside but determined not to show it. I wondered had he turned up deliberately here. He knew by now that it was darts night; he'd have seen our car driving out earlier.

'Are you OK?' Matthew materialised beside me. I saw his fingers twitching on a dart: that was all we needed, him to skewer Jason between the eyes and end up arrested.

'Fine. Just ignore him. He's hardly going to do anything here, in a public place.'

Jason was studiously ignoring us at the bar. Dominique plonked herself down on a stool, her mouth a thin red line. She was ignoring us too, yet I knew that her entire being was aware of my presence.

'Will someone please tell me what's going on?' Róisín insisted.

There was no way I was telling her now. Supposing she went over and confronted him?

But Matthew leaned over and squeezed my hand reassuringly. 'It's OK. She should know.'

It was like some kind of turning point. Some small fight-back.

And so we told her, starting at the beginning. Matthew listed off all the things that had happened, and as he went on, Róisín's face grew blacker and more outraged. She darted furious looks over at Jason, but he seemed to be embroiled in deep conversation with Dominique and paid us no heed.

When Matthew was finished, I was sure Róisín would launch into a you-have-to-go-to-the-Guards piece. She might even have said how she had never liked him anyway, and wasn't a bit surprised. Instead, she reached over and put an arm around my shoulders. 'You should have said something before. It must have been awful for you.'

I almost burst into tears. And I might have, had Dominique's loud, angry voice not captured all of our attention.

She was standing abruptly at the bar, and grabbing her handbag. 'You needn't think I'm going to hang around for this.' Her voice was shrill and high.

Jason, I saw immediately, was mortified. 'Sit down,' he said quietly, authoritatively.

'No man makes a fool of me, do you hear me? Not you, not anybody else.'

'Sit *down*.'

'Fuck you,' Dominique told him baldly. And with that, she grabbed her drink, and emptied it squarely over his head. 'We're finished.'

And she sailed out, her puffy hair springing up and down with each step.

Chapter Forty-four

'Are you sure you're going to be alright?'
'I keep telling you. I'll be fine.'

But he wasn't happy. For days now he'd gone about the house checking the smoke alarms, and giving the window locks a sudden, violent wrench, just to see if they held up. He'd put a new bolt on the side door – a massive, shiny thing with five pins and huge studs, and which took a bunch of keys the size of your fist to open.

'You have all the telephone numbers?'

'Yes.'

'The one for the hotel? And Mum's mobile in case for some reason you can't get hold of me?'

'I have them all.'

'OK.' He worried at his lower lip. 'I still wish you could come with me.'

So did I. But it wasn't possible. When you were a one-woman business, it was kind of tricky finding another staff member to delegate to.

Besides, it was an important gig: a summer party in a marquee for a hundred people. I'd spent ages preparing for it and there was no way I could get out of it at this late stage. I didn't *want* to; this could be a turning point for the business.

'It's only for a week,' I reassured him. 'It'll fly by.'

Matthew was going back to London for work. The whole of Team Tech was going. The mother ship was based there – Team Tech didn't 'belong' to the solicitors firm they worked for, they were outsourced by some other company, which had now called them home for a week of conferences and product launches. 'Basically, it's a big group hug.'

He'd tried to get out of it. Surely they couldn't *all* be needed. But one of the new accountancy packages was particularly relevant to them, and, as Eamon put it, 'You need to fucking turn up, man.'

There were advantages. He would get to see his mother. He was going to catch up with some of the gang, including Jo – 'Great! I've got tickets for a club!' – and Cool Art and a few others.

He would get some space from Ireland. He could relax, have a few drinks. Be normal. I knew he needed it.

'I hate you being here on your own,' he said.

'Well, don't. I'll be so busy I won't even miss you. Besides, in the evening I'll get the telly all to myself.'

Dance for Your Supper was reaching its culmination at the weekend. Thank Christ. The whole country was awash with excitement: would Paudie, the little fella in the shiny waistcoat, win? Or Stella O'Shea, with her beautiful long dark hair, and 'feet of fire'? And then there was the novelty act of a smiling man and his dancing dog, Duffy, who could keep time with him in a jig.

'They're tipped to win, they were saying it on the radio,' Anita phoned to tell me, livid. 'I'll go mad if they do. We'll have to look at them on every bloody television programme for the next six months, and Bangers and Mash go mental every time they see that stupid dog.'

I was taken aback at her anxiety. 'It's only a dancing dog, Anita.' ('Only'. Like they were two a penny.) 'There's no need to go blowing it out of proportion.'

'Oh, so now she's telling me how to feel as well as what to eat.'

'Now, that's not fair. Look, come over tonight, will you? I'll make dinner for us. We can catch up.'

'I can't. I have to drive Eddie to the train station. There's some kind of crisis meeting with him and her parents. So, naturally, I have to go too.'

'Oh, Anita. Didn't I tell you to keep out of it?'

'I will if they will! Eddie needs someone to stick up for him.' Her breathing was ragged. 'Here's Eddie now, I have to go.'

Matthew didn't look too upset at missing the finals of *Dance for Your Supper*. 'Put a fiver down for me on Stella to win.' He liked Stella's very short skirts.

We smiled at each other. It was genuine. Since Jason had vanished from our estate — Dominique had fecked all his things out in black sacks and he'd collected them under cover of darkness — it was like the sun had come out. We were no longer fearful of running into him on our front step. We'd put our blinds back up. It was like the big bad wolf had gone.

'You need to go,' I urged him. I was anxious for him to enjoy this trip, to get on well. We had a chunk of our lives back, and we needed to move on. 'Have you got the keys to the flat, in case they're out?'

Matthew patted his pocket. 'Oh, I have them, alright.'

Matthew was going to visit the flat, and our crabby tenants, in London. Mindful of rules and regulations, he'd meticulously telephoned ahead to signal his intention to visit. He'd got the asthmatic one, who sounded like he had a fine set of lungs on him, even though Matthew tested him by keeping him talking on the phone for a full ten minutes about the plastering job. 'Not a single wheeze.' Matthew had come off the phone in disgust.

He hesitated by the door. 'Are you sure you'll be—'

'I'll be absolutely fine. Come on. Let's forget about him now, OK?'

He might still rob our number plate, and get up to his fake-pizza-delivery tricks, but he was out of our faces. We hadn't seen Dominique since, either. Maybe she was too embarrassed after her display in the pub, although I had a feeling she was no stranger to scenes in pubs.

Maybe, just maybe, life was settling back into some kind of normality.

Kian was playing outside the front of his house. He seemed to have mislaid his trousers and was pottering about in his underpants. He saw Matthew's bag.

'Where are ya going, mister?'

'London.'

'Where's that?'

'In England.'
'Where's that?'
'In a galaxy far, far away.'
'Cool.'

Kian was still there when I got back from the airport an hour later, playing around in the dirt.

'Hi, Kian!' I was extra cheery as I got out of the car. It was great to just stand there in my front drive, like a regular person, and have a chat with the neighbours.

Kian looked at me hopefully. 'Have you got any sweets?'

'No. Sorry.' Anyway, I was afraid Ma would kill me if she caught me filling him with junk.

Like magic, her voice cut through the air from the bowels of the house. 'Kian. What did I tell you about washing your hands before dinner?'

'Nobody washes their hands before dinner,' Kian grumbled, but he got to his feet anyway.

Something stirred in the back of my mind. 'Kian?'

'I have to go.'

'I know, I just wanted to ask you. You said once that everybody looks into other people's gardens.'

Kian looked at me blankly, and I felt relief. My paranoia again. I was only confusing the poor child.

'Not everybody's garden. Only yours,' he said, after some consideration.

'Kian!' Ma shrieked again.

But I had to know. 'Who looks into my garden, Kian?'

'The man in the woods. I see him at night from my bedroom window.'

And he scampered in.

'Clara! Clara! Are you in there?'

I jerked upright on the couch, in full flight mode. My heart was in my mouth. I stared wildly around. What was going on?

The knocking started again. Although it was more of a pounding, really.

274

'Clara! For fuck's sake, open up! This is serious!'

The clock said ten past ten in the morning. I couldn't believe it. Too scared to sleep upstairs on my own last night, I'd taken up residence on the couch. I'd sat there, huddled, until I saw dawn breaking. Then I must have dropped off.

The voice, I realised, was Eddie's. Another fecking crisis with Eleanora, from the sounds of it. I staggered to my feet, groggy and cross. Honestly, that boy needed to wise up, and fast. And if he thought I was in the humour for some argument on the merits of artistic endeavour over the grind of child-minding, then he was in for a shock.

'Thank God.' He nearly fell in the door when I finally opened it, having disarmed the alarm and unlocked all the locks. He took in my dishevelled state. 'Are you sick or something?'

'No, Eddie, I'm not.' I tried to blink the sleep out of my eyes. 'I stayed up late working on the gig for Saturday, if you must know.'

It was partially true. It was a complicated party. They wouldn't stick to the menu and had wanted all kinds of fiddly things that I had to order in specially. It was someone's birthday and so they wanted a cake. And the napkins had to be red, for some reason, and the wine glasses long-stemmed, not short stemmed – all this via email – and for two pins I'd tell them to shag off, except that it was a really big party and I desperately needed the money.

'It's Anita,' Eddie said urgently.

'What about her?'

'I think she broke her diet.'

He'd make a drama out of anything. 'It wouldn't be the first time, Eddie. And if you paid her any bit of attention at all, instead of dragging her into your own problems, you'd see that she's finding things hard going at the moment.'

I knew I was being mean. Especially as I hadn't exactly been suffocating her with love and care myself the last few weeks.

'No, I mean she's *really* broken her diet. I came home from rehearsals early and I found her in the kitchen, all pale and sweaty, and she said that Eleanora had phoned to say that she was bleeding.'

I realised how white he looked. 'Leave Anita to me. I'll go over straight away.'

But Eddie was looking over his shoulder. 'She's in the car.'

I looked too. 'Your car?'

'She passed out on me. I didn't know what else to do.'

Chapter Forty-five

'Anita? Anita? Can you hear us?'

For a big woman, Anita seemed small, lying there in the hospital bed. Her skin was pale and she seemed a bit shrunken. But maybe that was because of all the tubes and drips hanging out of her, and the heart monitor beside her bed.

'Do you think she's going to die?' I asked Róisín.

'Don't be stupid.'

'Well, she looks desperate.'

'Thanks a bunch,' said Anita. She opened her eyes, dazed-looking, and licked dry lips. 'Can I have a drink? I'm very thirsty.'

'I'll have to ask them,' said Róisín. 'You're already getting a lot of fluid via your IV line.'

I didn't know whether it was reassuring or not to have Róisín there. On the one hand, she'd already spoken to the consultant, the ward nurses, the matron and possibly the hospital's board of management about our mother's condition. On the other hand she used a lot of terminology that was a little bit freaky, and I could get nowhere near Anita for all the fussing and adjusting Róisín was doing of various pieces of equipment.

'Do you know where you are?' she asked loudly.

'A hospital.' Anita rolled her eyes. 'I'm not stupid.'

'They got you here in the nick of time,' Róisín warned. 'You nearly went into a coma.'

Anita looked only mildly interested. 'Really?'

It had been very frightening. They'd whisked her to a cubicle in the Emergency Department and a whole team suddenly flocked around her, pulling the curtains closed. It was like something from *ER*, except that none of them looked like George Clooney. Thankfully nobody roared 'Stand clear!' from behind the curtain because in television-speak that usually meant some kind of resuscitation. Instead, the team all traipsed out a few minutes later, businesslike, and we heard one of them arranging to go on his dinner break.

There was a problem with her blood sugars, we were eventually informed. They gave us numbers that neither Eddie nor I could understand — Róisín hadn't arrived yet to decipher it for us — but from everyone's reaction they seemed to be impressively bad.

'Was it cherry bakewell tarts?' Eddie had asked in dread.

The medical staff, naturally, couldn't say for sure. But our mother's diabetes was completely uncontrolled, either through poor diet or lack of medication — it turned out that she'd been ignoring both — and something would have to be done.

At least she was looking an awful lot better now.

'Eleanora,' she blurted, sitting up in the bed. 'Is Eleanora alright? And the baby?'

The machine to her left began to blip a bit faster.

'We've no news yet,' I said. 'Eddie's gone up to her. He says to say hello, by the way, and that he'll be back as soon as he can. Anyway, they don't know what the bleeding is yet.'

'Probably a threatened miscarriage,' said Róisín carefully, no doubt to prepare us for the worst.

'A miscarriage! What are you two doing here? You should be up with her too! Róisín, you could put pressure on her doctors. Get them to prioritise her.'

'There's nothing anybody can do. They'll just have to wait and see.'

'It's all the aggravation,' Anita cried. 'That's what's done this. The petty fighting over jobs and money and who's going to do what. And that bedsit is damp, did you know that? It's no place for an expectant woman.'

Now the machine was totally stressed out, with green dots dancing up and down on it.

'Anita,' I said, 'we need to talk about you right now.'

'Me? I'm fine,' she huffed, and immediately threw back the covers on the bed. 'I need to get home to Bangers and Mash.'

'We're looking after the dogs. Anita, get back into that bed,' Róisín said, alarmed.

But our mother brushed Róisín aside and began hunting for her clothes. 'What did they do with them, then? Find my shoes for me, Clara, good girl.'

And then she clutched the edge of the locker, wavered, and sat back down heavily onto the side of the bed.

'Anita? Are you alright?'

'I just felt a bit weak there.' Her face had gone pasty white, and a clammy layer of sweat had broken out. 'I'll be grand in a minute.'

'See? This is what happens, you daft woman,' Róisín admonished. 'Clara, give me a hand.'

We loaded Anita back into bed, adjusting sheets and blankets. There were no more protestations or rebuttals from her. She was as quiet as a lamb as we pressed her back onto her pillows.

'This diabetes thing,' Róisín began eventually. 'What are we going to do?'

Nobody said anything. Neither Róisín nor I had the answers.

Anita seemed to realise this. 'I've been so stressed,' she said. 'And the bloody diet didn't work. I just gave up on it.'

'But if you give up on it, then what's going to happen? Are you going to end up here again?'

Nobody wanted to go any further. She might not come out the next time. Or she might end up in some care facility, unable to look after herself.

She looked frightened. 'I want to be around for Eddie's baby.'

Róisín looked at her. 'That's up to you.'

Chapter Forty-six

'It's not pretty,' Matthew warned me on the phone.

I felt my heart sink even further, if such a thing was possible. By now, it was lurking permanently somewhere down in my boots.

'How not pretty?'

'Downright ugly. Have you got half an hour?'

Ah, Jesus. Luckily it was my evening off from visiting our mother. Eddie was in with her. Fair play to him, he was spending long hours by her bedside, reading to her.

'Make him stop,' she'd begged me yesterday. '*The Complete Works of Shakespeare*, every single bloody day. He puts on different voices and everything. There are sick people in here, you know.'

'Just tell me,' I begged Matthew.

He'd gone round to the flat to see the tenants, as arranged. He just hadn't gone on the appointed day. The conference had run over, Team Tech had got stuck in at some networking do until late, and Matthew had had to put off the visit until the following night instead.

'Basically,' he said, 'I took them unawares.'

The question was, doing what?

Plants sprang to mind; rows and rows of carefully tended marijuana plants, irrigated by the shower hose in our newly plastered bathroom. You read about it all the time in the paper: 'Suburban Flat Conceals Drugs Empire'.

Our lovely, lovely flat. I was desperately homesick now for its cramped cosiness. We mightn't have had three thousand square feet, but we'd been happy there. We'd been able to sleep in our beds, safe in the belief that there was nobody lurking outside, watching.

Matthew had been right: we should never have let those two in, with their studenty clothes and starey eyes.

He was still reluctant. 'Are you sure?'

'There was a woman in the flat.'

'Who? One of their girlfriends?'

'I'd imagine so.' Matthew's voice was tight. 'Seeing as I walked in on the two of them in bed.'

'So what's the problem?' He seemed to think they'd signed up to celibacy as part of the tenancy agreement.

'Clara, it was Jo.'

I honestly didn't know whether to laugh or cry. Apart from all the hospital stuff with Anita, the big booking on Saturday was doing my head in. New emails came in every day: could I substitute one of the meat dishes for an extra vegetarian one instead? Could I cater for a nut allergy? Could they add twenty more guests at this stage?

I was stressed. I was missing Matthew like crazy. And I was afraid to go to sleep at night because of something a five-year-old boy had said.

I hadn't told Matthew. What could I say? He was in London; there was nothing he could do except feel worse.

Anita's house was empty. I'd gone over every day to feed Bangers and Mash and take them for walks. I could have gone to stay there. But I didn't know it like my own house; I'd forgotten its nocturnal creaks and groans. And it was in the countryside, practically. I'd be better off staying put.

But mostly I wanted to be brave. I wanted to prove to myself that I was still the same woman who'd left London; a capable, happy, positive person who was glad to be alive and who didn't dread evening time, when the light would begin to fade, and the town would grow still and quiet, except for the rustle in the woods behind the house.

'Clara?' Matthew was saying. 'Are you still there?'

I could hear the alarm in his voice. All week long he'd been ringing. Three times a day, sometimes four, 'Just to check that you're OK.'

'I'm still here.'

'I spoke to Eamon, you know,' he said suddenly. 'He said that maybe I could shoot off a day early. What with your mum in hospital.'

'But I thought the launch was happening tomorrow? Of that new package?'

'The lads can fill me in.'

'You need to be there, Matthew.' He was only on a contract, still.

'Not if it's a family emergency.'

But I wasn't going to let this be taken from us, too. 'Stay. There's nothing to come home for. Everything's fine.'

'Why didn't you tell me Matthew had gone to London?' Róisín asked, incredulous.

'There hasn't been time, what with all the stuff with Anita. Anyway, he's back in a couple of days.'

'I don't care. I'm staying over with you until then.'

'No, you're not.'

Róisín looked at me. 'Why are you being like this? Jason Farrell is making your life miserable and you're acting all brave and bolshy, like you've something to prove?'

'What do you want me to do? Crawl into a corner and pull a blanket over my head?'

I didn't tell her about Kian. In some ways, it was the final straw. Imagine being petrified by a five-year-old. If I admitted it to anybody else, then really, I might as well just give up.

And I wasn't ready to do that yet.

'Look,' I said to her, 'just give me your Le Creuset pot and let me go, OK?'

She got up and flung open a few presses. 'A marquee,' she snorted. 'In *Ireland*.'

'It is the summer, Róisín.'

'Again, a marquee. In *Ireland*.'

'I suppose they know what they're doing.'

The truth was, I was sick of this party on Saturday night. Piss artists, still emailing me with outrageous demands with less than twenty-four hours to go. And they still hadn't even paid the deposit, despite several reminders. At least their endless stream of requests reassured me that they hadn't gone cold. But, in all honesty, if I hadn't most of the food bought and prepped already, I would have pulled out. I wasn't even allowed to deliver anything in advance, as the marquee wouldn't be set up till early morning.

At least it kept me busy. I'd stayed up all last night, preparing for it. I'd be up all night tonight again. You can't have bad dreams when you're awake.

'What about moving back to London?' Róisín asked quietly.

I looked at her. 'Have you been discussing this with Matthew?'

'Of course I haven't. I'm talking about for a while. Just until things die down a bit.'

I hadn't thought of it like that: a break away from this knife-edge that we seemed permanently balanced upon. Almost like a holiday back to our old, happy lives.

It sounded so tempting. Right now every nerve ending in my body was over-worked, burned out.

'All this stress you're under,' Róisín said. 'He's not worth it.'

'Maybe,' I said. I picked up the dish she'd put on the table. 'I'll think about it, OK?'

'And, Clara? You should tell Eddie too.'

'No,' I snapped.

'Why?'

In all honesty, I didn't know. Maybe it was because Jason's stealth and secrecy made me feel like I was embroiled in something dirty too, and was too ashamed to tell anybody what was happening to me. What I had *let* happen; what I seemed to be powerless to stop. How could an apparently confident, educated, intelligent person like myself have ended up frightened of her own shadow?

Róisín read my face. 'It's not your fault,' she said fiercely. 'It's his. And you shouldn't protect him. The more people who know what he's doing, the better. Tell them,' she urged. 'Soon. Or I will.'

Warmed by her support and strength, I was able to let down my guard. Maybe I *would* ask her to stay over with me. It would be so nice not to face this on my own.

Then a voice rang out. 'Who's getting in the shower first, you or me?'

Catherine sauntered into the kitchen wearing only a pair of knickers and one of Róisín's T-shirts. She gave me a huge smile. 'Hi, Clara! I'm surprised Róisín let you in. Normally when I stay over she runs people out of here like they have an STD.'

Róisín looked from Catherine to me, mortification seeping out of every pore. 'Um, we're back together.'

'No kidding,' I said. I was smiling like a lunatic. It was so unusual to have something nice happen these days.

'I suppose with Anita getting sick like that, you realise that life is short,' Róisín said.

'So romantic, isn't she?' Catherine joked. 'Diabetes brought us together.'

I was curious, though, as to what arrangement they'd come to. 'So . . . is this going to be public?'

'Róisín's decided she's out and proud,' Catherine announced.

'I have not.' Róisín rounded on her. 'What I've *decided* is that maybe it's time I told a few people around here.'

Which was a momentous move for Róisín. I was so proud of her.

'I'm going to let word gradually filter out, that kind of thing.' She looked at me. 'Maybe you could slip it into the conversation with Sophie, for instance?'

'Are you sure? You know, if you want it to be gradual, as opposed to taking a megaphone and announcing it to the entire province?'

'Maura, then,' Róisín swiftly amended it to. 'And The Knob. They'd be decent about it.'

'Everybody's going to be *decent* about it.'

Catherine shrugged. 'So I keep telling her. I came out to all of my family and neighbours at my grandfather's birthday.'

'And he died two days later,' Róisín told me.

'The man was *ninety*.'

'But I'm not telling any of my patients.' Róisín was back to fretting again. 'It's none of their business. My relationship with them is purely professional.'

'Well, of course it is, Róisín.'

'And remember to carry some extra heart pills on your rounds in case word reaches them from the street,' Catherine advised her.

'Stop.' Róisín's hands flew to her face at the thought. It was all very well for Catherine to joke, but I knew how hard this was for my sister. 'One minute I'm fine with it, the next I'm absolutely petrified. What if everybody suddenly starts turning to look at me in the supermarket?'

'Why would they?'

'You don't get it. Being a lesbian is different. It's not as cool as being a gay bloke. People have all these preconceptions that we're butch and gruff and have desperate haircuts.'

'Not when I walk out to the post box like this,' said Catherine, flinging back her silky hair and flashing her knickers.

'Jesus Christ!' Róisín nearly took her down in a rugby tackle. 'You can't just walk out there!'

'You silly woman.' Catherine looked at her with great affection and said to me, 'Was she always this easy to wind up?'

Chapter Forty-seven

'Look. There's a foot. Do you see? And that's a hand. I know it doesn't look like much right now, but apparently those little nubs there are the fingers.'

I peered at the little black-and-white scan picture Eddie was holding up. To be honest, it just looked like a blob to me, but I made admiring noises.

'We don't know yet whether it's a boy or a girl. It's too early to tell. But the main thing is that the baby is measuring spot-on for dates.'

He was so excited about the baby scan that he didn't get any of his usual enjoyment out of getting dressed up in Matthew's trousers and putting on a long apron and greasing his hair back like a member of the Mafia. He was serving at the party today. Thankfully he seemed to have got over our little spat.

'Is Eleanora home from the hospital yet?' I enquired.

'Yes. Well, she's gone to her parents. They said there was no way she was going back to that horrible bedsit. That it was damp.' His enthusiasm waned. 'They don't want me anywhere near her, you know.'

'That's not up to them, Eddie.'

'They think I'm a layabout who's not going to provide properly for their daughter or our baby.'

Perversely, I felt protective of him. It was OK for us to be hard on him, but as for Eleanora's family . . . 'Lots of people have families in less than ideal circumstances, Eddie. You wouldn't be the first. Here. Take this.'

We were loading hundreds of miniature finger foods into the back of The Knob's refrigerated van. Well, he'd borrowed it from work, and had to have it back by five that evening before anyone missed it. Judging by the smell, it was normally used to transport fish.

Matthew was due home tomorrow. The thought of it was keeping me going. I was picking him up from the airport in the morning.

I hated the needy way I was counting down the hours. Jo and I used to loathe women who couldn't bear to be separated from their man, always texting and phoning him like their own personality had been swallowed up by his wonderfulness. '*No* dignity,' Jo always said disparagingly. 'Needs a man to complete her.'

If Jo knew I'd gone over to the dark side, she'd be amazed. *I* was amazed. I barely recognised myself any more.

But then again, Jo had gone over to the dark side herself. There had been no word from her since Matthew had caught her *in flagrante* with our tenant. Who turned out to be a twenty-year-old art student whose parents paid the rent.

'Maybe they're right,' Eddie announced. 'Maybe I *am* irresponsible.'

'Eddie . . .' We needed to get moving. I was due to pick Sophie up on the way – she was serving too – and she abhorred tardiness.

'You've said it too, Clara. Here I am, fast approaching thirty, and I have nothing except a second-hand car; no house, no job, no health insurance. I had to get Anita to be a signatory on a loan I had to take out last year to get one of my *teeth* fixed. Jesus, I can't even pay for my own dentistry, Clara,' he finished up rather sadly. 'But when I saw that scan . . .' He shook his head, awed. 'I didn't even know I wanted that baby until I saw it. I'm going to be a father, Clara. And now that Eleanora's out of danger, it's my job to support her and the baby.'

Well, you couldn't argue with that.

'I've got an agent who specialises in commercial voiceover work,' he said in a low, ashamed voice. You would have thought he'd engaged the services of a pimp. 'I'm trying out for an insurance ad on Monday.' He hung his head. 'The money's good, though.'

'That's great, Eddie.' Anita would be delighted. It would hasten her recovery by days if she could boast to all the other patients that Eddie was going to be on the radio.

'It's time to do the right thing.' With a suitably stiff upper lip, he turned away.

Blast. Just as I made my last trip to the van, Dominique came out of her house.

What to do? Ignore her? Pretend I didn't see her?

In the end I went over, just as she was clattering towards the car in a big pair of high heels.

'Dominique?'

Unfriendly eyes met mine. 'What do you want?'

'Look, I just wanted to say I was sorry about you and Jason.'

'Are you really,' she said flatly.

'Yes. Obviously I have very little time for him after his recent behaviour but at the same time I don't take any pleasure from your break-up.' Well, actually that was a lie. I was delighted not to have to look at his mug on my estate any more. But I didn't wish Dominique any harm.

Dominique planted a hand on her hip and looked me up and down slowly.

Admittedly, I wasn't at my best in my blue tartan chef's pants and plain white top. Plus, I was exhausted. Even a thick layer of make-up couldn't hide the lines under my eyes today. 'Honestly?' she said. 'I don't know what he ever saw in you.'

OK, I wasn't going to stand there and be insulted. I'd come over out of friendship but if she didn't want to meet me half-way . . . 'Whatever went on with you and Jason, I had nothing to do with it.'

She gave a harsh laugh. 'You're joking me, right? You might as well have been sitting on the sofa between us. Everywhere we went you seemed to crop up. Every time I stepped out of the house with Jason, there you were. That bloody pub – what's it called, Dirty Harry's – I had to look at you.'

'That wasn't my fault.' My voice shook a bit.

'He never stopped talking about you. Clara this, Clara that. I'd be sitting there some evenings, listening to him going on about you. Do you know how that made me feel?'

I knew how it made *me* feel: sick. 'I can't help what he talked about.'

But Dominique seemed to take the whole thing as some kind of personal insult. 'Let me tell you one thing. I've been out with a lot of men in my time. A *lot*. And every single one of them was mad about me. And it wasn't just because of the dirty books either. I've travelled, I'm educated, I know my *jus* from my foam.' Take that, Miss Chef. 'I've had two marriage proposals, did you know that? I turned them both down. Why choose one man when there are so many others clambering for my attention?' A shrug of her fake-tanned shoulder. 'Jesus, I can't get on public transport without half the men trying to give me their seat. So let me just assure you that I have more than enough to keep a man interested. *More* than enough.'

'I'm sure you have.' I just wanted to get away now.

'So to think that I could be bettered by the likes of *you* . . .' Another scorching look up and down me. I clearly hadn't improved since the last assessment.

'Is it the food thing?' she said suddenly. 'Some men like that. Women who can cook. Reminds them of their mothers and all that shite. Did you cook a lot for Jason?'

As always, my body jarred at the mention of his name. 'I have to go.'

Dominique wasn't going to let it go. 'Because I've been going over and over it, trying to work it out. What is it about you? You were so mousy when I knew you. And yet you seem to have left such an impression upon him. I just don't get it.'

I looked at her. 'Maybe it's him. Have you thought of that? Maybe it's not me at all.'

Dominique said nothing.

'Maybe you've had a lucky escape.'

I left her standing there.

Chapter Forty-eight

Sophie fanned herself furiously beside me. 'Roll down your window some more, will you? The *smell*.'

We were in the fish van on the way to the marquee. We were late. At least Eddie had gone on ahead, to start setting up. But even though I'd given him precise directions, he still somehow got lost.

'There's no fucking marquee,' he rang me up to complain. 'There's nothing, only fields.'

'Don't be stupid.' My temper was really short now. 'There should be a house. A redbrick. Can you see that?'

'No.'

'Oh, just hang on five minutes. We're right behind you. The bloody guests are going to be there before us at this rate.'

Then Sophie said, 'Do you realise you've put mascara on only one eye?'

Great. When I'd been in the bathroom, there had been a noise downstairs. I'd dropped the mascara wand and rushed down to investigate – just the kettle turning itself off – and had obviously forgotten to finish the job.

We drove on in silence through miles of countryside. Instead of nearing marquees and crowds and noise, we seemed to be driving further into the wilderness.

'There!' Sophie yelped.

'Where? Where?' We were on a tiny, bumpy road now; a lane, really. But we were following the sat nav's directions.

'Eddie's car.' She pointed, and I saw it, parked on the side of the road. 'If you were going to throw a party, wouldn't you think you'd do it somewhere *civilised*?'

'It's a family event,' I reasoned, trying not to panic. 'I guess this is where they live.'

The road grew narrower and more potholed as we neared Eddie's car. My stress grew as I saw him wandering around aimlessly rather than unpacking his boot.

'Put the skids under him,' I ordered Sophie.

'You betcha.' There was nothing she would enjoy more; Eddie, in her eyes, was another Valerie, only this time she had permission to bully.

We got out of the car to find a confused Eddie. 'There's no marquee,' he insisted again.

And on first glance, he appeared to be right. Before us was a great expanse of overgrown fields and trees. Up a winding, disused-looking driveway was an old redbrick house.

'At least there's the house.' They clearly weren't driven by appearances, but that wasn't our problem. 'The marquee is probably behind it.'

We craned our necks. Sophie walked up a bit, for a better look. Nope. No marquee. In fact there was no activity of any kind. No vans, or sound systems, or anything at all that would indicate that a hundred people were going to be wined and dined here shortly.

'Maybe they've moved the whole thing into the house,' Eddie said at last.

Nobody came out to greet us as we drove slowly up to the house.

'Give me the number of the guy who booked you,' Sophie said efficiently. No better woman in a crisis.

'It's in my phone.' I handed it to her. 'Frank Stein.'

She scrolled down my address book. She looked back at me. 'Frank N. Stein?'

'Well, I suppose if that's what it says, Sophie. He just texted me his business card . . .' I stared at her. Frankenstein. How could I not have seen it?

Sophie was trying to keep the scepticism off her own face. 'But you've spoken to him before? Right?'

I felt like such a fool. 'No,' I whispered. The list of demands had annoyed me so much that I hadn't picked up the phone to him at all, preferring the distance of email.

Sophie dialled anyway, and eventually broke the news that we all expected. 'That number seems to be out of order.'

Well, of course it was. Everything else came together in a rush for me. There was no Frank N. Stein and no marquee. Just as there had been no Anne Marie with her garden party that had never happened, or Ian Fleming, except, as Matthew had pointed out, the one who had written the James Bond books. They were fictitious, all of them, in every way.

I'd been taken for a complete fool.

Eddie was knocking on the door of the house now, calling, 'Hello! Anybody home?'

I watched him as though from a distance, a thousand things swimming through my head. Other enquiries that went nowhere. All that time wasted, when I could have been growing my business. And now there I was, in the middle of nowhere, with a van full of expensive food that would soon go off.

How he must have enjoyed himself, fucking me around.

Eddie joined us. 'There's no one home,' he said unnecessarily. 'I think the house is deserted.'

We stood there in the rotting driveway, surrounded by overgrown trees, Sophie and Eddie looking at each other, no doubt wondering whether I was losing it.

I turned around slowly, my eyes searching the fields, the trees. The old hay barn to the side of the house. He was there, somewhere, watching us. Enjoying our confusion. Having set me up for a fall, there was no way he would have missed this one.

'Come on,' I said to Eddie and Sophie, trying to keep the shake out of my voice. 'Let's get out of here. Now.'

★

'What's going on?' Eddie had come back to the house to change into his own clothes.

'There was a mix-up.'

He was watching me. 'It's not like you to make a mistake like that.'

I fumbled in my purse. 'Here.' I held out his pay.

'Don't be stupid.'

'Take it. I booked you. It's not your fault.'

He took the money reluctantly. 'What are you going to do with all the food?'

'Throw it out, I guess.' I'd palmed off as much as I could on Sophie. I'd do the same with Eddie. More had gone to The Knob and Maura, when I'd returned the van.

As for me, I couldn't face a mouthful of it. I'd been tricked, deceived, and hadn't been sharp enough to see it.

Everywhere I turned he won.

'Eddie,' I said suddenly, 'do you want to stay here tonight?'

He was still staying at Anita's. I didn't want to be on my own. If it wasn't too late, I'd have phoned Matthew and begged him to come home. I felt as fragile as glass.

And maybe it was time for Eddie to know what was going on too, as Róisín had said. Maybe it was time for *everybody* to know. This thing had gone too far.

But Eddie was putting his coat on. 'Sounds good, but I can't.' He looked a little shy. 'I phoned Eleanora. Told her about the voiceovers. She asked me if I'd go up. We're going to stay in the flat tonight. She can't wait to get out of her parents' house; she said they're doing her head in.'

It was so hard to put on a smile, to act happy, but I did. 'That's great, Eddie.'

'Is that OK? Because if you're nervous without Matthew . . .'

'Absolutely not. I've been here all week on my own. I just thought it'd be nice to catch up, that's all.' I was hardly going to keep a man from his pregnant partner, just as they were on the brink of reconciliation.

'Will you go over and feed Bangers and Mash? And put them in for the night?'

'Sure, sure. Off you go.'

'I'm sure Róisín's around, if you fancied some company,' he said as he left.

But Róisín wasn't. She'd gone to Dublin for the night; apparently a drawer had been cleared out in her bedroom for Catherine, and they'd gone to collect some of her stuff.

And Anita was still in hospital. When Eddie left, I phoned her up, asking if she'd like me to pop in to visit, but she was appalled. 'Do you not realise what's *on*?' At my stupid silence, she went on, 'The finals of *Dance for Your Supper*. We're all watching it in here. It's going to be Paudie against Stella O'Shea. We're evenly split, it could get vicious.' She hung up on me.

It was just me. After I went over to my mother's to feed the dogs, I locked the house up tight, and put the alarm on. Then I turned the telly on as loud as I could and settled down to wait.

Chapter Forty-nine

He came at 1.20 a.m. I was awake instantly, my heart nearly jumping out of my chest. I sat up on the couch and listened.

There it was again. A noise at the back of the house. I thought I was going to be sick.

I got up. My phone was in my hand. If someone was trespassing on my property, they could explain it to the Guards.

The kitchen was dark, save for patches illuminated by the moon. I stood inside the door, frozen, my eyes frantically searching the darkness outside. I'd left the blinds up, preferring to be able to see what was out there.

But there was nothing. The garden was empty. All I could see were the woods beyond the garden shed, silent and still.

I wondered whether maybe I'd dreamed the noise. I'd been in such a state going to bed, having spent an hour going over my emails from the person called Frank N. Stein. Trying to figure out how I hadn't seen it coming. How had I not known that it was all a ruse?

It was my own fault. I'd been naïve, never thinking that Jason would stoop so low.

I went through all the enquiries the company had received. Dead ends, a lot of them. But mine was a start-up business. I'd thought it was normal to spend a lot of my days providing quotes for people I never heard from again.

I wondered whose computers Jason had used to waste my time. I knew already he was too clever to be traced back to his own.

Something hit the window with a sharp clatter and then fell away.

I felt my knees give.

He was outside somewhere, in the middle of the night, throwing something at my windows.

I held on to the back of a kitchen chair. I felt weak with fear, and shock, and *disbelief* that this was actually happening to me. Because a part of me still couldn't believe that someone could make me feel this way.

I waited. I stood in the dark clutching the chair, my knuckles white, for exactly forty-seven minutes. That's what the digital clock on the microwave said. And nothing else happened.

Eventually, I realised that particular part of his plan for tonight was over. There would be nothing else thrown at the windows. He'd made me stand there, petrified, while he'd already moved on. Maybe he'd even gone home. The bastard.

I unpeeled my fingers from the chair.

I could ring the Guards. Tell them there was an intruder outside. Which there was.

He wouldn't wait around to be arrested, though. The very idea would make him laugh in that superior, arrogant way of his. No, he'd melt away, undetected; he'd turn it round to make it look like I was a nervous woman whose boyfriend had gone away for the week, and who was ringing up the Guards at the drop of a hat.

I didn't even know how he knew Matthew was away. But he knew.

He was in control of this whole thing.

It started again an hour later.

At first I thought it was an animal caught in some trap that had been laid for rabbits. They still did that round here, a few of the old boys. The howl was high-pitched and so clear that it sliced through the night.

The second time I heard it, the hairs rose on the back of my neck.

It was a wolf. The howl of a wolf. And it was coming from the woods behind the house.

Immediately, there was an answering volley of barks from every dog within a mile radius, including Bangers and Mash, who I'd brought back with me when I'd gone over to feed them earlier, just as insurance. They were locked in the shed in the garden, but I could hear that they were just as spooked as I was.

On instinct I went down on all fours. I could feel the blood pumping in my head. Adrenalin and fear and humiliation were all mixed up together, and before I knew it I'd vomited on the floor.

Matthew's home tomorrow. I clung to that thought like it was some kind of anchor. Today, actually. He would be home later today.

A-woo-ooo-ooo.

It was a pastiche of a wolf howl. Mocking. Immediately, there was an answering volley of furious barks from the dogs. He was frightening the shit out of me, and enjoying every minute of it.

And I was powerless to stop it. This was going to go on and on, I was only now beginning to realise. A pattern was emerging: just when I thought he'd finally got bored and gone away, he would come back at me again, having spent the intervening time coming up with new and innovative ways to make my life a misery.

I wished I'd never met him. I wished I'd turned up in that stupid restaurant that night and not embarrassed him in public. Most of all I wished I'd never come back to this godforsaken town.

A-woo-oooooo.

He was getting louder now, and nearer. No doubt imagining me exactly as I was, on the floor in a puddle of my own terror. And thinking, what? That'll teach the bitch?

But I'd already said sorry. And it hadn't made any difference. There was nothing left in my arsenal that would make him go away.

I didn't know if he would try to come in the house. If it would go that far. But I couldn't discount the possibility. Despite all our alarms and locks, he would probably find a way. By now, in my head there wasn't anything he *couldn't* do, at will, and without detection, no matter what the rational part of me said.

I'd made it to my feet again by the time the next howl came. This one was even more ironic, like something from a bad horror movie. He wasn't even trying to disguise that it was him

Shut up. Another howl. This time I said it aloud: 'Shut up.' Now, I was shouting. 'Shut up. SHUT UP.'

The dogs were going crazy now. Good. The more noise the better.

Feeling half crazy myself, I went round the kitchen turning on every single light. 'There! There!' I shouted, as each one burst to life. I even turned on the light over the cooker, and set the fan going for good measure, like I was going to whip up a three-course meal.

I felt naked standing there, in the blazing light, clearly visible to the world outside. The truth was, I felt a bit unhinged. But I couldn't stand any more of this. The waiting, the bloody waiting for what would come next.

Now I was unlocking the patio doors, my hands shaking like I had the DTs. When I turned the handle and threw the doors open to the garden, noise exploded all around me like a mini-bomb.

Jesus. I was paralysed with the shock.

Then: the alarm. I'd forgotten about the house alarm, and I'd set it off.

But at least you couldn't hear his fake wolf howling now. The dogs were louder now, though, the alarm spooking them more. They barked and barked.

'It's OK,' I told them. 'I'm coming.'

I left the alarm wailing into the night as I stepped onto the grass in my bare feet. I registered that it was cold and damp outside, and that I was in my pyjamas, but I didn't care. Every sense was fixed on the back fence, and the woods, where he was hiding.

'I know you're there.' My voice was drowned out by the shriek of the alarm. The trees ahead of me seemed huddled together in a menacing bunch.

'So you might as well show yourself.' I was shouting now, enraged.

A part of me knew that confronting him like that was stupid. And possibly dangerous. What did I think I was doing, out there in the middle of the night, trying to pit myself against somebody who'd shown them-selves to be far more malevolent and nasty than I could ever be? He might even have slipped away already, leaving me talking to a bunch of trees.

The injustice of it propelled me on, across the lawn, down towards the trees.

I walked till I got to the garden shed. I raised my head to the trees behind.

'You're a coward!' Not even the alarm could drown me out this time, or the dogs. 'A pathetic coward, do you know that? Come out and face me like a man! Say what you have to say to my face!'

My eyes probed the undergrowth, trying to see any movement. But the woods just stood against me, thick and dark, and as impenetrable as a wall.

Coward.

Hands shaking, I unlocked the garden shed. Even in the dim light, I could see the dogs' eyes glittering from their crouched position on the floor, the spittle on their snapping jaws. They were half-mad with rage at the pretend wolf, taunting them from the woods.

'Go, Bangers. Go, Mash.'

And I threw the door open. They leaped out from the shed and sprang over the high fence as though it were merely a minor inconvenience. Barking ferociously, they bounded into the woods to settle up with whatever had ruined their sleep. In seconds the trees had swallowed them up, and I listened to them crashing their way through the undergrowth.

I was so glad I'd brought them home with me.

Lights were snapping on in houses to the right and left. A blind went up in Burt Reynolds' upstairs window. I heard someone ask, 'What's going on?'

'Get him, Bangers! Go on, Mash,' I roared. 'I hope you're a fast runner, Jason Farrell! I hope they tear you to bits, you bloody creep!'

A voice came out of the darkness behind me. 'Clara.'

For a moment I'd thought I'd been blind-sided again. That somehow he'd got into my garden without me seeing him, and was going to finish the job off.

I swung around wildly, and saw Róisín coming out of the patio doors. She was in her dressing gown. I blinked; what was she doing here?

Then: I was so glad to see her.

'What's your alarm code?' was the first thing she said.

'One-four-ten.' My birthday date and month.

'Catherine!' she called over her shoulder. 'One-four-ten.'

And I saw Catherine through the kitchen window now, also in her dressing gown. She moved off towards the hall. A moment later, the alarm stopped.

I stood there, in the middle of my lawn, silent now except for my racing heart, and Bangers and Mash barking wildly in the distance. It sounded from here that they'd caught something. Or someone.

Róisín walked over to me. 'The alarm company rang.'

I realised then: she was a key-holder.

I couldn't say anything. She didn't ask. She just put her arm around my shaking shoulders. 'It's alright now. It's alright.'

I turned my head into her shoulder and I wept.

Chapter Fifty

Everyone was great. Róisín and Catherine stayed on and made me cups of tea, and the following morning Catherine drove to Dublin to collect Matthew from the airport. Róisín went around the garden picking up all of Matthew's practice darts, which appeared to be what had been thrown at the window during the night. She kept shaking her head; she didn't trust herself to speak. Maura and The Knob called over to express their support after hearing what had happened, both of them sick with guilt that they'd been out late, and hadn't been there to rescue me when the alarm went off.

'The next time you're to ring me, OK?' The Knob said, keying his mobile number into my own phone himself. 'Any time of the day or night.'

Maura told me that she'd leave her front door on the latch, and that I was to come over whenever I felt like it. Just for a cup of tea, or a chat. Anytime I felt like company, she kept insisting.

Various other neighbours called by over the course of the morning to offer support after my 'scare', as it was being called. Burt Reynolds offered to lay a trap. He knew someone who caught badgers for a living, he said. He could put a rusty trap in the trees just beyond my fence, big enough to take the leg off a grown man. 'And they won't be able to sew it back on, either.' He looked quite disappointed when I turned him down.

CLARE DOWLING

Bangers and Mash turned up back at Anita's house around midday. Eddie had come back from Dublin to wait for them. They'd drunk a gallon of water each, apparently, and settled down for a big, long sleep. They hadn't been hungry for their dinner, he reported.

I was out in the back garden, taking a break from all the well-wishers in the kitchen, when I heard, 'Howaya, missus?'

It was Kian, balanced on his slide and hanging over the fence. He wore a vest, and a purple, flowing scarf wrapped in a turban around his head. He reminded me of Eddie at that age.

'Hi, Kian.' I smiled.

'Where are the dogs?' He looked around my garden in great disappointment.

'Oh. They went home.'

'My da said you've gone bonkers.'

I considered this. 'He might be right.'

'My granny is bonkers.'

'Is she?'

'Yeah. She goes out during the night in her wedding dress and stuff. The last time the nurses found her on a bus, going to the zoo. I like the zoo,' he said.

'Me too.'

We both looked at the woods. They were pleasant and leafy in the bright morning sun.

'Was that man back again?' Kian asked. 'The one who used to go out with the lady over the road?'

'Yes. He was.'

'The next time, I'm going to get him with my laser gun,' he promised me.

'Thank you, Kian.'

Then, 'Kian! What did I tell you!'

He nearly fell off his perch on top of the slide as Ma appeared beside him. She was decked out in lurid Sunday best. 'Get in there and get dressed, we're going up to visit your aunties.'

'Not *again*. Why can't we stay here some weekends?'

'Because Dublin's our home. Not here. Now go on.'

302

She ran Kian, before becoming aware that I was watching over the fence. She returned my gaze. 'Howaya?' she said eventually.

'I'm sorry about the noise last night,' I said. 'I hope it didn't keep you awake too long.'

She looked at me, as though debating something with herself. 'I used to see him hanging around the house when you weren't at home,' she said eventually. 'That solicitor fella. He never looked like he was up to any good.' She looked at me gruffly. 'You can say that, if you want.'

She turned on her heel and went off, just as a car pulled up outside. I heard doors slamming, then there were voices in the kitchen, before the back door opened wide and Matthew stepped out.

'Clara?'

He was home. I ran into his arms. Then, after a little while, we went back inside and we phoned the Guards.

Chapter Fifty-one

The hospital finally told Anita she could go home.

'Oh, no,' she said. 'Thanks anyway, but I'm fine where I am.'

It was explained to her that her blood sugars were stable; she had a new plan worked out for her by the nutritionist, and various follow-up arrangements had been made for her to be seen at regular intervals by the appropriate professionals.

'Look,' they eventually had to say, 'we need the bed.'

Anita didn't want to go home at all. There had been great craic on the ward; always people coming and going, and she'd got very pally with some of the other patients. Apparently quite a crowd had gathered for the final of *Dance for Your Supper*, even though everybody had been bitterly disappointed that the novelty act – the man and his dancing dog – had won in the end. Still, that was what happened when you threw open the phone lines to the public and gave every lunatic a vote.

But now it was back to the solitude of her own house again, and another fecking diet, and no nurses around to check her blood sugar and heap praise on her when it was spot on.

'And if one more person tells me that I've had a wake-up call . . .' she grumbled.

'I suppose it is, in a way. You're going to have to take better care of yourself. Otherwise you're just going to keep ending up in hospital.'

She looked at me. 'You know they have me on happy pills?'

She was trying to be hip, but it was only to hide her mortification. Nobody in the family had ever been on anti-depressants, except for Uncle Joe, but he was a nutcase. And now she was being lumped in with him – talk about a stigma.

'Lots of people go on them for all kinds of reasons. Look, why don't you take all the help you can get?'

She sighed. 'I suppose.'

Matthew was waiting for us back at her house. He'd aired the place and done a few odd jobs. He stood in the hall, waving as we got out of the car.

'Bangers and Mash have missed you,' he called to Anita.

We'd been looking after them in our place since Eddie had moved back permanently into the flat in Dublin with Eleanora. The pregnancy wasn't going that well – there seemed to be lots of scares and bleeding and general frights – and everybody felt it was for the best.

At the sight of the dogs, Anita broke into a smile. 'How're ye, lads?'

She stopped and looked at them suspiciously. 'They look very healthy. Groomed. And they have new collars and feeding bowls and everything.'

It was true that we'd spoiled them a bit. Well, they'd been such good guard dogs for us over the last little while that we had to give *something* back.

The dogs didn't budge. Surely they couldn't have forgotten Anita that quickly.

'I, uh, think you might have to call them off,' Matthew called.

We discovered that they had him pinned up against the wall, making guttural noises in the backs of their hairy throats. I could tell that Matthew felt horribly betrayed – after all he'd done for them! – but they clearly felt they were just doing their job.

'Good boys,' I whispered to them. I'd never been much of a dog person, but these two had enabled me to sleep again at night.

Anita called them off and gave them a bit of a cuddle and a scolding. Then she turned to Matthew, her face lighting up maternally. 'I've a lovely steak and kidney pie in the freezer for your lunch.'

305

'Anita,' I told her, 'I made salad.'

'Salad's fine for us. But a man needs a proper meal. And you could do with some too,' she said to me. 'Skinny as a rake. Isn't she, Matthew?'

And she was like herself again, throwing off her coat and taking vicarious enjoyment in someone else's steak and kidney pie.

Matthew and I exchanged looks. She knew nothing about what had happened. After much discussion between us all, we felt it might only set her back. Best to let her get home, and on the mend. Then we'd tell her before one of the neighbours did.

'Hello! Anybody home?'

Without waiting for any reply, Róisín clattered in, followed by Catherine.

They were like a breath of fresh air, the pair of them. Róisín looked great. And Catherine, as usual, brightened up any room. There was a lot of chatter and fuss as they handed over a helium balloon and a bunch of flowers – 'Welcome home!' – and Catherine had several DVDs she thought Anita would like to see.

'Halle Berry's in that one,' she said. 'Apparently she has diabetes too.'

'Does she?' Anita was amazed. 'But she's skinny.'

'Well, there you go. So you're in good company.'

Anita looked through the DVDs. 'Robert De Niro, Meryl Streep, Judi Dench. All diabetics!'

'No, no. Just Halle Berry, I think.'

Róisín sat down at the table and looked at our mother sternly. 'Now, I hope you're going to look upon what happened as a wake-up call.'

'I knew it!' Anita exploded. 'I knew we wouldn't get two minutes into the conversation without someone telling me I've had a wake-up call! I know, OK? So you can stop saying it, the lot of ye. Consider me woken up.'

Then for some reason this tickled her funny bone, and she forgot to be cross any more, and she threw back her head and laughed. Thank God. We were all so relieved that we laughed energetically along with her. Bangers and Mash looked around at us all like we were deranged. I had a feeling they were hankering for the peace and comfort of my garden shed (we'd bought them baby blankets, and Matthew had installed a plug-in heater).

Anita eventually wiped her eyes. 'I think they must be working at last. Those happy pills. I might take another one.'

'Anita.' Róisín was appalled.

'I was *joking*. God Almighty. Nobody understands me around here, only Matthew.' And she squeezed his arm. He shot me a look: *how are we going to break the news to her?* 'Anyway,' she said to Róisín, 'you have other things to be worried about. I think the word might be out in certain medical quarters about your . . .' she lowered her voice dramatically, '. . . *sexuality*.'

Róisín froze. 'Who's talking?'

'Easy now,' Catherine murmured, like Róisín was a horse about to bolt.

'Just one of the nurses from up the town – Miriam Daly, you know her, she always has desperately cold hands. From what she was saying to one of the other nurses, she might have seen you and Catherine around the town and come to conclusions.'

'Thank God,' Róisín breathed.

Anita looked at me and Matthew in confusion. We were almost as confused. Was this good?

'Well, we've been dropping hints like mad, haven't we, Catherine?' Róisín said.

'All over the place,' Catherine confirmed.

'At the very least, you'd think we'd be a one-hit wonder, especially in a town this small. But there's been nothing.' Róisín looked a bit put out. If there was one thing worse than everybody talking about you, it was everybody NOT talking about you. 'Still, I suppose this pair have wiped our eye on the gossip front. Who's going to bother about hot lesbian activity when you have Jason Farrell trying to sneak home down Main Street with the arse torn out of his trousers?'

Immediately she clammed up. She looked at me. Damn. Anita didn't know anything about this yet.

CLARE DOWLING

She was about the only one in the whole town who didn't. What had happened in the woods that night seemed to have leaked out by osmosis, and without any help from us. We, in turn, heard morsels of gossip and rumour back: Jason had been spotted heading down Main Street in the middle of the night by some partygoers, with his trousers flapping in the wind, and one of his shoes missing. He'd turned up for work on Monday morning, apparently, with stitches in his hand that he said he'd received after an accident in his kitchen. Someone else said he'd made a colleague do all sorts of research into dangerous animals, and the prosecution of irresponsible owners. There might even have been a threatening letter drawn up, but we'd never got any such letter in the post.

I confess: we'd laughed our heads off at the trousers-flapping bit. His trousers were probably very expensive, Matthew had said. And as for him losing a shoe to Bangers and Mash, well, that was even funnier.

It was the thing he hated most; being laughed at. The whole town was breaking their sides, and he'd brought it all upon himself.

He'd denied the whole thing, naturally. The Guards had told me. Two of them had gone round and paid him a visit. Apparently he'd asked them – in his haughtiest solicitor-type voice – whether there was a law against walking in your local woods, and if so, could they direct him to it.

Matthew had gone very white upon hearing that.

'Listen, Anita,' I began. Róisín gave me an encouraging smile, bolstering me. She had been marvellous through this whole thing. 'There's something you should know.'

But Anita surprised us all by saying, 'I know about Jason Farrell and what he's been doing. I had other visitors in the hospital besides yourselves, you know.'

I couldn't tell if she was angry at me, or sad, or afraid that he'd turn up in her own back garden some day.

'I'm sorry, Anita.'

'What are you sorry for? *I'm* sorry I ever stood up for that fellow. Leaving him all those years ago was the best thing you ever did. Imagine if you'd stayed, and what your life might be like now?'

It hadn't occurred to me. But yes. I'd probably had a lucky escape, all things considered.

'String him up!' Róisín shouted unexpectedly. She composed herself again. 'Sorry. I just have to let it out every now and again. I'm fine now.'

She'd wanted to go around to his office and rip his head off. Well, it wasn't his head she wanted to rip off, I'm just substituting here. I'd talked her down; we'd done nothing wrong so far, and we weren't going to start now.

'What if he comes back?' my mother said suddenly. 'What's to stop him continuing to make your life a misery? Even if the law comes down on him hard, he could start this whole thing again somewhere down the line.'

She was right. It was something Matthew and I had discussed at length. We might have frightened him off for now, but did we want to spend the rest of our lives looking over our shoulders? And even if he never looked our way again, would the fear always be there?

It was one of the reasons we had come to a very big decision. It wasn't the only reason, but we would have been very stupid not to have taken it into account. As Matthew had said, we deserved to live our lives without that kind of worry. We deserved to be safe.

I looked at Matthew: *is it time to tell them? Yes,* he nodded.

'We have news.'

That got their attention. Every pair of eyes immediately dropped to my midriff. Oh shit. Not *that* kind of news.

It was Matthew who took the bullet. 'We've decided we're moving back to London.'

Chapter Fifty-two

wo other things happened to help us make up our minds.

Matthew didn't tell me about the first thing for a couple of days after he came home from the conference. Well, it was a busy time, and we were tired and raw.

But, after the fog had cleared, and we were sitting down one evening, waiting for a delivery from The Big Panda, I noticed that there was an air of secrecy about him. Excitement, even.

'Are you having an affair?' I enquired.

'No. Why, do you want me to?' he asked earnestly. (He would have done anything for me at that point. Run baths, ordered takeaways, had affairs.)

'Spit it out.'

'I don't want to land anything else on us at the moment,' he insisted. 'We're stressed enough.'

Me, he meant. I played along.

'But we're not.' We were curled on the couch, with the fire lighted, and I could honestly say that I felt better than I'd done in weeks. Outside my door, I had a whole estate on red alert, ready to protect me. Eddie and Róisín had their phones permanently switched on, in anticipation of a mayday call. The Guards had told me to get in contact at the slightest thing. They had kept repeating that.

And Bangers and Mash were in our garden shed still. It would take a much, much braver man than Jason to tackle them again.

In fact, I was feeling so safe that I was anxious for some outside news. There was a whole other world outside my estate in Castlemoy and I was hungry to hear about it. 'Tell me.'

'Well, if you're sure. They've left the flat. The students. Apparently the mould got too much for the asthmatic one.' I could see from his face that he didn't believe him. He probably didn't even believe in asthma. 'And the other one . . . well, we know what's on *his* mind.'

Yes. Riding Jo. She'd sent me a text the previous day saying, 'Sorry! I tried to tell you but . . . Forgive me? He's really nice. xxx'

Matthew had harrumphed at the kiss-kiss-kiss bit.

'He didn't say where he was going,' he said now, 'but I'm gathering it might be to Jo's place. They didn't ask for their deposit back.' He gave a huff as if to say, 'fat chance they'd get it'.

'So the flat's empty?'

'We'll find someone else quick enough. I'm going to get a letting agent this time. I've had enough hassle from tenants.'

He didn't seem as down about it as he should. And I realised that he was still keyed up. He was practically bouncing around on the sofa.

'Matthew. Is there more?'

'Well, yes. But it's about computers,' he warned.

'I can handle that.'

'Are you sure?'

'Just tell me.'

It turned out that, at the conference, Matthew had run into Sebastian from his old place of work. They'd begun reminiscing about the company – 'They still only buy Rich Tea for the kitchen.' 'You're kidding! We have Polo biscuits in my new place' – and ended up going on the razz together one night.

Things were going well for old Sebastian. It turned out that all those mysterious brown packages that he used to get in the post didn't contain X-rated material at all, but rather study materials for some super-geeky computer qualification that he'd just passed with flying colours.

311

'Are you still with me?' Matthew checked.

'Yes, yes.'

'Sebastian told me in the pub that, because he's now better qualified than anybody else in the company, they've asked him to head up a new division.' He paused for dramatic effect. 'I won't go into too much detail, because I know you haven't a clue what we IT people actually do, but trust me when I say it is very, very exciting.'

'Does it involve computer support?'

'Yes!' said Matthew, delighted at my grasp of the situation. 'But even *more* support. Hugging, kissing, massaging keyboards, you name it.'

'Lucky computers.'

'You'll get your share later on,' Matthew assured me. 'Anyway, you haven't heard the most exciting bit.' He stopped. 'Actually, I don't know if it *is* exciting. I don't know what it is.' He looked at me. 'It's a job offer.'

'What?'

It was the last thing I'd expected. And Matthew too, judging by the look on his face.

'Sebastian asked me to go to work in the new division with him. I would – brace yourself – get my own office. With a little name plaque on the door. Well, that might just have been loose talk, to win me over.' He was joking, but I knew that this was serious. 'It's a promotion, Clara. A big one.'

I looked at him. 'But . . . in London, right?'

I knew it was a silly question. I had to ask, though.

'Yes.'

We sat there, the ramifications sinking in.

'Obviously, I'm not going to take it,' Matthew said. 'I mean, we've just made this big move, and now that things are . . .'

We hadn't mentioned Jason's name for a couple of days. In a strange way, it was like he'd become diluted now that we'd passed the problem on – to Róisín, Catherine, Eddie, the neighbours, and the Guards. He was everybody's problem now.

'. . . under control,' Matthew finished. 'We can get on with things properly here.'

To a certain extent. Keeping one ear out.

'What things?' I enquired.

He looked surprised. 'Well, there's my job. And Food by Clara.'

'Which was a great idea. I'm proud of myself for trying it. But it was the wrong time for it, and maybe the wrong place. Can we honestly say it ever looked like succeeding?'

'Maybe if we gave it more time . . .'

I appreciated his support, I really did. 'I don't want to spend any more time on it, Matthew. I'm a chef. I want to cook. Yes, it would be lovely to strike out on my own, but I can't do it here.'

'Where, then?'

I looked at him. 'I could go back to Kitchen Queens – Brenda's sacked the new girl, and two more after her, Jo said – and start a business in London maybe somewhere down the line?'

I'd found the idea too frightening before. Compared to what I'd been through, I'd welcome the challenge with open arms now. I even felt a flash of excitement at the idea.

'What about your family?' Matthew asked cautiously.

Well, yes. They'd been such a big part in our decision to come back – especially Anita, with her diagnosis. But now that she'd had a wake-up call (it wasn't a banned phrase yet), maybe she'd need us less. And there was Róisín, madly in love and finally coming out (that would become a banned phrase in the near future). Eddie was busily preparing to become a father; he and Eleanora were their own little unit.

'We always flew home to see them. I suppose we could do it again.'

Suddenly we'd gone from Matthew absolutely not taking the job to finding reasons why he shouldn't.

'Look,' I said to him. 'Do you *want* it?'

'Honestly? Yes. It would be a new challenge. Team Tech is great, I love those guys, but I'm doing the same thing I always did.'

'Let's go for it then.'

'Clara . . .'

'No, I'm serious. You know what, Matthew? We have a choice here to do something that we actually want for a change. For a long time I was too afraid to walk out my own front door. My life totally ruled by someone else. And you know something? I'm not doing that any more. Yes, it would have been fantastic had things worked out here. But they didn't, for all kinds of reasons, he being one of them. Why shouldn't you take a promotion? Why shouldn't I try to set up my business somewhere else? What's the alternative – staying here to prove some kind of point to a guy who isn't worth spitting on?'

Matthew said nothing for ages. 'Well, when you put it like that . . . And I suppose the flat is free now, we could move straight back in.'

For some reason I kept thinking of what Ma had said to Kian the other day. Yes, we lived here, but did we truly belong? When I thought of London, I thought of home, and that was where my heart was.

And it had nothing to do with Jason.

Chapter Fifty-three

'We'll definitely be over to visit,' Eleanora gushed.

'Not until after the baby comes,' said Eddie, frowning. 'We don't want to risk anything.'

Eleanora just about refrained from rolling her eyes. For all the drama surrounding this baby, she sported the tiniest bump you ever saw. It was about the size of a tennis ball, incongruously protruding from her washboard stomach. Even so, she was killed giving out about how fat she felt; how she couldn't wait to shed 'all this baby weight'. And as for her hair . . . it was permanently tied up in a knot on her head because she was convinced it was falling out.

'Pregnancy can do that. Make hair shed. Something to do with the hormones.' Eddie looked beatific. 'Isn't it amazing what the human body can do?'

His transformation from feckless actor to diligent father-to-be was as amazing as it was complete. The only way we could explain it was that he and Eleanora were suddenly the stars of their very own show. And what a production! It had drama, suspense, a medical setting, and no two productions would ever be the same.

'This is going to change us so much, do you realise that?' he kept saying to Eleanora with great solemnity.

'Yadda yadda,' Eleanora normally responded. 'Here, isn't it time for your shift?'

In fact, the only downside to having a baby was that the money was, as usual, crap. If only someone would *pay* you to have babies, it would just be the best part in the world.

Failing that, Eddie put in sixty hours a week working for Jimmy and his team of ill-tempered chefs. The voiceover work had yet to start rolling in. So until it did, he was washing dishes, mopping floors and 'trying to be the best father that I possibly can'.

'Bloody hell,' Eleanora said to me. 'I'm only four months gone, and he's already this intense?'

She'd been glad of the excuse to get out of the bedsit and drive down to help us pack. This mostly seemed to involve picking over half-full cardboard boxes in the kitchen, while Eddie lugged stuff about.

She plucked out a book. 'Are you taking this with you?'

'Why, Eleanora – did you want it?'

'Just, if you weren't taking it, that's all.'

'Have it,' I said generously. The car was full to the roof already.

She was circling over another box as Eddie passed by. 'What about this? It'd be pretty cool for when we move into our new flat, wouldn't it, Eddie?'

It was our green lamp.

'We're keeping that.' Matthew swiped it off her. It had come all the way from our flat in London and was now on its way home, just like us.

He winked at me, and tucked the lamp securely back into the box, which he picked up, bound for the car again. 'Anything else?'

We were leaving the same way we'd come: with one carload of stuff. We'd considered shipping our new furniture home, but where would we put it all in the little flat? Besides, there was still something a little wild and exciting about just us and the trusty Renault Mégane, setting off on the road again, and we decided, to hell with it: we'd leave everything else behind.

'Just this, I think.'

I handed him a file of my Clara's Food stuff. It mightn't have worked out here, but I had plans for those files yet.

316

'I think after this we're pretty much full up,' he said, giving the place a last look round, before going out with the box.

Eddie and Eleanora had volunteered to take what was left – kitchen stuff, bags of clothes, that kind of thing – to the charity shop, once they'd had a look over it themselves. After Eleanora had finished with it, my guess was that the charity shop wouldn't get a whole lot. She wandered off now to see what she could cadge from the pile in the living room, and I was glad to get a moment with Eddie alone.

'Good luck with the baby. I want to be kept informed of every twinge.'

I had been joking, but he said, 'Sure. And I'll be sending photos too, on a weekly basis. Eleanora likes posing for them.'

No doubt. 'And I hope Jimmy is OK to you, Eddie.'

'I can handle Jimmy.'

'I know, but still. Hopefully the voiceover work will start coming in soon.'

So much soul-searching had gone into it all, and now it seemed to have fallen flat on its face. He'd spent a week's wages getting a demo tape done, but so far there hadn't been a sniff of interest in his ability to put on a flawless American accent.

But, happily, Jimmy had fired several minions in one of his rages, and there were more hours going in the restaurant than Eddie could handle.

'I'm happy just to be earning enough that we can move into a decent place,' he insisted. 'I'll worry about everything else after the baby comes.'

I admired his maturity. I just hoped Eleanora didn't end up driving him cracked.

'Keep an eye on Anita, won't you?' I said.

'Of course. We're going over to her for our dinner this evening. It's home-made fish and chips. She says she just wants to sit there and watch us.'

We'd said our goodbyes to her earlier. It had been emotional. She agreed that it might be best for her not to come to the house as we left. 'I waved you off once before and I don't think I can do it again.'

And Róisín and Catherine were in hiding. Well, Róisín was, after our leaving do in Dirty Harry's the previous night. Everybody had come:

317

Maura and The Knob, and all the darts team lads (they'd got quite upset at the end), and Eamon, Tim, Chris and Henry from Team Tech. Sophie had turned up, along with Valerie, who was actually great craic after two drinks. Even Ma and her husband had made an appearance towards the end, and had glowered in a friendly way at us from the bar.

Anyway, with the drinks flowing, Róisín had momentarily forgotten herself and had turned around and snogged Catherine in front of everyone.

She'd rung me up at dawn, whispering hoarsely down the line, 'I can't leave the house. I'm too mortified in case someone sees me. If the town didn't know about us before, they certainly do now.'

'I know. It was on the news this morning.'

'*What?*'

'You've knocked me and my stalker story off. Go back to bed, Róisín. You'll feel better later.'

'I won't, I'm giving it all up, I'm going to become a nun.' I heard Catherine laughing in the background. Then Róisín sighed and said, 'I just wanted to say that I'm sorry it's come to this.'

Róisín resolutely refused to believe that we hadn't left because of Jason. Matthew had even shown her his new employment contract, complete with big pay rise, and she just kept shaking her head and saying, 'Such a shame.'

'It isn't,' I said again, just for the record. 'We want to go.'

'I'm going to be watching out for him, you know. The next time I see his pervy face up the town, I'm going to make a holy show of him in front of everybody.' This was bluster, of course, but I appreciated the sentiment.

'That's if you can ever leave the house again,' I reminded her.

'Stop! I'd forgotten about that for a minute and now I want to go and be sick again.'

Now it was time for me to say goodbye to Eddie.

'You'll be back soon, won't you?' he said, uncertainly. 'I mean, you know, for the police stuff.'

'I don't know what's going to happen yet, Eddie. But I'm certainly not going to put my life on hold depending on whether they can make harassment charges stick.'

I could see he wanted to say more, but there was no way I was going to have my departure hijacked by my ex. 'I'll be home for the birth of the baby, in any case.'

Eddie's face lit up. 'Great! We're going to put the whole thing on video. Make a short film out of it. I've got a director lined up and everything. Naturally,' he said, 'I'll be doing the voiceover.'

Kian and Jennifer had formed a little departure committee on their front lawn.

'Did you remember all your shoes, missus?' Jennifer said, concerned. 'I did.'

'We'll miss ya,' Kian said.

'You little tyke,' Matthew said affectionately.

Kian took umbrage. 'Are you calling me names?'

'No, no.' Matthew gave up and turned to me. 'Come on. We need to move it out if we're going to make the ferry.' Travel arrangements always brought out the military side to him.

But our departure was being noted by someone else. The door across the way opened. Dominique stepped out.

'Start the car,' I told Matthew. 'I'll just be a minute.'

Dominique had been keeping a low profile lately. She was the one neighbour who hadn't called over to offer her support. But she came across the road now, to catch me before we went.

She came to a stop in front of me and scraped back her mop of blond hair. 'Look,' she said, 'I'm the last person you probably want to see right now.'

'Why is that?' I enquired.

'Because I brought that shit back into your life.' Good old Dominique; always said it like it was.

'You didn't. This started long before now.'

'Yeah, but it didn't help, did it? Me going out with him.' She looked a bit tired. 'I knew from the start that he wasn't really interested in me. Oh, he was a charmer, alright, and he laid it on pretty thick. And who wouldn't like being wined and dined like that? But anyone could see that I wasn't the kind of woman he normally went for.'

She wouldn't get any arguments from me on that one.

'And, in all honesty, he's not my type either. Too stick-in-the-mud. But I was suddenly landed back here on my own, my family gone, and my friends . . . well, I didn't seem to have many of those left from the old days.'

I wished now that I'd taken her up on the invitation for coffee. This might never have got so bad if we'd been closer.

'Anyway,' she said, 'hopefully that's the end of him in both of our lives.'

Amen to that.

She looked at the packed-up car, which Matthew was now revving meaningfully. 'You're heading back to London?'

'Yes. Matthew's got a great job, and I'm going back to the same place as before. We've got our flat there.'

At the thoughts of our little home, I was anxious to get going now too.

'You must be leaving soon too?'

Dominique looked more cheesed off. 'They rejected my book.'

I was shocked. 'The one you came here to write?'

'I just sent it off last week. *Indecent Exposure.*'

Oh dear. Oh *dear.*

'I know,' Dominique sighed. 'It was a shite title. The whole thing was shite, according to my publishers.'

I felt sorry for her.

'So what are you going to do?'

'Ditch the whole thing. Start over again.' No wonder she looked wrecked. 'The only thing they liked about it was the setting. So now I'm thinking, a couple of Irish colleen types, red hair, big breasted, going wild in a milking parlour, that kind of thing, what do you think? Corny enough?' She gave one of her big, dirty laughs. 'Anyway,' she said, 'I'm going to stay here to write it. I've extended my lease by six months. And I'm kind of enjoying the peace and quiet. It's a nice change from New York.'

'Send me a copy,' I made her promise.

'Good luck with things,' she said. 'I mean it. Oh, and say hi to Róisín for me, won't you? And, you know, if ever she's feeling lonely some evening . . .' She trailed off suggestively.

I was a bit shocked. And then I laughed. I wouldn't even mention it to Róisín, and trigger a fresh apoplectic fit.

'I think Róisín's taken,' I said.

'The good ones always are,' Dominique said cheerfully.

I waved goodbye, and then I got into the car beside Matthew and we drove out of the estate for the last time.

Deirdre could hardly believe we were putting the house up for sale so soon.

'It could take a while to sell,' she warned us. 'You're best holding out until the market improves.'

'We don't care about the market,' we said. 'Just sell it.'

'You'll lose money. No, the best thing you can do is to rent it out for a year or two, until things pick up.' She was already reaching for a filing cabinet. 'I have some prospective tenants here on our books, vetted and everything—'

'We don't want to rent. We just want to sell.'

Deirdre gave us a knowing look. 'Anxious to leave, eh?'

She'd heard too. Or maybe she'd seen the squad car going around to Jason's office last week, and the two Guards going inside to have a chat with him. I'd say they didn't miss much in this office.

Then Deirdre snapped into action, pulling out cabinet drawers and producing a sheaf of forms. 'Sign here. And here. And here.'

We did, and then we were handing over the keys, and Deirdre was looking at us and saying, 'I'll be in touch.'

'You mean . . . that's it?' Matthew said. Was it really that easy, to leave a whole life behind?

'Well, *hardly*. I'll have to go around and value the place, and you'll have to provide me with documentation saying all your household charges, et cetera, are up to date and then we'll take it from there.'

'Right, sure,' we said, chastened.

'And did you hoover before you left?'

'Every inch.'

She noted it down on a pad. I had an overwhelming urge to laugh, and we just about made it outside in time.

'So,' said Matthew, rocking on his heels a bit. 'We're all done.'

'Looks like it.'

'You want to hit the road then?'

'Absolutely.' I was looking forward to it now; a fresh beginning, even if it was back in the same place.

We saw Jason as we arrived back at our car on Main Street. He was rounding the corner from his office on Bridge Street. I'd like to think he hadn't spotted the car from his office and was waiting for us, and that it was just coincidence, but I didn't believe in coincidences any longer.

'Don't even look at him,' Matthew instructed quietly under his breath. 'Don't give him the satisfaction.'

But Jason clearly had some things to get off his chest. He intercepted us on the footpath.

'Running away?' he said softly to me.

'Careful,' I told him. 'People are probably watching. You know, now that they know what you're really like.'

His eyes flashed with rage. I wasn't afraid. There wasn't a thing he could do to me now.

'You bitch,' he said. 'Complaining to the Guards about me.'

He didn't mention the dogs. But that would mean admitting he'd been stalking my house that night, and he would never do that. The stitches in his right hand were ugly and black, though, and he shoved his hand into his pocket when he saw me looking.

'I didn't tell them anything that wasn't true.'

'Oh, really?' His lip lifted. 'Well, I told them that you were a loony. That the whole thing was made up because you were bitter and twisted over the way I'd broken off our engagement ten years ago.' He enjoyed my face. 'See? It's my word against yours. They know that too. So off you run to London. And when you're gone, I'm going to make sure that everybody in this town knows what a nutcase you really are. That your boyfriend here had to take you away in the end in case you ended up getting sued for defamation.' He pretended to consider this. 'Hmm, maybe I *will* do that. We're coming into our quiet time in the office; I'll have loads of time on my hands.' He was really enjoying himself now.

I was shaking, but I tried not to show it. 'You can say what you like about it. But the people that matter know the truth.' I turned to Matthew. 'Let's go.'

Jason looked at Matthew now, a sneer twisting his mouth. 'What's the matter? Cat got your tongue?'

'I don't speak to people who harass my girlfriend,' Matthew told him evenly. 'I just do this.'

And Matthew, pacifist, pragmatist, member of Greenpeace and all-round-reasonable-person gave Jason a left hook to his square, handsome jaw.

Jason's knees buckled and he sprawled to the ground. He lay there, glaring up at us, clutching his chin. 'I'll sue you too. You nearly broke my fucking jaw.'

'Shut up,' Matthew said, then he took my hand and we stepped over Jason and left him behind.

Chapter Fifty-four

'I didn't set out to sleep with your tenant,' Jo confessed miserably. 'It just kind of happened.'

'What, while you were collecting the rent?'

'Hey, I was doing you a favour.' She was still bitter over the handbag. Matthew had refused to get her one, on principle. 'Look, I ended up spending so much time over there, dealing with the complaints. Which were all from that guy Nigel, by the way. Freddie hardly complained about anything. He was so sweet, making me cups of tea, and listening to me give out about Brenda. And maybe I was glad for the company, you know? Maybe I was a bit lonely, with nobody to go out with any more. Then one night we had a bottle of wine and, well, you can guess the rest. I really wanted to tell you, Clara, but I couldn't because he was your tenant.'

'You couldn't because he's twenty.'

'Well, that too.'

'And you, Jo, are thirty-two,' Jane pointed out sternly. She'd become even more sensible since becoming a mother. A minute ago she'd taken out a wet wipe and cleaned off the table.

'I know, OK? I'm aware there's an age difference. You don't have to keep rubbing it in.' She took another slug of her wine. 'We're at completely different stages of our lives. He hasn't even finished college yet, and I want to get married and have babies.'

'Do you?' Mad Mags was amazed.

'Well, no, but I probably will any day now. Clara here has given me the want.' She squeezed my arm. 'So I've decided not to wait until it goes wrong, like all the others did. I'm going to finish it with him.'

'Jo.' I was taken aback. 'That's a bit drastic, surely?'

'Just go on having sex with him,' Mad Mags encouraged. 'It doesn't have to mean anything.'

'No, Clara's right. I'm forever picking the wrong kind of men.' She made her face very hard. Which didn't really work for Jo, she just looked like she had a toothache. 'This time, I've decided that I'm not going to let myself get hurt.'

None of us had met this Freddie yet. Jo had declared that we'd only make fun of his youthfulness and naïvety. Anyway, she kept insisting it 'wasn't serious', it was 'only a bit of fun', and that she was just in it 'for the ride'.

None of us believed her. She'd fallen for him, hard. He'd moved in with her, that was how 'not serious' it was.

I really, really hoped she wasn't headed for a fall. It would be just like her to be taken advantage of by some little scut who fancied a bit of a go on an older woman.

Mags checked her watch nervously. 'He's late.'

We snapped into supportive girlfriend mode. 'He'll turn up.'

'Yes, but he's never late. He prides himself on his punctuality,' she fretted.

We were meeting Philip for the first time tonight. Mags simply couldn't put it off any longer; he was, she said, beginning to be suspicious that she had no friends at all.

Jo, Jane and I were the most respectable she could muster; she was 'test-running' us before introducing him to anyone more hardcore. We were instructed to be on our very best behaviour and to mention absolutely nothing about her sex life in case the poor lad fainted.

'What the hell are we supposed to talk to him about?' Jo complained.

'Well, I don't know, do I? You can tell him about Ireland, Clara, can't you? He owns part of a thoroughbred racehorse over there, he said. I don't know which part. I don't suppose you did any horseracing over there?' she asked hopefully.

'Not a chance, Mags.'

A look of horror crossed her face. 'Sorry. I hope I'm not opening old wounds.'

Jo, on reflex, reached out to squeeze my arm again. Jane clucked maternally under her breath.

'Not at all,' I assured them. It was great having the support. But at the same time it would be nice to leave it behind.

We were in our usual haunt, Falvio's. We'd insisted, even though Mags was afraid that Logan would be on duty and she'd be exposed for what she was: a woman who liked sex. Shock, horror. 'It's the *amount* of sex,' she kept fretting. 'That's the difficult bit to explain.'

The door kept swooshing open, letting in cold air and fresh gaggles of noisy, happy people. Even though we'd been back a month now, I still sometimes felt a little out of place, unable to get settled in. It was nothing overly dramatic; I'd be on the Tube, as I was nearly every day of my life, or walking down to the little shop at the end of our road for a pint of milk, and I would feel strange and vulnerable, and I'd have to hurry back home.

Even the flat hadn't felt the same for a while. I thought it was just the smallness of the place, after our three-thousand-square-foot palace in Ireland. There was just something odd about it. Then one night I knew.

'The lamp. The green lamp. We never unpacked it.'

Matthew went and found it, and put it back up on the mantelpiece, in its proper place, and turned it on. And I waited for that feeling of rightness to spread over me, but it didn't immediately come.

It was me, I slowly began to realise. Not London. I'd thought that by leaving all that stuff behind me that my life would snap back to normal, like an elastic band. And I was angry with myself that I wasn't moving on fast enough. There were five hundred kilometres between me and what had happened; so why was I still letting myself be affected like this?

'. . . are you even *listening*?'

Jo was looking at me.

'Sorry,' I said.

'I was just telling Mags and Jane about Brenda ringing us up and asking us to bring her over fifty of those chocolate liqueurs we made for that party in Chelsea.'

'So?' said Jane.

'She's in *rehab*,' said Jo, exasperated. 'Liqueurs are kind of banned.'

Poor Brenda. It looked bad this time. Jo and I were running the place between us. Jo thought I was sick in the head to be enjoying slaving over hot ovens all day long, but I'd been away from real work too long, and I loved it. Besides, what choice did we have? We couldn't let Kitchen Queens go under.

There was a slight pause in the conversation, which Jane seized. 'Does anyone want to see a picture of Julian?'

That was what they'd named the baby. He was the spit of Don.

'Why, has he changed much since Tuesday?' Mags asked, with a tight smile.

Jane took it at face value. 'Oh, you wouldn't *believe*.' Out came the phone. 'I've got a little video of him trying to turn over onto his back. He's just gorgeous.'

You could see she'd been waiting for this moment all evening. We indulged her because we loved her. And Julian was, thankfully, photogenic.

'And here's one of him sucking his thumb.'

'Hmmm,' said Mags, trying to conceal a yawn.

One of the waiters dropped a plate near me and I let out a shout. People turned to look.

'Sorry, sorry.' I tried a laugh. 'I just got a fright. Phew!'

But I could see the girls exchange glances when they thought I wasn't looking.

Poor old Clara. Still a bit jumpy. And who could blame her, after what had happened? Naturally, these things took time to get over.

We didn't talk about Jason, Matthew and I. That was my rule. I'd wasted enough of my life on that man; he wasn't coming to London with us too. And I thought we were doing very well, all things considered. Yet I couldn't shake the feeling that there was something unfinished about the whole thing. But maybe it would always be that way; maybe it was the fear that someday he'd pop up again.

'I don't believe this.' Mags had just received a text. 'Philip has to cancel dinner. One of his aunts got injured in the hunt today and he has to go with her in the helicopter to hospital.'

Philip was terribly posh, just like the real prince, which was something else making Mags slightly nervous. It was all sherries and pedigree dogs and race meetings, which brought Mags out into a sweat whenever he invited her along to one, as she never had anything to wear, and it was a mad dash to some obscure boutique and she'd have to hand over half her wages for some awful tweed yoke that she'd never wear again.

'To be honest, it's a relief,' she said. 'Now I can have a proper drink. It's an awful effort being good all the time. You, there!' She summoned a passing waiter. 'A bottle of your cheapest house white. And what's this your name is again?'

It was a great night in the end. I probably had a little too much to drink, but in a way I needed it, and by the time the Honorary Girls were phoned to come and collect us, I was on top form.

Matthew was the first to arrive. He was there in five minutes flat, which made me think he'd been parked around the corner the whole time.

'Alright?' A searching look. Still a little over-protective, bless him. At least he hadn't hit anybody since. He promised me that he'd never do it again.

'Yes, fine.'

Good. Great. He could relax. As each day and week passed it was getting a little easier to relax. We knew nothing could happen, not in London, but old habits died hard.

'How was work?' I asked.

'Fantastic,' he said, without a trace of irony. He loved his new job. Sebastian, of course, had turned into a beast – the power of running his own division had gone to his head – but Matthew was cushioned away from it all in his own office, dreaming up fabulous new ways to make computers feel even more supported.

The money didn't hurt either. We'd – reluctantly – replaced the trusty Renault Mégane with a brand-new car, which was a snazzy red and did an astonishing number of miles to the gallon, according to Matthew. The flat had got a makeover too, and there was still some money left over for Matthew's savings account at the end of every month.

'Surrey, here we come,' he kept saying (he seemed to think that someday we'd move out there and have six children).

Cool Art arrived then, wearing a brand-new beard, and with an exotic pop singer called KuKi on his arm. Instead of going home, we somehow ended up ordering more food and wine, and the party really kicked off. Apparently Cool Art had come straight from shooting a promo with no fewer than three supermodels in it, and a fierce debate erupted over whether there was such a thing any more as a supermodel.

Cool Art languidly took out his phone. 'Let me just give Claudia a buzz and ask her.'

The guy was so jammy. If he wasn't so cool you would just hate him.

Then the door opened again. Jo got to her feet quickly. 'Here's the last Honorary Girl.'

We all exchanged alarmed glances, even Jane. Who the hell had invited Don? And how had he got past the bouncer in his polo neck? Worse, who was minding the *baby*?

It wasn't Don. It was Jo's boyfriend, Freddie.

There was a collective intake of breath. 'Shouldn't he be in bed at this hour of the night?' wondered Mags.

Jo led him to the table, very protective, and tried to shield him from the worst of the hostilities by begging, 'Please, *please*, be nice to him.'

This was primarily aimed at Matthew.

'Hello,' said Matthew to our ex-tenant. 'I didn't recognise you with your clothes on.'

I recognised him, though. He wasn't the one with the starey eyes, thank God. He was actually very cute, with gorgeous skin and luxuriant eyelashes. And beautiful hands too, which he kept firmly on Jo's waist.

She shook him off tersely, and said, unnecessarily, 'This is Freddie, everyone.'

He nodded round at us all. He was shy, you could see, but not intimidated by the scenes of drunkenness and debauchery in front of him. For all his youth, he had bottle.

'Very sorry about all the complaints,' he said to Matthew.

'And so you should be.' Matthew looked like he was going to bring up the bathroom mould again, but then lost heart and said, 'Ah, fuck it, I hated being a landlord anyway.'

'That dishwasher you got us was very good,' Freddie commented.

'Did you think?' Matthew brightened. The amount of background research that had gone into that dishwasher. 'We always put it on eco-cycle, now that we're using it ourselves.'

'So did we. Uses less electricity.'

'And water,' Matthew said approvingly.

The friendship was sealed.

Freddie insisted on buying Matthew a beer. He bought us all beers, in fact. Far from being a penniless student, it turned out that his father was a media mogul. 'I can't be sure, but I think he owns three daily newspapers and a couple of television stations,' he said, apologetically. 'He keeps trying to drag me into the business, but I'm determined to make my own way.'

'Quite right, quite right,' we all murmured.

'My mother's an antiques collector. She presents one of those programmes on the telly,' he said. 'But that's why we wanted the flat unfurnished.' He looked embarrassed. 'She filled it with all this art deco stuff, and priceless oriental coffee tables.'

'Must have been awful for you,' we commiserated.

It looked like Cool Art had just been knocked off his jammy perch by the Young Pretender here.

Freddie looked round for Jo eagerly, but she looked away, and then Cool Art pulled up a chair for Freddie and commandeered him. He knew an important contact when he saw one.

'Oh, Jo,' I breathed

She was terse. 'I know, OK? I'm not going to string him along. I'm going to finish with him tonight. I just need to psych myself up.'

'But he's perfect.'

'What?'

'He's good-looking, he's sweet, he's strong enough not to bow to family pressure. And, Jo, the way he's looking at you. He's obviously head over heels.'

She was a bag of nerves now. 'He's too young. There's always *something* wrong with the guys I go out with.'

'Does it bother you? The age thing?'

She wrinkled her nose. 'It bothers me more that he wants to be an artist.'

'Let him. He'll still inherit Daddy's money.'

'Clara!' She let out her breath slowly. 'I wasn't really going to finish with him,' she confessed. 'I just threw that out as a sop to the crowd.' She cast another look at him. 'I just don't know how it can work long term, though.'

'But isn't it great at the moment? Can you not just go with the flow and see how it turns out?'

She didn't need any more encouragement. A minute later she was sitting on his lap, arms around his neck.

'Give them five minutes and they'll be off home to have sex,' Matthew murmured. 'At least it won't be in our flat any more.'

Maybe it was the mention of sex, or the wine I'd drunk, but I suddenly said, 'Let's dance.'

'Clara.' He was half laughing, half embarrassed.

'I know it's a restaurant, but it's nearly empty, and there's a bit of a clearing over there, and, oh, just come on.'

And I dragged him up and put my arms around him – 'Woo-hoo!' shouted Mags – and we slow-danced to Beyoncé. I knew I was a little drunk, and maybe that was why I felt so light and carefree. I felt like I'd escaped, and in the nick of time too.

'Got room for one more?' Jo was up now, with Freddie, and we ignored the staff's exhortations to sit down, and eventually they gave up.

At some point much later on, when Mags was dancing around a waiter (so much better than a handbag), and singing 'Ain't No Mountain High Enough' whilst kicking her legs up like a showgirl on speed, her posh boyfriend, Philip, arrived.

'The helicopter was quicker than we thought,' he said, looking somewhat bemused at the scene.

Mags stopped dead; red-faced, inebriated, and utterly compromised.

Or so she thought.

'I was wondering when you'd let your hair down,' Philip said with relief.

And he shucked off his decrepit jacket and boogied on down with Mags on the dance floor, much to her surprise and delight.

'Will we leave them to it?' Matthew whispered. 'I'd like to go home.'

I held his hand tightly. It was too long since we'd had a bit of lust for each other. A bit of lust for *anything*. 'Me too.'

We'd been through a lot. But it was time to move on.

Chapter Fifty-five

A nita had big news. Correction, important news. Everybody was very
aware of using the word 'big' around her.

'I only had to buy one seat on the plane over,' she announced.

'It's true,' Róisín agreed. 'Although it was still a bit of a squash.'

'It wasn't, I was fine.'

'I meant for me. I had to sit next to you.' .

They'd arrived an hour ago and we'd just got past the initial line of
questioning. How was the weather forecast for the next few days? Was
Matthew wearing the required amount of underclothing, and of a suffi-
cient strength/warmth/durability? And who was stealing all those nice
new red pens from his office?

'Sebastian,' Matthew told her, shamelessly.

(He had got a bit 'hard' since coming back to London.)

Anita looked well. She was off the 'happy pills' now. She'd been a bit
worried that she might make a run for the freezer straight away, she said,
but that didn't happen, which was a relief. She still bitterly resented the
diet, and Dr Mooney, but she was stuck with the thing now, she maintained, so she might as well just get on with it.

I wasn't sure yet whether the sanguine attitude was real, or just a
precursor to another black mood, like the last time.

'Your blood sugars are OK?'

'Spot on.'

Beside her, Róisín nodded encouragement. 'I think it's the exercise that has kick-started things again,' she said.

Anita had enrolled for Susie's latest regime, Trim Those Thighs. Susie had got in some punishing new equipment that left you wobbling around for days on jelly legs, apparently. The woman was sadistic.

'Anybody for a cup of tea?' Matthew offered.

Both of them looked at him gratefully. He was going to be a marvellous addition to the family. Already he'd run their bags over to the hotel in the car. There wasn't enough room at the flat to put them both up. Besides, Róisín insisted that I would be busy enough before the big day without having to worry about them.

'Make mine nice and strong,' said Anita, giving him a little squeeze. So far he had been kneaded, patted, pinched, stroked and hugged by her. He was looking a little giddy at all the attention.

While the tea was putting in an appearance, it was down to serious business.

'We're dying to know,' Anita hissed. 'Is Brenda still in rehab? I've been saying a few prayers at Mass, God forgive me, and keeping my fingers crossed for a good outcome.'

It might be assumed that Anita was concerned for Brenda's wellbeing. But the good outcome she was hoping and praying for was that Brenda would keep merrily knocking back the hard stuff and that Jo and I could continue with our plans to take over Kitchen Queens.

Well, it was Jo's plan. She'd finally succeeded in opening my eyes to the extent of Kitchen Queens' troubles when Brenda hadn't shown up for three straight weeks and Jo had jemmied open the filing cabinet in the office.

'It's carnage,' she'd said crisply, thrusting unpaid invoices and bank demands at me. 'It's going down the tubes, Clara. Either we jump ship or we buy this place off her before the bank forecloses.'

I thought she was joking. But her face was funny, like she'd been bursting to say it for ages and had only now got the chance. '*We* are the Kitchen Queens, Clara. Not Brenda. She's only holding us back.

No!' she commanded, when I opened my mouth to interject. 'At least listen before you turn me down. I realise you've been burned, Clara. I realise it might bring back bad memories. But it'll be different this time, don't you see?'

She laid it out for me like this: I wouldn't be on my own, there would be two of us. (Well, three, if you included Freddie. He offered to do all the design work for a revamped website and promotional literature. For free.) We already ran the business, so nothing new there. Most importantly, we had a client base just begging to be taken care of properly. 'Plus, a whole new potential client base that we can tap through Prince Philip,' Jo said. (The name had stuck.)

'Jo!' I was appalled at the idea of exploiting Mags's boyfriend.

'Oh, get over it. I've already asked him if they get peckish at all those shooting parties, and he said that if we want to lash him in a proposal, he'd think about it.'

I had to hand it to her. She was really serious about this. The more we spoke about taking over Kitchen Queens, the more excited I got. Now all we had to do was approach Brenda.

'You bitches!' she shrieked. 'You think you can run this place better than me? Well, let me tell you something. I'll sell this place over my dead body!'

'That went pretty well,' Jo said afterwards, relieved. 'I think she really liked the idea.'

Brenda came round in the end, mostly due to being taken to court by one of her creditors. We promised to pay them all off if she would just let go. In the end I think she realised that she'd had a lucky escape.

'But it's not signed yet?' Anita said, still fearful that Brenda would sober up and wrest back control.

'No, but you can get a taste of our new menu on Saturday.' Before Róisín raised any objections, I said, 'I told Jo to adapt several dishes for diabetics, OK? She's already catering for vegetarians, coeliacs and lesbians.'

I only said that to rile Róisín up, but instead of blowing the required fuse, she just smirked.

'Catherine said to say sorry she got delayed, by the way,' she said. 'It's just difficult to take days off so soon into things.'

'They're still running her ragged?'

'It's outrageous! She worked sixty hours last week, can you believe it?'

Catherine had just got a great new job, after a year on the dole. But, as though Róisín's lies had come back to bite them both on the bum, the hours were ferocious.

'She'll definitely be here for Saturday, though,' Róisín assured me.

Anita had only been looking for an excuse to well up, and Róisín had just provided it. 'I can't believe it! My little girl, getting married!'

'I'm thirty-four,' I pointed out. 'Hardly little.'

But Anita was dabbing away at her eyes with gusto. 'I'm just so happy. You know, after everything.'

There was no need to elaborate. Everybody loved a happy ending. It would have been nice had ours been in Ireland, but at the end of it all, I considered myself lucky still to have Matthew, and my family and friends, and even a new chance at launching a business. Sometimes it wasn't possible to have it all, but the upshot was that you appreciated more what you *did* have.

'I saw him yesterday,' Anita announced, as though we were in the middle of a conversation about Jason. 'Walking up the High Street. You hardly ever see him out and about any more, and no wonder. People are still talking about him, you know. It's kind of a joke now, about him following people in cars, although apparently he goes mad if he hears anyone saying it.' She pursed up her lips. 'I never liked that man.'

'You did. You were always saying what a great lad he was,' I protested.

'Well, I've changed my mind,' she said stoutly. 'He's a creep.'

I don't think I'd ever heard her call anybody a creep before. She looked a little surprised herself, and erupted into a tee-hee. She set Róisín and me off, and when Matthew walked back in with the tea, he found us all rolling about on the couch.

'What's so funny?' he said, pleased.

I wiped the tears from my eyes and scooted over on the sofa to make room for him. 'Nothing worth talking about.'

Eddie rang just as we were finishing dinner.

'Oh my God, oh my God,' Anita started up. 'Is it the baby?'

Eleanora was overdue by two weeks. Obviously, she and Eddie weren't going to make our wedding on Saturday. Eleanora was livid; apparently she was complaining that we'd deliberately scheduled it so that she would miss out, because even if she'd delivered on time, she'd still have ended up looking like a pig in a frock.

It wasn't the baby.

'Listen,' Eddie said, in a small, ashamed voice, 'I got a part in a film. Don't tell anybody.'

'You're going to be in a *movie*?' I screeched.

Anita, Róisín and Matthew abandoned their dessert and did some rubber-necking. This was nearly better than a baby.

'It's only a small part. And I'm just doing it for the money, OK?'

'Yeah, yeah, that's what they all say.'

'This is the big time,' Anita was swooning. 'I knew it would happen sooner or later. Never mind those blessed chicken voiceovers.'

'Ask him who's in it,' Matthew pitched in.

'I'm not sure. Some guy called Depp, I think?' Eddie reported back. 'Oh my God!'

'Everybody has that reaction.' Eddie sounded baffled. 'To be honest, I'd never heard of any of the cast before this. Anyway, the script is *terrible*.'

'Thank God,' Matthew muttered, when I relayed this back. 'If he'd said it was great, I'd have been worried.'

'I'm playing some pirate guy who helps to kidnap a girl and I have to say things like "me beauty".' His anguish was coming down the line in waves. 'I'm contracted to go to the Caribbean for a month to film the thing.'

This was the jammiest yet. Cool Art and Freddie would have to move over.

'The thing is, Eleanora wants to come out with me. Once the baby is born, obviously.'

'Obviously.' She would be in her element, hobnobbing with film folk.

'We have a slight problem, though, in that we need someone to look after the baby.'

'It'll be with you, won't it? He or she.'

Surely they didn't plan to leave the baby behind?

'Well, yes, but Eleanora doesn't want to be completely tied down. I'll be working all the time. She'll need some help, you know.'

Hmm. Most women managed to cope with their babies all by themselves. But then again, I didn't have children myself, so I'd have to give Eleanora the benefit of the doubt.

'Eddie, if you're asking me to go the Caribbean with you . . .'

'Not you. Anita.'

As though she heard her name mentioned, my mother looked up sharply.

'Is that wise, Eddie?' I said, neutrally.

'She needs a purpose. You said it yourself. And it'll be a holiday for her. Plus, we're going to pay her.'

I wasn't going to get too excited about that. Eddie was used to terrible pay in Jimmy's.

'When are you going?'

'Two weeks after your wedding, presuming the baby has finally arrived by then.' A little embarrassed, he remembered to say, 'I hope everything's going well with the preparations and all that?'

'Yes, yes.'

'You and Matthew deserve each other,' he said. 'And I mean that in the best possible way.'

I heard a voice in the background, querulous and insistent. Eleanora.

'Put Anita on to me,' he said. 'I'll run it past her.'

I suddenly wondered whether she was up to it. 'Would you not ask Róisín instead?'

'Róisín?' Eddie scoffed. 'You couldn't drag her away from Dirty Harry's these days. Did she tell you they're running a gay night in there now every Wednesday? I never thought I'd see the day, but it looks like Castlemoy is the new Irish hotspot for people of all sexual persuasions.'

★

'No, no,' Róisín corrected me with a sigh. 'You see, this is the kind of misinformation that's going to get us all into trouble. It's not a "gay night". Jesus, they'd be coming down from Dublin in busloads if it was that kind of free-for-all. No, *Hens* – that's what we're calling it – is a night for ladies from the midlands, and their friends. Harry insisted on the ladies bit; he's a bit old-fashioned like that. We're not excluding any other group, mind. They're perfectly welcome to come along if they want. The bar is big enough for us all,' she said generously. 'But it's been set up first and foremost for women. We don't have a lot going on for us in the countryside, you know,' she said, as if I could possibly be in any doubt.

This development, of a lesbian night in Castlemoy, was so out-of-this-world that it actually seemed quite normal, and I found myself enquiring, 'Whose idea was it, anyway?'

Catherine's, surely. She was probably finding the place a desperate backwater after the thriving scene in Dublin.

'Hilda came up with it,' said Róisín, unexpectedly. 'The night we got told off for snogging in the corner at your leaving party – do you remember? – she said she realised there was a business opportunity staring her in the face. That bar only serves auld fellows with comb-overs, and the lads who play darts on a Thursday night. Oh, tell Matthew they're going for the Six Counties Darts Cup next month, by the way. There's massive excitement. They'll send him a photo if they win. Anyway, Hilda and Harry got to thinking of all the toasted sandwiches and gin and tonics they could sell to a pub full of women, and they approached Catherine and myself to see if we'd support it.'

It was hard to believe that she was the same Róisín. A few short months ago, if anybody had come near her about such a thing, she'd have had to be resuscitated. But now she sounded calm, confident. Comfortable in her own skin.

'We put some conditions on it. They have to upgrade the toilets for starters. They're a bloody disgrace. And there are to be no posters up around the place or anything like that, like it was the circus coming to town. We agreed to float the idea on a few forums online – Catherine's into all that – to see whether there'd be any interest and, Clara, there is.'

She still sounded a bit amazed not to be the only gay person in rural Ireland.

'So we're going to start it off small. Just me and Catherine, and a few people we've invited online. We'll see how it goes.'

'It sounds fantastic, Róisín. Can I come along?'

I'd only been joking, but Róisín immediately said, 'Oh, do. We'd love to see you.'

'I'm going along too,' said Anita chirpily (unsurprisingly, she'd taken the all-expenses-paid nanny job in the Caribbean).

'You are not,' said Róisín. 'You'd only mortify me, by asking everybody what lesbians get up to.'

'I wouldn't. Because I know now, thanks to Catherine. She filled me in on everything. I might even become a lesbian myself.'

'You don't "become" one, Mum.' (The Mum thing was thrown in to annoy Anita.) 'You either are one or you're not.'

Diplomatically, I said, 'Matthew? Do you think it's time to drop everyone back to the hotel?'

It was getting late and we still had so much to do. The wedding was going to be small – just fifty people – and we were pretty laid-back about the whole thing, but at the same time it was only a couple of days away.

Every time I thought of it, a little thrill ran through me. 'Well, naturally,' Matthew kept saying. 'You're marrying me, you lucky girl.'

But I knew he was just as thrilled as I was. 'Surrey, here we come,' he kept announcing.

He was doing his bouncer act now, bundling a tittering Anita out the door. 'OK, ladies, can we move it out, please? Have you no homes to go to?'

'See you tomorrow!' Anita and Róisín called. We had a dress fitting first thing in the morning. Anita kept losing weight, and the dressmaker was going mental at each new report of another two pounds lost.

Róisín took something out of her bag and tossed it into my lap as she was leaving. 'For you. From a mutual friend.'

With a wink she was gone.

★

Matthew arrived back fifteen minutes later to find me in fits on the couch.

'What's wrong? What's the matter?' That old worry was back on his face as he rushed towards me.

Then he saw I was cracking up laughing. Twice in one evening, a recent record.

'Read that.' I handed him the book I'd been engrossed in, and pointed at a page.

A little mystified, Matthew did so. '"The tight leather of his trousers creaked and groaned under his urgent desire . . ."' His eyes widened as he shot me a look. '"He turned to her, crotch thrusting forward aggressively. 'Get ready, honey,' he said, handing her a whip. 'This is going to get nasty.'"'

Matthew was agog now. 'What *is* it?' Although I think it was beginning to dawn on him.

'Read, read,' I urged, convulsed again.

Matthew did so. '"She raised the whip and brought it down hard against her thigh. He flinched at the crack of it. Suddenly, the tables had turned. 'Bend over,' she commanded softly. Slowly, thighs quivering in expectation, he did as she ordered, presenting her with his back as he leaned submissively over the couch. It was then that she saw that the leather trousers had been artfully cut away to expose his buttocks. Nothing new there. But, on closer inspection, she saw that the trousers were serrated at the edges – almost as though an animal had taken a bite out of them."'

If Matthew's eyes got any wider, they would pop out. He flipped the book over. The front cover was all jolly bondage – lots of ribbony whips twirling about, and handcuffs glinting merrily in the background. The author name was splashed across the bottom in sexy pink.

'Dominique!'

'Her new book, hot off the press. She sent a copy over with Róisín.'

'The trousers,' Matthew said, already starting to snort with laughter.

'I know. I haven't read the rest, but I bet she made fun of plenty more, too.'

341

She'd got her own back, old Dominique. And on my behalf, too. In cheeky purple pen, she'd inscribed the front of the book with the words, 'From your friend, Dominique.'

'Róisín texted me to say that the bookshop in Castlemoy is coming down with advance orders. Everyone wants to see if they're in it.'

It looked like I mightn't be the only one who should leave Castlemoy behind.

We put the book away – Matthew said we'd save it for some cold winter's night, wink wink – and we put the green lamp on, and we dreamed of Saturday.